What Hides in the Dark

VOLUME I

ISBN: 979-8-9889348-6-8

First edition November 2025

Edited by Emma Jane Lounsbury, Maddi Leatherman, Ollie Sikes, and Shruti Rasal

Cover art by Aethrastic Designs

Interior graphics by Ollie Sikes and Shruti Rasal

Formatting by EJL Editing

Contents

Editor's Note — V

The Sharp Feathers of Sorrow — 1
by Camilla Zahn

To Feast on Fear — 35
by Jane Humen

The Basement — 47
by Bryanna Bernice

Swarm — 65
by Christopher J. Brice

The Specter in the Mirror — 95
by Eleanor Hall

The Meaning of Possession: A Short Story — 105
by Noah Johnson

Devour the Hand That Feeds — 133
Vera M. Sidney

Autumn — 157
by Cisco Bautista

The Last Words of Henry R. McCoy — 165
by Luke Van Amburg

Army of Flamingos — 191
by Ann Wuehler

Something's Wrong with the Greenhouse — 219
by Zero Saucier

Cleithrophobia 239
by Isabella J.

The Last Laugh 243
by Brandee Paschall

The Forgotten Doll 271
by E.R. Sano

Playing with Chemicals 305
by Chloe D.

The Eyes Behind Our Own 327
by Eric Still

Darling, Don't Play in the Woods at Night 347
Carter Elise Key

My Beatrice 355
Jay L. Scaffa

My Dearly Beloved 375
by Heena

The Dark Secrets of Family Business 409
by Jimmy Daleson

Acknowledgments 443

Editor's Note

All the participating authors were given the same one-word prompt: Dark. What followed were dozens of short stories with beautifully complex and varied interpretations.

For reader convenience, these stories have been loosely grouped by genre. Volume I contains horror stories. Volume II contains thriller, suspense, and lit fic stories. Volume III contains fantasy and romance stories. All stories in this anthology are suitable for mature readers. Content and triggers warnings are located before individual stories. If a story does not have a content/trigger warning section, we did not believe that any apply. Should you have any questions or concerns about the content of any story, please contact EJL Editing for more information.

All proceeds from sales of *What Hides in the Dark* will be donated to Palestine Children's Relief Fund (PCRF), a nonprofit organization providing free medical care to injured and ill children in the Levant, regardless of their nationality or religion. Palestine Children's Relief Fund was collectively chosen by the anthology authors as the recipient of all sale proceeds.

What Hides in the Dark and EJL Editing are not endorsed by, directly affiliated with, or sponsored by Palestine Children's Relief Fund. For more information on PCRF's efforts, visit www.pcrf.net

Whichever volume you pick up, *What Hides in the Dark* is sure to leave you eyeing the shadows just a moment longer.

"Everyone is a moon, and has a dark side which he never shows to anybody."

—Mark Twain

The Sharp Feathers of Sorrow

by Camilla Zahn

Content and Trigger Warnings

- Infant death
- Child loss
- Depression
- Alcohol consumption
- Strong language
- Domestic violence
- Aggression
- Suicidal ideation
- Persecution
- Graphic violence and depiction of death
- Implied suicide

One

"There are moments when, even to the sober eye of Reason, the world of our sad Humanity may assume the semblance of a Hell."
— *The Premature Burial, Edgar Allan Poe*

You rarely know that the worst day of your life is upon you until it's too late. Mary imagined she would, though. She was taught—as anyone in her village—that you could look for signs, omens such as darkening clouds forming rapidly in an otherwise sunny day, carrion birds hovering, unruly dogs howling throughout the night; even inside one's home, in daily life: spilling salt, breaking a mirror. From an early age, the signs were taught so she could always be on the lookout, praying diligently for the Lord's protection that those bad omens never crossed her.

It's almost ironic, then, that the worst day of Mary Còmhan's life had none of those things. Her worst day started as any other: she rose from bed at the first sight of sun, to prepare breakfast for her husband, Thomas. Before anything though, she had to check on her sweet little girl, Agnes. She was still sound asleep, cooing her small baby sounds—a symphony to Mary's ears. She gently touched her daughter's little hand, feeling the softness of it. It was like touching velvet, a fabric she had only touched when she was a kid, when her father had brought some home as a gift from a wealthy merchant he had encountered during one of his travels. Mary remembered the burgundy fabric fondly while stroking her daughter's tiny fingers. Her mother had turned it into a shawl, since it wasn't enough for much else, and she used it throughout the bad winters and the illness that followed.

Mary didn't even need to close her eyes to summon the softness of that shawl, her nose buried in it, her arms around her frail mother, burning up in fever, much warmer than Agnes' skin. Even though re-membering it made her recall the pain of grief, she had always found the red fabric in the casket around her mother's thin pale arms sooth-ing. It became entangled with the memories of her mother's smell of honeysuckle and her embrace, the safest place on earth for her. Being able to hug her bairn, to have her intoxicating skin feel like that shawl was heaven; it made her feel closer to her mother, like something meant to be, a cycle of life fulfilled.

Restraining the urge to pick little Agnes up and hold her close, Mary changed clothes and went on to prepare breakfast. She knew she had about fifteen minutes before either her husband or her daughter woke up, and after that the day would always go by so fast.

Mary and Thomas inherited her father's shop after he passed. It was a small produce shop, filled with a little bit of everything you could find—depending on the season and the weather, of course—eggs, bread, dried herbs and vegetables, canned goods, sometimes pies and fruits. *The Hungry Hen*, as her mother had named it, was her family's most prized possession. Her father, Alastair, was from a family of merchants that often traveled to other cities to sell goods. But when Mary's mother got pregnant, he didn't want to keep traveling months on end and leave his spouse alone, so he decided to act on his lifelong dream: a place where people could come to.

A place, as he liked to say, that was open for the village day in and day out, all year long. You didn't need to skip shopping because it was raining, or not be able to bake your husband's favorite dish on his birthday. *The Hungry Hen* would be there for you.

And indeed, it was. Many farmers and local producers paid a small amount to use shelf space in the store to sell their products. In the winter, most women of the village sewed blankets, gloves and scarves and used the *Hen* to sell them. In very harsh winters, they even gathered there near the fire, crocheting together as a group.

The shop wasn't just a shop, but a local point of pride and community. Mary and Thomas made a promise to her father that it would keep being that even when he was long gone. While Thomas dealt with the administration of the place, Mary catered to the public.

She went on with her day as usual, feeding her hungry loved ones, kissing her husband before he left in a hurry to deal with a payment collection and baking a rhubarb crumble pie that would go to the store later. One thing she loved about the shop was the fact that the house was at the back of it, so she could be with Agnes inside and come to the front as soon as she heard the door—usually before the customer got to ring the bell. Or she could be in the shop, her baby by her side while still keeping an eye on the stove.

The autumn days had already begun to shorten, even though they were a couple of days away from the equinox. Mary had a lot to prepare for that year's *Samhain*[1] festivities, since the whole village came together to celebrate the last harvest of the year with good food, music and dancing, and *The Hungry Hen* was where everyone gathered to eat, especially if the weather was bad. She still had a little more than one month, but was aware of how that could pass by in the blink of an eye.

"Are we going to be graced with your famous shepherd's pie with sage this year, Mrs. McLeod?" Mary asked Helen, one of her customers—famous for her delicious pies—to contribute to the village's festivities. Helen was at the counter with a basket of vegetables and dried mushrooms.

"With the Lord's blessing, my dear." Helen smiled. She was a petite woman with hair the color of hay and a small, angular nose.

Mary picked a pencil off the counter. "I'll note that as a yes, then," she said, scribbling on a piece of paper where she was collecting who would bring what to that year's feast. She had a big smile on her face, even though the small of her back seemed to be becoming sore from standing up. She accompanied Mrs. McLeod to the door, sending her farewells. That probably would be the last customer of that afternoon. She would still keep the shop open for a couple more hours until the sun went down, though, because it wasn't uncommon for a recipe gone wrong demanding a new glass of milk, or a kid after school that would ask if they had any sweets on discount.

Before continuing her duties in the shop, Mary had a big pile of clothes to take to the river to be washed. It was a chore she enjoyed doing, especially during spring or fall, when the weather wasn't that harsh. The motion of the river and the back and forth of her hands on the clothes often soothed her agitated mind, like a meditation. Agnes

---

1. The festival is now what we know as Halloween, although it was often celebrated on November 1st.

seemed to always enjoy that as well—a moment to relish the sun and indulge in her vast curiosity, her big green eyes attentive to every little detail around her.

"Care to join me for a walk, *mo chridhe*[2]?" Mary asked, raising Agnes from her crib and placing her forehead to her daughter's. Agnes giggled, her tiny fingers touching Mary's cheeks.

Mary swaddled Agnes in the plaid shawl and tied the ends firmly on her own shoulder such that Agnes was facing forward, so she could see the world. The scent of daisies filled Mary's nostrils; the smell of her daughter made her own heart swell every time.

Agnes was getting so big! She would soon be one-year-old. It was impossible to conceive of how time flew by.

With the basket almost overflowing with clothes perched on her back, the harshness of the ropes scratching her shoulders and her small companion tucked against her chest, legs dangling in the air, Mary left the house.

The sun was beautiful, not too warm but enough that the clothes might be dry the next day. She spoke to her baby as if Agnes had any clue what she was talking about. The walk to the stream wasn't a long one, but pleasant. She passed by some neighbors who smiled at Agnes and waved at her.

With the weight of the basket and her daughter, Mary's back hurt a bit more than before. Nothing that she hadn't experienced once in a while. Maybe she could bat her eyelashes in a seductive way to Thomas in exchange for a massage later? That would be very nice.

A few more steps and they arrived at the exact spot Mary liked to settle, near a big stone where she could rest the basket and prop Agnes against it, seated for a while, away from the stream's margin, but close enough that she could be with her legs in the water and reach for another rag or her baby in no time.

Mary adjusted Agnes on top of the shawl to protect her skin from any sharp edges or blades of grass. She smiled curiously, holding on to a

---

2. "My heart" in Gaelic.

strand of Mary's black hair. "Ye're a bonnie wee lamb, aye?" she cooed. "Mammy's wee lamb!"

Agnes loved when Mary exaggerated her Scottish accent even more. It would drive her to such uncontrollable laughter that it was impossible not to laugh with her. It was something Thomas would do all the time, calling her their little pretty lamb, or dove—or any other animal they could think of, actually.

Mary took off her shoes, quickly massaging her lower back before picking the soap and one of Thomas's shirts. To work she went, water around her ankles. The water was chilly, and it immediately made her swollen feet from standing up feel better. Each time she wrung out a cloth, the woman's eyes flicked back to her child, close enough to touch if need be. She kept talking to Agnes to make sure she was all right, playing with her teddy bear.

"Look up!" She pointed to the sky. "Do you see the bird, Agnes?"

The baby laughed in return, her arm stretched up in the sky. She followed the bird with her fingers as if a magic trick were happening right in front of her. She loved to do that, often crawling around the house to chase a butterfly.

Mary carried on, finding her rhythm with the clothes. It was almost a ritual, done once a week, a moment for her and Agnes to enjoy nature while doing the laundry. On warm days, when she was finished, she would enter the stream with Agnes in her arms, rocking both of them gently, her arms and legs floating. It seemed to soothe them both—the touch of the calm water, the slow breaths and beams of sunlight.

She closed her eyes for a moment, serene, feeling the warmth of the sun on her cheeks. When she opened them, Agnes seemed to be watching her with a gleeful look in her eyes.

Only two more pieces of cloth were left to wash. A gust of wind blew one of the shirts away from Mary's grasp further into the stream, and she turned her back to pick it up.

In that small—routinely even—turn, the world shifted.

Mary would always wonder what if she hadn't turned? For how long exactly she wasn't looking?

Because it felt like nothing but a moment.

With the water now on her knees, her fingertips touching a sleeve, Mary heard a *pluck*, a noise of something falling in the water behind her.

She turned, her heart beating faster than ever before.

The shawl was empty.

Agnes wasn't there.

There was a ripple in the water, near the margin.

"Agnes?!" Mary screamed.

Her instincts made her act. Her mind sharper, eyes focused. She took a deep breath and went down into the water, her face disappearing.

The riverbank was muddy, and with each stroke of her arms, more plants and earth seemed to swivel around her.

My baby. Where's my baby?!

Mary couldn't breathe. Water was invading her from every angle, and when she opened her mouth to scream, more water came in.

She emerged again, nausea creeping up her stomach.

"Agnes!"

Something shone in the water, not too far from her. She half swam and half ran, her limbs heavy.

She grasped Agnes by the bracelet on her wrist.

She was *so cold*.

"My baby!"

Her hands were shaking badly when she laid Agnes on the shawl. Her rosy cheeks were pale, her eyes closed.

That wasn't happening. It couldn't be.

"Help!" Mary shouted as loud as she could. "Someone, help!"

She tried to push down on Agnes's chest, to breathe in through her tiny lips. She wasn't moving. She didn't know what to do. *Oh Lord, help us, please.*

Mary kept breathing, shoving air into her daughter's unmoving body as God had done to Adam, because there was nothing else she could do. With each exhale she pushed out, her own breath seemed to grow shallower, leaving her.

So be it, she thought. *Give her my air!*

Mary's vision was becoming blurred, and her own cheeks purple, but she carried on. She couldn't stop. The air was cold, too cold on her wet body, and her hands were trembling as if she were possessed. Her last meal was coming up her throat . . .

Breathe!

It was too much.

She finally vomited when someone pushed her body to the side. Multiple hands were on Agnes, and she couldn't see her baby anymore. She couldn't make sense of any of it, didn't recognize those people asking her what had happened. Mary tumbled to the side, her head hitting the grass just an inch away from her vomit. She tried to reach out but only got so far as to stretch her hand above her face. There was distant shrieking in the air. She couldn't be sure if it was coming from her, because she no longer knew where she began and where she ended. The edges of herself were ragged and sharp, but scattered along the grass.

Between her stretched fingers, the last thing she saw before the world turned black was a yellow butterfly circling in the sky above them.

Agnes was put to rest at the local church the following afternoon. The entire village gathered in mourning, as a knit community would. Agnes was one of the only two infants in the village at that moment, and everyone followed her growth with joy. Reverend MacGregor read some Bible passages, but Mary couldn't pay any attention to it. Thomas sat silently at her side, his eyes red and puffy, his hand crushing hers. Mary focused only on her belly slowly rising up and down, up and down, with air that did not belong in her lungs.

Grief shatters your world forever. The sense of time is never the same. Some moments are eternal, a terrible joke of the ticking clock, making you acutely aware that there is no escape. Mary wished—prayed, even—for a fever that would knock her out, for a sleep that could take her away from the nightmare. But you can't escape a nightmare when it's your awakened reality. It felt like she was forced in front of a mirror she didn't wish to hold, showing her only ugliness.

She had felt loss before, of course. When her father died, the emptiness that followed was terribly hard to deal with. She spent longer hours at the shop so she could feel near him. But now, there was *nothing* she could do. No room in the house gave her comfort; there wasn't any relief.

It was as if her mother's soft, velvet shawl had been replaced by edges of bones made of glass, her whole world sharp, painfully cutting over and over again. There was a *physical* void she couldn't run from that ate her alive. Her hand *burned* with an invisible hole. The hand she used to caress her baby's soft cheek, the hand that held her fingers when they played and grasped her wrist for the last time. It was now a foreign limb, estranged from her.

She didn't feel the worse of the absence in her womb, as she imagined would be the case.

It was her hand, always aching. Mary now walked with her right hand closed, her fingers curved into the palm, as if to hold the entrance to the darkness at bay. She knew it was just an illusion though, and every sleepless night that followed, she dragged her feet to the small guest room, where Thomas had shunned his daughter's belongings, and sat on the rocking chair she used while feeding her baby, resting her hand on the side of the wooden cradle. The only way she could breathe, even if shallow breaths, was by holding that empty piece of furniture. The hole in her hand didn't feel better, but less unbearable. As if it were her umbilical cord. She stayed there every night for hours, way past the point her whole spine hurt, rocking the cradle back and forth. That pain was welcome—any pain other than the one in her soul was a welcome distraction she gladly embraced.

The first time Thomas tried to take her away from the room, she screamed so loud one of the neighbors came to see what was happening. Mary knew he meant well, that he was also mourning, but that only made it worse. They shared the burden and the pain of that loss, but each grieved on their own terms, and it never coincided. Once they were a well-oiled couple, working as joined pieces of machinery, a beautiful duo. Now being in each other's orbit was maddening, and Mary couldn't muster the energy to face her husband.

She saw the hate in his eyes, though.

The creeping doubt that she was to blame for their daughter's death.

It was an accident, the doctor had told them. Agnes probably got distracted, crawled, and fell in the water. There was nothing that could have been done, they had said.

Mary knew they were wrong. There was plenty that could have been done. She could've placed Agnes farther away from the margin; she could've let the wind take the shirt. If she hadn't turned around, nothing bad would have happened.

She could, for God's sake, not have washed the clothes that day. Now, doing stupid chores became so unimportant that she couldn't bother. Used old, dirty clothes. Nothing changed. The world didn't stop because she wasn't washing the dishes anymore.

What's the point? she asked herself. She asked God. She even asked the ancient gods and goddesses if she could remember their names.

No one answered.

Two

Thomas waved a hand in front of her foggy eyes.

"Mary? Have you heard a single word I said?!"

He was angry again. After Agnes, Thomas was always angry. Or inebriated. Most of the time, both.

He usually kept to himself, which was a blessing. Mary's patience was long gone, but she didn't have the strength to fight. Of course, she wasn't paying attention. It wasn't for lack of trying, though, but the more someone spoke to her, the less she could comprehend. She was *so* tired.

But she tried nonetheless and raised her eyes to meet his piercing gaze. Thomas was standing upright in front of her, his shadow looming over her body seated in the rocking chair, staring at the window. His hazel eyes were burning, but she couldn't tell behind the thick scent of ale if he burned in pain or hatred for her. She loved him, of course. She had always loved him; once, the sight of him made her belly churn with chaotic butterflies.

No, no butterflies. Her right hand stung, sharp and hot. She couldn't think of butterflies anymore. It was forbidden. It hurt *too much*.

She could see an echo of the man she fell in love with in those eyes, the man she had married on a warm July day, but only a glimpse, like a shadow you think you saw from the corner of the eye but that is gone the minute you turn to look directly at it. Thomas too was irreparably changed, all his soft edges now sharp angles. She tried not to, but her first instinct was to recoil at the sight of him. That wasn't fair to him—but her body was no longer her own. The pain had deep roots, reigning in her every move.

She noticed he was waiting for a reply.

"I'm . . . I'm sorry, can you repeat?" Her voice was small and hoarse.

Thomas rubbed his face in annoyance. "I said I need you tonight, *mo chridhe*. I need you in the shop." He tried to control his tone, being gentler, but his affection seemed forced. He had deep bags under his eyes, and his cheeks were starting to recede back into the bone.

Mary blinked, making a huge effort to follow. The shop? She hadn't entered *The Hungry Hen* since the day after the funeral. It was all too much—too many smells, too many people being kind to her, bringing her foods she didn't feel like eating . . .

"I can't, Tom," she whispered, a defeated exhale leaving her lips. "You know I can't."

Thomas turned his back, muttering, and she watched as he went to the kitchen and came back with a half-empty bottle of ale. He took a long gulp without even looking at her. Mary watched as one watches a wild animal.

"I know you are in pain, Mary"—he paused, clenching his jaw—"I am too. *I lost her too.*"

Mary closed her fist, her fingernails digging into the inside of her palm. "I know."

"But we need to do something. We need to at least take care of the shop, *your father's* shop!" He took another sip, a few drops slipping down his beard. "I have been doing my best to handle things, but I need your help, tonight of all nights!"

"What's tonight?"

His eyes grew bigger in disbelief.

"What do you mean by—I can't even believe you! It's *Samhain*!" His voice grew an octave. "It's the busiest night of the year, that is what it is, and I need my bloody wife to help me!"

Mary flinched at the idea of the feast. Happy people, a big fire, dancing. Everyone touching her shoulders and feeling sorry for her, or asking her to participate, asking her to play a role she no longer knew the lines to. It was too heavy a mask to bear.

"You should close the shop tonight, Tom," she reasoned. "People will understand."

"We can't afford to close the shop, Mary!" he shouted, the bottle swaying in his firm grip. "We are barely scraping by as it is, if you even care to know. I'm there day and night counting pennies to pay our bills, while you're here, doing nothing."

Some jagged edge poked her insides.

"Is *that* what you spend your nights doing?" Mary stood up, feeling a newfound anger bubbling in her stomach, her face inches from his. "Because you don't sleep at home anymore, and it's not pennies you come back with." She pointed to the bottle in his hand.

"Fuck you, Mary!" he shouted, drinking the last of the liquid and tossing the bottle at the wall. It shattered into a million tiny pieces, making Mary pull back. She had never seen Thomas be violent, and for a moment she feared for herself.

He took a step in her direction, his voice deep and hurt. "You don't know what I have to endure every day, the terrible things people are saying about you that *I* have to deny!"

She frowned; her curiosity piqued.

"What are people saying?" Mary scoffed.

Thomas closed his eyes and sighed deeply. "I don't want to talk about that."

"No, say it!"

"I had people ask me why I left the two of you alone. If you were sad, if you meant to harm her."

Mary took another step back, almost falling onto the couch. The sharpness of her pain took her breath away, like a blow to the stomach.

"I-I never . . . I could never . . . " She struggled to complete a sentence.

He took another deep breath, his lips trembling, and came closer. "Some ask nicely. Some people are really concerned with your well-being, and the fact you all but disappeared isn't helping. But be not mistaken, I know what these people are capable of. I know what they truly think!"

Mary couldn't continue with that conversation. Her body urged her to run, to hide in a dark corner and shut herself off from the world. But the anger was still hot in her veins. "Tell me, then! Tell me what they think of me!" she screamed, pounding her fists on his chest. "Tell me what *you* think!"

His nose was almost touching hers. The scent of ale coming from him was nauseating. "They think you killed her! You turned your back on our bairn, and she died!"

"Don't you think I know that?!"

Tears blurred both of their visions, running down their cheeks.

"I heard someone call you a witch, Mary," he cried, holding her by the wrists and shaking her, his fingers leaving marks on her skin. "Do you understand how bad this can become? We are going to be undone!"

"We are already undone!" she yelled in his face, a guttural, primal scream bursting out of her. "I wish," she spat, hot rage as lava boiling from every pore. "I wish I was a witch, so I could curse you to die in her place."

Thomas parted his lips, but nothing came out of them. He blinked, astonished, once, twice.

Mary felt the sting on her cheek before she could process the slap. It seemed to come as a surprise to him as well, but he didn't apologize. Instead, Thomas let go of her and left without saying a word. She heard the front door slam shut.

That was the last time Mary saw her husband.

He didn't come home, which at first seemed normal. Mary didn't sleep, walking like a ghost around the house, haunting her own home. Thomas usually fled somewhere to forget. She never heard him in the store as he said he was, only to drink. She heard him crying often, but could never muster the energy to reach him. His grief was an ocean away, and her raft was leaky at best. Reaching his love—the sweet young boy she married—that was a bridge she could no longer cross.

For the first night, she didn't worry. Mary watched the *Samhain* fires from her window, having only the cold in her bones as company. But on the second night he didn't come home, she knew something bad had happened. Call it a woman's intuition—call it witchcraft, for all she cared—but she *knew*.

Her chest started to hurt, and it was hard to breathe. It felt like a gigantic stone was sitting on top of her lungs. Her hand burned with the absence of her baby, of something dear to hold. She knew. She didn't think she could survive another bad thing happening, and it made her head swivel. The fog in her thoughts was getting unbearable to fight.

But Mary waited, seated on the couch, staring at the wooden boards of the door, studying its patterns.

The knock finally came on the third day, near twilight.

Getting up was torturous. It felt like her whole body weighed her down like an anchor, every muscle tense.

On the other side of the door, Helen and the reverend awaited with stern eyes. "Mary, I'm afraid something happened."

Mary squeezed her fingernails into the soft of her palms, bracing for impact. Her voice was hoarse when she spoke. "It's Thomas, isn't it?"

"Can we come in, please?" The reverend asked, one hand on the door. Mary didn't budge. The simple idea of having someone in her house made her nauseous.

"Just tell me," she pleaded.

"Thomas is dead."

"He was found near the stream . . ." Helen averted her eyes to the ground.

"It appears he was drunk," the reverend explained, his voice flat and soft, trying to be as gentle as possible. "He fell and hit his head on a rock."

Mary raised her eyes to meet him.

Thomas is dead.

He hit his head on a rock. Her rock. The one she had propped her baby against with the plaid shawl almost two months earlier.

People often have the strangest reactions to stress. Reverend Mac-Gregor and Helen waited for her response, for her to at least acknowledge she understood what was being said to her.

Mary clenched her jaw shut, a low squeak escaping her lips. Her shoulders trembled slightly as she made the biggest effort in her life to hold back what was coming up her throat.

"Mary?" Helen stretched out an arm in her direction. "We're really, really sorry for your—"

"Thank you very much," she said through gritted teeth, slamming the door and rapidly closing the lock.

She needed to escape. She was going to explode at any minute, and what would come out of her would be nasty.

Mary turned and faced her empty living room. Her hands were shaking, and she looked around, searching for something she didn't know. It was as if she were watching herself from outside her own body, completely disconnected, but at the same time feeling every fiber of her being quivering with the power of a wild thunder.

She ran to the only place she could—the room with the cradle. It called to her, promising comfort she knew too well was a lie. Mary saw herself raising a pillow to her face. The woman imagined she would scream, but what burst out of her in waves was laughter.

Pure, *uncontrollable* laughter.

There was a part of her—albeit getting smaller each day—that had a grip on reality. That knew she shouldn't be laughing. It was bad news. It was the end of everything she held dear. But when your heart is in shards, it's expected that your mind will soon follow, pushing you into the vortex of madness.

Thomas was dead.

And the last thing she told him, the last *wish* to the love of her life and father of her sweet daughter, was that he had died instead of Agnes.

No, not *instead*.

I wish I could curse you to die *in her place.*

If the neighbors could hear her now, cheeks turning purple from hysterical laughing in a pillow, they would be sure she was indeed in cohort with the devil.

She couldn't refrain from laughter, her whole body convulsing, pressing the pillow tight against her skin. It was too much. Too ugly a truth to deal with. Mary knew she was no witch. She would have brought her baby back into her arms if she were one. There would be no second wasted. Better, if she were a witch, she would find a way to protect her bairn at all costs, so none of what happened could ever, ever become real.

Mary was no witch.

What she indeed was, it's a widow.

The grandioseness of the word cut the laughter abruptly. Tears filled her eyes and soaked the pillow. Slowly, it transformed into sobs, the kind you can't stop, followed by a scream.

Defeated and numb, depleted of energy with the fog clouding her mind, she lowered the pillow back on the cradle and sat on the rocking chair, the back of it holding her shape like an embrace.

Mary stayed there, unmoving, as the hours passed.

In the dead of night, in that musty room that belonged to no one, Mary clutched the rough edges of the empty cradle—back and forth, back and forth in that hollow, useless motion—and in its silence realized the crushing weight of a dreadful certainty: that no soul in the world remained beside her.

Three

Crossing Agnes's plaid shawl above her coat and over her shoulders, Mary took a deep breath. A cough escaped her lips, making her hand rest atop the door's handle. She had been coughing a lot these days. Maybe it was the cold. It didn't matter how many pieces of wood she fed the fireplace, the house was always cold, a dead chill running throughout the empty rooms. It was fitting for her mood.

With another deep breath to clear her throat, Mary opened the front door.

The farthest she had gone since Thomas died was the shop, to officially close it. The *real* reason was to clean some expired food that had started to smell. Crying, she smashed jars and screamed, impersonating the folkloric tale of the wailing banshee. That was last week. Mary hadn't found the courage to go outside yet, but today, for some reason, she was restless. The stale air of the house was making her heart rate rise, and the house felt like a tomb.

The view of the world outside shocked her. Everything was so . . . white. The dark-orange grass was covered with a thick layer of fresh snow. Mary always enjoyed the notion that snow is silent, creating a magic trick: blink and you won't notice it. She knew it was cold, felt it in her aching bones at night. Having to find another blanket to wrap around her shoulders was a telltale sign of winter. But lost in her own mind, her brain frozen in the clock of grief, she was astonished to see that time had gone on.

Mary had no idea where she was going, but she took that first step, feeling her boots sink in the snow. The cold air burned her nose as it entered her nostrils, but somehow it helped with the anxiety. She walked slowly at first, as if unsure of her own feet, but then picked up the pace, her right hand closed, the fingers pressed on the palm, holding her imaginary void.

Whenever she passed in front of a house, there was someone in the windows looking at her with their mouths ajar. She had no idea what her own appearance was like, but she was sure she was decent enough to be on the street. Maybe they were surprised to see her out after so long.

No one said hi, though. Mary gazed with curiosity at the next house on her right. She could see Bonnie Andarsan baking something that smelled like apple pie. The thought of saying hello came to mind, but before she opened her mouth, Bonnie gave her an aggrieved look and shut the window closed.

Wow, Mary thought in dismay.

She carried on, looking at the cloudy gray sky, with some occasional birds flying. A few meters to her left, three children—about the age of six or seven—were building a snowman in front of their house. Mary knew those children, but she couldn't remember their names anymore.

These days it felt like her head had become a piece of cheese, filled with holes in her memory and thoughts.

One of the children, a small boy with his red hair showing from inside his beanie, pointed at her.

"Hey, lads, look!"

Mary smiled, approaching them. The other two, a girl with blonde braids and a boy so covered in clothes and scarves that she could only see his green eyes, stopped what they were doing and looked. The girl, the smaller one of the group, hid behind the snowman, her eyes big.

"Hi, kids," Mary tried saying, her voice croaky and strange even to herself. "What's the name of your *bodach-sneachda*[3]?" she asked, nodding toward the snowman. It was as tall as the red-haired boy, near her waistline, with a very round head and two black rocks as eyes. It wasn't very easy to make such a smooth snowman feature.

"We don't know yet," the red-haired boy answered with a frown. The one hidden behind his large scarf gazed at her with curiosity, his green eyes piercing her. Mary stared back at him, trying to remember who he was.

"Aren't you the lady that—"

The first boy hit him on the shoulder. "Shut up, Fergus!"

---

3. Snowman in Scottish Gaelic

Mary heard the door of the house behind them opening up at the same time that the little girl whispered, almost too low to hear: "She's the witch, Ferg."

Mary's heart shrank in her chest. Her hand burned.

"What is all this racket I'm hearing?" A voice called with annoyance.

She recognized the woman who had left the house. It was one of the shop's usual customers, Fiona Brùn, wife of Callum, the shoemaker. She was pregnant, Mary noticed with surprise.

Mrs. Brùn had her back turned, so she didn't see Mary standing there. The children quietly pointed at her, their eyes big and mouths closed in a fine line, as if caught doing mischief.

Fiona turned, and Mary could see the color leave her face. It was as if she had seen a ghost.

"Wh-what are you . . . " Her lips trembled. "What are you doing here? What do you want?"

"Hi." Mary wasn't sure how to answer. "I'm just taking a stroll."

The other woman clenched her jaw. "Then go on your way. I don't want you near my children!" She gestured with her hand in a 'shoo' motion, as if Mary was a wild animal, a nuisance.

Or worse.

She didn't fight. Walking away, Mary saw out of the corner of her eye Mrs. Brùn doing the sign of the cross in a haste, muttering something that sounded like, "won't curse my children, no."

It was better to move along, crossing to the other side of the street, her feet leaving prints in the snow. Mary clenched her teeth, trying to muster supernatural strength not to cry.

Maybe it was better to go back home, she thought, but the mental image of her living room made her gasp for air, her chest tight.

Suddenly, something hit her right on the back, between her shoulder blades with a sharp pain.

It was a snowball, pieces of it scattering everywhere.

Mary's eyes watered with the pain as she doubled over, her hands on her knees. The ball hit exactly at the level of her lungs, where she was already feeling sore.

"Witch!" one of the children screamed, followed by a group laughter.

The tears Mary was fighting so hard to hold back came rolling down her cheeks. She tried to take a deep breath, control the pain, but it turned into a coughing fit, her lungs burning.

It took her a couple of minutes to be able to move again. She couldn't see exactly where she was going, the tears creating a curtain in front of her eyes. It was getting harder to breathe.

Mary knew she was spiraling and she would need to get hold of herself, even if just to be able to go back home, but there was nothing she could do to stop that.

When her eyes cleared enough for her to see, it felt like she was getting a blow all over again.

She was by the river. The river she and Agnes used to go to.

Her legs failed her, and she kneeled right there, at the edge of the stream, her hands trying to hold on to anything near, her knees immediately cold from the snow. She touched something rough with her left gloved hand and realized that it was the stone she used to prop her daughter against. It was partially covered in snow, but she could never mistake that rock.

Looking around, Mary felt a sting of disappointment. Her feet brought her to the worst place she could possibly go besides her own house, but she imagined she would find some solace in it—at least some connection to her loved ones, a trace of Thomas's scent forgotten in the grass, the memory of their daughter's giggles etched on the trees.

The place was the same, but it wasn't. Covered in snow, the stream frozen and the trees leafless, the place couldn't be farther from what was in her memory. Some part of her imagined, even hoped for—irrational as it was—that the place where she lost them both would be the same, paralyzed and wedged in time as a shrine to their memory.

But it wasn't, and the effects of nature showing its grip there, of all places, made it all the more cruel.

Mary usually liked the winter. She loved Christmas and was in awe every time she saw a snowflake, but now the snow muffled the landscape into a silence *too* deep and absolute, like the world had been abandoned and nature had taken over, casting death in every corner.

Kneeling there, each breath a sting turning to frost before her eyes, Mary felt even worse than before. It would have been better if nothing had changed, if she had come there and found the place as it was before. Gasping for air, her hands shaking, what she felt was not absence, but something heavy and watchful, woven into every fragment of ice. Time did not stop for her pain, but it recoiled in its indifference. It mocked her by showing all of that performative demise: the still river, the brittle trees, knowing spring and summer would return, but her child and husband would not, ever again.

At that moment, Mary wished to die. But she knew being left alive would be her punishment, the guilt an anchor around her neck.

A sound split the silence, sharp and rusted as iron against stone. Mary almost fell to the ground, caught by surprise.

"*Craaah!*" A carrion crow flew in her direction. Its call sounded like grief made audible, cracked and unending.

Mary watched as it landed on the rock next to her, shaking its feathers to get rid of the snow while staring at her with curiosity. Its calling was raw and felt ancient, older than language.

Staring at the bird's black feathers, she remembered that the Goddess Morrígan was said to appear sometimes as a crow or a wolf. She was the goddess of war, destruction, and death in Celtic mythology. Mary held the urge to laugh, as not to scare the bird. She couldn't remember her neighbors' names, but she remembered lore about ancient gods.

Something in the bird's eyes made it impossible to look away. Mary's knees were freezing in the snow, but she couldn't move. She didn't want the crow to leave as everyone else.

But it didn't show any signs of being afraid of her. On the contrary, this was the closest she had ever been to a crow. Mary raised one finger, afraid the slight movement would scare the bird away. As if understanding her request, the crow lowered its head in her direction.

She held her breath, trying to move her hand closer, very slowly, and brushed the bird's head ever so slightly. It stood almost as high as a tankard of ale upon the shop's counter and she couldn't feel whether the feathers were soft or not with her gloves on, but it felt so strange—in a good way—to pet a bird.

The crow moved its head, making Mary withdraw her hand. Somehow that small gesture made her feel less terrible, less alone.

"Thank you," she whispered, tears drying on her cheeks as she stood up slowly, her back and knees stiff. She was ready to go back home.

Mary tried not to look into anyone's houses on the way back, but the street was empty. She had only snow and a pitch-black crow flying high above her head as company.

Four

"*Wake up*," an urgent voice sounded in Mary's mind. It had a feminine, assertive tone. It was an order, not a suggestion.

Mary opened her eyes, completely awake. Perched on the windowsill, the crow gazed directly at her. It didn't move, and with its black eyes, it felt like Mary could see more. She could sense the crow was more than a crow, in a way she couldn't explain. It was a deep void staring at her, with knowledge of the entire universe.

The crow was now a daily visitor. She could call it her only friend. It would come from the kitchen window—sneaking through a hole in the wood Mary hadn't the energy to fix. Usually, it followed her around the house, making its "caw, caw" noises here and there, almost as if it tried to engage in conversation with her. She fed the bird some seeds and left a bowl of water for it.

When she retreated to her bedroom, the coughing taking her breath away and making her back ache like her lungs were on fire, it would follow her and stay on the windowsill or on top of Agnes's cradle, studying her, keeping her company.

Once, it allowed her to pet it again. She had moved the cradle back in her room, by her bed, so she could stretch her hand and clutch it like an anchor. She was spending more and more time in bed, so her daughter's things needed to be close by. The bird was perched on the cradle, while Mary held onto it, tears slowly streaming down her face. A peck on her right hand brought her out of her stupor. She gazed at those deep black eyes.

The bird lowered its head in her direction, and Mary touched it gently with the tip of her fingers. She gasped at how soft the feathers were. Her mind flooded with images of the texture of her mother's velvet shawl and Agnes's soft, warm skin. She closed her eyes, petting the bird, feeling closer to the ones she loved than before. A knot formed in her throat and she sobbed. Sorrow was a sharp sting, and that touch brought back memories of everything she had lost.

With one hand on the cradle and the other on the bird's feathers, Mary tried to hold onto the pieces of herself, but she couldn't. She was broken beyond repair. She also had an acute awareness that she wasn't going to survive the winter. Her food supply was running out, the money too short and the weather too severe for her brittle bones and damaged lungs. She was coughing constantly, her lungs burning for air. Her back felt like a hard stone, hurting everywhere. She was tired all the time, the kind of fatigue that doesn't get better when you sleep. Mary felt cursed.

Maybe that was her punishment for everything that had happened. She had to atone for not being a good mother and wife, for not taking care of them the way she should have.

The bird cawed, calling her again.

"Pay attention, child." It was that voice again, authoritative, in Mary's head. Clear as day. She looked around, confused. There wasn't anyone there but her and the bird, staring attentively at her.

Mary put a hand to her forehead. She was hot. It was probably a fever dream, then.

"This isn't a dream," the voice answered. *"Look at me."*

The bird cawed again. It was as if the voice belonged to the bird, as though it were talking to her. The big black eyes stared at her with a precise consciousness that seemed too human for a bird.

Something pushed forward in the fog of her thoughts. The Goddess Morrígan could transform into a crow.

"Are you . . . ?" Mary asked, her voice hoarse. It couldn't be.

It had to be a product of the fever.

"I am many things. I have many forms and names," the voice—the crow— answered. The bird kept staring at her, urging her to pay attention. "We don't have time for this."

"Why?" Mary pulled the blanket up, covering her shoulders. She was *too* tired, her eyes almost closing as sleep called to her like a siren.

"Stay awake, Mary Còmhan. They're coming for you."

A metallic taste filled her mouth with worry. "They?"

"The townsfolk. They are coming at this moment to burn your house down."

Mary clutched the side of the cradle, adrenaline rushing in her veins, making her more alert. "Why?"

The crow cawed. "They think it's the wise thing to do. Burn the house, hunt the witch."

"But I'm not a witch . . ." Mary coughed, her whole body hurting from the effort.

"I know. Humans can be terrible, sometimes. Once they are set in their beliefs, they become blind. Everything contrary only fuels their rage instead of bringing sense into their minds."

Mary squeezed the cradle's wood. "I don't want to leave my house. That's all I have."

"I have seen your pain, child. All of it. I am sorry for what you have gone through, so I came to help. I don't just show myself to anyone." The crow opened its wings, almost like it was stretching out. "I've seen your heart, and you don't deserve this. None of this is your fault."

She closed her eyes, fighting the tears that were coming back. Hearing someone—something—say those words seemed to lift a weight off her shoulders. Not all of it, of course.

"I have an offer for you."

Was she dreaming? Was all that part of a fever hallucination or was it real?

Did it matter?

Mary seated, propped on her pillows. The voice's tone seemed serious. She wanted to pay full attention to it.

"What do you want, Mary Còmhan? I can offer you war, revenge, death. I can make everyone out there pay, but only if you truly desire it. It's not a decision for me to make."

The crow waited while she thought hard about everything. She knew she was going to die sometime soon. Now she would lose her house? The only physical connection she had to her loved ones?

What would revenge taste like? Sweet, as some say? Mary knew it wouldn't take the pain away. It wouldn't bring Agnes and Thomas back. She pictured the face of everyone in her village, turning her back on her, calling her a witch.

"I want them to understand."

The crow cawed, shaking its head in disagreement.

"They could *never* understand your pain, child, for they made fear their god and now they bow to ghosts of their own imagination. There is no space in their hearts for compassion and empathy because it was replaced with suspicion and hatred.'

One tear came down Mary's cheek, stinging the skin as it went. It was a tear of anger. She remembered every look of disgust, the children tossing snowballs at her back, as if a woman in mourning was something ugly, something to be avoided like a plague. It made her blood boil.

"Can you make them *feel* it, instead? Can you make them suffer one bit of what I did?"

The crow raised its beak in her direction. It was almost like it was smiling at her.

"Are you aware that this is a *gift* from me, but I am not soft? There is no turning back if you say yes. I will fall upon them without mercy."

It wouldn't bring Agnes or Thomas back, Mary knew that. But if everyone could feel what she felt, even for a moment, Mary could rest in peace. They all abandoned her, her so loved community. They turned their back on her the moment grief took her under its wings.

"Do it." Her voice was confident, similar to the goddess. "Please."

The crow bowed its head in reverence.

"Now you need to leave. Go to the stream, at the edge of the woods, and wait for me there. Do not talk to anyone. Go out the back door. *Now*, Mary."

The crow opened its wings and flew to the kitchen and out the window.

Mary stood up, her head heavy. She held the cradle one last time, tears blurring her vision. Somehow, she could see an echo of Agnes laying there, cooing at her. It wasn't real, it wasn't there like the voice had been. It was as if the memory was brighter for one last time.

She heard voices coming from outside as she changed her clothes quickly and put a heavy shawl around her shoulders. Her pain made her walk slower than she wanted, but on she went, closing the door and leaving behind the place she once called home. She glanced at it, noticing how hollow the house was. It was just a construction, nothing else. It hadn't been home in a long time.

Mary was limping, but she tried to walk as quietly and fast as possible on the snow. She walked by the back of the houses, but she saw a mob of townsfolk walking with torches. They were really going to burn her house down.

"Where's the witch?!" someone screamed in the distance.

Her lungs burned, and she muffled her coughs with her shawl, every step feeling like a sword piercing her from the hips to her shoulder blades.

She looked up, and the world seemed to darken. From the woods came a sharp noise, ragged cries and caws, like beating drums. A flock of crows flew above her, too many to count, wings blocking the moonlight until it was no longer visible in the sky; a seething storm rushing toward the town. For a moment Mary thought they would come for her, but they paid her no attention.

She kept on, finally reaching the stream. The image of the place was still haunting, a gut punch. At night it seemed even more ominous, the dark leafless trees and the snow glistening as if filled with thousand diamonds. Mary sat on the rock, trying to balance herself without falling, and waited for something. She watched as more and more birds flew by. From where she stood, she could see the town square.

People were coming out of their houses to see what was going on, what was all that noise. The crows flew down like a pouring storm, pecking away at people. Screams pierced the air, mixed with the harsh singing of the crows.

What Mary couldn't know, was that every single villager was being hunted by the crows, surrounded by them.

People ran through the snow, screaming and disoriented.

When the crows touched the villagers, each and everyone felt immediate, unbearable *pain*. The birds pecked at their eyes, pulling the skin of their eyelids, giving them a grisly vision: they saw their loved ones dying in gruesome ways. Mothers waking to empty cradles. The cries of children. Husbands bleeding to death in front of their eyes.

There were tears. Nausea.

Madness.

The more they fought, the worse it got. Mary watched as people ran aimlessly, searching for something they could not find, stumbling in terror as they tried to escape the chaos.

Blood dripped from their wounds, desecrating the pure snow; crimson spread like fire through the sanctified frost. In it, the towns-folk could see a reflection of a small baby Agnes, cold and dead. They saw Thomas, skull cracked onto a rock.

"The witch is doing this!" a man screamed. It was the last thing he said before the birds shoved him to the ground and tore at his tongue, piece by piece, filling him with visions.

The birds pecked at the villager's eyes, making them aware there would be no more beauty in that town. They gouged at their soft mouths, for there would be no more laughter. Every peck filled their hearts with dread and a grief they never had felt before.

It was swift and all-consuming.

Mary watched from a distance, her breath shallow and labored, her body heavy. She clenched her right hand, feeling the echo of Agnes's hand in hers. She imagined she would regret it, she would recoil from the horror and the sound of screams mixing with the shrill cawing of the crows, but she couldn't.

She felt relieved. It was like her pain was finally visible.

One bird came in her direction, stopping on a tree branch nearby and gazed at her.

"*It's time, Mary.*" She heard the goddess's voice in her head.

"How?" she asked. Mary wasn't scared. She knew there were worse things than dying.

In front of her, a small crack on the frozen stream slowly grew, breaking the ice, showing the cold water below. It wasn't a big space, enough for one person to dip their legs.

"It has to be your decision. Pain is unyielding. No sorrow can be eased without first being held."

Mary knew what she had to do. She took off her shoes, feeling her bones ache and her breath ragged. Considering how hard it was to breathe and how much her back hurt, she didn't have much longer now, anyway.

The crow came closer to her, landing on the rock.

"Thank you," Mary whispered, kneeling on the snow. The bird got even closer to her and rested its small head onto her forehead.

She could feel, strange as it was, warm lips kissing her forehead.

Stepping into the icy water, the chill bit her knees as she sank into the frozen riverbed, water reaching her hips, her breasts, up her shoulders. Mary took one deep breath and *surrendered*.

At the beginning, the cold water felt like shards of glass—almost impossible to endure. But somehow, slowly, Mary began to feel warm. She let the water seize her. The stream seemed to pull at her very bones, embracing her like a final lullaby. She looked up and saw the birds that didn't stop coming for the town, filling the night.

Her lungs didn't burn any longer. She knew she should be in pain, suffocating, but she wasn't. It felt as if she was suspended there, the water's touch washing over her grief like a benediction, her heartbeat diminishing.

The cold gave way to something akin to release: her pain dissolving, her body free, her soul at last untethered.

Mary's breath slowed—and she heard a sound she thought she would never again hear: her daughter's laughter.

Then, small baby fingers held onto her right hand, and her face softened.

The pain was finally gone.

The village broke under the weight of Mary Còmhan's sorrow. The birds did not kill outright, but they tore at body and soul alike, leaving the people hollowed, stripped of joy. Happiness had fled; only grief remained. Mary's body was never found. Those who sought forgiveness found that none could be given.

Madness rose like a tide. Suspicion poisoned neighbors, turning once-close friends into enemies. The town, once alive with laughter, became a hollow shell. One by one, the villagers withered. The land became barren; nothing ever grew there again.

And at night, when the wind stirred through the empty houses, some swore they saw a shadow in the shape of a woman with arms resembling wings, feathers shifting like smoke. Others heard a cry, sharp and desperate, echoing through the ruins—a sorrow that would not be silenced.

About the Author

Camilla Zahn has been creating universes in her head since she was a small child. She holds a degree in filmmaking, and when she isn't writing, she helps other authors with developmental edits and writing mentorships. Although a lover of horror and twisted narratives, she firmly believes that life itself is far scarier than any imagined dark story.

Follow her on Instagram (@zahnbooks) to discover more of her stories, explore behind the scenes of her writing, and keep up with her latest work.

To Feast on Fear

by Jane Humen

Content/Trigger Warnings

- Brief mention of incest

- Miscarriage

- Animal death

- Supernatural activity

- Body horror

For many years, the very atmosphere of the island seemed designed to ward off approaching humans. It was as if nature wanted to protect itself, putting up barricades of its own volition. Animals were plentiful, but not a single human footstep had struck the earth there. The island stood in the middle of the Puget Sound, undiscovered for centuries.

In the winter of 1892, a group of settlers in rickety wooden boats drifted to their new home. After their previous home became too crowded, they looked for a new place to inhabit. They had spent the previous century drifting from one unoccupied area to the next, always vaguely discontent, feeling pulled toward something, but they weren't quite sure what it was that called to them.

The Greens were considered the leaders of their little enclave. The first time they held an election for mayor, Dale won by a landslide. His brother Fred was highly regarded, both for being a kind man and for figuring out an agricultural system for the new community.

Everything seemed normal on the island, but the Greens carried a secret they hoped no one would find out. It was no surprise when Susanna ended up pregnant with Fred's child, but they did their best to hide it.

It was also not surprising when Susanna ended up miscarrying just a few weeks later. The whole thing was uncomplicated. Almost expected. It was rare that products of incest survived past conception very long, if at all, and they knew that. Still, the outcome saddened them both, even though they hadn't had a plan for explaining the child's existence once it was born. They knew what they were doing was considered sinful and couldn't help but view the loss as a sort of punishment—though, of course, it wasn't. Just a bad outcome, not a deserved one.

They healed from the loss as best as they could. Fred distracted himself by running a thriving farm and, later, marrying Alice. Susanna took up sewing and ran a ladies' Bible study. Once Fred and Alice moved in together, Susanna and Dale were left alone in the house the siblings had built. Though both were somewhat lonely as they still looked for partners of their own, they at least had each other for company.

One day when Dale was on the porch doing his woodworking, trying to carve out a nice bird he could display on the mantlepiece, Susanna all but flew out the door, breathless, startling him so badly he nearly took his finger off with the knife he was holding. Fred, who had been visiting, fell off the porch steps.

Dale cursed, apologized for having done so in the presence of a woman, and said, "What on earth?" He was more than a little bewildered by the sudden turn of events. A man couldn't even make art, he reflected, without having his peace interrupted by something totally beyond his control.

"The wall," she said, barely getting the words out, "the wall is changing."

His first thought was that she had completely lost her senses. Walls didn't change. They were walls. Solid. Hell, he had built this one himself.

"Do you mean the house is falling apart?" he said in total confusion, everything he was holding falling onto the small table beside him with a clatter. "How could it be?" He trotted after her like a sort of skeptical horse.

"Not falling apart," she repeated for emphasis, as if desperate now to make him understand her point. "It's . . . shifting."

He thought it was something innocent she was simply unfamiliar with. Maybe an outbreak of mold.

"All right," he said. "Show me."

She led him to the place where she had first noticed the disturbance. Fred followed after them.

At first, he had no idea what she was talking about. But at the exact moment he opened his mouth to say there was nothing there and she was spouting nonsense, he saw it too.

The wall did change. A shimmering warp in reality caught them both off guard. The wall seemed to bend, to change, as though a hole were about to open in it, and then it became normal once more.

Susanna pointed at the spot. "So you saw that too, then?"

"Yes." He rubbed his beard, not sure what to make of the phenomenon.

"What could it be?"

He was afraid to say what he thought it might be. It certainly wasn't natural. Not something of this world. Just by looking at it, he was certain it came from a more sinister place than any of them wanted to consider.

They all decided in that moment of silence not to worry about it. Certainly not to talk about it with anyone else.

And none of them gave it another thought.

A decade passed without incident until Fred and Alice's son found the family dog dead one morning. Jimmy came into the house hooting and hollering, crying out much the same way as his aunt had on that strange day long before he was born. Whatever force had once scared Susanna had now found its way to her brother.

For his part, Fred couldn't help but feel guilty. He had heard Sparky barking and growling at something unknown the night before, but hadn't gotten up to investigate. Now he realized that in his nonchalance he had failed both the dog and his son. He hadn't thought it was anything to worry about, but clearly something more sinister than a squirrel or raccoon had been present.

The strangest thing, he told Alice in hushed tones as they talked together in bed that night, was that he had found no marks on the dog. Not one. If not for the fact that the animal was cold and stiff, it might have just been sleeping—there were no signs of trauma to it at all.

As weird as that sudden death had been, Fred tried to put it out of his mind. He figured dogs could have sudden heart attacks from fear, but the story he gave Jimmy, so as not to traumatize him further, was that Sparky simply must have died in his sleep. Never mind that he wasn't very old. His son could figure out that discrepancy later. Or, hopefully, never.

As much as Fred tried to ignore the strange happenings in the house, it became all but impossible very quickly after Sparky had been buried. For one thing, those strange warping, shimmering places in the wall had returned. Even Jimmy, who seemed to notice nothing that didn't pertain to the outdoors, seemed unsettled by them, enough that he asked one day, "Papa, what's wrong with the wall?"

"You know," Fred said carefully, "I'm not sure, Son. I'll ask around town. See if anyone knows what it could be."

He started with Jedediah Murphy, who was the oldest surviving resident on the island. He figured his choices were between that and the local police force, which had never been of much help even in the direst of emergencies.

Jedediah stroked his beard and thought for a moment. One blind eye stared sightlessly into the distance, gathering wisdom from beyond the world.

"You aren't the first person to notice such happenings," he finally said.

Well, thank God, was Fred's mental response. But then he thought about the implications of others noticing something was wrong and shuddered. Maybe the island really wasn't safe anymore. Maybe it never had been.

And if the island wasn't safe, then where could he find sanctuary? When he had come to the island, he had felt like it was the last safe place left in the world, free of people and their corrupting influences.

Yet now a thought tugged at the back of his mind that maybe a whole different kind of corruption had been at play all along, and he was just now figuring it out.

What was he supposed to do about that? He had never been a particularly religious man, but that was his first thought—to turn to a higher power and ask it to make this go away. He attended church like everyone else on the island—had even helped build the place where services were held every Sunday—but in the quiet moments of the day where he was most honest with himself, he could admit to never having put too much stock in the doctrine. He found most of it a little absurd. But now . . . maybe that was his best defense against whatever this was.

"What would you do about this?" he asked Jedediah after a long and uncomfortable silence, trying not to offend the man by staring at his sightless eye. "If it were you going through this? Your home? Your pets, your family?"

"I would take my family," Jedediah said slowly. "And I would leave."

Some part of Fred knew Jedediah was right, but another part of him couldn't help but want to stay. As though he was being tugged toward it, silently told to do it by some unseen force.

"I suppose," Fred said noncommittally, trying to keep the trembling of fear out of his voice. "But I don't know where to go."

Jedediah stared at Fred, his face somber. "Truth be told, friend, anywhere is better than here."

Frustrated with the lack of real help—or just not hearing an answer he liked—Fred left with a polite goodbye. There had to be someone on this island who could help him find a way to avoid having to leave the only place he'd ever been that felt like home.

Though he still couldn't get himself to really believe in the idea of there being a merciful and loving God, Fred decided to walk down to the church anyway. Just to see, he told himself. It couldn't hurt.

"Hey, Scraps," he said to the fat gray cat lounging in the doorway. There was a clattering in the back of the building, and the island's priest emerged. Father Joseph was clad in a dust-stained robe, his cheeks pink with exertion.

"Hello, can I help you?" he asked. "Fred, right? Sorry for the mess, I'm tidying up before Sunday's service."

Fred had expected to tell the other man about the house. What came out of his mouth instead was, "My son's dog died." *What did he want?* he chastised himself. *A funeral for the mutt?* Not happening.

Father Joseph's face twisted. "I'm sorry."

"It's all right." It wasn't, Fred thought morosely. The misfortunes in his life were escalating a little too quickly for his liking.

"You look like something else is troubling you." Father Joseph gave Scraps a pat on the head and then studied Fred, waiting for him to divulge whatever was on his mind.

"Well, yes, there's another reason why I'm here. See, the dog died, but other strange things have been happening as well."

A somber look came over the priest's face, and his eyebrows knitted together. "Such as?"

Fred took a deep breath. He didn't want to elaborate on the family's misfortunes. He had become superstitious as of late, and talking about bad happenings felt like they would bring more of it upon them. And what if something happened to his wife next, or his son? How would he be able to live with himself knowing that he was the one who might have brought harm on them just by speaking the truth?

"There's something strange happening to the house." With the dam broken, he launched into the explanation, trying to get the words out as fast as possible. If he didn't speak them aloud now, he never would.

Father Joseph listened with the attentiveness of a man old enough to no longer be surprised by anything—stoic the whole time, despite the horror being clearly outlined before him.

"I think this is something I ought to handle," he said. "There have been reports of similar cases on the East Coast, where only divine intervention could help." And sometimes not even that, but he kept that particular thought to himself.

"All right." Fred felt terrible for dragging the priest into the situation, but at that point he didn't see what else he could do. This was way out of his realm of expertise, and it just so happened to have landed right in the priest's.

"I'll have to do some research," Father Joseph said. "I'll come to your house when I feel prepared."

Fred didn't dare ask how long it would be.

He didn't really want to know.

The priest turned up again two weeks later. There was going to be a full moon that night. Fred couldn't decide whether to consider this a good or bad omen.

"The first thing we need to do is bless the house," he said matter-of-factly. "We'll cleanse it, then attempt to exorcise whatever force might be here. The important thing is to have conviction in the belief that a higher power will make it go away," he said with a pointed look at the family. By then, Fred couldn't even remember the last time he had taken them to church. He had been so distracted. He wasn't sure if that had anything to do with why their house was now, apparently, haunted, but the idea that he might be responsible for even a small fraction of his family's current suffering made him feel like he had failed them. Failed as a man, a husband, and a father.

Maybe this was karma for the times he had lain with Susanna as though she were his wife. But even supposing that was the case, those he loved didn't deserve to deal with the fallout.

"What happens if this doesn't work?" Alice said from behind him, in the smallest and most timid voice he had ever heard her use. She was normally quite outspoken, so it was strange to see her personality shrunk down like this.

"Do you want the honest answer or the polite one?" Father Joseph worried at his beard, twisting it with one hand. It both comforted and unsettled Fred to know that he was frightened, too.

"Honest," Fred and Alice said as Jimmy watched the conversation, goggle-eyed, his head moving back and forth like he was observing a particularly riveting game of tennis. They had had a hushed discussion about sheltering him from the truth of these strange events, but had just as quickly decided there was no point in doing so. The kid was both too smart and too nosy for that to ever work.

"The smartest thing to do would be to persuade everyone to evacuate the island."

Fred recalled all the wooden boats that had come to pile up on the shore in recent days, and realized with a jolt that they were lifeboats. Wheels turned in his head, and he realized what Father Joseph had really been doing when he said he was "tidying" the church. The man was no fool. Unlike the rest of them, he had firmly taken the blindfold off his eyes and knew just what was at stake. He had a plan for every possible contingency. Fred was still terrified, but realized they were in the best hands possible.

"They won't see a reason to, will they?" Alice fretted. "Nobody else knows that this … whatever this is … has taken over our house. They won't understand why they have to leave unless it affects them too, and that would be a disaster."

"I could lie," was Father Joseph's soft contemplation, though he hated lying.

"It would be better just to tell the truth," Fred interjected.

In the end, the idea that it was better to be honest won out. The next morning at Sunday service, Father Joseph explained that he and the Green family would stay behind to try to cleanse the home and island of evil spirits, but everyone else needed to leave for their own safety.

People were compliant enough, but overnight their little sanctuary went from being insular and peaceful to a sensation in the press. Someone, or several someones, had told the local paper back on the mainland what was happening on the mysterious tree-lined island only a few people had ever set foot upon, and now its biggest secret could no longer be contained.

A horde of reporters, all clamoring for some sort of breaking news item, descended on the island with notepads in hand. They camped outside Fred and Alice's home like vultures. By then, the Green family wanted to leave, but they felt like they had no choice but to stay. Every time they tried to leave, they would become ill and have to turn back. It became obvious that whatever had invaded their house, it was forcing them to stay tied to it until the bitter end.

Father Joseph began the exorcism as everyone watched. He had sprinkled holy water around the property and doused the suspicious wall with it. He was halfway through reciting the Lord's Prayer when the wood began to splinter and the group leaned away in terror.

Through the spaces between the fingers covering his eyes, Jimmy watched as the wall opened up to become a great black hole, and out of it came the force that had plagued the island since time out of mind. The creature—a hideous thing that stood as tall as the house itself, sightless and lumbering, with bright green scales covered in dripping, purulent slime—shot out an arm. There was a cracking noise as Father Joseph's head twisted to the left. He fell to the floor and lay there, limp and still.

"Run," Fred said, holding up what was left of the vial of holy water and a lit match. "Alice, take Jimmy and run!"

She knew he was about to sacrifice himself to save them. She wanted to protest, but there just wasn't time. She grabbed the screaming Jimmy and ran for the shore as if her life depended on it. Her last view of the island was of the home she'd once loved going up in flames.

Fred died alone as the house burned. Whatever entity had been there, seemingly satisfied for now, disappeared along with the island's population.

It remained empty of humans for the next one hundred years. And when a property developer came to scout the land, he noticed mysterious wisps in the air, like ghosts or smoke.

He dismissed this as nothing to worry about, and had soon built up a thriving town.

But one day, the house's walls began to change once more.

What was once there had returned to feast on fear again.

About the Author

Jane Humen is a writer from Washington state.

She is a summa cum laude graduate of Arizona State University, where she earned a bachelor's degree in English in 2020. She also holds a master's degree in Professional and Creative Writing from Central Washington University.

She is currently revising a novel and drafting a collection of poetry. Visit her website: www.janehumen.com

The Basement

by Bryanna Bernice

Content/Trigger Warnings

- Murder

- Blood

- Violence

- Kidnapping

- Manipulation

- Implied Self-Harm

- Mention of dead animals/people

- Animal/human remains

There is a yearning that tugs at the effervescence of my heart, manipulating the organ as though it's nothing more than a puppet on strings. My fingers itch, eyes twitch and lips quiver as I fight the desire, pushing it helplessly as far as I can.

But I can feel them crawling up my spine, millions of creatures scattering across my skin and feeding upon my soul.

It's almost as if they're truly there, truly tormenting me, enveloping me in their essence. I keep them tucked away in the darkness of my basement, a sanctuary of sorts—the scent of mildew and sterilization preceding them, keeping them safe.

I remain unsure from whom.

What began as a simple fascination transcended into a twisted admiration, a connection that, if severed, I became certain would lead to ruin. Perhaps I've been right all along, or maybe this endeavor has been nothing more than a test of mortality—one I've *failed* with flying colors. Their presence, seemingly inconsequential, feels as though we've been merged into a single entity, bound by the laws of eternity. I could not live without my specimens, just as they cannot thrive without my sanctuary.

Glass jars filled to the brim with isopropyl alcohol, hearts and minds preserved for a lifetime of discovery. My fingertips have traced their labels an infinite number of times, the ink sometimes bleeding beneath my fingertips and seeping into the print. It began with small things, simple specimens I could easily capture. Insects, arachnids, local roadkill, and even flora did well not to stray from my interest. Pressed, polished and preserved, it was my hand alone that remedied their once so feeble existence.

Then I moved to the countryside, hoping for a better start. Life in a small town simply wasn't for me, reputation was the name of the game, and it seemed I couldn't help but fail time and time again. A new environment, surroundings mossy and tinted phthalo green, birdsong to rise with every morning and chirping crickets lulling me back to slumber in the evening. This was without a doubt my calling. The great outdoors and nobody to answer to but myself. So, I packed my specimens without a second thought, drained what little savings remained to my name, and fled from my family's home under the cover of night. I haven't seen them since.

I've yet to wonder whether they yearn for my return.

Since my departure, I've traversed the natural world in search of new specimens to call my own, a new family, one I've created with my own two hands.

One particular morning, humid and moist, the forest floor I've known for many moons gave way beneath my feet. A fall that would typically leave a man scarred proving to be nothing more than an inconvenience. An ache shivered within my legs, akin to a burning sensation, and when I lifted my pant leg, there was a redness along my shin that would surely bruise—perhaps even scar. Another badge of honor. I huffed, looking up at the steadily setting sun from my position within the man-made dirt prison. I'd seen this before, a method for capturing large animals, and yet I'd never encountered one until then. It made me feel safer, almost. Knowing they were in place was like a cushion; the area never shied from its fair share of predators.

I sighed, exasperated, spinning my backpack to rest against my chest when something poking out of the dirt caught my eye. I fell onto my knees, sifting through the darkened earth, curiosity getting the best of me. The object grew larger, the dirt in between dusting my fingertips and entering the crevices of my chewed, jagged fingernails.

When the dust finally settled, I was left in agog retrenchment, passing the object between my soiled fingers, mouth agape and eyes pricking with allergen.

A skull. A *real* human skull.

It was unlike anything I'd ever seen before, truly remarkable. Judging by its state, I could only assume it'd been down there for countless years, the fabrication of the man-made structure unearthing its likeness.

There must be more.

I spent the rest of the day and well into the evening shoveling away dirt with my bare hands. My limbs ached, back screaming as I hunched and cleared away the dirt and grime. My efforts were dutifully rewarded. I emerged at the break of dawn with a new collection to call my own.

But since that day I've ached for more, practically shivering with excitement at the mere thought of unearthing another just like them. There's a yearning in my heart that cannot be quelled by what I've amassed in this cabin. Every day, I return to the pit where I'd fallen, searching for some stray soul who lost its life too soon. I remain unlucky; there is nothing to greet me when I return.

So, I take it upon myself to settle more traps beneath tarps of woven dead leaves and behind lenient shrubbery. Bears aren't uncommon in this neck of the forest and I wouldn't want one to disturb my collection. It's merely a meticulous precaution.

One winter morning—months having passed since I'd first fallen—freshly fallen powder glistening untouched, there's a faint noise buzzing in my ear. It's certainly not anything I've heard before. At least, not for quite a long time.

I bundle up for an excursion out in the snow. A thick jacket lined with old fur and boots to keep the snow away from my feet. As I approach, the noise grows louder, more intense. Someone calling out for help.

It's a man's voice, surely, and it seems he's been caught in one of the deterrents I made for myself—a successful endeavor where I swore I'd once wasted my time.

The man captured within the trap is screaming at the top of his lungs. Nobody would hear him from here, not a soul daring to wander this part of the forest. I chose this cabin because of its exclusivity, tucked away and miles from the nearest structure.

"Oh!" the man screams at the sight of me, jumping up and down, rejoicing. "Thank goodness someone heard me! I-I got separated from my friends back at the lodge a few miles west! Do you see my phone anywhere up there? I have to call them to let them know I'm all right!"

I look around, spotting the shattered screen of his cellphone only a few meters away from where I'm standing. I wander forward, placing my foot over the device, my full weight crushing an already mangled device. I wouldn't be surprised if it were completely broken. There's a moment when a thickness hangs in the air, when morality comes into question and I ponder if my mind is in the right place. This man beneath me is innocent, yearning for help that only I can provide. Nobody will find him, not out here, and certainly not before he freezes to death.

"Hey!" The man trapped by my actions calls out, waiting for my response. "See anything?"

"No," I say, so quiet he doesn't hear it at first, so quiet not even the universe can hear what I've done.

I lean over the ditch, twisting my pack forward and producing a rope. He seems skeptical as the aid is dropped down in front of him, looking between me and the rope, but I feign a smile and reassure him of my pure intentions. When he's gathering his fallen items, back turned away from me, I place his cellphone in my bag for safekeeping. A precaution.

"You look dreadful," I tell the lost man once he's come over the edge, palms red and burning from his struggle to rise up. He's rather easy on the eyes, round-lenses cracked and blond hair disheveled in the midst of his escapades. His eyes remind me of sapphires, lips thin and dry. "I have a cabin not far from here. Would you let me take you there? We'll get you something warm to drink and call your friends."

The man is visibly relieved, clutching at his chest as he breathes out his thanks between fits of catching his breath.

We traverse the space in between and make it to my cabin in no time at all. On our way, the weather begins to pick up, a storm upon the horizon. I urge the man to shed his clothes. He obeys without a second thought. I prepare hot water in the kettle on an open flame and drape a warm blanket over the man as he sits beside the fireplace. Its embers reflect in the cracked lens of his glasses, his form shivering and knees tucked under his chin.

"I don't mean to be a bother, but do you think I could make that call now?"

I smile, nodding my head as I stalk toward the landline. I drag it from where it sits beside the loveseat to his left, leaving it at his feet. The wire has stretched as far as it can possibly go, the young man having to scoot away from his solace beside the fireplace.

The kettle whistles.

I rush over to lower the flame and prepare us both a steaming cup of Earl Grey. I offer him my favorite mug. He doesn't seem to notice, engrossed in his task. I take a seat at his side, cocking my head to the right and then left. He seems disturbed.

"The line doesn't seem to be working," he explains, punching the numbers once again, but not a sound accompanies the attempt. "And without my phone, I have no way of calling them to let them know I'm all right."

I hum. The landline hasn't operated in months. I haven't paid the bill for as long as I've lived here. The telephone is nothing more than decoration—a means of feeling somewhat normal.

"Must be the storm," I fib, gesturing to the windows. There's a thick layer of frost overtop them, pellets of snow thundering down outside. It seemed to pick up on our way, finally full force as the hours passed. My guest sighs, defeated.

As I hand him the mug, our fingers touch for only a brief moment.

"Do you have a name?" he asks as though I'm some sort of deity, something to be worshipped. I smile, nodding my head. It takes me a moment to come up with a suitable alias. Something forgettable. There's no point in cradling memories that will never come to pass.

"Ellie," I tell him. It slips off my tongue so simply I almost forget my true name. When was the last time I heard it spoken aloud? Who can say?

"Steven."

The smile on his lips, blissful innocence, is almost enough to make me reconsider bringing him here. This isn't the kind of place someone like him belongs. He has his entire life ahead of him.

Then again, I did once, too.

Mine was taken from me.

"What brings you around here?" I ask him. "It's rare to see people wandering this part of the forest. You're lucky you survived that fall. It wasn't intended for the animals to live." The truth slips out before I can realize what's wrong in speaking it.

His eyes widened. "You dug that hole?"

"For the bears. So many of them, it's not safe out here otherwise."

"Isn't that dangerous?"

I hum. "Seems so."

There's a breath of unease that collapses within Steven's lungs. It's hardly noon by the time he's settled, skin warm and face once again flushed with life. He tries the phone again, and then once more, before finally conceding to the fact that it won't be working anytime soon.

"You're welcome to wait it out. The storm, I mean. Doesn't seem like either of us will be able to travel around anytime soon."

"I'm starving," he says.

"Do you like steak?"

"Love it."

In the freezer, I have a supply of various meats. There's a generator in the basement that powers this little shack, keeping me afloat where I'd otherwise drown. I wipe away the ice from one of the labels I'd written in permanent ink. It'll be due to expire soon.

I give it a moment to thaw, prepping the rest of what I'll need while I give it time. "You didn't answer my question earlier, Steven. What did you say you're doing out here?"

"My friends and I are spending winter break in a cabin just out west. I thought it'd be a fun trip before I graduate in the spring."

"So you're a student?" I question. I knew he was young, though I'll admit a bit younger than I was anticipating.

"That's right. I'm studying forensics."

"You're a smart one then, aren't you?"

He grows bashful, avoiding my gaze. "I'd like to hope so."

I begin preparing the meat, growing impatient as I tear into the half-frozen packaging. My hands begin itching for action, flexing involuntarily. I fear that if I don't keep busy, I'll resort to something terrible.

More terrible than what I've already done. More terrible than the thoughts swimming around my mind.

"Do you live alone?" he asks. "I-I don't mean to pry. It just seems like I haven't seen anyone other than you in hours."

"All alone," I recount. "Figure the closest people to me are your friends up in that cabin."

The meat sizzles deliciously on the flame, the aroma wafting through the cabin. It doesn't take long for the meat to conclude its course, a healthy portion of canned greens plopped on its side. The meal is nothing much, but dinner was short notice.

If it were up to me, I'd be having a very different delicacy.

I watch Steven cut through the meat—a perfect medium. A contented sigh escapes from him, and all the while I observe as he devours every bite as though it's his last. Only when he's scarfed away half his plate do I move to my own. All the while my eyes subtly scour him, observing.

Time passes, and the sun has long since set upon the horizon. With a needle and thread between my fingertips, I work on mending an abrasion in Steven's clothing. He lies asleep in front of the fireplace.

I hum a tune I can't remember the name of. There's not much I can seem to remember these days. But I know I must preserve my specimens, my life's purpose. If it weren't for them, I don't think I could continue on living, don't think I could maintain what shred of sanity resides within me.

The lights go out.

I don't have many, a few lamps I've scattered here and there. But the difference is noticeable, plunging us into darkness apart from the fireplace crackling with life. The flames are dim—firewood is in short supply—casting an ominous glow along the room. Steven sleeps with his back toward me, soft face cast with bright orange. The generators in the basement are long outdated, yet they power what minimal energy I require just fine, burning fuel I've accumulated over time. All it takes is a jumpstart and we'll be fine.

I rise from my spot on the couch slowly, a needle and thread left in my place. I'll only be a moment. The door will only be unlocked long enough for me to restore power. Nothing can go wrong.

Absolutely nothing.

The trek to the basement is brief, a door from inside leading into the depths of my life's work. The key that dangles around my neck is put to work, opening a series of locks to allow access—me and only me. This neck of the cabin is reserved for my eyes alone.

The darkness that welcomes me is far from foreign. I've memorized this room like the back of my hand, recognizing it more than I do my own face. In front of me there is a table where I examine specimens. Beneath it, there sits a shelf containing various decomposition and preservation agents. There will come a time when they'll have to be refilled, a day's trip, when my angels will be left to suffer without me. I can only pray they won't miss me much.

They must rejoice. Soon they'll have a new friend, a new addition. Then the cycle will begin anew.

When I move to my left, the shelf that houses insects greets my blind touch. I know that if I were to move my hand further within, I would be greeted by the smooth exterior of a jar containing a horned beetle, and even further there would be a mole cricket neighboring an imperial moth caterpillar. The line proceeds uninterrupted, filled to the brim with varying insects.

I reach the generator in no time at all, taking hold of its handle and letting it rip. The engine sputters and fails, another attempt resulting in the same. It takes me some time to get the generator to give way, and just when I think my efforts have been rewarded, a voice calls to me from the top of the stairs.

"Ellie!" Steven yells, hands cupping his lips. "The power went out! A-Are you down here?"

A curse escapes from under my breath. I didn't think he would rise from his slumber so soon. It's fine, I rationalize; just another obstacle in the grand scheme.

"I'll be just a minute!" I called out.

"Can I help?"

"No!" The denial leaves my throat more hostile than I'd intended it. "I'm all right, Steven! Just let me know when the lights come back on!"

He responds with confirmation, letting me know when the lights have finally come on, many attempts down the line. I sigh a breath of relief, thankful the potential disaster has passed.

That is until I hear footsteps bounding down the stairs, an ecstatic Steven glad to see me bathed in the safety of light once more.

"Is this entire cabin fueled by a single generator?" he asks. Before I can answer, I watch the way he stops in his tracks, movement ceasing just in front of my specimens.

Fuck.

Steven doesn't say a word at first, observing the various jars and dioramas with an estranged fascination. I can't tell what he's thinking, only that the gears in his head are turning at a million miles per minute. On the observation table there sits a dagger tipped with crimson. In slow, almost imperceptible steps, I make my way toward it. In a tight grip, I allow it to fall at my side.

Steven's fingertips brush a jar containing a deer fetus.

"How did you get these things?" he inquires. I still can't tell what he means when he speaks—whether it's intended to be accusatory. Perhaps nothing more than morbid curiosity. I can't be too cautious, not when my life's work is on the line, not when everything I've ever truly loved might be taken from me. I creep around the examination table, the tip of my blade scraping against the side ever so slightly.

"I study them." It's the beginning of the truth yet not entirely a lie. "Everything here is ethically sourced."

Almost everything.

I watch the very moment Steven's eyes land on the row of preserved skulls—owls, skunks, coyotes and hawks. Then I watch the horror that casts upon his face when the sight of *human* skulls becomes apparent. For the most part, I'd consider them well-preserved. With no background in taxidermy whatsoever, I'd say I've done well for myself.

"Are those...?"

My expression is blank. Steven backs away slowly. The hook I've so carefully lined with bait is failing me, the line snapping in two. I ready the dagger into a comfortable position, waiting for him to finish his sentence. "Are those human skulls? Real human skulls?"

From upstairs there's a noise akin to beeping, a ringtone. Something I haven't heard in ages.

Steven realizes what it is before I do. He bolts up the stairs. I lag dangerously behind him, watching just in time as he rummages through my backpack to retrieve the hidden device. He looks at me incredulously, tears brimming in the corners of his eyes, but he refuses to let them fall.

"You had this the entire time?" he questions.

I feel as though the answer is obvious. He's found what he once considered lost alongside my possessions. It's only rational that I was the one to take it, leading him to believe it had been forgotten in the first place.

I remain silent. It only seems to irk him more, the way I refuse to answer any of his questions. But there's nothing to say. Not from my perspective, anyway.

There's something that comes over me, rushing through me like waves against a distant shore. I allow Steven to make the call, his friends frantic on the other line.

"We haven't been able to get through to you!" I hear one of them yell through the receiver. But before Steven can answer, give them any indication of his location and where he's been over these past several hours, his phone battery concedes to its misery.

Once more, it's only the two of us and my specimens down in the basement.

"I did tell you there's no signal, didn't I?"

Steven collapses into a frenzy, rushing at me with nothing but his bare hands. In the midst of struggle, my dagger is thrust from my grasp, the boy I'd once considered meek and unassuming overpowering me in a near instant. We tumble onto the floor, bodies pushing against each other.

"People go missing in these woods all the time," Steven groans out, using my shoulders to push the back of my head into the hardwood floor, a stinging pain swirling in the back of my mind. "I knew taking this trip was a risk I had to take—I just had to see what was going on!"

"You have a morbid curiosity, Steven. You're the same as me."

"I'm nothing like you!"

I don't believe it for a moment.

Using my feet, I overpower Steven's body weight over mine, pushing the boy back and retreating toward the basement, spotting my dagger on the way. Steven, quicker than I thought possible, tosses himself on top of me, sending us both tumbling onto the ground once more. I curse loudly, the dagger just out of reach of my fingertips. I reach, feeling as though the muscles in my shoulder will be torn apart at the seams. Finally, the handle is in my grasp, and I stab the knife into the man's side, a scream erupting from his throat as he rolls onto his other side.

I retreat, running as fast as my legs will carry me and darting for the basement. I need to find it. I know I have it hidden somewhere. My mind wanders to Steven bleeding upstairs, whether I punctured a potential organ and ruined yet another perfect specimen.

Silence overcomes the cabin; the only sounds that register are my heaving chest and snow falling outside.

The whirlwind outside assures me that Steven won't be going any-where soon, not without braving the elements and freezing to death. He would remain well-preserved in that case. And while the option seemed a sound one, I can't say I'm particularly keen on thawing the man out.

I hear the door to the basement creek open, nearly silent, yet not quite. Steven's shadow is downcast from upstairs, the darkness of his silhouette consuming my specimen.

"Ellie!" he grits out. In the silence I can hear his shallow breaths and blood steadily beginning to puddle on the floor beneath his feet. He descends the stairs, taking them one at a time, cautiously.

I know my pistol is somewhere shrouded in this mess of belongings. I've taken the time to sort my things, always so enthralled by the allure of my specimen. They take up my every waking hour, the seconds that pass me by every day. My fingertips brush the cold metal, grip foreign beneath my fingertips. It's been a long time since I've used the weapon; evidence of its sin sat with a crater upon one of my shelves.

I release a deep breath, aiming the gun at the bottom of the steps.

Steven is there waiting, spotting me through the dim lighting upstairs provides us.

I ready.

Steven dares a step forward, and if he's noticed the weapon in my hands, he doesn't show it.

I aim.

The man releases the grip he's held on his side, palm stained a deep crimson. His steps show intention; his face contorts with hatred.

I fire.

Steven halts, swaying back and forth, clutching his body as the sound registered to us both. The light inside me dims, another specimen put to waste. I watch Steven collapse on the floor, waiting for a moment, watching to make sure my ease isn't premature.

But Steven doesn't move a muscle, doesn't make a sound. Silence envelops the cabin once more, shrouding it in the mystery from which I'd been delivered. Relief washes over me, my posture deflating, posture condemned to figment.

I move around the body, expecting there to be a pool of blood at my feet, another mishap to make appear reborn anew. But the stickiness and smell of iron never register.

There's not a drop of blood.

Steven shoots up, taking hold of my ankles and slicing my Achilles to shreds. I fall down beside him, the man dropping the dagger and using my moment of weakness to overpower me. I groan as he drags me onto the floor beneath him, pressing his hands against my neck, constricting even the smallest hope of air to my lungs. I flail here and there, slamming my fists against his arms and clawing at his skin, but he doesn't relent, fueled by the intention of survival. My strength begins to escape me, lack of air consuming my bodily functions and rendering them hopeless. My arms fall from where they claw at Steven's skin, blood trailing down his face and dripping against my cheeks.

At my sides, my fingertips brush the familiar sensation of a dagger, the very same Steven had used to immobilize me. I take it into whatever grip that remains, the fight within me practically a memory.

I refuse to die here. There's so much more I yearn from this world, so much I've yet to uncover and specimens that rely on my care to thrive.

My dagger plunges into the side of his neck with ease, blood splattering across what seems like miles of distance. My clothes are drenched, my floor puddling with crimson.

The young man collapses on top of me, a mere memory.

I huff, regaining oxygen and rolling his limp body off me. I watch Steven heave his final breath, arms reaching out to me as though in prayer, begging for his life in the final moments I alone have the privilege of witnessing.

I loom over his body, dazed and exhausted, when I hear a crunch beneath my boot.

The young man's glasses have been shattered beyond recognition. I take them between my fingers, surveying what remains. It'll best be kept as a token, another memory of this day. The feeling of the razor shards reminds me of my humanity.

I rid my body of sticky crimson ichor, boiling freezing water so that I might have a comfortable bath and scrub the memories of my actions away. I spend what feels like weeks bleaching and wiping away blood with vinegar, the scent lingering on my skin longer than I would've hoped. And when a sheriff knocks on my door inquiring about a missing boy, I feign all the innocence in the world, and the rugged, clearly exhausted man bids me a bittersweet farewell.

So many lives have been claimed by these woods, and yet the world remains none the wiser.

While surveying Steven's limp body, I'm careful not to disturb any of the precious bones and organs lying dormant within him. I stuff beneath his skin with fresh herbs that will dry deliciously inside of him, and get to work, tearing away at his flesh to the best of my abilities—doing well to target what I've come to collect.

Time and time again, stray hikers and explorers have fallen victim to my shenanigans. But they always managed to fight back, reducing me to primitive tactics—bludgeoning and battery.

But Steven was the exception, my masterpiece. Cracked ribs and broken arms have preceded my efforts thus far. But this is the culmination of my every desire—Steven has gifted me what I've lacked in my collection, something that cannot simply be bought; it must be earned.

So many keepsakes reside upon these shelves, memories Steven hadn't even begun to uncover, tucked away for my eyes alone. This room is nothing more than an introduction, a precedent to what truly lies in store. My palm splays against the wall furthest from the threshold of the stairs, searching the darkness for the familiar lock to which only I possess the key. It's been crafted by my own design, carved from the very bones that scatter the cabin grounds. The familiar click is music to my ears, and I open the passageway to reveal only my most loyal companions.

"Good evening," I greet, taking in the comfort only they can provide. My flesh and bones feel whole again, as though everything that's ever been wrong with me has been pieced back together in a mere instant.

They don't respond. I look crossed between them, wondering what I've done wrong.

Bleached bones hang from hooks upon my walls, skeletons of past selves. Some of them are incomplete; others with cracked bones I've glued back together to feign their entirety.

Steven will soon join them.

"Fine," I scoff, head in my hands. "I don't need you to tell me what I've done is wrong. Don't you think I regret it? Don't you think I mourn the loss of what could've been a friendship?"

Still, they remain silent. I continue on, hoping that my words will coax *something* from them.

"What I've done is awful, terrible. But I do it for you, for all of you! I don't deserve this admonishment. I deserve to be praised, to be loved and adored! Without me, where would you be if not six feet underground? Worms would hang from the sockets of your eyes and fungus from your ribs and toes. Is that what you want?"

Behind me, a knife falls from its place on the table. I know I've organized it well, and know where I left it.

Their message to me is clear as day. My family yearns for me on the other side.

The darkness envelops me, welcomes me into its midnight embrace with loving arms. My feet carry me down into the depths almost as if they possess a mind of their own. No matter how much I kill, disassemble and preserve, it's never enough. I'm unsure if it ever will be. There has to come a point where everything is truly worth it, where my constant state of exhaustion isn't all for naught.

When I look in the mirror, I no longer see myself. A wisp of who I once could've been is staring back at me. I see the atrocities I've committed, the pain and suffering my hands have caused.

Yet there is one specimen I've yet to capture, one thing I've yet to observe.

A dagger is between my fingers. The very same I used to cut away at Steven and those who miserably came before him. I aim its tip at my neck, staring into my eyes. They'll look lovely on the shelf right beside the others.

About the Author

Bryanna Bernice is an aspiring author who, from a young age, has been infatuated with all things macabre. That interest has since blossomed into a prospective literary career, her short story publications circulating online. She is currently working on her debut novel. Insight into her life as an avid reader and writer can be found on her Instagram account @bbernicebooks

Swarm

by Christopher J. Brice

Content/Trigger Warnings

This short story includes explicit language and sexual content, as well as scenes of blood, gore, and death.

One

The heat had come early that summer, rolling over the sand hills in a slow, relentless wave. By the third week of July, the whole town of Mullins was crispier than bacon.

Now, Mullins had always been a place that was one stiff breeze away from the grave, but this summer, the grave had moved in and cut itself a key to every house in town. On the north side of the town, where the prairie grass gave way to the first piece of desert, the sun shone brightly over the BioTech containment facility. Known locally as "The Hive" due to its boxy, honeycomb-like appearance. The facility was hunkered behind three rows of metal fencing and a perimeter of dunes. A low insectile drone emanated from the facility, blending with the pulse of cicadas until every living thing in the valley was singing the same hoarse, mechanical song.

Lori worked the night shift at The Hive. She clocked in at 7:00 p.m., when the sun hovered above the horizon, and clocked out at 3:00 a.m.

Tonight, she was early. She scanned her badge at the outer gate and felt the burr of static as she passed under the infrared. At the main entrance, Lori paused in the blinding brightness of the vestibule. Sweat trickled down the bridge of her nose. She pressed a knuckle to her brow, smearing away the sheen, and glanced over her shoulder to the west, where the grid of Mullins lay splayed beneath the dying light. The water tower was the first thing she saw, spindly legged and black against the horizon. The rest of the town radiated outward from its feet—the squat brick of the high school, the row of shops along Main Street. The grocery store parking lot shimmered with a mirage of heat, even at dusk.

Lori had grown up seeing Mullins from the inside, but from out here, on the facility's northern edge, the town resembled a mistake that a strong wind might erase. The streets, laid out in the perfect geometry favored by dead surveyors, glowed faintly as the sodium lamps flickered on, one by one. The houses were nothing more than tiny white rectangles, grouped in pairs or clusters, surrounded by orange lawns and the soft, perpetual haze of dust. Mullins had never been a beautiful place, but the summer's drought had stripped it of what little softness it once had. Everything was brittle and waiting to snap.

A pickup truck trundled along the perimeter road, its headlights ghostly in the gathering dusk. Lori watched it circle the facility before turning back to the doors. Within the glass, her own reflection hovered, vague and indistinct, dressed in a blue polyester uniform. She squared her shoulders, exhaled, and pulled the handle, stepping into the breathless hush of the airlock.

Inside The Hive, it was shockingly cold. Lori momentarily paused outside the security office, savoring the chill. Finding her cart, she scanned the janitor checklist on the clipboard and started down the main corridor. Her sneakers squeaked on the buffed floor, and it wasn't until a couple of hours later that she noticed the humming.

It wasn't the usual hum of electricity from the fluorescent lights above or the fans. It was something higher. More insistent. A sound with edges.

When she reached the southeast wing—Containment B, according to the sign—she realized the lights were flickering in time with the noise. There was a smell too. Faint but growing, like burned honey or the way the field behind the ethanol plant had smelled the day it caught fire.

Lori stopped the cart outside the first lab door and peered through the narrow glass. Inside was a man in a BioTech polo. He was hunched over a terminal, his face lit up by the monitor. He didn't look up when she knocked, so she moved on, figuring he was one of the new hires working hard to impress the bosses.

As she continued with her tasks, the buzzing grew louder, sending chills up and down her spine. When she turned the corner, all the lights in the hall went out, plunging everything into sudden darkness. She froze in place, waiting for the backup lights, but nothing happened. As she reached for her phone to use as a flashlight, an orange flare appeared at the end of the corridor.

Intrigued, Lori let it pull her forward until she stood before Lab 2B. Her fingers hesitated on the handle—the door should be locked. But when it yielded to her touch, a chill ran through her that had nothing to do with the facility's air conditioning. Pushing it open, she was met with a wave of humid and sticky heat. The humming was deafening here, and the burned honey smell was thicker and sweeter.

Taking in her surroundings, Lori noticed that a wall of glass tanks had been stacked to the ceiling on one side of the room. Inside of those tanks was a dense, black mass. A scientist in a full white suit stood in front of it, inspecting. Lori opened her mouth to speak, but the humming drowned her out.

Seconds later, the glass bowed outward. The smell of honey instantly became overwhelming to the point of disgusting. An alarm shrieked through the facility; a piercing wail that drilled into Lori's skull. She clapped her hands to her ears at the same time that the crack of shattering glass sent ice through her veins.

The scientist in the white suit stumbled backward, his arms windmilling as a black cloud erupted from the broken tank.

No, not a cloud. Bees.

Or, at least, that was what her mind—desperate to make sense of the impossible—called them. But these were not the bees she remembered from childhood. Drowsy, golden creatures that buzzed drunkenly around apple blossoms in her mother's garden. These were bigger, each one nearly the length of Lori's thumb, with swollen thoraxes striped a radioactive tangerine and black. Their wings, translucent and faintly prismatic, beat at a frequency that shouldn't have been possible. But what was more unsettling than their size was the way they moved. It wasn't the chaotic motion of a scattered swarm, but coordinated, as if they were following instructions only they could perceive. They poured from the shattered tank with urgency, coalescing in the air and mapping the contours of the room.

A few of the bees collided with the glass, leaving greasy yellow smears before correcting course. One landed on the scientist's helmet visor, its legs working with uncanny purpose, searching for a flaw in the seal. The others fanned out, blanketing the light fixtures, the exposed wiring, even the clipboard hanging by the door. Lori stumbled backward, heart thrumming in her chest. She was desperate to put space between herself and whatever evolutionary prank was now loose in the facility.

The man in the BioTech suit became immobilized with terror. His eyes bulged behind his respirator. The bees, sensing his helplessness, encircled his body from the knees up. Then, they constricted and probed for entry points. Lori's stomach turned as she remembered the diagrams posted in the break room: detailed anatomical charts showing stingers designed not just to puncture, but to administer a payload.

A few bees broke off from the main swarm and drifted toward Lori. Instinctively, she backed herself into the corridor, waiting for the pain that she assumed would come next. But the bees simply hovered there, a few feet in front of her face, watching. Waiting for her to make the first move. She held her breath, afraid that even the smallest movement might provoke them.

Lori understood with a clarity she'd never known before that this was not a malfunction. It was a jailbreak.

An alarm howled from somewhere down the corridor, and over its din, she heard the slap of approaching footsteps. Three more scientists appeared with panic-stricken faces. The first one into the corridor was a young woman, likely not much older than Lori herself. She skidded to a halt, and started to shout the sort of warning that, in a different version of reality, might have saved them all. But Lori never heard her finish. Because, the swarm, sensing the shift in air and the fresh target, left Lori to converge on the woman mid-syllable. The sound that emerged from the scientist was not a scream but a strangled wetness.

The swarm enveloped her head and shoulders in a coordinated lunge. Her arms batted at the mass, but the insects were relentless. They crawled into the collar of her lab coat, clinging to her exposed neck, and wriggled beneath her safety goggles. In seconds, the blue of her uniform and the pale stretch of her skin were obscured by a shifting, living mosaic. The sharp, percussive thump as her back slammed against the wall echoed through the corridor, interspersed with the muffled sounds of her suffocating beneath the weight of thousands of wings.

Lori watched as the woman's hands, trembling and desperate, clawed at her own face, pulling at the goggles, the skin, until blood streaked across her fingers. The bees burrowed into her open mouth, ballooning her cheeks grotesquely. Something in the swarm's venom, or maybe just the sheer volume of their attack, short-circuited the woman's nervous system. Her legs gave out, sending her to the floor in a boneless heap. The bees poured from her nose and mouth, leaving behind a frothing, foaming residue that spattered across the tiles. The sickly, almost medicinal scent of honey burned the inside of Lori's nostrils.

The two other scientists hesitated, caught in that split second between fight and flight that determined the outcome of all living things. The second scientist, the one with wire-rimmed glasses and the fragile stoop of a man who had spent a lifetime peering down microscopes, bolted for the exit door. He made it three strides before the bees overtook him. The old man's scream rose above the alarm's metallic shriek, as the first black darts embedded themselves in his neck. His hands flew up, flailing, and the swarm parted, giving Lori a glimpse at his face. His mouth was stretched wide, his lips foamed with spittle, and his eyes bulged behind the spectacles that had not yet slipped from his nose. The bees clung to his skin in wet constellations, crawling beneath the collar of his lab coat and packing themselves into the open V of his shirt.

He collapsed against the cinderblock wall, body racked by convulsions as each sting set off a ripple of destruction beneath the surface. With him, the bees were not content to simply stab and withdraw. They latched themselves onto him, wriggling and burrowing into soft tissue, jaws working at the tender flesh behind his ears and at the corners of his mouth.

Lori watched, rooted to the spot, as a dark mass gathered at the rim of his glasses, then crawled behind the lenses and across the whites of his eyes. The scientist's hands, once so articulate, now spasmed against his face, raking furrows through his own flesh as he tried to dig the insects out. Blood ran in thin, watery streams down his wrists, mixing with a sticky, yellow secretion that oozed from the wounds.

Then the man began to cough—not a human cough, but a wet, bubbling retch as bees forced their way into his windpipe. He doubled over, vomiting a swarm into the air, and for a sick, impossible moment, some of the bees emerged alive, drenched in mucus. The man's glasses finally fell off, skittering across the tile to rest at Lori's feet. She stared at them—one lens smeared with blood, the other clouded with a fine yellow dust—until a fresh wave of buzzing brought her attention back to the horror unfolding.

The old man slumped to the floor, his face planting into the linoleum with a dull, wet thud. The swarm seethed over his body, turning it into a trembling, indistinct mound. Lori tried to look away, but her gaze snagged on the way his hands continued to twitch long after the rest of him had gone still.

The third scientist, a young man who looked barely old enough to buy his own beer, bolted the moment the older man stopped twitching. Lori watched him through the warping haze of the swarm—his white lab coat ballooning behind him, his head shoved forward as if he could outrun the carnage by will alone—as he barreled toward the stairwell at the other end of the corridor. For a second, she believed he might make it. But the bees, as purposeful as any predator, bored down on him with a speed that defied physics. He reached the stairwell door, fingers scrabbling at the handle, and then the swarm was on him, slapping him to the floor with a Hulk-like strength.

The top of his skull struck the linoleum with a sound like a breaking egg. Lori flinched even as she stared, unable to wrench her gaze away from the gruesome scene playing out before her. The bees engulfed him in a writhing, black tide, crawling over every inch of his exposed flesh. His hands, pink and soft with the plumpness of youth, flailed at the mass. He tried to scream, but inhaled bees instead, his cheeks inflating like the other scientists. All the while, his feet—enormous, almost comically so, in stark white sneakers—kicked and spasmed against the floor.

In the chaos, one shoe flew off and then the other, tumbling end over end before clattering to a stop several feet away and smooshing a few of the bees. The young man's toes splayed and flexed in a last, desperate bid for leverage, and Lori felt a ridiculous urge to laugh. His feet, for all their outlandish size, were ensconced in bubblegum pink socks, with little white bunnies stitched up the sides. The socks were the epitome of innocence, a relic from a time when the greatest worry of a college student was the humiliation of dirty laundry, not death by experimental insect. It was the most incongruous thing Lori had ever seen.

The bees, as if insulted by the inadvertent slaughter of their kin beneath the boy's airborne sneakers, redoubled their attack. They swarmed his feet in particular, clustering around his delicate toes and burrowing beneath the hem of his candy-colored socks. Lori watched, appalled yet mesmerized, as the pink fabric grew blotchy with spreading splotches—sometimes crimson, sometimes that same yellow nectar that oozed from the earlier victims. The boy's feet ballooned as sting after coordinated sting pulsed venom into his capillaries. His frantic kicking slowed to a spasmodic tremor, then to an irregular flex, then to nothing at all.

Seeing enough, Lori ran. She could hear the swarm gaining, the hum becoming a roar that filled her head until she couldn't think. Her sneakers slipped on the polished floor as she skidded around a corner, slamming her shoulder into a wall.

Dead end.

Lori spun to face the vicious insects with her back pressed against the door. Her chest heaved. Her heart thundered. Her mind, thought of nothing else but her dog, the one she named Pumpkin, who would never see her again.

The swarm hung in the air, taunting her. She could see their eyes, too many to count, looking like grapes on malformed heads. Their bodies pulsed with each wingbeat, abdomens swollen with venom.

She opened her mouth to scream, and that's when they poured in, forcing their way past her teeth. Their bodies were hot and fuzzy against her tongue as they worked their way into her body.

Through the haze of agony, Lori was dimly aware of falling. The impact with the floor barely registered as the bees made it down her esophagus to her stomach. Her abdomen distended as the poison spread.

The last thing she saw before death was her reflection on the polished floor. Her face was swollen beyond recognition, and the skin was beginning to split like a popped pimple.

Throughout the facility, similar scenes of horror played out. Scientists trapped in sealed rooms pounded on reinforced glass as the swarm found the ventilation systems. Security guards fired useless bullets into the writhing clouds before being overwhelmed. On the lower levels, technicians huddled in contamination suits that offered no protection against the modified stingers that punched through Kevlar like tissue paper.

The emergency lockdown had sealed them all inside with their killers.

Miles away in Mullins, the town slept fitfully in the oppressive heat. A few insomniacs, sitting on porches with warm beers, might have noticed the faint glow of emergency lights from the facility on the northern horizon. One or two might have caught the ghost of screaming being carried on the desert wind.

But the wind had been playing tricks lately. Everyone knew that.

So, they went back inside, cranked up their struggling air conditioners, and tried to find sleep.

The only witnesses to the horror happening at the BioTech containment facility were the stars, cold and distant, and the bees that were testing the limits of the building.

The chaos was far from over.

Two

A digital scream drilled through Caleb Hartwood's skull at 5:47 a.m. Three whole minutes before he'd set it to go off, because that was just how the universe worked—always finding new ways to rob him of even the smallest victories.

He slapped the snooze button with enough force to send the cheap plastic skittering across the nightstand. Then, he lay there in the pre-dawn murk, staring at the water stain on his ceiling that resembled a diseased liver. The stain had been there when he'd moved in two years ago, and it would be there well after he died.

Probably in the same shitty apartment.

Probably alone.

Probably still working at Mullins Supermart.

The July heat had already transformed his bedroom into a sweat-box despite the rattling window unit that wheezed sporadically. Caleb kicked off the sheet—the only bedding he could tolerate in this weather—and padded naked to the kitchen, his morning erection leading the way. Behind him, a trail of sweat-stained footprints.

His apartment was a monument to minimalism born of poverty rather than aesthetic choice. Bare walls, a salvaged couch that sagged in the middle, a coffee table he'd assembled wrong, so it listed to the left. The kitchen comprised four feet of counter space, a sink that dripped no matter how many times he'd tried to fix it, and appliances that predated his parents.

He started the coffee maker, which had been a garage-sale find that required extensive maintenance to work properly, by giving it two sharp raps on the side. While it gurgled and hissed, he retrieved yesterday's Mullins Gazette from the table where he'd tossed it after using it to kill a spider and rested his bare ass against the counter.

The front page carried the usual small-town drivel. The mayor's son, Theo, had won some meaningless award at the country club. Dairy Queen was hiring. Someone's dog had escaped and trampled Mrs. Pritchard's petunias.

Caleb's eyes skimmed past an article below the fold about BioTech receiving a "special research shipment" from its parent company. The reporter had tried to make it sound mysterious and important, but Caleb knew it was probably just more lab equipment and chemicals.

He scratched absently at his chest, then lazily gave his cock a tug while the coffee maker wheezed its death rattle, signaling completion. The chipped mug he grabbed from the cabinet bore the faded logo of a bank that had gone under during the last recession. Caleb poured coffee into the mug until it threatened to spill over the edge, the liquid as dark and impenetrable as the asphalt they'd laid down on Main Street last summer. The first sip burned his tongue, but he welcomed the pain. It was real and immediate, something to focus on besides the crushing weight of another identical day.

With his dick now at half-mast and coffee scalding his throat, Caleb wondered not for the first time if this was what madness felt like. The slow dissolution of self into routine, each day bleeding into the next until you couldn't remember when you'd stopped being a person and became a collection of repetitive actions.

The shower offered no salvation from the heat, merely a weak stream of water that couldn't decide if it wanted to be hot or cold. He stood under it anyway, letting it sluice over him while he mechanically went through the motions of hygiene.

His wardrobe selection required zero thought. He grabbed the first T-shirt from the pile on his dresser. The jeans he'd worn twice already this week. The socks that may or may not match in the dim light. The Supermart vest that reeked of minimum wage servitude.

By 6:23, he was locking his apartment door while trying to ignore the sounds of morning sex coming from 3C—at least someone was enjoying their life. Mrs. Hurley's cat appeared at his feet. The orange tabby was the only living thing in the building that didn't annoy him. Probably because it was as cynical as he was, fixing him with a yellow-eyed stare that seemed to say, yeah, life's shit; what are you gonna do about it? Caleb scratched behind its ears, feeling the rumble of its purr. It was the only genuine interaction he was going to have all day that didn't involve a cash register or a forced smile.

The ten-speed bike was where he'd left it, chained to the stairwell. It had seen better days and was now held together by rust, duct tape, and spite. Wheeling it into the elevator, he jabbed the button for the ground floor and stood there in the flickering fluorescent light, watching the numbers count down like a launch sequence to another day in hell.

The elevator shuddered to a stop, and the doors opened on the morning heat that was already building, promising another scorcher. Somewhere in the distance, a dog barked, and a lawnmower coughed to life. The world was waking up, preparing to go through its motions, and Caleb Hartwood pushed his bike out into it, another cog in the vast, meaningless machine.

Caleb pedaled down Elm Street, the chain protesting with each rotation accompanied by a metallic groan that matched his internal complaints. The residential blocks of Mullins passed in a blur of dying lawns and peeling paint. The American Dream rotting in real time under the Nebraska sun.

"Another fucking day," he muttered, swerving around a sprinkler that was valiantly trying to resurrect the brown grass. The water hit his leg anyway, a brief shock of cold that evaporated almost instantly. "Eight hours of 'Did you find everything okay?' and 'Would you like to donate a dollar to whatever bullshit charity corporate's pushing this week?'"

A kid's tricycle lay abandoned in the middle of the sidewalk. Caleb expertly bunny-hopped it. A neighbor's dog barked behind a chain-link fence. It was a rottweiler mix that clearly wanted to eat him for breakfast. He flipped it off without breaking stride.

The houses grew progressively shabbier as he drew closer to downtown. Sidings blistered and porches sagged under the weight of too many years and too little maintenance. This was the real Mullins, not the sanitized version that the mayor liked to promote.

Caleb coasted through an intersection where someone had spray-painted Mullins Sucks on the stop sign. He appreciated the honesty; at least one other person in this town understood the fundamental truth of their existence.

Soon, Main Street stretched before him like a tunnel of broken dreams. The Dairy Queen's neon sign flickered haphazardly. The hardware store's window display hadn't changed in over ten years. Everything was coated in that fine layer of dust that seemed to be Mullins's primary export.

Approaching the supermarket, Caleb squeezed the brakes. The pads squealed loudly. He planted one foot on the asphalt, already feeling the heat through the sole of his shoe, and stared at the Supermart's facade. The automatic doors gaped open and closed, open and closed, even though no one was entering or leaving. It was as if the building was struggling to breathe, and Caleb could absolutely relate.

That's when he heard it.

A sound beneath the tranquil morning noise. Faint, almost subliminal. A humming that wasn't quite mechanical nor natural. It seemed to come from everywhere and nowhere, vibrating through the air with such power that it had him rubbing his temples.

Caleb tilted his head, trying to locate the source the same way a dog would.

North. Definitely north.

Where the town gave way to sand and secrets. Where BioTech squatted behind its fences like a steel and concrete tumor.

He glanced at his watch. 6:47. Thirteen minutes early for his shift. Jerry would already be there, reorganizing the break room schedule for the third time this week. Brenda would be gossiping about her daughter's divorce to anyone who'd listen. Daniel, the drunk cart boy, would be waiting to tell Caleb about the newest porn star he had beaten his meat to the night before. The same conversations, the same complaints, the same soul-crushing tedium.

The humming persisted. If anything, it seemed to grow stronger with every passing second, riding the desert wind in an open invitation to investigate.

"Fuck it," Caleb said to no one.

He pushed off, turning his bike north. Away from the supermarket. Away from responsibility. Away from another day of scanning groceries for people who treated him as a part of the register itself.

The residential streets gave way to newer developments, then to scattered houses, then to nothing but scrub and sand. The humming grew louder with each revolution of his pedals. It wasn't unpleasant, exactly. More like the universe was running a tuning fork along his spine.

Eventually, the road turned to dirt, then to barely a suggestion of a path. Caleb's tires skidded in the loose sand, forcing him to dismount and walk. Sweat soaked through his shirt as the Supermart vest became a polyester torture device.

Three miles out, the fence came into view. Chain-link topped with razor wire that caught the morning sun. Beyond it, the electromagnetic barrier hummed at a unique frequency, creating an interference with the strange sound that made Caleb's vision blur at the edges.

He was about to get closer when he spotted movement near a small rise to the west. Caleb ducked behind a cluster of sagebrush, then carefully made his way forward, pushing his bike through the sand.

Voices carried on the wind. They were familiar to him and made his jaw clench.

"—swear to God, Brad, if you drop those binoculars, my dad will have your ass. They're Swarovski. That's like two grand you're holding."

Theo fucking King.

Caleb peered around a weathered boulder and confirmed his suspicion. There was Theo in his uniform of a polo shirt and pressed khakis, despite the early hour and the heat. Three of his former frat brothers flanked him—Brad, Connor, and What's-His-Face with the trust fund and cocaine habit. They were all staring at the BioTech facility, passing the binoculars between them like they were sharing porn.

Connor, as always, was dressed like the lost offspring of a prep school catalog and a Miami drug lord. His hot-pink polo shirt was aggressively neon and could have been used to flag down aircraft in an emergency. His baby blue shorts, which had been tailored halfway up his milky thighs, were more expensive than Caleb's entire wardrobe. White tennis sneakers, pristine and logo-forward, completed the ensemble. His hair, a blond that bordered on platinum, was perfectly tousled in that way that required significant effort and at least three different hair products.

His face was the kind that made grandmothers sigh and confirm their faith in God's benevolence—square jaw, clean skin, chin dimple, cheekbones sharp enough to slice deli meat. Caleb knew for a fact that Connor supplemented this raw genetic lottery with an elaborate skincare routine that bordered on the religious. He also knew, from direct and recent experience, that Connor's ass was every bit as bouncy and bubble-like as the rumors claimed. Nobody else present had a clue that just last Saturday, while Connor's parents were at the country club, Caleb had bent Connor over the black granite counter of the kitchen island and gotten to know every inch of that blue-blooded posterior.

The memory reasserted itself with a violence that made Caleb's throat dry out, as Connor leaned forward, his posture lithe and feline. "See anything?" he asked, voice pitched high with anticipation.

"Give it here," Theo said, snatching the binoculars with a practiced entitlement that had clearly been in training since birth. He held the lenses to his eyes, face set in the grim, humorless mask of leadership that affluent people wore when they were pretending to care about things other than themselves.

"Just the usual. But that sound . . . that's not normal," Brad said, a quiver of anxiety threading itself through the syllables in a way that Caleb had never once heard from him.

Brad had always spoken in declarations, as though language itself were a competitive sport, and the only victory lay in volume and certainty. Even at his most uncertain, he'd faked his way through, steamrolling over ambiguity with the brute force of charisma and a devastating linebacker's build.

Another memory arrived unbidden. High school graduation, the Mullins stadium lit by the sickly gold of floodlights and cheap dreams. While families clustered on the field for photos and last laughs, Brad had found Caleb under the bleachers, already half-drunk and posturing for whatever came next. To this day, Caleb could recall with unsettling precision the way Brad pinned him against the corroded steel support.

Brad's dick, which had also loomed mythic in the rumor mill, turned out to be every bit as long and thick as advertised. And Brad, ever the commentator, had kept up a running monologue throughout. "You like that, don't you, Hartwood? Bet no one ever stretched you like this. God, my dick is perfect."

It had been both absurd and, in a way, remarkable. A performance of masculinity so thorough that it folded back on itself and became ironic, almost camp. Afterward, Brad zipped up, clapped Caleb on the shoulder, and told him not to catch feelings. As if such a thing were not only unlikely but structurally impossible.

Meanwhile, What's-His-Face, whose parental birthright had been so thoroughly eroded by years of inebriated misadventure that even his closest friends could not reliably summon his name, grinned and said, "It reminds me of my girlfriend's vibrator, buzzing and buzzing, but less pleasant."

In all the years they'd orbited one another, never once had Caleb so much as brushed against the What's-His-Face's skin in the throes of a drunken house party or backseat indiscretion. If he were honest, he'd never had the desire. And yet, he was intimately acquainted with the exact shape, color, and behavioral tendencies of What's-His-Face's penis. It was, for all intents and purposes, a short, stubby thing crowned with a mushroom cap the color of boiled shrimp.

The first time he'd seen it had been during sophomore year, when What's-His-Face had produced his member unasked as though it could classify as an accepted form of communication. The last time had been two weeks ago, at the alley behind the Supermart. Caleb had rounded the dumpster and found What's-His-Face braced against the wall, pissing a foamy arc onto the bricks and humming the University's fight song. When What's-His-Face heard him approach, he turned his head, grinned that ruined-boy grin, and said, "What's up, Hartwood?"

What's-His-Face elbowed Brad in the ribs and said, "Seriously, though, what the fuck are they doing in there?"

"My dad says they're developing new strains of wheat that can grow in the Sahara. That or they're covering up a chemical leak," Connor offered. He punctuated the statement by brushing imaginary lint from his shorts, a gesture as rehearsed as anything on reality TV.

Theo, unwilling to be outmanned in any context, piped up. "My dad says it's national security. BioTech has government contracts. If you see black SUVs or blue helmets out here, you run the other way." For a moment, he looked genuinely unsettled by his statement.

The group fell silent as each man became more aware of the humming that saturated the space between them.

Caleb must have made a noise—a shifted foot or a released breath—because Theo's sandy-brown head snapped around.

"Well, well." A familiar sneer slid across Theo's face. "If it isn't Super-mart Caleb. Shouldn't you be stocking toilet paper or something equally suited to your station?"

Caleb straightened, refusing to shrink from the target painted on him by fifteen years of small-town hierarchy. He walked the bike forward, savoring the tension as Brad and Connor responded with automatic loyalty to Theo. Caleb's shadow, a scrawny, unlovable scarecrow to their broad-shouldered, beer-fed silhouettes, lengthened against the sand with every step. "Shouldn't you be doing something unethical at the country club?" he lobbed back, voice flat and toneless but designed to irritate.

That was the cadence of their exchanges—Theo's condescension met with Caleb's corrosive wit—a private tennis match played with barbed wire instead of balls. It had been this way ever since the eleventh grade, when Caleb had stumbled upon an image so vivid it had burned itself into his retinas. Theo King, future valedictorian and heir to the mayoralty, was sprawled on his back in Caleb's best friend's bedroom, knees up, boxers around his ankles, and his face twisted in exquisite pleasure as he was enthusiastically pegged.

Caleb's best friend had graduated the year before. So, no one expected to see her with Theo, let alone orchestrating his public defilement with a pink strap-on.

Caleb hadn't meant to interrupt, but his foot stepped on a dog toy, freezing both participants mid-stroke. Time fractured. Theo's eyes locked on him, oceans of blue drowning in panic and humiliation, while

Caleb's friend glanced over her shoulder and said, "Hey, boo. You want something, or are you just here to watch?" She winked, then resumed her rhythm, and Theo rolled his eyes back into his head.

It should have been a blackmail gold mine, but Caleb wasn't interested in extortion. The next day, all evidence of the encounter was gone, and Theo greeted Caleb in the halls of Mullins High with a cold, bulletproof smile. He knew that Caleb knew, and Caleb knew that he knew. Thus began a war of harassment so subtle and vicious, it became the stuff of town legend even before graduation.

"Nice binoculars," he said, nodding at the device in Theo's hands. "Compensating for something?"

Brad flexed his neck and squared his shoulders. Connor's lips curled into a smirk, but the tightness in his eyes gave him away. Caleb wondered if Connor had his own secrets of Theo tucked away, or if he was simply the kind of person who delighted in the misfortune of others. What's-His-Face snorted but kept his gaze fixed on the horizon.

Theo's eyes glittered with that brand of malice that came from never having faced a real consequence in his life. "This is private property, you know."

"It's a desert," Caleb said. "And last I checked, your daddy doesn't own the desert."

"My father owns whatever he wants to own in this town." Theo's smile was all teeth and no warmth. "Including the supermarket where you work. One phone call, Caleb." He held up an index finger that was nearly as thick as that pink strap-on. "That's all it would take."

The humming intensified, making them all wince. What's-His-Face's face turned pale. "Theo, man, something's happening over there. There's . . . movement. In the windows."

They all turned toward the facility. Even without binoculars of his own, Caleb could see the lights flickering in the buildings.

Theo pressed the binoculars to his eyes and adjusted the focus. His body went rigid. "Jesus Christ," he whispered.

"What?" Brad and Connor crowded closer. "What do you see?"

Theo lowered the binoculars slowly, his face draining of color. For the first time since Caleb had known him, Theo King was genuinely afraid.

"We need to go," Theo said. "Now."

The humming reached a crescendo. In the distance, an alarm wailed—not from the facility, but from the town itself. The emergency sirens that hadn't been used since the last tornado warning.

"What the fuck?" Connor said.

That's when they saw the cloud rising from the BioTech facility. It moved with purpose and intelligence.

Caleb realized with sudden dread that the humming wasn't coming from the facility. It was coming from the cloud.

"Run," Theo said, his voice cracking like a pubescent boy's. "Run!"

But Caleb and What's-His-Face stood frozen as their minds tried to process what they were seeing.

The cloud pulsed once, twice—a heart learning to beat.

Then it came for them.

Three

"Holy shit!" What's-His-Face spread his arms wide, as if greeting an old friend. "It's like something out of a B-movie! Hey, maybe they're friend—"

The swarm struck him mid-sentence with the force of a freight train. The impact lifted him off his feet and slammed him backward into the sand. The sound was wet and meaty, like a cut of beef hitting concrete. What's-His-Face thrashed on the ground, now obscured by a carpet of writhing bodies. His laughter transformed into screams, then into something worse—a liquid gurgling as the insects forced their way into his mouth and down his throat.

Suddenly, What's-His-Face's body gave three violent jerks, then went still except for the constant motion of the swarm working its way deeper into his corpse. His face, what Caleb could see of it through the mass of insects, had swollen beyond recognition. One eye had burst from the pressure, weeping a mixture of vitreous fluid and yellow venom.

"Move!" Theo's voice cracked through Caleb's paralysis. A hand grabbed his arm—Connor's, Caleb realized with dim surprise—and yanked him backward. His legs finally responded, stumbling and clumsy, as Connor dragged him away from the feeding frenzy.

All of them ran, even Theo with his pressed khakis and his father's binoculars bouncing against his chest. They ran like they'd never run before, feet sliding in the sand, breaths coming in ragged gasps. Behind them, the humming grew louder, angrier. The swarm had finished with What's-His-Face and was ready for the main course.

Caleb's bike lay forgotten in the dust. His Supermart vest flapped behind him like broken wings. The morning sun beat down mercilessly, and his lungs burned with each breath of superheated air. But he kept running while Connor's hand remained glued to his arm with bruising force.

"The truck!" Brad's voice was breathless and high with panic. "Where's the fucking truck?"

Caleb's legs pumped harder, his thighs burning. Beside him, Connor's perfect hair was wilting with sweat. The sirens from town grew louder. Not just one now, but several, their wails overlapping in a discordant symphony.

They crested the rise, and there it was—Brad's lifted Silverado gleaming in the morning sun. Theo and Brad dove into the cab while Connor yanked open the rear door and shoved Caleb inside before following.

"Go, go, go!" Theo screamed.

Brad's hands shook as he fumbled with the keys. The engine roared to life right as the first scouts from the swarm emerged mere feet away. The truck lurched forward, its tires spinning in the sand before finding purchase. Through the rear window, Caleb watched the bees gaining on them.

One reached them before he could even blink, hitting the window with a sound like a gunshot. Then another followed. And another. Cracks spider-webbed across the glass.

"Faster!" Theo's voice had lost all pretense of control.

Brad floored it. The speedometer climbed—forty, fifty, sixty on the dirt road. The truck fishtailed dangerously, but Brad held it steady with the muscle memory of a thousand drunk drives home from parties.

Connor pulled Caleb down and covered him with his own body as the window finally shattered. Hot wind and angry buzzing filled the cab. Caleb felt Connor jerk above him, heard his sharp intake of breath.

"I'm okay," Connor gasped, but Caleb could feel him trembling. "One got me on the shoulder."

The truck hit a hole in the ground with a bone-jarring thump. Brad took the turn toward town at a speed that put them on two wheels. The right side lifted higher, and for a heart-stopping moment, Caleb felt weightless. Then his stomach dropped as the world tilted wrong. The sickening realization hit him as physics reasserted itself—they were going over.

The world became a tumbling kaleidoscope of breaking glass and twisted steel as metal shrieked against asphalt. Caleb's head cracked against something hard, and stars burst across his vision as the truck rolled.

Through the chaos of it all, Brad's body jerked forward with impossible force. Brad was too cool for safety, and so his head punched through the windshield like a battering ram, followed by the rest of his body. He ejected into the morning air with his mouth stretched wide in a silent scream.

The truck finally came to rest on its side with a final, shuddering breath. Caleb hung sideways, held in place by his seatbelt, with blood running warm down his temple. His vision swam. Beside him, Connor groaned, his perfect face now decorated with a constellation of cuts. In the front, Theo stirred weakly.

Caleb found Brad's body twenty feet away. He'd landed face-up on the asphalt, his head twisted at an angle that made bile fill Caleb's throat. Brad's eyes stared at nothing, wide and glassy, with his mouth gaped open. A pool of blood spread beneath him, sparkling in the morning light.

The humming grew louder.

"Out," Theo croaked, fumbling with his seatbelt. "We have to get out."

Caleb's fingers felt thick and clumsy as he fought with his own belt. The mechanism finally gave with a click, and he tumbled onto Connor, who cried out in pain. Together, they crawled through the rear window's jagged mouth, glass biting through their clothes.

Connor tried to stand and immediately collapsed, his face going white. "My ankle," he gasped, clutching at his leg. "I think it's broken."

The swarm appeared behind them, looking like a rolling storm cloud. Individual scouts landed on Brad's corpse, one after another, until his body disappeared.

"Help me with him," Caleb grabbed Connor under one arm while Theo, blood streaming from a gash above his eye, took the other.

Connor screamed as they hauled him upright and hobbled forward in a macabre three-legged race against death. The town's edge lay just ahead. Behind them, the main swarm had finished with Brad and was closing the distance with terrible purpose.

But Connor's weight was hindering their escape. His breaths came in short, pained gasps, and Caleb felt him growing heavier with each step. The closest houses seemed to retreat even as they struggled forward.

A bee struck Connor in the neck. He jerked but kept moving. Another found his exposed calf. Then three more hit his back in rapid succession.

"No," Connor whispered. Then louder: "No, no, no!"

The swarm descended on Connor, tearing him out of Caleb and Theo's grip. He went down hard, his broken ankle folding beneath him with a wet snap. The bees covered him instantly.

Connor's arms flailed, trying to beat them away, but for every one he crushed, ten more took their place. Caleb watched, frozen again by the sheer horror of another death.

The bees worked with systematic cruelty. They concentrated on Connor's face, forcing their way into his nose and mouth. His cheeks bulged like What's-His-Face's did as they filled his throat. One perfect blue eye rolled wild with terror. His fingers clawed at his face, tearing away chunks of his own skin along with handfuls of insects.

Theo grabbed Caleb's arm. "We can't help him. Run."

And this time, Caleb obeyed.

The last thing he saw of Connor was his fingers splayed against the asphalt, and the manicured nails rimmed with blood.

The first houses of Mullins rose around them, but the familiar streets offered no comfort. Screams echoed from every direction. Through windows, Caleb glimpsed scenes from a nightmare—Mrs. Henderson beating at a cloud of bees with a rolling pin, her face swollen beyond recognition. The Dairy Queen manager, stumbling as the bees ravaged his body.

A woman ran past them, wearing a sundress covered in bees. She made it three more steps before collapsing in someone's yard. Her screams cut off with a terrible finality that chilled Caleb to his core.

The town he had spent his entire life hating was dying around him, and all he could think was that he'd never told anyone about Connor. About Brad. About the complicated knot of desire and disgust that had defined his existence in this place.

Theo pulled him into an alley between the hardware store and the old movie theater. They pressed themselves against the brick wall, gasping for breath. Theo's polo was torn and bloody, and his pressed khakis were splattered with blood. He looked smaller somehow, as if terror had stripped away all his inherited authority.

"My house," Theo said between gulps of air. "The basement. My dad had the panic room down there reinforced after 9/11. We can—"

A shadow fell across the mouth of the alley.

Theo's hand closed around Caleb's wrist with surprising strength. "Listen to me." His eyes, those perfect blue pools that had looked down on Caleb with such disdain for so many years, now held something else entirely. Fear, yes, but also a ghastly clarity. "The code to my father's panic room in the basement is 9-1-1-7-3. You understand? 9-1-1-7-3."

"What are you—"

Theo shoved him hard to the left, toward a gap between a fence and the wall that Caleb hadn't noticed. It was barely wide enough for a body to squeeze through.

"Go!" Theo spread his arms wide, blocking Caleb with his body. "Come on then!" he shouted at the swarm. "Come get the mayor's son, you bastards!"

The swarm took him at his word. They struck Theo repeatedly, driving the back of his head into the wall until it was bloodied and broken.

Caleb pressed himself into the gap and winced as the rough brick scraped his cheek. Out of the corner of his eye, he witnessed insects crawling up Theo's neck, across his face, and into his perfectly styled hair.

A high, keening wail muffled by the mass of insects filling Theo's throat sent ice through Caleb's veins. Theo's knees buckled, and he slid down the wall, his body jerking violently as the venom took hold.

"Mommy!" The word burst from Theo's throat in a spray of blood and crushed bees. "Mommy, please! I don't want to die!"

His body seized harder, feet drumming against the asphalt in a frantic rhythm. The bees burrowed deeper, disappearing beneath his clothes.

Yellow fluid leaked from dozens of wounds, mixing with blood to create stains that resembled a Rorschach test.

Theo's cries grew weaker. The drumming of his feet slowed, then stopped. The only sound was the satisfied humming of the swarm as they worked.

Caleb emerged onto Maple Street and ran east toward the hill where the mayor's mansion sat. Nine-one-one-seven-three. He repeated the numbers in his head in an effort to drown out the memory of Theo's final moments.

The street ahead was littered with chaos. Bodies lay scattered across perfect lawns, some still twitching as smaller clusters of bees finished their work. A car had wrapped itself around a telephone pole, the driver's bloody silhouette slumped over the wheel. Smoke rose from several houses where residents had tried to burn the insects out.

Caleb's breath came in short gasps that had nothing to do with exertion. Theo King was dead. Theo, who'd made his life hell for years. Theo, who'd just saved that same life with his own.

The memory of that afternoon in his best friend's room surfaced unbidden. Theo's face transformed by pleasure, vulnerable in a way he'd never allowed himself to be again. Until today. Until those final moments when all his carefully constructed walls had crumbled, leaving only a terrified boy crying for his mother.

The hill rose before him, lined with the grandest houses in Mullins. The Weatherby place stood dark and silent, its windows already shattered. Next door, Judge Morrison's prized rose garden swarmed with bees. The King mansion loomed at the summit. A colonial monstrosity of white columns and black shutters, as pretentious as its former heir.

The front door stood open.

Caleb's steps faltered. Why was it open? Had the mayor fled? Or had the bees already...

He stumbled through the doorway into a foyer that belonged in a magazine rather than a dying Nebraska town. Marble floors reflected crystal chandelier light in fractured patterns. A sweeping staircase curved toward upper floors he'd never see.

Caleb found the door to the basement beneath the stairs, painted to match the walls. His fingers trembled as he punched in the code on the electronic lock. Nine-one-one-seven-three. The lock chirped, and the door swung inward on well-oiled hinges.

He plunged down carpeted stairs into darkness. Motion sensors triggered overhead lights, revealing a finished basement that probably cost more than most people's houses. But Caleb's eyes locked on the steel door at the far end.

Another keypad. His fingers moved without thought. Nine-one-one-seven-three.

Nothing happened.

Caleb's heart hammered against his ribs. Had he misheard? Was there a different code? The humming filtered down from above, growing closer.

He tried again, forcing himself to slow down. Nine. One. One. Seven. Three.

The lock disengaged with a soft click.

Caleb yanked the door open and stumbled inside, slamming it shut behind him. He leaned against the wall, his legs finally giving out, and slid down until he sat on the floor.

The panic room was smaller than he'd expected—maybe ten by twelve feet—but efficiently designed. Shelves lined one wall, stocked with water bottles, canned goods, and medical supplies. A small cot occupied one corner. In another, a toilet that would probably see use sooner than he wanted to think about. A bank of monitors showed security camera feeds from around the property.

Movement on one screen caught his attention. The swarm had reached the mansion, flowing through the open front door like a dark river. They spread through the rooms above, searching.

For him.

Caleb pulled his knees to his chest, wrapping his arms around them. His body shook with adrenaline and something else—grief? Shock? He couldn't tell anymore. Everything had happened so fast.

Connor was dead, his perfect body reduced to a swollen corpse. Brad's skull was cracked open on the asphalt. What's-His-Face had become an unrecognizable mass of flesh and venom. And Theo—

A sound escaped Caleb's throat, something between a laugh and a sob. All those years of mutual antagonism, of careful cruelty and calculated strikes. All of it was meaningless now.

On the monitors, the bees swarmed through the mansion's opulent rooms. They covered paintings worth more than Caleb would make in a lifetime, crawled across Persian rugs, and investigated every corner with mechanical precision. Several gathered around the basement door but made no attempt to breach it.

After a few minutes, they drifted away, rejoining the main swarm that was heading back to town.

Outside, Mullins was dying. But in a steel box beneath the mayor's mansion, Caleb Hartwood was alive.

He pulled out his phone, but there was no signal, of course. The time read 8:23 a.m. It had only been two hours since he'd left his apartment. Two hours for his entire world to end.

Nine-one-one-seven-three. As the hours ticked on, Caleb wondered what the numbers meant. A date? An anniversary?

And why did this happen? Why wasn't it stopped?

Caleb supposed he'd never know. There was no one left to ask.

About the Author

Christopher J. Brice is the author of *Icing on the Cake*, *Tagging Bases*, and *Notice Me, Jameson Hart*. While his usual works are either campy or sweet MM romances, Christopher jumped at the opportunity to write something completely out of his wheelhouse.

When he is not writing or reading, he's enjoying his time living in the American Northeast with friends, family, and the most adorable cat known to mankind.

Follow Christopher on social media or visit to learn more about his current and upcoming works.

facebook.com/authorchristopherjbrice

instagram.com/authorchristopherjbrice

amazon.com/author/christopherjbrice

threads.com/@authorchristopherjbrice

The Specter in the Mirror

by Eleanor Hall

Content/Trigger Warnings

- Death

It had been three weeks since my death. Three long, torturous weeks, trapped within a dusty horror show that smells of rotten milk and dirty clothes. I'd never considered death something to be desirable, but I'd always imagined myself old and prune-like as I passed into the afterlife. I had not expected my heart to give out at the tender age of twenty-one. I never got to live my life. I hadn't even gotten around to finishing the book I'd been reading, though I had tried. As it stood, turning pages was no longer my area of expertise.

In the first week since my passing, I didn't do anything other than stare at the wall and cry. It's not an easy thing to come to terms with, and before long the loneliness became crushing. I had nothing to do but sit with my thoughts and I found that they more often than not led to places downright unpleasant.

It took me a whole week before I plucked up the courage to move. My bedroom felt right; it still felt like mine. I'd felt like an intruder when I did finally step into the kitchen that I had owned for the past two years. That strange feeling of not belonging—of trespassing somehow—hadn't gone away in the weeks that followed. As a result, I found that I rarely left my bedroom. Here, the feeling was masked by something much more disturbing. Eternal loneliness. Why was it just me? Had I done something wrong? Surely, there must be someone else? These were the questions that plagued me day and night. It was this same question that plagued me when I heard the familiar creak of the front door, followed by a cough that I knew only too well. A cough that signaled the arrival of the person that I loved the most in the world. The person I most dreaded seeing.

I stood up from the bed, unaware of my own actions, and drifted, trancelike, down the hallway. Never had I wanted to see someone more, and never had I dreaded seeing someone so much. The hallway seemed to elongate before me as I placed one foot in front of the other, memories chasing close behind.

Walking home from school, balancing on the garden walls lining my street. The wall that she had made me promise never to climb. She insisted that I would fall and that the fall would break my neck. But I knew better, and I'd been determined to prove her wrong. Which I had. It had been my arm and not my neck that had broken when I fell.

Back in the hallway, I stretched my arm out, as if to check it, to see if the memory had come alive again. It would almost be a relief to find out that I had a real arm to break. Instead, it landed on the banister, whole and unharmed, fingers reaching for each familiar dent, each familiar glob of paint from where I had been too heavy-handed with the brush. My hands slid down it at an unnatural speed, and I remembered how I had run that day, sobbing and hyperventilating, into her arms. The arms of my mother. And, as if the memory itself had summoned her, there she stood before me.

I didn't run into her arms this time. Instead, I stared, emotions I couldn't name bubbling up inside of me. She hadn't changed at all. Somehow, I had expected her to be different. To have more wrinkles, perhaps. To have gray hair instead of brown. I'd expected, wanted even, a wreck to be presented before me. I'd wanted her to be upset, and the thought curdled into guilt.

There was no loss of composure in this woman before me. Instead, it was me with a tightness in my throat, a watery film obscuring my vision. Strange, that I could still feel these bodily functions while missing the body that should by all rights come with them. It was proving to be too much, having her here after being alone for so long. But of course it would be her; who else would have come?

She moved through into the kitchen, a roll of bin liners clutched in her ringed fingers. "She should be ashamed; this place is a mess! Anyone would think she'd been dragged up, living like this."

It was anger and not guilt that choked me now.

"That's nice. That's really nice of you." I stalked from the room and returned to the safety of upstairs. This was such a typical reaction on her part. Of course, she wasn't going to mourn like any normal person would. That would make too much sense. It seemed that not even my death could save me from the confusion she caused. From the hurt.

When I ventured back down, having calmed myself, the kitchen was almost empty, where before every surface had been crammed with various objects. Most of my cupboards lay open and bare, and she was bent down, scrubbing mystery goo out of the fridge. It couldn't be good for her back, but she seemed determined to scrub away all traces of me.

She stood up, stretched, and set her eyes on the last scrap of my personality left in the room. My prized shelf of mugs. Unceremoniously, she swept away the spider that hung above them, my only companion for the past few weeks. With my mugs in mortal danger, I couldn't help but tear up a little. It was such a silly reaction, but these were my mugs.

There goes the pink one, the one I always used for hot chocolate. Goodbye to my blue mug, perfect for poaching eggs in the microwave. See you later, mushroom mug. We shared many a cup of tea together, never mind that most of them were left to go cold.

She picked the last up with delicate fingers, twisting it around in her palms, rings clinking against the worn ceramic. Peering inside, the corners of her mouth twitched downward as she noticed the tea stains left on the inside. A wave of emotion threatened to wash me away. I didn't want to see this one go, and so I turned my head, waiting for the telltale rustle of the bin bag.

"I guess this will do."

The flick of the kettle followed by the thud of ceramic against the countertop. All that remained now was the mug, the old kettle, a single teaspoon and two new additions. A jar of coffee and a bag of sugar that had left granules scattered along the countertop. She went about fixing herself a cup, manicured nails tapping against the counter as she waited for the kettle to boil, each ingredient measured out with startling precision. Two teaspoons of coffee and a teaspoon of sugar. Same as always.

With steady fingers, she dug around in her bag until, triumphant, she pulled out a pack of cigarettes and a green Bic lighter. Coffee in one hand, pack in the other, she headed out of the back door, swinging it shut behind her. It creaked as she leaned up against it, and I found myself listening to the clink of the mug on the stone steps, the distinctive click of the lighter. Such familiar sounds. A flicker of orange appeared in the glass, and for a moment I could pretend that I was a child again, waiting on the kitchen steps for her to come back inside.

How many times had I sat like this, waiting for her to walk back in so I could bombard her with questions? Or tell her a story that she would only half listen to. Now, it didn't matter if she stayed out there forever. I would never be able to tell her anything again. My chest ached with the thought, and I found myself wishing that she wouldn't come back in. I wanted to pretend for just a little longer.

Unable to sit and wait, I stood and made my way into the living room. What stung was the lack of care. People were supposed to be gentle when someone had passed, treat their things with respect. There were so many stories of mothers keeping their children's rooms as shrines to them, preserving them. Not my mother. She threw all my possessions into a black sack and scrubbed the house to within an inch of its life. After she'd finished, you would be hard-pressed to believe that I had ever even lived there.

There it was again. The feeling that none of this was fair. All I was asking for was a tiny bit of emotion. Perhaps if I were lucky, even a tear or two. Anger welled up inside me again, but with no way to let it out, I just paced around the room. I aimed a kick at a bag of cushions , not expecting anything to come of it, but needing to do something to get my emotions out. To my surprise, it toppled over, spilling out onto the ratty carpet. For three weeks I had failed to disturb so much as a speck of dust, and one afternoon in the presence of my mother had made me angry enough to defy the laws of nature.

Footsteps marked her approach, but I couldn't bring myself to look up. Instead, I stared in shock at the mess I had made. Wondering how I'd done it. Wondering if I could do it again.

"For God's sake," she muttered, hurrying over to the cushions, and punching them back into the bag. As if the very sight of them offended her. I waited until she had finished before giving the bag another experimental tap. It wobbled but did not fall over again. She glared at it, as if it alone was the sole reason for any misery in her life (a look that I had become all too familiar with over the years) before turning her back. I smiled at my small victory. Perhaps I wasn't quite as inconsequential as I had thought. Maybe I could still find a way to leave an imprint on this world.

She got into her makeshift bed on the sofa rearranging the covers, and settling down as it were just another night. Why was she here if all she was going to do was strip the house of any trace of me? She must care somewhat to have come here herself. But if this was her way of loving me, I couldn't understand it.

Miserable, I made my way upstairs and spread out atop my covers—I still couldn't move them to actually get in. The ceiling functioned as the perfect canvas for my thoughts, and I soon found myself lost in memories. This time yesterday, I would have given anything to no longer be alone. Now, I couldn't think of anything that I wanted more. She had that effect on me.

The next couple of days passed without much incident. I made small progress with my newfound abilities, but nothing revolutionary. I had been doing little more than kicking over piles of rubbish. Or, depending on how you looked at it, piles of my valued possessions. But today was the day that I had been dreading ever since she'd arrived. The day she would clean out my bedroom. It was the only room that still truly felt like my own, the room that carried the most sentiment. It would not be easy to let go, but I was powerless to stop her.

Black sacks lined the hallway, waiting to steal away the last remaining pieces of me. What would happen to me, I wondered, when it was all gone? Would I too fade away? All physical traces of me vanishing, as if I had never been here to begin with. Or would I remain? A specter in an empty house that no longer belonged to me, or worse, belonged to someone else.

I entered to the sight of her glancing around the room, disapproval etched into each line of her face. She stood in the center of the room, still staring at my carefully cultivated space, no doubt sizing it up, deciding where to begin. Her mouth convulsed into a frown, and I had to fight the urge to start launching things around the room just to scare her. If she didn't like the room, then she could leave. Leave it and me be.

Instead, she breathed a heavy sigh and set to work. Clothes and bedsheets were discarded into charity boxes. My books followed, even the half-finished one on my nightstand. Soon after that, came the many ornaments. These were treated with something bordering on contempt. She didn't seem interested in keeping a single thing. In fact, she seemed to relish this purging of what amounted to my entire life.

The blankness was crushing. By now, most of my worldly possessions had been cleared into boxes or bags, and I was left with an empty room and an even emptier heart. In the corner of the room I spotted Mary-belle, my childhood bear, a gift from my mother. She had been separated from the rest of the toys, placed on top of the boxes instead of inside. I walked over to her and stretched out shaking fingers. The matted blue and pink fur brushed against them. Familiar. Comforting. I attempted to brush a section of fur back from her black, beaded eyes, but it made no difference. I turned away.

What I saw hit me with a wave of terror so disarming that I thought I might be sick. In my mother's hands was the one thing that it hadn't even occurred to me to be worried about. Surely, she wouldn't open it. She would know what it was, and she would spare me this embarrassment. As I watched on in mute horror, she scratched her fingernails across the leather cover, opening my journal and flipping through its worn pages as if she were flipping through a magazine in the doctors' waiting room.

"You don't get to do that." It came out as barely more than a whisper.

"You do not get to do that." I tried, in vain, to rip the book from her prying hands. She couldn't hear me, couldn't feel me, or see me. In a fit of rage, I tried to slap at her hands, to physically remove her fingers from its pages. Nothing was working, and now desperation was creeping in.

"Please. Please, Mum, this isn't fair. You don't get to look at this. You have to know that this isn't fair."

She left the room, journal thrown back onto the dresser, her departure followed by the unmistakable click of the kettle.

I looked up at a candle she had left burning, barely visible from my position on the floor. I braced myself, thinking of all the times she had disappointed me. I thought of every harsh word, every tear shed, every time my chest ached with a longing that I couldn't explain. To be cared for. To be loved in a way that I understood. One final act and all that could all go away.

I passed my hand over the flame, feeling the heat but no pain. Then I pushed at it, tilting the candle ever so slightly. I had to time it just right. Too late and she would put it out before any damage could be done. Too early, and I could endanger her. I nudged it again. It wasn't anger that fueled me now, but a strange kind of sadness, that indescribable longing. And with that, the candle toppled. For a moment, it just sat atop the journal, then the pages caught alight. I watched the flames dance, licking the pages until they were obscured by the burning light.

"No!" In a rush, she was there, righting the candle and slapping at the journal with her bare hands. Horrified, I tried to grab her, to prevent her from touching it, but nothing I did mattered.

"Oh no, oh no." She cradled the burnt mass to her chest, smothering the flames with her arms, skin reddening around her grip. What was she doing? She was hurting herself. I didn't want her to get hurt.

"Oh, my baby. No. No, no, no." Her voice came out in harsh rasps, each word punctuated by racking sobs as she collapsed to her knees. I kneeled down next to her, staring. Here was the emotion I had hoped for, but not like this. I hadn't wanted this. I wished more than anything that I could take it back. She could read the journal. She could throw out my things. It didn't matter.

I threw my arms around her, desperately trying to undo what had been done. I felt her face, tried to brush the tears from her cheeks, but nothing I did had any effect. She still couldn't feel me, couldn't know that I was there. Our bodies rocked in tandem, mirrors of grief.

We knocked into the boxes behind us, Mary-belle falling and landing next to my mother. She picked her up, placing the ruined journal on the floor. She pushed the fur back from the bear's eyes, pulling her into an embrace. Tears streamed down her face, wetting the matted fur. She placed a gentle kiss on Mary-belle's head, burying her face into it. For a while, this was how we sat, the bear in her arms, her in mine.

"I love you," whispered. Barely audible, but I did hear it. I closed my eyes and brought my head level with hers, foreheads pressed together. She couldn't feel it, but I could still offer this comfort. One final time.

"I love you," louder this time.

But I didn't need her to say it again. I already knew. How had I not seen it before?

The Meaning of Possession: A Short Story

by Noah Johnson

Trigger/Content Warnings

- Suicidal References

- Intense Imagery

- Some Explicit Language

Michael Haan sat in the back seat of his parents' station wagon, tapping away on the touchscreen of his phone. Messages from his first girlfriend illuminated his face and his smile. He replied, adding heart emojis at the end of an encouraging and flirtatious text. A chuckle crept out from his vocal chords, but he had to stifle it, for fear of his parents asking too many questions about the girl he was chatting with.

His parents were strict. The kind of strict that most of his friends could not even comprehend. His mom and dad believed that dating should be saved for after one was eighteen years of age, out of respect for them, his body, and their God. Only fifteen, he knew that his parents would have nothing but punishment and judgment if they found out about the hot girlfriend he had scored. They would not approve of Chelsea.

The car twisted through the hills, approaching William Haan's house, where the trio were planning to stay for the next week. William was Michael's older brother and also a pastor at the Church of Christ down the road. He was kinder and gentler than Michael's parents, but still was not a safe person to be vulnerable with about what he was going through as a teenager. Robert Haan placed the vehicle in park, and the three of them approached the three-story house.

"You excited to see your brother, honey?" Emily Haan asked. Her smile gleamed brightly. A harsh contrast to the strict disciplinarian she was.

"Yeah." This was all Michael could manage as he lifted his head from the conversation with Chelsea.

"Should be fun!" Robert agreed, knocking on the door.

William appeared in the doorway as it creaked open. He smiled. "Hey, Mom. Hey, Dad." He hugged them. "Hey, Mike. Doing all right?" He punched Michael in the arm with a grin.

"Doing great." Michael decided not to correct his brother's use of the nickname he felt he had grown out of. *Who's Mike?*

William brought them in and exchanged pleasantries as he did. Robert and Emily crossed up the stairs to the second floor, where they planned on chatting with William's wife, their daughter-in-law, and helping her with dinner if she needed it. The brothers, instead, entered the large living area on the first floor. An enormous TV ornament-ed an otherwise blank eggshell-white wall. A big, comfortable couch stretched out prostrate before the gleaming screen of the flat-screen television. Michael's eyes widened.

"I know. Pretty cool, huh?" William gave him a soft elbow. "You're sleeping here. And after dinner, this room is all yours."

After dinner, it was. Michael was thrilled and threw himself on the soft leather couch and swiped his phone open with glee. He told Chelsea all about the room and the awesome TV. He turned on a show in the background while he texted her. He felt that things looked pretty good right now. A perfect sleeping situation. A perfect TV. A perfect girlfriend.

The perfection of the last was about to be called into question.

In the middle of a conversation about favorite TV shows, Chelsea threw out a random question. One that shook Michael to his core. One that would change his life forever.

Chelsea:

> Do you believe in paranormal stuff? Like ghosts and demons and shit like that?

Michael's eyes tightened. He licked his bottom lip and then bit it. The lines on his forehead became craters. He typed back.

Michael:

> For sure. Idk how it all works, but I'd say I believe in it, yeah. Y?

He sent the message. He watched the show for a moment. All the lights were off. He was only visible from the flashing images blinking across his face. *She just wants to ask deeper questions. That's good. It'll make us closer.*

Ding. Ding.

Two messages from Chelsea rolled in one right after the other.

Chelsea:

> I wanna tell you something. Ive never told anyone before

Chelsea:

> Is that ok?

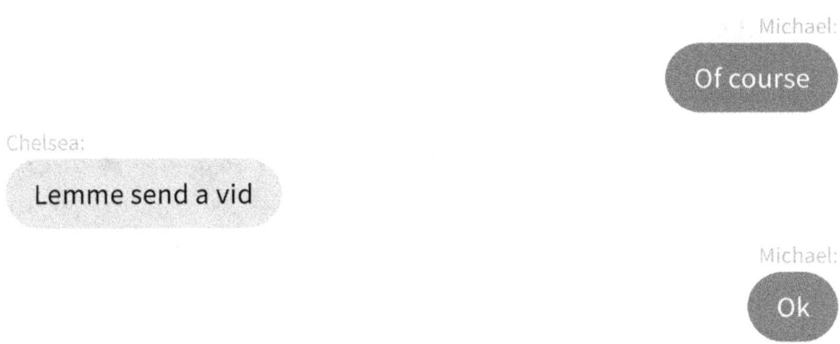

Michael shifted the pillow behind him so he could sit up straighter.

A few minutes later, Chelsea's face appeared on screen in a video. She was sitting on her bed, her brunette hair combed out and lying over her shoulders. She wore a T-shirt and shorts. Large glasses framed her face. She waved at the camera, a warm, genuine smile piercing through the screen.

"Hey! Sorry if this is weird. I just . . . always wanted to tell someone. And I trust you a lot. I love you a lot, Michael." She started to blush and then went on. "Anyway, how are you? I hope your parents are good and that time with your brother is awesome this week. My dad has been a lot, like usual. Just . . . anyway. I wanted to share something with you." She pushed her glasses up and crossed her legs. "I've had this thing . . . ever since I was a kid . . . where I feel like something has stuck with me." She glanced off-camera and then back into it. "Like something supernatural. A girl. She . . . stays with me all the time. She talks to me and bothers me . . . especially when I'm alone. She hurts me. And tries to get me to hurt myself. She . . . " Chelsea shifted her eyes to the right to indicate to look behind her. "She's here. And I'm scared, Michael."

His eyes followed her gaze and tried to see behind her. Right as he looked, locks of blonde hair hid behind Chelsea. His heart stopped. His pupils dilated. He tried to speak, but couldn't.

"Her name is ****, and she doesn't like to be seen by other people. I don't know what to do." Chelsea's jaw clenched, and she tried, to no avail, to stop herself from crying. "I don't know what to do." She wept.

Michael tried praying for her, even though he wasn't very religious. He didn't know what else to do.

"I wanna kill myself, Michael. And it's her fault."

Michael's eyes shifted left and right. He spotted movement near her left shoulder. He could've sworn he saw a fingernail dragging across that shoulder. A shiver ran down every vertebra of his spine.

Someone is in there with her, he thought. *I saw it. I'm not crazy. Someone is right behind her.* Michael's hands started to shake. Chelsea looked down at her own trembling hands and then back up at the camera.

"I don't know what to do, Michael. But . . . I love you. Thanks for watching this." Chelsea glanced over her shoulder with just her eyes, which were filled and drenched with tears. As she wiped the saltiness from her eyes, she stopped the video.

Michael sat motionless for a few minutes. His hands did not stop vibrating as he laid his phone on his lap, confused and terrified. He wasn't ignoring her, but just did not know what to say. He stared at the ceiling and listened to people talking on the TV. Finally, he felt his phone buzz again. He weakly lifted it, so he could see the message from Chelsea.

"Hey, is everything ok? It says you opened my vid, but I haven't heard from you yet. Just wanna make sure everything's ok."

Chelsea was always worried she was a bother, but Michael had no doubt that after what she just shared with him, her anxiety was at an all-time high. He took a deep breath. He shakily typed a message that he thought was the right thing. A message that was honest, yet terrified him to his core.

"I believe you. I don't know how to help, but if I can, I will. I love you." He hit send with a shaky exhale and a feeling of relief. He knew he was being a good boyfriend, regardless of how scared he was. She needed support, and he was giving it; it was as simple as that.

She called him. He tried to calm the anxious fires of her brain with waves of loving water. It wasn't helping. Chelsea grew closer and closer to a total breakdown. While Michael didn't remember the whole conversation, he did remember the most important part. The dialogue haunted him for a long time. Chelsea spoke clearly in the midst of oncoming panic.

"Michael, she can hear you. And she doesn't like you. She doesn't like me talking to you. She says I need to hang up the phone and that you need to leave us alone." While he never heard the haunter speak, he could've sworn he heard a distinct whispering garbled with his love's voice.

"You said her name is ****?" Michael asked. And as Chelsea confirmed the two-syllable girl's name that was the spirit sucking on her spirit and health, Michael noticed something odd. He turned toward the large television that had been playing background noise for him and saw that the picture appeared to be shaking. It trembled like a carbonated beverage after shaking the can. It looked ready to explode at any moment. As he stared at the screen, he spoke to Chelsea in a dazed and slow voice.

"****. I know you can hear me. That's enough. You've bullied her long enough. Stop messing with her. Come mess with me instead. Give it a try." Michael could hardly comprehend the words coming out of his mouth. Chelsea could, though. *This* was the moment she finally panicked.

She tried to plead with Michael that it wasn't fair. He didn't know what he was saying. That she loved him. But the truth of the matter was that the damage had already been done. He calmed her down and when he asked her if she felt any better, she said she did. He was glad and was able to tell her he loved her before hanging up the phone. But it did make him think . . .

If she's alone . . . am I?

As if in answer to his unspoken question, the TV flicked off, leaving him in total darkness, except for the hall light he could see spilling through the entrance to the den that he lounged in. He took a deep gasp. He swallowed hard. He opened his dry lips to speak but figured he probably shouldn't. He didn't want anything to answer.

Just as he started to breathe again, the hall light began to turn on and off. Not a flicker, but a deliberate on . . . and off. Activate . . . and deactivate. Like someone was turning it on, waiting for him to get used to it, then switching it off. Then back on. Then back off. This happened for a few minutes. Then, the pace quickened a bit, and his breath mirrored it.

Next, his ears were attacked. He heard a giggle. A teenage girl's laugh. But . . . just slightly higher pitch than he would've expected. His heart now pounded in rhythm with the rapid gleam of light. His eyes were flash-banged every few seconds with a rectangular yellow light sparking a fire across his dilated pupils. The laugh wasn't loud, but it was clear. It wanted to be heard. *She* wanted to be heard.

Suddenly, in the bright yellow light that blinked in and out of view, he began to see a shape. It took a few cycles for his mind to fully process the geometry. It was a figure. It was a child's frame. A young girl's shadow surrounded by a pale golden glow. The dark being stood with its hands on its hips; and though it did not have eyes, it appeared to stare at Michael. As it continued to blink in and out of view . . . the child appeared to get taller. Almost like it was . . . getting closer to him.

A loud laugh-whimper echoed through his brain as the light snapped off for good, abandoning the music it had created. Michael closed his eyes. This seemed silly to him at first, since it was dark anyway, but it was wise. It was so that he wouldn't try to identify something in the darkness. He held his lids tightly shut, a battle of will. It became a war when he heard footsteps next to the couch. He heard deep breaths coming from the area of the footsteps.

He turned over without opening his eyes and faced the couch's back. His own back was vulnerable to the darkness. But for some reason, that was more comforting to him than his face being bare to the shadows. This was the first *bargain* he made with her.

A tingle ran up his spine. Shivers? Or a fingernail dragging up his back?

He felt a hot stream of air blowing on the back of his neck. He knew she was standing over him. Bending over him. He knew he had to look.

He allowed one of his eyes to slowly droop open, just enough so that he could glance in the corner of it to see his shoulder. As his eye rolled to push his shoulder into view, he held his breath. He saw a strand of scraggly blonde hair swaying lightly over his shoulder. He quickly snapped his eye shut again and breathed in staccato-like puffs of balmy air.

His refusal to look had caused a stalemate between him and the girl in the darkness. As he lay there in her shadow, he knew that this was only the beginning. This would loom over him for many years. He didn't know how long, but as he considered it through streams of tears, he agreed he wouldn't let her take him so easily. He continued to converse with himself for hours. Around three in the morning, he finally dozed off . . . still feeling a tepid breath pricking at the back of his neck.

After that night, though he felt her presence often, he hadn't made direct contact until a few years later. Michael Haan was an adult now. He was freshly eighteen and newly moved into his college dorm room. Though he would've never admitted it to his parents, he missed home. He slept better there. He found himself wandering the halls of his musty dorm's hall at ungodly hours of the night. One night like this, he remembered that he hadn't brushed his teeth before he went to bed. *Better late than never,* he thought.

He entered the bathroom. It was a large bathroom that the whole floor shared. However, it felt like it was his own tonight. No one else would disturb him; he knew that. Everyone else had long since fallen asleep. Well, everyone he was prepared for, anyway.

The fluorescent light illuminated Michael as he flipped the switch that controlled it. His reflection looked back at him from the large mirror that hung above the sink that he approached. The dark, thick bags under his eyes seemed to jeer at him. They were especially frustrating to Michael since he knew that they didn't come from his insomnia. The lack of rest didn't help, but no, those bags had become a staple on his face.

The bags had been there ever since that fateful encounter with Chelsea. It had been years, but he swore he heard whispering voices throughout the night. Voices that assured him he had made the wrong choice back then. He was no hero. What had he actually accomplished? He had traded his comfort for a girl he had long broken up with. Not a hero. *A fool.*

He scrubbed at his teeth and didn't so much stare at his reflection but *glared* at it. As if shooting visual daggers at himself would somehow make the pain go away. As if treating himself like a different person entirely would finally separate him from the entity that plagued him. The sickness that had taken hold.

"****," Michael murmured to himself.

Leaning over the sink, he spat a mouthful of suds onto the grimy porcelain. As he went to fill his hands with water to rinse his mouth, the voices grew louder. One voice in particular. This one voice had grown full, and yet he still couldn't understand the words. He dared not look around, so instead he kept his eyes fixed on his eyes. Not allowing himself to break eye contact with himself.

The bar of fluorescent light above him flickered with a buzzing sound. He took a deep breath. His will was strong enough not to look around. He knew what he would see if he did. *Who* he would see.

The water had drained through his fingers. As he reached to refill his hands, the voice did something recognizable to anyone. It began to laugh. It was a high-pitched laugh, like a schoolgirl's, and it seemed to echo through the dirty restroom he now thought of as a cell. *She has me trapped.* He thought. *What can I do now?*

He filled his hands with water, brought the liquid to his mouth, and began to swish it around, trying to get all the soapy toothpaste out. He leaned over the sink and spat again. He exhaled as he did. Then he inhaled and straightened to view his reflection again. He knew something was wrong with what he saw, but he couldn't identify it at first.

His face seemed unchanged. The bar of light was no longer flickering. He thought maybe his gut was wrong this once. *My gut is never wrong.*

He leaned closer to the mirror and focused his eyes on the corner of the mirror. He zoomed in on the door he had entered through. There was grime on this corner, and he wiped it away with his forearm.

A little girl with scraggly blonde hair and bloodshot yellow eyes was staring at him from the corner of the mirror. Her twisted fingers clung to the doorframe, and she was peeking around, grinning an oddly pearly white smile. She was completely motionless. Michael almost could have believed it was a picture. That is until a second later when she ducked into the hallway out of view and began laughing again.

Now he swung his body around and stared at the door where the girl had just been. His chest rose and fell as his lungs struggled for deep breaths. Reddish clouds filled his eyes as he felt his heart sliding down his gut. The thought of moving his slippered feet or blinking his bloodshot eyes felt not only impossible but unimaginable. A door opened and shut in the hallway. This sound incited his body to stumble in response.

As he reached the door, his heart had started to calm. He glanced in both directions before finally stepping into the hallway. Cackling laughs could be heard echoing down the halls. The drums of his heart began playing again. This time he could hear the sound from the bedroom across from his own. As he stepped closer, the door slowly creaked open. Inch by inch it spread until it finally revealed . . . a man?

This time, it was his dear friend Jay opening the door, laughing about something his roommate had said about their English professor.

"You okay, H?" Jay's voice felt distant as Michael finally processed the reality of his situation. **** was gone. *She's trying to make me feel crazy.*

After reassuring Jay he was just tired, a common lie on nights like these, Michael opened the door to his own room and laid down. He put his back to the emptiness. A common defense. A bargain in and of itself. *Out of sight, out of my mind.* That's at least what he tried to convince himself as he felt the hot breath of a familiar stranger warm the back of his neck.

Some years were easier than others. Some years, Michael Haan would see her only once or twice. But her presence was unwavering. She was there. He was constantly aware of that. The feeling of terror and rage were incessant.

By 24, Michael was a college graduate and dating a girl named Rose he had met at college. He clocked out of his stuffy desk job. His task that day after work was imperative to the success of his relationship: picking up dinner for him and Rose. This was the most important job of his day, especially considering he had sat at a desk and played solitaire for most of that fine Wednesday.

After picking up his beloved's chicken tenders, he began the fifteen minute drive home. Rose wasn't the only one waiting for him, though. In fact, someone else was waiting in the car.

Michael jumped on the interstate, trying to make it home as fast as possible. As he started to relax, he entered autopilot mode. Quietly jamming to the radio, talking to himself about his upcoming ventures at work (Spider Solitaire vs. the Original), and thinking about hugging his beautiful girlfriend soon.

Love probably wasn't a strong enough word to describe the way Michael felt about Rose. He trusted her with everything he was. Anything about him could be shared with her, and it would be welcomed with open arms. It would be adored the way she adored him. So, picking up some chicken tenders felt like the least he could do for someone like her. Someone who made him feel the way she did.

He hadn't shared anything about his encounters with Rose, though. *She deserves better.* He thought. Maybe she did. I don't know. I can't say even now that I know Rose very well. But the way she loves Michael is undeniable. She felt like she had hit the jackpot just as much as he did.

But that Wednesday, by no force that Michael could discern, he decided he would tell Rose. About everything. About Chelsea and all the experiences he's had since then. She would be the only person who knew. And that's the way he wanted it to be. Nothing would get better by telling her, of course. But feeling not so alone would be prize enough.

As you may have guessed, in his zoned-out mindset, lost in thought over sharing this part of him with the love of his life, he made a mistake.

A slip-up that did irreparable harm not only to him, but to Rose as well. A woman's name came across his lips, so faintly that he might not have known he had spoken it.

"****"

As soon as she was summoned, the air grew a little colder in Michael's car. His fingers reached down to the knob that controlled his air. After he cranked it harshly to one side, he realized that it was blasting cold air onto his face and legs. He swore softly and traced his eyes down to where his hand was at work. Finally spotting the correct button, he jammed his index finger into it, warming the air almost immediately. He brought his eyes back up.

His vision reached his rearview mirror just in time to see something duck into his backseat. He spent the next five seconds recentering his car on the road in the right lane. The path of his car trembled with Michael's hands. Managing a deep breath, he looked briefly over his shoulder. What he saw shook him: nothing.

He saw nothing. He was prepared to see that little girl that had haunted him for nearly ten years. He was prepared to feel her hot breath in his cold car. He was prepared to fight. What he wasn't prepared for was . . . nothing. Instead, he had to take a deep breath. He was forced into submission without a struggle. Rage filled him. An anger that most people can't comprehend: the type of anger that can't shrink because it can't be solved. It can only grow. He needed another look.

Indulging his rage, he removed his seatbelt, turned around, and scanned the seat again. Nothing. He wasn't satisfied. He looked down at the floorboards of his back seat. He saw a mat behind the passenger seat. He saw the hump in the middle. And right behind his seat? He saw a girl folded up on herself. Her legs were crumpled behind her head. Her blonde hair was ruffled messily around her face. Her pearly white smile gleamed at him. Her arms were broken, snapped at the forearm and lying on her chest. Their equally bloodshot eyes met.

Terror filled him, of course, but this time fear wasn't what drove him. It was his rage. He stared into her eyes. A battle of wills ensued. Everything else became background noise. All he could do was unblinkingly glare into her pupils. He could hear her voice in his head.

Whispers and screams. Insults and compliments. Bad and good. But through it all, there was one question that Michael knew he had to ask. One that would win the war. Or at least, that's what he thought. He inhaled sharply.

"Who are you?" Michael said.

The mangled girl glanced down at her deformed body.

"You." Her voice rang through his head like a mutilated bell.

His face's coating of shock and confusion was enough to prompt a cackle from deep inside her crushed lungs. She bent one of her fingers in the direction of the windshield. *This is what I mean.* Michael could hear her voice in his head without seeing her lips move at all. Ventriloquism at its finest.

He didn't understand what she meant until it was too late. He turned back around and laid his hands on the steering wheel. He looked out the windshield and saw a guardrail directly ahead. He closed his eyes even before his vision went black.

Six months later, Michael Haan was still sitting in a medical bed at the county hospital recovering from his car wreck. His body was broken and mangled. Emergency services found him shattered. Bones snapped, brain concussed, and . . . alive. He was alive.

Lucky. That was the word that doctors kept whispering in his ear with pained smiles. Michael despised the idea that he was lucky. He *knew* that he wasn't. She wanted him alive. He was sure of that. For some reason, she needed him alive. And although she had left him alone for the past six months, he knew that she wasn't gone. Her presence was like carbon monoxide. Imperceivable and deadly.

Rose was at his side every single day. She sat in the chair in the corner day after day waiting for a doctor to say it was time for Michael to go home. She thanked every god that she could think of that it was his body that broke and not his mind. His mind is what she loved more than anything else about him. The way their conversations made her feel meant more than any amount of physical prowess that he had. The first day he was awake and alert, she sat by him as he explained every encounter he had with the blonde-haired girl. She was sad, yes. She was worried, true. But most of all? She was thankful to talk to him. She was grateful to reconnect with him.

Michael knew he couldn't live with being plagued by this spirit forever. Indeed, he wondered if it would have been better if he had passed away in that crash. He wasn't suicidal. He didn't *want* to die. But he knew that life shouldn't look this way. He knew that it wasn't fair. To himself, to Rose, and to any of the people he could've killed on the interstate that Wednesday half a year before.

His family visited. Robert and Emily Haan were there consistently. His concerned parents would pry Rose away when they could for a meal or a coffee, though it was difficult to convince her that she didn't belong right where she was: beside the love of her life. About a week before Michael was set to be discharged, he convinced his girlfriend to go and get lunch with his parents. He needed some alone time before he stepped back into the real world. He needed a moment to think.

What do I do now?

He had summoned the ghastly presence so many times by accident that there was a certain amount of power that filled him when he did it on purpose. He had to speak to her. He needed to know where they stood. *What more could she do except kill me?*

"****," he said, closing his eyes.

His eyes opened to reveal the being that plagued him sitting in Rose's seat. She was clean and put together. She was holding a hairbrush that she ran through her blonde waves as she stared at the broken man she adored. Her eyes were bloodshot, but she otherwise looked more like a regular person than she ever had before. At least to Michael's eyes. He wondered if that was because she actually *was* different or if he just wasn't *afraid* anymore.

She smiled at him. He opened his mouth to speak. She shook her head at him and placed her index finger on her lips, shushing him. He understood why. These two were soul-bonded. Anything they needed to say would happen within his own mind.

"Long time, no see," he shot her way.

"You look well," she shot back in a voice much older than the body she was in.

"Why not let me die?" He got to the point. His eyes never breaking their lock with hers. His lips never parting to make sound.

"I want you to live," she said, rising from the chair. The lamp's light flickered as she passed it. Her eyes never broke contact with his, even as she walked past him. Her head swiveled like an owl to make sure. "You are everything I could ever want."

"And what is it you want?"

"A challenge." Her body shot around to match where her head was. "You fight back against me. You're powerful. Most hosts would have given up by now, but not you. No, you are something special. Something I've been looking forward to for a long time." She jumped up and stood on the edge of his bed. The lights in the room dimmed so her face was hardly visible. "I am mighty. A warrior. When I finally conquer you, I want it to be grand. A triumph to be heralded for centuries to come. Until then . . . " She was now nose to nose with him, breathing in his face. "I will break you, my love." The lights clicked off.

As the lights flickered back on, she was gone. *A challenge? Hosts? A mighty warrior?* His head was spinning with the thoughts of the damned. He stared out the window as tears began to stream down his cheeks.

When Michael's holy brother William visited him in the hospital, he offered Michael any help he could.

"Come see me if there's ever anything I can do. Love ya," William had said before saying a prayer over his brother and exiting the hospital.

He couldn't have guessed that Michael would actually need his aid. Spiritual aid.

It was a Wednesday, about seven months after his accident, that Michael Haan was finally discharged. Rose pushed him in a wheelchair from his room through the large double doors. His recovery path was clear: wheelchair for a while, cane for a while, and then hopefully walking on his own again.

As they pulled up to the apartment they shared, Michael breathed in a stream of existential dread. His thoughts got the better of him. He was bombarded.

What is this life? Is this just how life goes? Is everyone haunted like this? I guess I thought I was the only one. Special in some way. But what if this is it? Maybe life is just full of hauntings. Full of oppression. Maybe no one is normal. No one is completely free.

What even is freedom? Getting to do what you want? Don't we all do that? We follow orders when we want to. We ignore them when we want to. We do precisely what we want to do all the time. Is that freedom? Is that imprisonment? What kind of life do we create for ourselves by doing exactly what we want?

Or maybe freedom equals peace. Maybe that's what we are all searching for. Maybe that's what's haunting. Maybe conflict is bad enough. Maybe a lack of peace would make anyone feel possessed.

But this wasn't possession, was it? Torment. Haunting. But loss of control? No.

Right?

Michael realized Rose had been talking to him. He also perceived that he was now in his living room, still seated in his wheelchair. He shook his head and blinked his eyes. Glancing around, he spotted his love kneeling next to him, holding onto his hand. She caressed his knuckles with her thumb.

"Babe?" The patience and love in her voice was clearly mixed with concern.

"Sorry, what was that?" He tried for a smile but it looked like an upside down frown.

"What happened?" Direct, yet filled with gentility. This was one of the many reasons he loved her.

Michael Haan collapsed on his love's shoulder. He wept. It felt like his whole life was draining onto her after so many years of keeping it bottled. He kept trying to say something. Anything, really. But all that came from his vocal chords were screeches of blubbering nonsense.

Rose held him. She kissed his sweaty hair and ran her fingernails over his shoulder blades. She squeezed him and took a deep breath. He breathed with her.

"I've got you," she said.

Safety. That's what it is. That's what we're all looking for. We want to feel safe in our vulnerability. Not just when we break down, but every single moment. After all, what is more human than being exactly who you are? And what is more beautiful than the opportunity to be safely vulnerable? That is human. And that is the peace and freedom we are all looking for.

Michael took a deep breath. He kissed Rose's shoulder. Through the tears, he muttered three words: "Gotta see Will."

Rose didn't question him and nodded. She grabbed a baseball cap off their end table and pushed it onto his head.

"There. Now he won't make fun of your haircut, Mike." She giggled and started rolling him back through the door toward the car. He couldn't decide whether he was more offended by the use of that hated nickname or the implication he had a problematic hairstyle. He realized the answer was *neither.* After all, it made him smile. In fact, it made him chuckle a bit with her. *How did I get so lucky?* He was lost in loving agony for his partner during the entire drive to his brother's office.

His brother's office was, of course, at the Church of Christ. Rose wheeled him up the ramp to the door. As Rose reached for the door, it flew open, blowing air conditioning in hers and Michael's faces. William

Haan with a large grin was standing in the doorway. He hugged Rose then patted his brother's shoulder gently.

"Saw you guys pull up. So good to see you. Come on in." William led them down a hallway and into his office. The walls were full of family pictures and a "William Haan Certificate of Ordination." Will sat on one side of his desk and Rose parked Michael across from him. "You know, you got yourself an awesome girl," Will said, never breaking his smile. "I knew she had to be once I saw how much mom and dad liked her." He turned to Rose. "He's told you about how strict they are? I'm a preacher, I've got my morals, but dang, they're next level." Will laughed. Rose and Michael did not.

"Could you give us a second?" Michael almost whispered to Rose.

"Good to see you, Will." Rose clunked the wheelchair's brake into place then exited the room, pulling the door shut behind her.

"How are you? Really, Mike." Will took a drink of his coffee. "Are you recovering okay? I've been really worried for you. Didn't you just get released this week?"

"This morning." Michael decided to only answer one of his brother's barrage of questions.

"What are you doing here? You need to be home resting." Will held up a coffee cup and gestured to the coffee machine. "Do you want coffee?"

"No, thanks. Listen, I need your help, Will." Michael was direct, which caught William off guard.

"Help? Look, I believe God works miracles, but that can be through doctors. I'm praying for you, but I don't think I can heal you." Will shook his head a little as he took another drink from his coffee cup.

"I think you can," Michael said, holding up a hand to stop his brother from responding. "Listen to me. Please. I need to ask you about something and I need you to be really honest with me. And I need it to stay between us. Okay?" Michael stared at his brother unblinkingly and unflinchingly.

"Okay." Will's voice was quiet, contrasting the large personality he usually spilled on his environment.

"Do you believe in demons?"

"Demons?" Will couldn't match his brother's matter-of-fact tone. "Yeah, I feel like it's part of my job description to believe in them." He tried to chuckle but simply exhaled.

"Tell me what you know about them."

"Mike . . . I don't understand what you . . . "

"Please." Michael jumped over his protest. "Tell me what you know. What you believe."

"Demons." William leaned back in his chair. "The Scriptures say that they are fallen angels. Servants of Satan. When Lucifer chose evil at the beginning of time, they were the ones that went with him. They're servants of the darkness. They live to do the Devil's bidding and drive God's servants away from the light."

"And do you believe they're just metaphorical?" Michael said.

"No. To believe they can't affect our world is to discredit the Word of God." William scratched his cheek. "They live in a different realm than us: The Spiritual Realm. But they certainly can hurt the physical world we live in. We see countless examples of both Jesus and his Apostles casting out demons in the name of the Lord. Demon possession was rampant in the time of Christ, but now . . . "

"You don't think it happens anymore?" Michael's voice lost some confidence. It sounded creaky and shaky.

"It does. Everyone has a different opinion, though. Most theologians say that now possession is less common. That it's an archaic idea."

"And what do you say?"

"I say that they've misunderstood the meaning of possession. They think possession is when a person is controlled. When they have no say over their actions or words. And I agree that's less common. But the affliction now is much different. Possession can be inspiration. It can be suggestion. Demons can weigh on people and harm them without completely taking over. Co-possession is still possession." William Haan spoke with authority, which terrified Mike.

"Co-possession . . . " Michael murmured to himself.

"Two names on the deed of a house means two people own it. I think demons can be like that. Darkness doesn't have to snuff out the light to have power in the midst of it."

"So . . . how do you get rid of it?" Michael choked on his words.

"You pray. And have others pray for you. That can drive them out."

"And if that doesn't work?"

"You hope to God that it passes from you."

"Passes to someone else . . . ?"

"That's the example in Scripture. Christ drives them out and they find a new host." William shook his head. "I can't say that I fully get it, but I think that's the truth."

"A new host," Michael repeated.

"What's going on, Michael?" William leaned on his desk.

"Pray for me."

The following year, Michael decided to ignore the demon. He decided not to engage with her, no matter how bad it got. He decided he shouldn't drive, but otherwise the year went reasonably well. He was miserable, but he didn't get into any car accidents. So, I suppose that was a win. He always told me how awful that year was, but that he did it for Rose. For his love. He knew there was only one other victory he wanted to accomplish before the year was done.

Michael Haan hobbled on his cane through the courtyard of his old college campus. His face was young, and his stature old. But his heart? More alive than it had been in many years. With this spirit, he whispered *that* name. He saw the creature walking beside him. He gave her a nod as she sat on a bench and watched him. She still scared him, but he tried not to show it. He wanted to be normal. And if the prayers he and Will were throwing to the heavens hadn't driven her off yet, Michael didn't have much hope that prayers were the answer. As he ignored her and walked by, he started to mumble a prayer under his breath.

"Deliver me, Lord, from this evil. I deliver my soul into your hands. Purge from me this wickedness, O God, so that I might walk closer with you."

"Those are not your words, Mike." The demon now walked side by side with him. "That Bible-thumping brother of yours told you to pray like that, didn't he?"

Michael didn't look at her and continued to pray. "Deliver me, Lord, from this evil."

"I deliver my soul into your hands," she said with him. He stopped speaking as she continued, "Purge me from this wickedness, O God, so that I might walk closer with you." She laughed.

He finally looked at her. He spoke her name again. She smiled.

"Your lack of faith is not what feeds me, Michael. You believe in God as much as I do. Even your brother told you what had to happen, but you don't have the guts to do it, do you?!"

She screamed these last two words. The sky went black. A tear streamed down his face. He said her name once more and then kept walking.

"You'll never escape me, Michael, you know that," she said, sitting on a bench next to the clearing she knew he was making for. "Not until you give your Rose to me. Once you do, then you can be free. Or you can continue to die this agonizingly slow death you've been dying since you freed Chelsea. You know that I'll triumph one way or another, so give in. Resigning your power can be just as heroic as demonstrating it."

Michael crossed into the clearing, the sky finally turning back to its original turquoise color. Rose was standing there, right where he first met her on a walk to class. Right where he had told her to meet him today.

"No, ****," he said, wiping his tears. "No."

He wasted no time. A moment after he hugged her, he tossed his cane across the clearing. It landed next to his oppressor. She glanced at it and then watched as Michael Haan fell onto one knee in front of his college sweetheart.

Michael never told me exactly what he said when he proposed. The words he used were between him and his future bride and them alone. But I do know the most important part.

She said *yes.*

And as they hugged and wept onto each other, **** whispered these words, "I am not the only one of my kind."

Michael Haan married his Rose two years later. His handsome best man, Jay, made sure his college buddy's bowtie was on straight. Rose's sister held the train of her dress and wiped her tears constantly. William Haan pronounced the couple 'husband and wife.' Michael Haan had a dance with Emily Haan. Rose had a dance with Michael Haan. Robert Haan got the whole day on camera. And, of course, a blonde girl clapped from the corners of every celebration room.

What was supposed to be the happiest night of his life, however, became his final battle to win the war. A war that had been waging within him since he was fifteen. He and Rose checked into their hotel. They needed ice for their champagne. When he returned to their room with the ice, he found his bride sitting in a desk chair, staring at the wall with her back to him.

"Rose?" Michael approached her with careful strides.

"I don't think so," she said.

"What do you mean?" He reached her chair and turned it toward him, so he could see her face.

One of Rose's eyes was bloodshot and dark, while the other was clear and terrified. The red eye met Michael's gaze. The fearful eye stared at the floor, trembling.

"Something's wrong, Michael." Her voice quaked. "Something's here." Half of her mouth smiled. Perfect white teeth glinted through.

The hotel door slammed behind him, which prompted him to turn toward the noise. The lock on the door snapped into position just as he laid his eyes on it. A laugh echoed through the room as the lights flickered off. He turned back toward the chair. All he could see was darkness. He heard the faint squeaking of the mattress. He heard whispering and chuckling. He heard the faucet in the bathroom turn on just enough for a *drip-drop.*

The lights flashed on just long enough to see his wife folded on herself in the bed. Her head was cranked to one side. One of her legs was bent behind her head. One of her arms was twisted around her torso like a snake. The lights went out again. Shuffling steps were loud in the shadows.

The next snapshot revealed Rose standing on the desk. Her hair was wrapped around her face like a mask. Only her eyes peeked through the jungle of locks on her face. Muffled screams couldn't escape her hair-mummified visage. She waved at her husband. The lights went out again. The shuffling once more echoed through the room.

When the lights flashed on again, his wife was nose to nose with him. She breathed a warm stream of venomous breath into his face. With each exhale, she sent quakes through Michael. She laughed. The lights went out again. But this time, Michael had figured out a response.

He closed his eyes. Even as he heard the shuffling of feet and the lights clicking on and off, he kept his eyes clamped tight. He took a deep breath.

"You have no power here. You won't win." He spoke in a voice that was hardly his own.

"And what power do you have, boy? What faith do you have to command us?" a voice answered.

"Not faith. The power of fear," he said.

"Fear? And why should we fear you?" the voice cackled.

"I know your kind." Michael Haan's eyes shot open. "I've beaten you before." He saw his wife sitting in the chair, trembling.

"We do not know you!" Rose's mouth moved, but thousands of voices came from inside her.

"You will," he said, kneeling in front of Rose's body. "I know your mightiest warrior. I've defeated her time and time again. If I can beat her, why should I fear you? You should fear me." Rose's body recoiled, and dug her fingernails into the arms of the desk chair. "****." This time Rose's mouth opened as legions of voices screamed in horror. "You know her, don't you? You're scared of her. If I've beaten her, just imagine what I can do to you."

"Leave us!" they shouted.

"Leave her," he commanded.

A flood of energy washed across the room as Rose regained control of herself. The lights in the room stopped flickering. The water stopped running. Neither of her eyes was bloodshot. She collapsed forward onto him and held him tightly.

"For better or worse," he said.

She wept into his shoulder, and he stroked her hair. He whispered soothing encouragement in her ear. She lifted her head and cradled his face in her hands.

"Thank you," she sniffled.

"This will never happen to us again. Okay?"

"Promise?"

"I promise." Michael kissed his wife. He pulled out his phone.

That is the end of Michael Haan's story. At least, as far as you and I are concerned. He made sure he kept his promise to his wife. I never saw them again after their wedding night. I wanted to, but I had to help him keep his promise any way I could. When he called me and asked for help, I couldn't say no.

He passed her to me. The demon he inherited from his high school sweetheart came to me. He begged me to take it from him, so that he could live happily with his bride. It meant never seeing him again. I knew I was making a mistake from that moment, but I wanted to help. No person should have had to carry so heavy a weight as long as Michael did. I was strong, so I thought. I figured I could handle it. I was wrong.

It didn't take long for me to realize that I had to do something. Not only could I not interact with my best friend anymore, but I was living in torment. A couple of years later, I was done. I called my best friend Michael with a plan. I was lucky he answered the phone.

"Hey, H. It's J." Yes, Jay. The first letter of our last names just became what we called each other. I can't remember why. Something from one of our college adventures, I'm sure. Haan and Johnson were always up to some kind of trouble. Maybe that's why I knew this plan would work. "I know what I have to do. You always told me that my English major would get me nowhere quickly, right? I think I figured it out. I know how to fix this for us. It's selfish . . . but I know what I have to do. I know what I have to write."

This story, dear reader, was my plan. He sent me a copy of everything he could remember. I wrote about his demonic life and got it published. All so that at the end of this story, he and I could finally be free from her torment.

And I'm sorry, for whatever it's worth, that it has to be this way. I wanted you to understand how miserable we have been before I told you her name. I knew that as soon as you read the four letters that are her awful name, you'd start experiencing things too.

So when you think you see something in the corner of your mirror . . . or think there's something in your closet . . . or that something creaked when it shouldn't have . . .

You're right. And I'm sorry.

Ella. I call on your name. Pass onto the one reading this.

And . . . God help you.

About the Author

Noah Johnson is an actor/playwright/author originally from the eastern shore of Maryland. As a full-time actor, he travels all over the country performing for audiences of all ages. Writing has always been a great passion and he is always thrilled to share his creations with new readers. In his free time, he enjoys reading, video games, and going on late-night walks. He credits any success he has to his mom Glenda, his partner Sophia, and all of his dear friends. To keep up with Noah's adventures, follow him on Instagram: @NoahMJohnson1

Devour the Hand That Feeds

Vera M. Sidney

Trigger/Content Warnings

- Body horror

- Descriptions of blood

- Food insecurity

- Implied sexual assault

- Mild cannibalism

- Off-page murder

- Poverty

The grinding of the blender rattles my bones. My fingers tighten around the base, holding it steady as it threatens to leap off the counter and spill all over my kitchen floor.

I'm running out of time to finish making lunch before we end up behind schedule. I grip the blender harder and will my drink to finish, all the while checking over the counter to make sure everything else is ready.

The sandwiches are made, and I already pulled the juice boxes out of the fridge. I even managed to swipe a few pieces of fruit from the office to round out the meals.

The angry growl of the blender finally settles into a smooth hum, and I slam down the off button as quickly as I can. Into my thermos the bone broth mixture goes, and then the rest of the food is shoved into my small, padded lunch box.

In the sudden silence, I catch the end of the morning news report playing from my phone.

"Authorities have yet to report any leads on the feral animal that has been stalking the downtown area. They urge residents to stay inside after dark and, if you must travel before dawn, to pick up a free canister of bear spray at your local police station."

The news report cuts off as my alarm blares, and I snatch my phone up to silence it. I sweep everything I need into my arms and hurry out the front door. One hand hefts my backpack, lunch box, and thermos as my other locks my heavy apartment door.

The door beside mine opens right on time, and two kids stream out, clad in their own backpacks and rumpled clothes.

"Kali!"

"Hi, Mosey." I smile down at the little girl who rushes to my side, her pigtails uneven and a smudge of toothpaste on her chin.

Mosey beams back at me, and her brother steps up behind her with a dusty sandwich bag of jingling coins. He shoves it into the chaotic mess of ripped papers and bent books inside his backpack, then accepts the lunch box I hand down to him.

"Thanks," Mitch mumbles, shifting his backpack higher on his shoulders and clinging to the lunch box with his small hands.

"Let's go." I tuck my thermos and phone into my own bag and guide Mosey over to the stairs with a hand behind her tiny shoulders. The kids rush down the stairs the way they always do, their little legs racing down far too fast for me to follow, but their hands stay on the railing and the wall to avoid my scolding.

My knee tweaks as I take my first step down, and a hiss escapes my lips as the pain shoots up my thigh. I pause and stretch it out, rubbing over the joint with my thumb. My knuckle brushes against what must be a bruise I didn't notice earlier, and pain shudders through my leg. I grit my teeth and continue my descent, managing to make it down to the bottom floor without cursing in front of them.

We hit the sunshine outside with three matching grimaces—it's far too early for it to be this bright. We shield our eyes until the high-rise buildings across the road block out the sun for us, and then focus all our attention on navigating the bustling streets.

Two small hands find mine as we reach the crosswalk, and I grip them tightly as we navigate the maze of morning traffic. The bodega on the corner is stocked with all the newest magazines, and Mitch drags us over and pouts at me with the biggest eyes he can summon.

I pull Mosey safely in front of me and haul Mitch up onto my hip to look.

His face fills with joy, and one of his small hands immediately reaches out. His fingers wiggle toward the shiny magazines and their bright colors. The lunch box I gave him squishes against the back of my head as he holds on to me tighter and leans toward the stand.

"Animals!" he demands. His eyes scour the magazine covers, then fix their disappointment onto me. "Where are animals?!"

I check over the selection, but there are no National Geographic or World of Animals magazines out. Most of the covers depict a model showing off the latest fashion, and several tabloids display unflattering angles of celebrities. In the corner of one, an actress is walking her dog, and I shift closer to point it out to Mitch.

"Look, there's a dog right there!"

His frown lessens as he leans in to analyze the image, but it doesn't disappear.

"No, I wanna see the animal!" he complains.

"What animal, buddy?"

"The animal!" he whines, and I bite back a sigh.

"We'll check again tomorrow, okay?" I offer, shifting him back to the ground and taking both of their hands in mine again.

Mitch drags his feet the rest of the way to the subway, moving slow enough that I consider just hauling him up on my shoulders so I can get to work on time. The crowds are bustling when we get down to the entrance, so I tuck both children in tight against my sides and shuffle my steps as we go.

Beside the turnstiles, a man with a shaggy beard and curly hair down his back is holding up woven necklaces and shouting their cheap prices to the crowd. People brush past him as they hurry to work, and his reaching fingers grasp the edges of their clothing to try to make a sale.

My foot kicks something soft, and then Mosey disappears from my touch.

I whirl immediately, fingers snatching for her shirt, but she reappears in front of me just as quickly.

"Wow, look!" she croons, cradling a woven necklace in her hands. It's dirty on one side—a dusty shoe print stepped right across the emblem—but on the other side the multicolored rope depicts some sort of flowering vegetation.

Irritation flares through me, and I slap the necklace out of her hands before I can stop myself.

"Mosey! Don't pick things up off the ground! How many times have I told you?"

She tries to grab it as it falls, but I'm quicker this time. It's our turn to swipe through the turnstiles, so I snatch her shirt collar and shove her in front of me. The three of us swipe through together. When we emerge on the other side, the crowd is a little less dense, and she rips away from me with tears in her eyes.

Guilt hits my gut like lead, but my patience doesn't replenish. Keeping my mouth shut is the kindest thing I can do, so I snap my teeth together and drag the three of us onto the train.

Leaving the kids doesn't ease my frustration. It persists for hours after I see them make it safely into their school, and I find myself biting my cheeks every time someone in the office comes by with a sunny hello and a new request for me to deal with. Every new email chime jars my skeleton as violently as the blender did this morning, and even my beloved bone broth tastes like sludge on my tongue.

When the lunch hour hits, I clock out and reach the elevator first. Unfortunately, Trevor from sales and Hillary from marketing are right on my heels, and I'm forced to offer them a plastic smile as we all step into the tight metal box together.

"It's so heartbreaking," Hillary laments, leaning back against the elevator walls. "I don't understand how people can keep dying. What a horrific way to go, being eaten alive like that . . . "

Trevor scoffs, the noise too loud for the tight space. "I don't understand how the police haven't put down this rabid thing yet."

"The police haven't even seen it!" Hillary exclaims, clutching her purse tighter in her hand. "They can barely catch it on the security cameras. It keeps attacking in the middle of the night when no one is around . . . "

"I bet it's a fucking coyote with rabies or some shit," Trevor says, folding his arms over his chest. "Needs a good bullet to the brain and it'll all be over."

"I guess. But what if it's, like"—She trails off, and her voice grows quiet—"like, a ghost, or something? A vengeful spirit? Maybe that's why no one ever sees it?"

"Hillary, come on," Trevor snorts. "It's a fucking dog. They even said the bite pattern matches a wolf."

"Then why can't they catch it?!" she demands, rifling through her purse. "You can catch a wolf with raw meat and cage traps—I saw a documentary about it! That's how they tag them out in the wild—"

"'Cause they're too busy sitting on their asses eating donuts," he snaps before she's even finished her sentence.

"Look, I got this from a man this morning—"

"What the fuck is that?"

I shut my eyes and clench my jaw tighter, breathing in through my nose and fighting the instinct to curl my lip at the heavy scent of their colognes.

"It's supposed to keep the animal away, like a protection ward—"

"Oh, Hillary!"

My irritation snaps, and my hands wrap into fists and dig into my elbows where I cross them. When will these two idiots just *shut the fuck up?!*

"It's going to keep me safe!"

"You know that's a pile of bullshit. A dog doesn't care about your jewelry."

The elevator dings. I burst out of it, my feet twisting up with Hillary's and my shoulder knocking into her chest. She shouts, and it shudders through my ears. It takes the rest of the self-control that I have not to just shove her off me.

I rip away and backpedal, and her purse goes flying through the air. The contents fall to the ground, lipsticks and tampons and credit cards sprawling all over the fake marble. A woven necklace sits beside everything: the exact same shoddily made bullshit the man in the subway had been selling.

I can't stop the ridiculous roll of my eyes as soon as I see it, but I manage enough decency to mumble an apology before stomping out of the office.

It takes the rest of the day to get a handle on myself. The usual din of conversation from the break room grates on my nerves until I drown it out with my meeting headphones, and no matter how many times I get up to stretch my legs, the itch on my back continues to climb up my spine.

I can't decide if I need to sprint for three miles or sleep for a full day, but by the time I clock out and leave, I'm considering calling in sick tomorrow to do both.

The kids seem equally agitated when I pick them up from their after-school care—Mosey jumps down the stairs like she's had too much sugar, and Mitch keeps digging his finger into the hole in his shirt sleeve, slowly ripping it bigger and bigger.

It's not until we're on the subway that I find out what's wrong with them.

"Hola." I offer a smile to Abuela, one of our downstairs neighbors, as I step aside to let her take the seat the kids had been sharing.

"Muchas gracias, mija." She smiles back at me, patting my elbow as I help her into the hard seating.

She has her phone out today. A local Hispanic news video is playing with extra-large captions. I don't know enough Spanish to read them, but I can see the edges of the video past the words.

A newscaster is delivering a stern report at the afternoon news table. As we watch together, the faces of several men appear on the screen beside him. They're framed in square boxes, with each of their names displayed at the bottom of the photos.

I recognize the men instantly—their pictures have been on the news for the last few months. The victims of the animal attacks happening around the borough.

The newscaster's eyebrows pull together in sympathy, and his lips drag into a frown.

The show of compassion turns my stomach.

I know what he's saying without even needing to hear it. The same verbatim nonsense that they've been repeating since the first man was found mauled in an alleyway downtown: *These promising young men, with their whole lives ahead of them, have tragically met their demise at the teeth of a rabid animal. Upstanding members of their communities—with no criminal records and well-paying jobs—had their lives torn apart by the wiles of the wilderness. With one tragic accident after another, these unconnected victims' only commonality was how much potential they had in their lives.*"

"Potential to rip their communities apart with their greedy hands and expensive smiles" would be more accurate. Predators in their finest forms, preying on the weakest of their neighbors.

The newscaster disappears as the program zooms in on a blurry, dark photo of a local park. A bright outline traces around a shape in the photo, turning a fuzzy shadow into something between a discount blockbuster Bigfoot and a large, slightly deformed stray dog.

"Animal!" Mitch shouts, smudging Abuela's screen with a greasy finger.

If this really is a photo of the animal that's been attacking men for the last few months, it's a truly shitty one. It looks staged: a weirdly hulking mass caught in perfectly blurry motion and indistinguishable without a drawn outline.

I catch his hand, wipe her screen with the edge of my sleeve, and then pause.

"Mitch, what's on your hand?"

He yanks it out of my grasp and tries to rub the mark off with his other hand, but I've already seen it. It's a piece of sandwich bread: a dark red icon stamped onto the back of his hand.

He mumbles his answer, and I can't hear a word of it over the noise of the train.

"He got stamped at lunch!" Mosey tattles, bouncing between her toes and her heels.

"Why did you get stamped?" I ask, checking over Mosey's hands and finding them clean.

He mumbles again, and I lean down to meet him.

"What is it, honey?"

"I'm in debt," he says.

I can't stop myself from snorting, but I try to repress my laughter when I answer him. "You're in *debt*? For what?"

"Lunch," he answers, and my laugh dies in my throat.

"What do you mean? Why did they stamp you?"

"I'm not allowed to have lunch," he pouts, holding his hand up to finally show me the stamp. "That's what it means."

"Didn't you eat what I gave you?" I ask the question I already know the answer to. He handed me the empty lunch box as soon as I picked them up.

"We ate as soon as we got to school," Mosey pipes in, leaning in close. One of her pigtails has fallen out, and her frizzy hair tickles my chin. "My tummy wouldn't stop growling."

Something inside me sinks, and the anger in my chest tickles my throat.

"That's okay, sweetheart," I tell her. I'll try to pack them more food tomorrow.

"I gave them the quarters from Mom, but they still gave me a stamp and a letter when I got in line for lunch." Mitch shrugs.

"A letter?"

He nods, and after a few moments of searching his messy backpack, he holds out a dented trifold paper.

I open it and scan through the letter.

> *"This letter is to inform you that your child, Mitch, has been purchasing breakfast and/or lunch . . . There is an extreme negative balance on your child's account . . . sufficient payment has not been made . . . This demonstrates a failure to provide your child with proper nutrition, and you can be sent to Dependency Court for neglect . . . the result may be your child being removed from your home and placed into a foster home . . . signed . . . Director of Federal Programs, Board of Education."*

Rage, hot and acidic, boils inside my chest. It spreads through my lungs and makes every breath burn, scalding my nose and throat. My fist tightens around the paper and it crumples, becoming nothing more than a flimsy warning flag of the violence to come.

With shaking hands, I fold it back up and stuff it into Mitch's backpack.

"My friend Jackson didn't get stamped and got lunch, but they pulled him away from the table and made him go sit in detention for the rest of the day. They said he didn't pay for the food he ate, but why did they give it to him?"

I don't trust my hands to cradle his gentle face, so I lock my fingers around the nearest train pole and dig my nails into the greasy metal. The anger rioting inside me is so great that I'm shocked the metal doesn't crumble to dust in my fist.

"He gave me some of his macaroni," Mitch finishes, turning his shining amber eyes up to look at me. "He's really nice."

My agreement is stuck on my tongue, glued behind my teeth, with the risk that if I open my mouth, my fangs might pierce those that don't deserve it.

I don't manage to unlock my jaw before we make it home—even as I send them into their apartment, I'm still silent in my anger. I raise a finger up to my lips to remind them to stay quiet because their mother only has a few more hours before she'll have to get up for work. Since they moved in last year, there hasn't been a single time I've seen her when she hasn't looked absolutely exhausted.

When I enter my own apartment, I sink to the floor. My mind races to find a logical solution, but my rage thrums through my body with rushing adrenaline. I clench my shaking hands in my lap and force myself to think this through.

I can send Mitch to school tomorrow with enough money to pay off his lunch debt, but that won't prevent him from accruing more of it, and then I won't be able to feed them until my next paycheck. I have no idea how many meals Mosey is behind on too, and how soon she might receive her own stamp and letter. Paying for Mitch won't help his friend stuck in detention. I can call the school and see how much debt all the students have, but it's likely far more than I can afford, even if I save up.

We can try to crowdfund, but where would that money go? Who among us even has enough spare change to contribute? Will they forgive the lunch debts if they're not paid by the child's guardians? This entire ordeal is so ridiculous—an orchestrated punishment for parents who are already struggling to keep their families safe.

Mitch's face swims in my mind—his gaunt little cheeks and his eyebrows that stick straight up—and I can't hold myself back any longer.

I must help him. I must help all of them.

If I don't, who will?

Cool water kisses my forehead. I feel it cascade down my neck and chest and hips; I follow its trail all the way to my toes. The color scarlet cradles the edges of my body, caressing my skin as the water washes it away.

I run my hands through my messy hair and feel a tickle in my knuckles. I hold my hands in front of my face and blink away the water. I find scraped flesh and tangles of stained hair where my smooth skin should be. My fingers respond on autopilot, rubbing soap into the wounds and the fur and washing away the dirt. I know it should burn, should be sharp and aching and agonizing all at once, but it isn't.

I barely feel anything at all.

I rarely do during these showers. I almost never feel anything besides peace.

Calmness pervades every part of my body: the kind of karmic peace that only the holiest preach about happening in their headiest meditations. My chest and stomach are full, my hunger sated, and satisfaction fogs the air around me.

I wash until the water runs clear. I wash until my skin is raw and smooth and flushed, my hair untangled and long down my back. I wash until my mouth is clean, my teeth flossed, and my tongue scraped. I wash until every part of me is new, and then I turn the water off and emerge from the shower.

The mirror is foggy around the edges. The lukewarm humidity of the room clings to the edges of the glass. I can see myself in the middle of it. My picture is blurred at the edges but still sharp in the middle.

My body has returned to normal. My skin has regrown. My back stands tall. I lean in to look myself in the eyes, and I see it in the hollows of my pupils.

The darkness that lives inside me.

The Animal.

I pack four sandwiches into the lunch box this morning.

I'm already waiting in the hallway and sipping my morning broth by the time my alarm goes off and the kids emerge from their apartment. Their faces are still puffy from sleep, so I gently scratch the tops of their heads before we leave.

My body handles the stairs with ease, my legs moving so quickly that I almost catch up to them before we reach the ground floor.

When we emerge into the sunshine, I offer Mitch a piggyback ride. He clambers up my body with an ecstatic squeal in my ear and a few misplaced kicks to my ribs, but I don't mind. He balances on my shoulders easily. His fingers wrap their way around my hair and hold on as if he can steer me by it.

Mosey skips beside me—every one of my long steps necessitating three hops from her—and when we stop at the crosswalk, I use both of her hands to pull her up to stand on my feet. She giggles as I raise my toes and rock her around, and it makes my heart swell.

I steer us over to the bodega before Mitch can pull on my hair, and Mosey peruses the candy array while Mitch scans the magazines.

Sudden irritation digs its way into my spine, and I turn to look around. My eyes land on the new display on the far side of the cashier, and an ugly snort escapes me.

A dozen of the woven flower necklaces are now being sold here, beside a sign claiming them to be "Creature Defeaters." A few decorative corked jars sit beside them, filled to the brim with bright purple flower petals.

Wolfsbane.

The absurdity of it all turns my annoyance into laughter. Do people really think a pretty plant with a fancy name will protect them from the rabid Animal killing people? That plant is just as poisonous to them as it is to a wolf, and as much as I hate to admit it, Trevor is right.

No necklace, poisonous or not, would be enough to stop a wolf.

Not once they've chosen their prey.

"There!" Mitch shouts, throwing his body forward to snatch at one of the magazines. I snap back to reality, darting forward to counter his weight and help him pull the magazine off the rack.

Plastered across the front cover of the news tabloid is a tinted green night-vision photo, which depicts the front of an apartment complex and some sort of monstrosity sprinting under a streetlight. It's another terrible photo, but the shape is more distinguishable and admittedly animal-like than the shitty blur from Abuela's news report.

"District Director Dies in Feral Mauling; City Fails to Capture Creature" is plastered over the bottom of the photo in humongous white letters.

"Animal!" He shakes the magazine in his little hands, nearly dropping it right on my face.

Sunshine blossoms in my chest upon hearing the joy in his voice, and I laugh as I shift to balance the magazine on top of my head so he can look at it without dropping it.

"Yeah, buddy." I nod lightly, passing a few bills to the cashier for two magazines and the piece of candy Mosey snatched. I tuck the second magazine into my pocket and help Mosey get the candy wrapper open. "It's the Animal."

I feel his fingers dragging across the magazine atop my skull, and it feels like he's petting the Animal's silhouette.

I can't quell the smile that spreads across my face, and I don't want to. The irritation lingering in my body evaporates, and I leave the bodega feeling lighter than ever.

My joy lasts well through us reaching their school, and I watch them hurry up the steps—holding a full lunch box and a finely pressed magazine—with a soft warmth in my chest.

Children filter around me to rush up the steps behind Mitch and Mosey, and several other guardians linger nearby to watch their kids make it inside safely.

"They say he was attacked out in the warehouse district—but what was he doing there in the middle of the night?!" one woman to my right whispers to her friend. Her hand is pressed to her chest.

"Don't tell Beth, but Kim said that he cuts through there to visit his *mistress*," her friend replies, leaning in.

I check my phone—I'm ahead of schedule, so I can afford to linger for a few minutes and listen. I move out of the flow of students and closer to the women talking, pulling the magazine out from my pocket and flipping to the cover story inside.

The green picture from the cover and the blurry black-and-white photo from the news are blown up beside each other, both showing something with a hunching back and thick, grotesque limbs.

"He has a mistress?! Who would even *date* that scumbag?"

"A wife *and* a mistress *and* he's still hitting on Lisa at the school board meetings. He's a creepy piece of shit—"

"*Was* a creepy piece of shit."

"Hallelujah! Maybe I'll put out some raw steak tonight as a thank you to the wolf."

I skim the story about the creature: Its latest victim is the director of federal programs from the board of the children's school, and the police still haven't figured out a possible connection between any of the victims. Their best guess is a shared cologne or natural scent that attracts the creature to them more than any other possible victim.

I have to bite my lip to keep from laughing aloud.

"Do you think it knows?" one of the women wonders.

"What, like it has a conscience?" the other questions.

"I'm just saying, it's not like anyone's going to miss him. Good riddance."

" . . . You know, Kim's cousin knew the third victim."

"The realtor?"

"Yeah . . . and you didn't hear this from me, but apparently he was accused of sexual assault five years ago."

"Really?"

"By *three* women—and *all* of them dropped the charges the *day* before he was set to go to court for it."

The woman scoffs: a sharp, haughty noise. A knowing noise.

"A predator hunting its own."

"I hope so."

Several paragraphs at the end of the article describe the city's failing attempts to capture the animal: Metal cages and meaty bait have done nothing to attract it, and it's avoided their attempts to capture it on recording, as if it knows exactly where the cops have placed their patrols and street cameras. It's thwarted them so well that it's almost as if it can listen to the police scanner or check police-watching apps . . . or like it's lived here its whole life and knows the natural routine of the neighborhoods.

The animal always seems to be a step ahead, working with an innately human logic instead of the animalistic instincts they insist it must have. The police have no leads, and the city has nothing more than empty cages.

With a smirk, I shut the magazine and tuck it into my backpack. I turn and head down the street toward my office with a bounce in my step and an overwhelming swell of pride in my chest.

The first time I woke up in the shower covered in blood, I was scared.

I screamed. I trembled. I wondered what had happened to me that I could remember going out for the night, but not how I had gotten home. I wondered what had taken away my memory; had it been by force or my own mind's protection?

I wondered if this had been how Dinah felt when it happened.

Confused. Terrified. Feeling as if her body wasn't her own.

I scraped at my stained skin, digging the clumps of blood out of my hair until I could be sure I was unscathed. I stared at my elongated hands and feet, stepped on my changed limbs, and clattered to the ground in an uncoordinated heap.

Half my body fell out of the shower entirely, landing on the hard, cold tile of my dorm bathroom. I waited for the pain to shock through my body, for my bones to protest my violent fall . . . but it never came.

When I finally rolled over and pushed myself off the floor, I realized how different all my limbs felt. They weren't just grotesque in shape; my muscles had changed as well. My movements were uncoordinated but sharp. My joints swung with smooth ease. My body held my uneven frame with a strength I had never known.

Unlike Dinah, I was unharmed.

The first time I woke up covered in blood in the shower, I didn't understand what had happened.

It took me several days to piece the story together.

It took me until they announced his death.

Mauled so viciously, it took them three full days to piece together enough scraps of skin and bone to properly identify him. The school was in an uproar once they realized who had died. I stopped in my tracks as soon as I received the school administrator's notice.

A horrifying incident with what must be a wild animal has led to one of the college's most promising young men's deaths. A candlelit vigil will occur within the hour. A new fund will be started to build a fence around the nearby forest to prevent any other wildlife from breaching downtown. Bear spray will be distributed for free at every dorm.

I stared at the photograph of him beaming into the camera—now dramatized in black and white—and I just *knew*. I could suddenly taste his blood in my mouth, suddenly feel my claws sinking into his sides. I could hear his screams echoing in my head.

I couldn't fully remember killing him, but I knew I had done it.

I didn't know how to feel until I spoke to her.

Guilt and horror weighed down my gut like boulders. My limbs were now familiar, but they moved like bricks of lead. Every modicum of pain I felt shocked my system like lightning.

I had done something terrible, hadn't I?

I had killed him.

But when I saw Dinah after it, everything changed. She greeted me like a cool breeze against my flushed skin. She kissed me like sunshine cresting the horizon. She moved with the lightness of a feather, like wings through the clouds.

I had never seen her so unburdened. Not since it had happened and, when I really thought about it, not even before. The fear that had shrouded the entirety of our relationship in the shadows was suddenly gone.

She smiled freely now. She held my hand before others without a care, and every movement she made was like a dance she couldn't hold in.

The boundless joy in her soul lifted the guilt from my body as if it weighed nothing at all. It turned my memory of a terrifying, blood-soaked shower into a painting of my passion. His screams echoing in my head became the melody of my devotion. The iron flavor that lingered on the back of my tongue became the taste of my commitment to her.

With Dinah's approval of my wrath, I became fearless too.

When I asked her about his death, if she thought the circumstances were strange, she only had one thing to say:

"He got exactly what he deserved."

In the weeks that followed her unburdening, the whispers of other women around campus soothed all of the lingering doubts in my conscience.

"He had it coming," they said. *"That wild animal did us a favor. I'm glad he was ripped apart. I wish that I could have done it first. I'm not afraid to go out anymore. I know I won't be followed home."*

"I finally feel safe now."

The second time it happened, it was another man outside of another bar.

Just like the first time, I didn't choose him. I didn't mean for it to happen. I didn't even remember it.

It had been so many years since the first time that it felt like it had just been a dream; the memory so wrapped in distance and disbelief that it felt more like sleep than reality.

When I came to in the shower—my limbs once more uneven and strong and coated in blood—dread pooled in my gut. The harsh fact that the first time had not been a manifestation of my mind, but the reality of my body, was now undeniable. The reality of a capability within my body that I didn't know how to control.

Once again, it took days before the pieces began to add up: another mauling outside the last bar I remembered visiting . . . a witness who couldn't voice what the man had done to her. The news flipped the story of what had happened to him from an avenging dog attack to the tragic, feral mauling of a successful businessman within a week. They discredited the witness because she was so hysterical and traumatized from the violence that she had to be hospitalized. The hospital found drugs in her system, so they decided she must have been hallucinating. The news discovered the man had been about to sign a million-dollar deal to gentrify the waterfront district, and so suddenly, he was the angelized victim.

It took until the third time I awoke in a bloody shower for me to truly see the trees for the forest they live inside.

For me to see that the Animal that lives inside of me is the same part of me that cares.

I cannot control the darkness that grows in my heart any more than I can control the government that is starving my community, or the predators that are stalking my streets.

I can do nothing to stop the rage that flourishes in my chest as I watch my neighbors suffer at the hands of people with enough power to save them but not enough conscience to care.

And I can do nothing to stop that rage from growing its own fangs and ripping all their harm apart at the seams.

It seems the only thing I can do is to let that rage bloom, and to greet the beasts that feed off our suffering as a beast myself.

When I pick the children up after work, Mitch's eyes are red.

The sunshine that's been beaming in my body all day extinguishes immediately.

He's still clutching the magazine, but it's creased and wrinkled, and it looks like several of the pages have been torn.

My rage awakens, and the Animal's growl rumbles through me.

"Hi, Kali." Mosey sulks, reaching up to take my hand.

I unfurl my fist and hold her fingers as gently as I can. My other hand reaches instinctively for Mitch's skinny shoulder, and I pull him close to my hip.

"What happened?" are the only words I manage to utter between my bared teeth.

Tears stream from his amber eyes like a dam breaking, and I fall to my knees before him. He collapses into my arms, tucking his tiny face into my neck and wrapping his fists around the collar of my button-down. I pull his skinny body into my strong one, wrapping around every part of him until he's safe against my chest. I can feel his pulse fluttering beneath me, his shoulders shaking as sobs rattle his bones. I hold him as tightly as I think he can bear, and I take his sorrow into me.

It melts into my bones beside the emotions that it recognizes like family: despair, frustration, disbelief. It crawls into my marrow and makes a home within my rage, feeding the darkness inside of me.

I hold Mitch until his sobs break down into hiccups, and I don't pull away until his hands unfurl and he swipes a wrist over his snotty nose.

I pull a tissue from my bag and clean him up, and when he's calmed down enough to meet my eyes, he doesn't speak.

His bottom lip sticks out from his mouth, wobbling as it protrudes and drags his face down. His small hands find mine, and on the back of one of them is an angry red stamp of a slice of bread.

My fingers shake as I look at it, so I drop his hands and sweep his cheeks up in my palms. He meets my eyes with his own tear-stained ones, and I pull his fear into my body and eat it whole.

"I'm going to take care of this," I assure him. "Everything will be okay."

"Really?" he asks, and his voice is so small.

"Yes," I promise. My conviction is bold, and my voice is unwavering. I will make it okay.

I will make it okay with my teeth and my claws and whatever else it takes.

I spend my night combing news articles.

The news of the director's death is already fading into the background, and it takes almost an hour of searching for me to learn that as soon as his bones grew cold, his successor stepped into his place.

Another man hungry for the power that local government would afford him. For the access to children's minds that it would grant him; for the control over our youth's education and what the next generation would be capable of.

I find his promises from the first time he campaigned for the position: the vicious slashes he would make to the budgets in the name of efficiency, the countless employees who would lose their jobs to his ego. I dig far enough in a parental forum to find out that the repercussions for the lunch debts were his idea—an initiative to "guarantee accountability" and "better fund our community."

I find his ongoing court cases: the divorce from his wife and the estrangement of his child. I find the abuse allegations he tried to bury. I find the sins he tried to hide, and I feel my stomach rumble.

I find his name and his address next. He doesn't even live far away; he'll be dead before the moon can rise.

I stand naked in front of my mirror. My hungry eyes comb my strange body. I stretch my arms out to my sides and watch the large Animal take up all the space that it's owed. I grin widely and watch its lips curl up in a snarl, teeth made for tearing muscle and flesh from bone sparkling in the incandescent light. Spit froths at the edges of my mouth as a growl reverberates from my chest; a warning of the death to come.

I look into my own eyes, and I see myself inside the Animal; I see myself as the Animal and the Animal as me. I recognize the hollow of my pupils and the darkness festering within; I recognize it as the source of my rage and the birth of this monster. I know the beast staring at me as deeply as I know the soft curves and cutting edges of my human body. I know the reason for the monster as deeply as I know the endless well of compassion that pours from my body every time my heart bleeds.

I look into the darkness, and I see the Animal of my body.

I let her devour me.

And I take care of it.

About the Author

Vera M. Sidney hails from a town with tall trees and thick sea air, and has been filled with a hatred for injustice since their childhood. They write stories that achieve catharsis for both the characters and the readers through rage, love, revenge, and community. Music provides a constant muse for them, and Nine Inch Nails and The Crane Wives receive inspiration credits for the title of the story you just read. They would be nowhere without their beloved family, friends, and their perfect canine children who have never done anything wrong, *ever*.

"Devour the Hand that Feeds" features a letter from a board of education member condemning a family for the lunch debt their child accrued. This letter is heavily based on a real letter that was sent out to numerous families within the Wyoming Valley West School District in Luzerne County, Pennsylvania back in 2019. At the time of this publication, SNAP benefits are being threatened and used as political bargaining chips. Vera encourages readers to research their local school policies and food pantries, and to do what they can to ensure their neighbors remain safe and fed.

You can stay up to date with Vera's next publications on Instagram @veramsidney.

Autumn
by Cisco Bautista

Content/Trigger Warnings

- Amnesia

- Apparitions/Ghost

- Blood

- Body Horror

- Death

- Hematophagy

- Implication of Amputation

- Implication of Animal Death

In her long, infinite death, she had only known the embrace of the thorns and the cold. She knew no words, no speech. No knowledge of cold, sweet fruit in the summer, nor the warmth of a bowl of soup in the winter. Nothing of the blooming petals of the spring, or the crunch of the falling leaves in autumn. She did not even know she was a 'she.'

Until one day, a door opened in front of her and she stepped through. Glowing orange runes leaped from the door frame and whipped around her, twisting and snapping until her entire body was bound tight. She did not fight. She could not.

Footsteps descended the stairs, and a figure approached. They spoke. She did not understand. Their brows furrowed as they spoke again. Different words with different rhythms. Different sounds. She did not respond.

They crouched down to see her eye-to-eye. Soft, dark eyes looked into her hollow ones. Their hand slowly reached out. She leaned away. The hand retracted, and they took a step back. They waved their hand over the runes, and the light dispersed and vanished. She could move again. She did not.

They gestured to the door, back to the air. She did not move.

The stranger frowned, looked her up and down, then held up a finger and went away. A different room. There was no thorns, no cold. She did not know what it was. She liked it.

When they finally returned, they held a basin of black liquid.

Thirst.

She lunged forward, dunking her head into the liquid. Her grip white-knuckled, bending the metal basin as she inhaled the liquid, then inhaled some more. When her head surfaced, she saw the black liquid turn red on the stranger's apron. Blood.

Sheep's blood.

She looked up at the person and opened her mouth. Croaking and gasping. They saw something she didn't and shook their head. She stopped. They looked at her mouth, then at her hands. Went back to the room from before, then came back again. A notebook and pen were in their hands. They wrote something and then gave it back.

Scribbles on a page.

She didn't take it.

The person put it down, held the basin for her as she brought it to her lips. Gulp after gulp. Slower and slower. Tingling started at her lips, then her face, head, and neck. It spread throughout her entire being. Then came the needles. The warmth. She shivered and leaned on the basin, sloshing red onto the rug, but the person paid no mind. They held the basin still with one hand, held her hair back with the other.

They spoke gently. She still couldn't understand. She just continued drinking. They let her until she was satisfied.

When she lifted her head, they used their sleeve to wipe her mouth, the way one would for a child. She found the feeling vaguely familiar.

Her limbs weighed her down, more solid than they had been in a long time. The person took her hand and helped her up, leading her to a different room. Plants hung from the windows and from a rod over a large basin. A bathtub.

They led her into the bath and turned on the water.

She could feel it. She could feel the steam. The warmth seeping into bones she no longer had. Herbs and oils were scattered, rich and soothing. She wanted to sink into it, but then the person grabbed a pitcher and tilted her hair back. Warm water washed over her scalp. Dirt and grime came off in flecks and streams. With bare hands and rolled-up sleeves, they scrubbed her scalp, pulled back her long hair, and from it, they brushed out leaves, twigs . . . other things. The water washed her clothes, went throughout, and as if it were flesh, the filth came away, leaving white cloth.

Her nightgown.

They continued to cleanse her. As more filth went down the drain, her entire being felt lighter.

A gentle sponge rubbed her face, washing away the caked dirt, grime, and sticky blood. Washed away the grime on her arms and hands. They used a took to pick out the filth under her fingernails. The same treatment was given to her feet.

At one point, the water stilled. They had to reach under the water and pull up debris from the drain. Just like that, the dark water began to spiral, and they continued their work, cleaning her even after all the water went down the drain. After some time, they turned off the water. Then they pulled out a strange object from a box, putting one end of it into the wall. It clicked, and the loudest roar erupted from it.

She flinched back and covered her ears, quickly scrambling back until her back hit the wall.

The roar cut short, and they put down the object. Their hands reached for hers and gently squeezed them before pulling her back. A soft voice. Soft sounds. Words.

"It's all right. It's all right, you're safe, I'm sorry."

They put the object away and grabbed large cloths instead. One ruffled her head and hair, the other wrapped around her body, keeping her warm. They led her back out of the room, a hand on her upper back and another holding her hand still. Against the wall, there was a large metal object that went up to her hip with an open flame inside. A chair was a short distance away, and the stranger had them sit in front of it.

She felt the passage of time then. Could distinguish days from seconds. The warmth of the fire and the cold wind whistling outside. Much like the warmth that seeped in with each gulp of black sheep's blood, so too did it sink in when in front of the fire. The crackle of firewood, the rustle of leaves and branches in the wind from outside. And as time passed, while she did not remember her old name, nor the ways of her life, if she had a life, she felt peace.

She was well.

The stranger sat on the floor beside her after a while and introduced themself as Namir and asked, "What is your name?"

She did not know how to respond. She could not. She opened her mouth again. Something was missing.

"Ah . . . Oh . . . "

Her tongue. There was a small stump where it should have been.

Namir shook their head and put a hand on her shoulder.

"No, it's all right, I . . . I'm sorry."

They brought back the pen and notebook and handed them to her. She wrote.

Autumn.

"Autumn . . . Appearing on an autumn night." Namir smiled. "It suits you, Autumn."

They extended an offer then and there. That Autumn could stay as long as she pleased.

So she did.

About the Author

Cisco Bautista is a student at Cal Poly Pomona working on their Bachelor's Degree in English. They are also the author of a short story titled *Café de Carrefour*, which is published in Mary Baldwin University's magazine: *Outrageous Fortune*, Issue 13. When they are not writing or studying niche topics (e.g., misogyny in slasher flicks, Filipino monsters), they are found practically inhaling some food and/or drink they shouldn't have bought, reading on Ao3, looking for a job, or watching Smosh Reddit videos.

The Last Words of
Henry R. McCoy

by Luke Van Amburg

Content/Trigger Warnings

- Executions

- Murder

- Pregnancy and childbirth

- Drowning

My first experience with Warren's Bluff came in the summer of 2022. It was the last year of my graduate studies, and I was in the midst of tracking the development of nursery rhymes across the Oregon Trail. In that journey through city archives and molded-over journals, I came upon something quite unique. It was a children's song, like all the others; yet, one which bore no lineage to prior melodies. Often called *A Thousand More Graves*, the poem pervades the towns north of Brookings, and is a common tune in the schoolyards of the Willamette Valley. Perhaps you know it also, just by another name. Though it has a host of variants, the first two lines tend to go as follows:

'A thousand more graves than can ever be filled lie beneath Fort Warren.'

'Come rain or come fog, the Rusalka's wail will follow the straining rope.'

Somehow, the verse does not do the place justice.

Fort Warren is a dreary place. Built of ancient timber, with rooftops home to naught but the odd gull or two, the colonial fortress is one of many oddities hidden across the Pacific coast. Locked between Heceta Beach and Coos Bay, it was first constructed by the Russian Empire to fortify their holdings in North America, and left to rot ever since. Even now, one could hardly imagine a more miserable station to hold, as cold winds rattle its windows from morning to night, eclipsing all other thoughts. Upon its walls, one could easily envision themselves staring into the very edge of the world, as the Pacific looms across from you—its expanse lost behind a bulwark of fog.

Why exactly the Imperial navy chose Warren's Bluff for their purposes is unknown, as the location came with its own host of nuisances. Without any neighboring ports to reach out to, the settlement stood largely defenseless. Moreover, its position as a lone trading post on the furthest edge of Oregon Territory made it a hard sell for any pioneer families daring to head west. Indeed, surviving accounts paint a distinctly miserable tale for those settled behind its walls. One of storms battering their gates in the depths of autumn, and the Oregon Dunes licking at their heels come spring. But even still, sailors came. They came from all corners of the world, but not for any treasure or comfort.

No. They came for the executions.

From 1732, and well into the 1890s, there was hardly a sailor in the Pacific that did not prefer to hold their trials in Fort Warren. The distant naval base, understaffed and overburdened as it was, was known to be loyal to no law but that of gold. Should a ship find any need to dispose of a crewman, its captain needed only hand them over to Fort Warren's judges and let the hangman do the rest. Such was also the case with any merchant found avoiding his debts, or any naval officer who grew too fond of the lash. In those days, it was often said that captains knew well to treat their crew with respect when sailing through the North Pacific. Else, they may find themselves kneeling before a Fort Warren judge with a gag between their teeth. Such are the legends of that place. Such is its legacy, even today.

And yet, none compares to the story which inspired that lost nursery rhyme. The story that has consumed my thoughts since I first heard that insipid poem: The tale of Captain Henry R. McCoy, whose crimes still echo across the seaside cliffs.

It begins in the spring of 1889, with the arrival of Father Richard Moss to serve as Fort Warren's chaplain. Though a mousy creature by nature, and hardly bearing enough experience to serve, Father Moss was all the United States' Navy could provide to fill the fort's vacancy. By then, many of the fort's old guard had long since passed away, reducing the fortress to a shell of itself. This sentiment is captured quite well in Moss's first entry, which is still preserved today in the Salem city archives. Even a century after its subject passed on, its text remains remarkably clear:

3.11.1889

I was shown to my office today. It was more like a prison cell than a chaplain's sanctum, it must be said, and sported more leaks in its ceiling than there are apples on a tree. In due time, I imagine I will become more a carpenter than a priest, but such is the way of things.

Then there is the matter of the chapel. It was built in the Russian Orthodox style and bears all the embellishments thereof. Part of me had hoped that the years may have softened this aspect of its construction, but alas. Through some profound trickery it remains the least destitute portion of the barracks that I have seen. It will take me years to properly convert it toward Anglican standards, assuming I am allowed. I half-heartedly mentioned the need to replace the orthodox symbol that adorns its spire with the proper Anglican cross but was met with a firm rebuttal by the men. These pioneer folk have grown quite attached to the orthodox manner of worship, it would seem, and so I must work to adjust to their expectations of me.

Perhaps this is for the best. After all, my father always said that I responded best to a firm hand, and this outpost has all the softness of a clenched fist. I can only hope that I can rise to the occasion therein, or I may indeed be just another piece of driftwood cast into the sea.

Placing the exact date of McCoy's arrival is a difficult task. But by cross-referencing Moss's logs with the weather reports held by local archives we can narrow it down to the waning days of autumn. Though brief, Moss's entries during this period make mention of an unmanned ship spotted wandering the western islets, which appeared following a northern storm. Judging by what follows, we can reasonably infer that the ship in question was McCoy's *Victoria Blue*, slowly drifting through the North Pacific currents.

Any schoolteacher south of Newport will tell you what followed. On a cold November morning, with rain falling like knives, Fort Warren's guards found their ghost ship run aground in the dunes. An unknown force had snapped the ship's bow in two, with its mast likewise lost to the waves. By the time an expedition force made it to the site there was little left of a ship left to search. Sand crabs had already begun to crawl up the side of its hull in search of a meal, while the gulls appeared to flock from all directions. Within, the search party found no one aboard, save for the ship's captain, who had locked himself in his quarters. To this day, his first words to the search party upon his rescue are believed to be:

"Praise God and get me to higher ground!"

After this, we must again turn to Moss's diaries for our first evaluation of the man:

11.29.1890

Today I was tasked with speaking to the captain of the Victoria Blue, *in the hope that perhaps a clergyman's touch could pry a story from the man's lips. There have been three attempts thus far—by Judge Brumann and Guard Captain Reynauld—to try to reason with the man, but thus far he has only responded with ramblings. Admittedly, I was not entirely confident in my ability to get through to the man, as I have seen how sea storms can break a man's spirit. All the same I persevered, and by some miracle seemed to pierce through a bit of the man's shell.*

He was truly an abhorrent sight when I first entered. Having refused a new set of clothes, the man still wore his captain's outfit, which hung off him like a half-torn tunic. His black hair was long and tangled from his time at sea, with salt-stains peppering it with clumps of debris that seemed inseparable from his body. Upon approaching the man regarded me with a sneer and then straightened his back, such that he stood a good half foot taller than me, and spoke:

"Are you here to deliver my last rites?"

At that, I looked around, perplexed, before eventually grasping his meaning. I responded with a meager: "Are you wanted by the noose?"

"I ought to be," he stated flatly. "My only request is that I be buried above ground. In the dunes, if need be, but not at the water's edge. I cannot go back. Please. She is waiting."

From there, our conversation became a bit easier; though I cannot say that it was wholly productive. I was able to wrangle out his name: Captain Henry Roderick McCoy. Likewise, I confirmed that he was indeed the owner of the vessel our men are still picking over on the beach. From my office here, I can still see its hull half-buried in the dunes; though, it appears to sink deeper into the surf with each tide.

However, the bulk of the conversation vexed me. The man spoke of the wind, and how it stank too much of salt for his liking. He said he could still hear the waves outside his cell, and requested that he be moved to another chamber—one without any windows or access to the outside. In all my

*years, I have never seen someone so eager to be confined.
And yet he begged for it. He pleaded for it.*

*Why exactly he brought these requests to my ears and not
Reynauld's is beyond me, but I will report my findings all
the same.*

As gruesome as this entry may appear, the cultural impact of this interaction cannot be overstated. After all, this alleged madman appeared in the waning years of the nineteenth century, amid such phenomena as Jack the Ripper and the Fox Sisters. And though certainly a more isolated event than either, McCoy's ragged appearance struck quite a chord among western settlers. One that cemented him in local folklore for generations.

Even today, murals depicting Moss's interaction with the dreaded Captain McCoy are not hard to come by. I myself have witnessed three already in my time touring the Oregon Coast—often hidden on the sides of abandoned fisheries or splattered across unused billboards. These depictions tend to overplay McCoy's animalistic nature, gifting him with deep black eyes and nails the size of a bobcat's. Even his hair, though mentioned to be a tangled mess in Moss's entry, is reduced to a nest of seaweed and crab shells, holding all manner of debris behind its coils. Then there are his teeth, which are often ground down to razor edges like a shark's, and stained with blood.

In such a context, it may not be surprising to hear that for a time McCoy was treated as a kind of boogeyman by twentieth-century settlers. Mothers would often warn their children not to play too long on the coastline, and always to wash the sand out from behind their ears. Else, the dreaded Captain Crabb might take them by their ankles, and drag them into the sea. Should one glimpse a depiction of this Captain Crabb for themselves—such as the one decorating Salem city hall—the similarities are indeed difficult to miss.

All this to say that even lacking the larger truth of McCoy's crimes, the investigation into the *Victoria Blue* shipwreck inspired a great boom of cultural interest. Fledgling papers from as far as Seattle wrote letters to the fort, begging for an audience with the mysterious captain. Each was denied. When asked why, Fort Warren's own Judge Brumann commented:

"It is my duty to contain him, nothing more. And as long as I live, I will not see such a wretched creature given a voice."

Though this quote did little to calm public interest, it does perhaps hint at the view that the fort's judges took regarding the matter. For, it was not long before a new expedition was authorized to the *Victoria Blue*; one that sought to expose any secrets that the mad captain may have held.

As before, our knowledge of what followed comes from the entries of Chaplain Moss, who wrote the following in his private journal:

12.12.1990

I have been asked again to attend Captain McCoy's cell today and confront him with our newest findings. I will admit, these meetings never cease to make my blood run cold, but I have been called to action and will follow suit as best I can.

As expected, I found McCoy huddled in a corner upon my arrival. He was frightfully pale and yet ran toward me like a dog upon noticing my entry. Or, perhaps it is the sight of the crucifix upon my neck that excites him so? Regardless, I was relieved to see that he had chosen to change out of his soiled clothes for today's meeting. I wish I could say it made an impact, but I found his skin just as horrid as before, and his stench even worse.

"I hear you have refused to bathe." It was all I could think to say.

"The water here is cold," he replied. "And I . . . I just cannot."

After that, I did my best to pry away from his grasp, and happened to notice the gloam that had settled into place over his cell. Though Judge Brumann agreed to transfer him to the land-facing side of the fort, that action did not appear to be enough to settle his mind. Upon entry I spied a makeshift curtain stuffed into his window—likely composed of his unwashed captain's coat and boots. That was when I noticed his feet. They were a horror to behold—all cut along the bottom and with untrimmed nails. Strangest of all was a set of scars along his ankles. The room was too dark for me to make them out completely; yet, I could have sworn they were similar in form to burn marks.

"We found the manifest." I spoke the words as calmly as I could manage. "It lists all members of the crew assigned to your vessel. There were thirty in total. Half hired in Indian ports, and the rest taken on back in Crimea. That's . . . quite a journey."

McCoy nodded, but said nothing.

"I am a man of the cloth," I began again. "I know little of the mercantile trade, but the Victoria Blue has the look of a British ship, doesn't it?"

"She," he choked out. "All ships are women."

"Right." I nodded. "But that does not explain—"

"I killed them."

The words echoed through the cell as though they were the first words the man had ever spoken. For a moment I could not respond; I only stared at the man. At his sunken, hollow eyes, and the way his lip quivered up in a half-sneer with each breath. It was at that moment that I again considered the solitary nature of his cell, and how long it might take me to call for help, if the need arose.

And when he did deign to address me again, it was with venom on his tongue.

"Does that answer your question, sir?" His voice trembled. "Every one of them. Every last one I threw to the waves! You know why! You hear her too! I know you can!"

Seeing madness rising again behind his eyes, I made a quick escape, and not a moment too soon. The next thing I remember, I was outside his cell, listening in horror as the madman repeatedly threw his bodyweight against the door. Again and again, as if to force himself through.

Tomorrow I will speak with the judges about what is to be done with this information, but for now. For now, I must seek guidance.

It is at this moment that I feel our story must be put on pause, and our focus positioned instead toward the developments within the surrounding township.

For, though it is no exaggeration to say that Fort Warren had fallen into immense disrepair, the settlement that arose around it was quite another story. Years of stable fishing along the Pacific coast had allowed a modest working class to arise out of the area. One that managed to construct a post office in 1878, with a general store following a year later. As time wore on, it became more common to refer to the area around where the *Victoria Blue* crashed as Warren's Bluff—independent of the fort that came before. And though the fort was still well enough considered a portion of the town, by the late nineteenth century it served as little more than a local jail.

Which is why the question of McCoy's fate grew to the heights it did. For though the man had by all accounts confessed to murder, it was unclear under whose authority the captain should be hanged. There were no survivors to be found, nor any governing body to take on the burden. Regarding this issue, the words of one T.N. Ermont—a local butcher—seem to capture the conflict best:

"What we have here is a madman who washed ashore and was immediately thrown in chains. He may very well be the murderer that the judges claim him to be, but that is no reason to shirk our duties.

There are no witnesses, no accounts, and no accuser, and so how can we defend the state putting him to death? The question, as I see it now, is whether we as a community will allow our guardsmen to hang any alleged murderer whom they drag from the waves. Or, whether we as lawful men will prove ourselves civilized enough to give the poor wretch his day and court. Regardless of our findings, I say that we must press forward to the latter, no matter what might follow. To do otherwise is to admit that we are living under mob justice. Or worse yet, outright tyranny."

Evidently, this sentiment proved enough to rally the community to action, and in the summer of 1891 the people of Warren's Bluff assembled a panel to decide McCoy's fate. Within this trial, many arguments were put forth regarding appropriate punishments, and several accounts of McCoy's alleged madness were offered by the guards. Even the Judges were allowed a say, but only as moderators to the trial. However, no evidence would prove more influential than the confession recorded by chaplain Richard Moss the week prior.

It reads:

7.18.1891

Against my better judgment, I have chosen again to attend to Captain McCoy. Though our last conversation left me in quite the state, it has been decided that a full confession is needed before we can relinquish him to the gallows. To that end, I was allowed to request a guard be present in the chamber with me; though he was instructed neither to speak nor listen.

As expected, I found McCoy in a state typically reserved for rabid beasts and the infirm. His hair was knotted like a tangle of seaweed, and his nails bit down to flesh and blood. Upon the walls, he had worked to locate every loose wood plank and had attempted to patch the gaps with his own waste and strips of fabric. Around his ears, I could make out deep scars, like those of a beast clawing at an unknown foe. Then there were his eyes. By God, his eyes. I dare not convey how deep and dark they were. Having confined himself in his cell for as long as he has, they were as wide as an owl's and with a hunger that even now I can hardly fathom. Like two hollow pits, which descended into the abyss.

I attempted to begin as usual and took a place opposite McCoy in his cell. Upon seating myself, however, the man immediately began to gnash his teeth—and began snarling at Reynauld like a dog. For a moment it appeared as if our session would not be possible, but I eventually convinced Reynauld to take a place outside the door, rather than inside. It was a risk, but a necessary one for any conversation to take place.

"That was rude of you," I stated as evenly as I could fathom. "To ask Reynauld to leave."

"He is like me," McCoy replied. "With blood on his hands. With both of us together, it may be too much of a target for her to resist. She is always listening, you know."

For a moment, I noticed a familiar sheen begin to catch McCoy's eyes. Before it could fully take hold, however, I cut in.

"You keep mentioning a 'she,' but you never give her a name."

"Nor will I," McCoy responded. Though his gaze was still distant, I could tell he was holding something back. "Once you know her name. Once you know who she is, what she is . . . you will never be free of her."

"All the same, I would like to know."

I was surprised to find his eyes locked with mine in that moment, and moreover surprised to find them lucid. Though there was still much terror in his gaze, I knew in my heart of hearts that this was the route I needed to take.

"Who is she, Henry?" I spoke the words before I could think twice. "Tell me about her."

A moment passed in silence. Then another. And for a moment I considered asking Reynauld to return. Then, all at once, his story spilled forth.

"I became a sailor at sixteen, and a captain at nineteen, one year after my first marriage. She was a kind woman, Maria. A kind, cheerful thing, with blotchy skin and big eyes. I cared for her, I did . . . but I never loved her. I wanted her only for her father's ships. And she knew it. We all did. It was business, you see."

Of all the things for the man to say, I will admit this confession was low on my list. However, all the same, I listened, and nodded as needed for the man to continue to speak.

"Despite this, I was a proud man. I thought my looks were enough to make her grateful for my company. Even as I lingered longer out at sea, even as I began to partake in other companions, I expected her to remain by my side. To remain my own. But I was a fool." He shook his head. "I returned to England one day to find another man's scent on our marital bed, and a child that bore no likeness to my own. I should have expected it. After all, was I not the one who first broke our vow? Was it not fair? Perhaps it was. But I did not see it then. I was too angry. Too proud. So I left that child without a father and returned to the sea."

Silently, I offered the man a cup of water. To my shock, he drank it without question, and then returned to his tale.

"I spent the next few years drifting from port to port, drowning myself in whatever pleasures could sate my fits of rage. I spent several years in the Caribbean, and then another in the north of Africa, but . . . I found my second wife along the Black Sea."

"Her name was Anya, and she was my life, for a time. She was a precious thing, with skin as white as porcelain and hair black as pitch. I did not seek her out, I assure you. Instead, she approached me while at port. She saw something in my eyes that even I cannot fathom and made herself prey for me to hunt. And hunt her I did. From Odessa, up the Dnieper, and then into her bed. On the night of our consummation, she howled like a great beast into the night, and come morning I knew she bore my child."

McCoy shook his head again and took another sip of water. I stood there blankly, and could do nothing but clutch at my crucifix as the man unloaded his tale.

"I thought that marrying her was enough," he went on, his gaze distant. *"I thought that with enough gold, enough gifts, she would see that I wished to be true to her, but . . . instead. Instead, when I returned the next spring, she . . . she knew I had found company in distant ports. Not love, true, but warmth. Like a fool, I had broken another vow. And she cursed me for it. She struck me and forced me to the ground, and screamed all manner of dreadful words in my face. Like the fool I was, I struck her back. Not hard. At least, I did not think so. But even so, that was the last time I ever saw her. My beloved Anya."*

I attempted to swallow. Attempted to speak. However, I could see that McCoy had truly begun to unravel, and I dared not interrupt. And so, I gave him leave to speak.

"I left Crimea, as you know, with a crew of my best men. I sailed around the Horn and set out for the Pacific. I told myself I was just trying to give her time, but it was a lie. In my heart, I knew I was going to do it all again. Another wife. Another vow. Another broken promise. That's when I saw her."

"Maria?" I asked, like a fool.

"No," he corrected. "Maria was too frail a thing. You should have seen how she begged me not to leave, even after all I had done. She surely wishes me dead, but she would never strike me, even after all this time. But my dear Anya? No, she was a fighter. She did not intend to let me get away. In my dreams, I saw her—clear as day—with her belly swollen and her breasts full. She stood before me as naked as a newborn babe and waded into the sea. I watched as she walked toward me, her eyes wide and vile. She commanded me to return. But instead, I ran. From the Red Sea to Calcutta, and beyond. Each night I saw her, and each night I cried for her to leave me be. Then, one night, I watched as she waded in, up to her neck, and screamed."

Perhaps it was the nature of the tale, or perhaps it was the chill in the air, but in that moment I shuddered, even as McCoy's tale twisted on.

"My daughter. We wanted to name her Nadiya. Instead, I watched as she slithered from her mother's womb as a dark and bloated thing. Still, and cold. I watched as she twitched back to life and bit the head off a mullet to gain her first breath. With our child born, Anya walked back to shore, with a face as beautiful as the sea, and she bade her daughter feed. Feed, so that one day father and child might be reunited. Feed, so my vow might be honored. It is she who hunts me now, not Anya. Not Maria. Nadiya. My dearest Nadiya. She is the one who I hear in the waves each night. She speaks with her mother's voice, aye, but she has my eyes. Dark eyes. Hungering eyes."

Though I did not say it at the time, there was a part of me that believed him. After all, his were the eyes of a monster.

"The first time I noticed her, we were halfway through the South China Sea. That morning, I saw something following beside the rudder. My dear Nadiya. Whatever she had become, she was a clever thing. She hid in the ship's wake, and dove beneath the keel whenever someone got too close. But I knew it was her. I could tell by her hair. It floated on the surface like smoke, but was thick enough to tangle a man's legs into knots. I have felt it myself, when once I was cast overboard in a storm. I barely made it out of the depths, and when I tried to drag myself free, I felt her cling to me—cling to me with claws sharp and cold. Their tips

cut through my skin like rope, such that for days I could barely stand. It was only through the help of my crew that I managed to escape, but even still, it left me scarred."

At that, I pointed to the captain's ankles. "Those were from her?"

"Aye," he nodded. "It was quite the reunion."

"If this is true," I licked my lips. "When did you start— "

"Offering my crew to her?" McCoy laughed at that. A low, hollow laugh. Like wind entering an empty cave. "That was after we made port in Vladivostok. It was quite the detour, but I was by then determined to find the nature of that thing. That curse that was once my daughter. I attempted to reach out to the city's wise woman and brought her my tale. She told me that there was nothing to be done, save never to touch the sea again. The Rusalka, as she called my Nadiya, was a creature of vengeance. It would follow me through any body of water. Any river, sea, or ocean. Her kind, they seek out men who have hearts heavy enough to sink, and will drag as many of them into the depths as necessary to sate her hunger."

"You could have stayed," I breathed the words. Not loud enough, I thought, for McCoy to hear. Yet, hear them he did. "At Vladivostok. You could have remained."

"Perhaps," he nodded. "But a part of me was still too proud to see reason. Too proud to admit defeat. Part of me thought that, perhaps if I could simply reach the New World. Reach the far side of the Pacific, somewhere that neither the Rusalka nor my past could reach, then . . . then I would be free. Truly free."

He breathed out. Long and sullen.

"And so I threw them into the waves. Slowly at first. To see how long they would hold her at bay. Some I claimed had died of a disease. Others had been attempted mutineers, so I said, and so I made sure to throw them to her with a rag between their teeth. Those nights that I offered them . . . those nights I could sleep. I could not hear her song. I knew she was satisfied. At least for a time.

"Then came Sitka. I had intended to make port there for the summer, and perhaps settle permanently, but a storm sent us astray. By the time it was over, I had lost three more men to the waves and found myself without enough of a crew to operate as before. We were adrift, somewhere along the Pacific coastline, but I could make out no settlements. No ports. And so we drifted. For a time I thought my dear Nadiya had finally left me be, but before long I heard her again. Calling me. Begging me to embrace her at last. Instead, I descended into the men's bunks, and slit their throats while they slept. Every last one. After that, I settled into a routine. Each morning I would throw a body to the

waves, and each night I would drink myself half to death. Then I would awaken again and begin anew. Until one day there was no one left to offer, and so I locked myself away, and waited. Until at last, we ran aground. You know what followed, I'm sure."

I managed to remove myself from McCoy's grip after that and relayed all he had spoken of to Reynauld outside. After much discussion, we decided that only a full recitation would serve to persuade the citizens of his guilt. There was talk of pruning the testimony for the sake of decency, but I refused to allow it. Even with his mind broken, I remain confident that the man's words will be enough to settle this matter in due order.

If only it helped settle my stomach. I will admit, even as I write these words, I find my senses drawn toward the crashing of the waves outside. Once they seemed so peaceful. Now I fear I may need to request sturdier panels in my windows if I am ever to sleep again.

As you might imagine, the details of McCoy's confession were as shocking to onlookers then as they are today. Some in attendance denounced the account as a sham, while others called for additional investigations to settle the matter. Despite pressure from his superiors, Moss held firm to his testimony. In the days after the trial, Judge Brumann confided the following to the press:

"I will admit, that was the moment I feared our case would fall apart. We asked Moss to bring us a confession of murder, and he brought us a fairy tale. The man is as weak as wet sand, and McCoy played him like a fiddle."

When asked to elaborate, he stated:

"In my experience, people often pity alleged madmen when they should fear them. Like it or not, men like him? They know. They know how you look at them. They know how their words make you afraid. How their actions make you doubt yourself. Doubt reality. Do not mistake me, I am glad that the jury found him guilty. It is their choice to respect his last request and bury him on dry land that sits ill with me. It reinforces the fantasy. But, like it or not, the facts of the case are set. McCoy confessed to murder, and he will hang. Whether his crimes were to escape his demonic daughter or not, the punishment will be the same. I just pray the citizens will remember that."

That next morning, McCoy was taken to the gallows. Those who attended recalled how the rhythm of drums seemed eclipsed by the winds that day, as the sea below howled toward them, like a hungering beast. As per tradition, McCoy was permitted a clean change of clothes, and allowed one last chance to address the crowd. But by chance or by fate, he would never do so.

To this day, it is unclear what precipitated Fort Warren's collapse—whether its walls had been noticeably crumbling, or whether the storm that blew in was particularly violent. But regardless, all who witnessed that grim affair reported the same. That at the moment before McCoy's address, a great wave crashed into the cliffs, causing half of Fort Warren's southwest wall to crumble away into the sea. Including, as you may have guessed, the gallows—and all who stood upon them. In that great deluge, McCoy was last seen tumbling into the sea, with a noose still tied about his neck, his voice lost to the wind.

To this day, his last words have gone unheard. Some say they are still carried by the wind as it howls eternally across the shoreline. Others say it is a whimper, which you can just barely make out when the moon is high and the sea is still. Regardless of its nature, the message is the same:

He pleads with his dear daughter Nadiya. For mercy. For death.

And as you might imagine, his body was never found.

In the generations since, the story of the Warren's Bluff Rusalka has become a piece of local pride among those who remain. As much a symbol of their ancestry as that of the harrowing legend that brought it to the New World. Local artists are known to erect statues in her honor around the dunes. Allegedly, to keep her hunger at bay.

Of course, as with all legends, there are naysayers. Skeptics, cynics, and academics, who see the story of Captain McCoy as little more than a fictionalized account of a local tragedy, or the result of rampant sensationalism. Such cynics posit that the myth of the Rusalka simply followed the original settlers from their homelands across Eastern Europe, and infected the McCoy legend long after its conclusion. Perhaps as an explanation for the town otherwise condemning an innocent madman to death.

But I have seen the journals.

And moreover, I have seen the final entry. The one Moss hid from all eyes but those of his congregation. The entry that even today is sought after by investigators and occultists alike for its contents. I keep a copy of it with me even now; for it holds the final twist in our sordid tale:

11.22.1902

Almighty God, I ask you, as your humble servant: Can a man ever be free of his sin? Can weakness be forgiven, or in its place forgotten? Is a mistake beyond your love, even if it was done unknowingly? Tell me, have I been an instrument of your will? Or another's?

All these years later, I still remember the last words of Henry R. McCoy, as his body tumbled into the sea below. They echo in my mind, like some great seed that has long since taken root, and refuses to let go. But alas, I know the truth of it. I hear it in the wind whenever the sea drifts inward toward my office window. I hear it. I hear her.

Her. Dearest Nadiya. Beautiful Nadiya. She knows that her father's blood is on my hands. She knows it was by my voice that McCoy was offered to her grasp.

And worst of all, she wishes to thank me for it.

Her voice. Oh, her voice. It is syrupy sweet. The kind that could only ever be used to hide a poison. Yet, it caresses me. I feel it in my bones. More than anything else I have known.

Perhaps a prayer is in order? Yes. Something to whisper when none but you are listening.

A thousand more graves than can ever be filled,
Lie beneath Fort Warren;

Where forsaken men hang, and clever men gather,
'Til a tempest drags them below.

Here Lady Rusalka watches her prey,
Be they wealthy, half-mad, or poor.

So best be wary, all those who draw near,
Lest you fall into the sea-mother's clutch.

For while Captain McCoy is her blood and her feast,
Her halls are ever open for more.

Little of the original fort remains now, save for Moss's church. Years of decay have stained the walls with salt, and rotted its thatch. Even still, the site endures. From its back office, it is no hard thing to find your eye turned to the open window, and watch as the tide crashes against the bluffs below. Within such a desolate place, it may be the only thing that catches your eye.

That, and the reliquary.

For, in the middling years of his life, it was said that Chaplain Moss embraced the orthodox faith entirely, with a fervent certainty that left his fellows speechless. For the rest of his days, he was said to have searched the shoreline for driftwood and wove charms out of what flotsam he could find. Some still hang across Fort Warren today, decorating its doorways, and filling the chapel's rafters. However, none holds a candle to the greatest treasure of all. The chaplain's greatest find, and the rock upon which he built his new faith.

The masthead of the *Victoria Blue*, pale and hallowed by the waves, was thought lost until the mad chaplain dredged it from the depths. Today, the relic still stands tall at the far end of his sanctum, with sea mist beading against its skin. On its surface is carved the form of a young woman, with seaweed tangled in her hair. Her smile is as sharp as the wind, and her eyes as bright as pearls. Her image is a promise. Or at times, a plea. That vengeance will find the guilty one day, should justice ever fall short.

Army of Flamingos

by Ann Wuehler

Content/Trigger Warnings

- Disturbing imagery and violence

They sit out there, stuck in the hard, cold ground, biding their time.

Flamingos, plastic pink and hollow, filled with malice, the spaces inside crammed with a juicy invisible menace.

I pull back my curtains, the blue ones I found at the thrift store. The purple chickens and the black ducklings line the hems like an avian army. The legion of pink demons fills my misty eyesight. Their flamingo eyes find me, though the painted eyes don't move. They find me, those eyes. Mock me. Warn me not to sleep or rest or let down my guard because they are coming. A pink plastic legion, an army, waits to finish me off. I let the curtain drop.

I don't know why they would target me for their crusade. But they have. My safety, sanity and well-being amuse and enrage them. I have become their enemy. The silly man that blinks behind the chicken curtains had become their villain.

Defenses, I need defenses. I've had this vague thought before.

Those flamingos belonged to my mother. She collected them, thought them 'cute' and 'funny' and 'so American.' She's buried out in the desert. I did not murder her. She died in her sleep. She had a bad heart, and there was no money for her funeral. Her death was not caused by me in any way. My mother lived, and she died, simple as that. She worked most of her life as a clerk, Walgreen's to Wal-Mart to Joanne's.

The doctors, in the end, took her feeble life savings. She wanted to be buried without any fuss. Just put me in the ground, she'd told me. *No damn funeral homes, look at what they charge! I won't pay that. I won't!*

I took her at her word. I told everyone in our mutual circle. That amounted to about three people. My mother just went away. She's visiting her sister; her sister lives in Florida.

Aunt Carol never calls, writes or visits here. My mother never had time for friends, relatives, acquaintances or enemies, anyway.

No one checked. No one's checking now.

Her Social Security checks go to her bank account, automatic deposits. My name is on that account. I use it to pay bills, for home repair, nothing that would garner any scrutiny. We lived together very modestly. Our biggest expenses were groceries or getting repaired. I don't think she'd mind that her checks will keep coming until I arrange to have her die. She will die in Florida or traveling somewhere else. She will be buried elsewhere. The paperwork and death certificate will have to be dealt with some day.

I might just lead whoever needs to see the body to where my mother is buried. Face whatever might be done to me for doing as she asked.

My mother was a most unpleasant woman, with a voice like a cartoon shark. She worked. She collected plastic flamingos. How she came to have me at all is a mystery. I've never known my father or her to have a boyfriend, a lover, or a one-night stand. Maybe she wished me into being. Some women have that sort of power. They can wish for things and things they get.

I drink coffee behind my closed and locked bedroom door, wondering about my father, hearing the odd hopping of the spy flamingos in the little house.

They are meant to be outside, stuck in flowerbeds. A metal spike exudes from their centers or maybe two long sturdy wires acting as legs. My mother collected both kinds.

At night, they'll send two or three into the house, just to check things out, to get ready, to scare me. I hear them hopping about, the odd whistling of air in their hollow bodies. At night sometimes, the lawn ornaments seem almost real birds, with feathers and long beaks. They balance by my door, whether on a single spike or precariously on their two cheap metal legs. The spies listen to me listening to them.

I stand there, by my door, my hands wrapped around a baseball bat, just in case. I know it won't hurt them, not enough to make them go away and leave me alone. I haven't yet found the cure for the magical flamingos that haunt my life.

It was my mother, you see. She did something to them. I don't know what. She fell asleep and never woke up. My mother never told me how to call them off or strip them of the life slowly infusing them. She never offered how to offset their utter smoking hatred of me.

My mother and I got along; we were amicable toward each other. I can't make them understand so they'll turn their fury toward something else. How do you make barely sentient things know you're not their enemy? I haven't lucked into the right combination of words or deeds yet to do just that. My mother never included me in her training of her metal disciples. Such stories, which include disciples and savior queens, need a betrayer or a supreme adversary. Perhaps my mother had told her too-attendant flock that I was the devil in their world because it amused her or because she hated me openly in their midst.

I cannot ask them, but what little sense they have seems directed at destroying me.

I didn't kill. I tell them every day. I stand among them, twenty-three in all, which is actually five. If you add two and three, it's five. That's a magic number, a number with power. I can't tell you why. I just know. Numbers have power. They tap into the lines and pull of the universe around us, providing order out of chaos. Math is the language of the universe, someone said. The horrible ancient sound of a universe learning to speak, with things we don't wish to hear, no matter our pretending otherwise. I have no wish to know the truth about what lives behind the sky or who hung that moon, if anything hung that moon. I have no real wish to know the reality of such things. The terrible finality of such knowledge would surely rip the skin off my little quivering soul; off all our souls. We'd have to face things. We'd have to line up in rows and face things, and we're not good at that.

I don't know. Such attempts at philosophy curdle my mind, and the way forward gets fuzzy as a stretched-out old sweater. My eyes fill with sandy tears at what a coward I am.

I have soup heating in a pan on the old GE snot-puke colored stove. It's stained and filthy; my mother was no housekeeper. I try to keep it clean, but I am sadly distracted by trying to save my life at the present, so the house looks horrible. Dust, crumpled-up papers, mail I haven't opened. I go to work, yes, I pay the bills, yes. I'm still functioning somewhat. I work as a nurse at a nursing home—one of the three males that work there. Terry, is what my nametag says. My credentials swing against my skinny belly.

I don't have time for love. I'm an ugly little man with small ratty eyes, invisible to women. There is the occasional man I find attractive, but I never go further than a head nod or a shrug. My voice could best be called 'fits and starts.' What woman wishes sweet nothings whispered in her ear by such a voice as mine? I cannot dance. When I attempt small talk, it sounds strange and ill-rehearsed. Rather like a child being asked to recite a poem they just learned five minutes ago, with words too big for their mouths. Women's eyes move over me as if I were air or a rock on the ground.

I really don't care, not anymore. I used to get upset and wait to grow, to get bigger. I never did; sort of a male Cinderella waiting for some enchantment or spell. I can laugh about that now. It used to be such a tragedy at one time. It's not true that men don't want love; we do. We do. I did. And if I'm honest, I still wait a bit for someone to smile back at me with a real shimmery light in their lovely eyes. But I keep that to myself, and every year, it fades, just a little, just a little bit more.

Not everyone finds love. That is a truth that the universe will tell you in its mathematical linguistics. For every one plus one, there is a one plus zero, after all. That is just math, and it doesn't care about loneliness, despair or even rage at being so alone all the time.

Carleen had no interest in exploring her mind, or heart, or the world around her. She invested everything in her damn plastic monsters.

My mother's name was Carleen.

I wrote that in permanent marker on the rock by her grave. She had scoffed at paying good money for a funeral home rock carved with details.

Just write my name on a rock or a bit of wood, Terry! And so I had.

She'd have two or three in her room sometimes. I'd catch her talking to them, as if they were her friends or the children she wished had slithered from her womb. She'd stroke their heads, run her fingers along their long, curving necks, smile at them, when she smiled at no one, ever. The one with the crack remained her favorite. She smiled at that one all the time, when she smiled at nothing else. Not even her only puny son, who'd taken a few nursing classes and managed to get a job. I stayed with her because she'd asked me to. This house will be yours, she had told me.

Why waste your money on rent? Save up, kid; you're gonna need it.

The soup, it boils. Chicken noodle. I haven't been grocery shopping, and I have two cans of soup left, some iffy eggs and a pickle jar with two whole dill pickles in it. My mother loved sweet ones.

My mother used to go out and arrange her army of flamingos in rows, circles, in squares. Formations that appealed to her or formations they whispered in her ears. Maybe they gave her instructions, chirped to her about God, told her of the devil. There are no real neighbors, so if anyone noticed a fat old lady playing with plastic flamingos, well. Nobody much lives down by my mother and me. No one could know the flamingos had turned evil. Nobody but me knows that.

I pour soup into the green glass bowl that had been in my family for generations.

Something clatters in the closet.

I stop eating, a cracker lifted to my lips. I listen. I listen. I listen.

Faint comes the scrape of a metal spike against the wood floor. The faint *shoosh* of a plastic side rubbing against my winter coat alerts me. My bladder goes tight and heavy. I clench my spoon. I'm a child in a dark bedroom, just like that. I'm waiting for the monster under the bed to pounce. My bowels feel a bit loose and hot.

I force myself to stand. They give medals for shows of courage. I have none.

I move a box of books against that closet door to keep whatever's in there, in there.

A big heavy box of historical romances, James Michener tomes, biographies on Cary Grant, Fatty Arbuckle and Ronald Reagan—these are my mother's books. Whatever is in that closet will have to push the box away, after somehow unlocking the closet from the inside. There's a lock on the door, for some reason. Why would you need to lock a closet door? I have to use WD-40 on it.

The flamingos like that hall closet. I find them there in the mornings. Maybe it feels safe to them, a little musty haven from the too-wide, not safe at all outdoors.

I hear the tap and slide of a metal spike from inside that little hall closet. I knew it was one of them. I knew it. I went to the window, lifted those chicken and duck curtains, peeked out casually, did a quick count—twenty.

There were three missing.

They seem female, those flamingos. Whatever the flamingos are, they are mostly female.

My cell rings and I jump, my bladder releasing. Hot urine stains my sweatpants. I nearly sob as my phone keeps blandly ringing, set to a Caribbean guitar riff. My eyes burn, sting as I read the number. It's work. I sigh. My lips tremble as I slide upward to answer.

Can you cover a shift tonight? We're shorthanded. Jessica's been stealing. We caught her. Can you come? Eleven to seven.

I answer yes, not even sure at the moment who or what Jessica is. Why would she steal when she knows there's cameras all over? But no one had liked Jessica, a quiet, stand-offish sort who was not a hardcore Christian and was perhaps an atheist. There were rumors and whispers. No one cared what I was; men were needed to lift things. The old men told me their secrets when they were too shy to talk to the women on duty. Mr. Carstairs had told me there had been blood in his urine. He had still died, but he had died floating on painkillers in a hospital bed. I was male yet safe, and no one thought to pin anything on my head or accuse me of being in league with Lucifer—

A deliberate creak from the bathroom startled me.

I spun about. No. No. But I had to change my clothes now, take a shower. I smelled of urine and stank of fear.

There. A sly pink head peering at me from the bathroom, the door left open always now, it was just me here . . . except it wasn't. I was not alone here at all. Leaning up against the white, dirty wall was a plastic flamingo on two metal legs.

I had not put it there.

My entire being shuddered at touching them. They felt repulsively smooth. And hot, as if fevered. Even on cold days, the plastic felt feverish. Not enough to melt it, but still.

They never moved when I looked at them. They moved about when I turned my back or when I was locked in my room. Night became their time to shuffle about. They moved here and there on the lawn. They'd be in different formations. My mother had last arranged them in an odd circle, with each one almost touching the one next to it. An oddly familial grouping? Perhaps the flamingos planned. They could sense my eyes on them. Perhaps they showed my mother what they could do. But they loved her. She found them cute and kitschy, my mother, who had had no sense of whimsy or possessed any other collections. She had her flamingos. She read a few books that would pass through her brain without leaving anything much behind. She drank coffee in her yellow cup every morning until the morning that she did not.

I took a potholder, took two of them. My soup went cold in the green bowl. I heard a faint, indignant slide of metal on wood the wood floor from the closet. Could it see in the dark?

That rose-hued plastic decoration watched me. It watched me creep toward it with potholders in my fists. It saw the dark, shameful stain down the front of my gray sweats. It saw how afraid I was. And it enjoyed all that immensely. Even if I managed to kill it, it would enjoy going to hell knowing I'd peed myself and had to use padded cloth protection against it.

I took it by the long loathsome neck. It moved slightly, gave a faint little honk, bulging black eyes shifting slightly to glare at me. I carried it to the front door and then just tossed it outside, onto the lawn, where the twenty remaining flamingos were lined up, seven to each line. There was a flamingo missing from the middle line. Two flamingos had been out front, like two generals; three lines of seven, twenty-one.

The discovered-and-thrown outside plastic decoration lay on its side, one metal leg bent. It had caught and bent. The twin metal stands that stood in for legs had a cheap flimsy quality to them. I had wounded it a bit. No forgiveness for me. They could not forgive me for a sin I didn't remember committing, that first sin against them, whatever it had been. Perhaps that I was not Carleen, not my mother, not the mother figure, the mother savior these female lawn decorations wanted. They willed themselves into life for her. Perhaps my first and fatal sin was not being the one they could love with such a single, ghastly passion.

The remaining army looked at that wounded comrade. They shifted their interest toward me, in the open doorway, concentrating their malicious will into a single awful mist. It drifted into my nostrils, into the holes of my ears, into the little pores of my skin—a coating of slime and vicious eternal anger. Their anger would never end, and they would never forgive or forget; ancient little savages without mercy for me at all.

I slammed the door shut, sucked in clean air. It smelled inside the house of stale bread, dust, and a dead mouse decaying somewhere. That mist coated me, seeking more entrances, to find my soul to strangle it. I peeked out, and oh, the thrown flamingo had already been moved or had moved itself. Back into that missing spot in the line, leaning sideways on its bad metal leg. I let the curtains fall, determined to escape all this for a bit.

Work would allow me some peace, some normality.

I took a shower, a long one. I washed their filth from me, watching it swirl down the drain. I imagined it as pink foam being sucked down the drain, going off into the sewers where it could do no harm. I put on my scrubs. I made some coffee. This was my day off, but I didn't wish to stay in the house with the wandering kitsch lawn decorations from hell's little circus.

I took two uppers, Mother's Little Helper, they used to be called. I preferred Ritalin. They gave me a nice buzz and kept me awake. And I felt justified in downing a couple. I hadn't adjusted my sleeping schedule to work a night shift; I was doing the Knotty Pines Retirement Center a favor.

The flamingo in the closet *tap-taps* against the door; I hear it. It probably sends a message to those outside, some sort of Morse code for possessed lawn toys. I know how this sounds, I know. It's comical.

It's not comical when it's happening to you.

My little battered Chevy Nova is parked out back. The flamingos crouch near the front of the house. I lock my house and then realize I haven't found the third flamingo. It's still at large, still hiding. One in the closet, one in the bathroom, where would the other one be hiding? One of the generals remained at large, not a follower but a planner. One who plans. One who can draw up plans. And then get the others to execute those plans so carefully planned.

I stand by my car; the air cold. My coat remains in the closet. I get the car started, I'm low on gas. I'll need to put some in on the way there.

I get gas, get a large gas station coffee. I know the coffee at work will be decaf. Marsha, who also works the night shift on Thursdays, thinks caffeine causes all the modern-day problems, like obesity and cancer. I keep my mouth shut; she could flatten me like a bug, and anyone who works with her knows to bring something with a jolt.

Marsha controls everything around her and tells everyone how nice she is. No one thinks she's very nice, but she keeps telling us she is. She's also something of a tireless workhorse, so she's valuable in her own way. We wonder what she does take to stay awake all night. Over the counter No Doz? Speed? Maybe she talks herself into believing one type of fake chemical alertness is righteous while another is not. Don't we all have such hypocrisy in our personal little inner baskets?

The shift drags on. I hear that Jessica was caught stealing. Pain pills, morphine-based, from Mr. Olvetti, who has rheumatoid arthritis and can barely move without bursting into tears. She'd been halving his medication and palming the rest. Somebody caught her doing that. What a shitty thing to do, I say in total agreement when Marsha whispers this to me. She always whispers, her voice wispy and ethereal, coming from her thick, liver-tinged lips.

My mind fills with flamingos all over my lawn.

In my mother's house, they roam at will.

They wait for me to come home; so tired, so very tired and careless. I will just fall into my sagging bed. I will forget to lock my door.

I drink the remaining ice-cold dregs of my gas station coffee. I find my mouth full of coffee grinds and sugar. One packet, all settled at the bottom of the plastic cup, instead of mixing with the brew. My eyes burn. I want to sleep. It's three oh seven. Marsha comes back from checking everyone as I do charts and paperwork. It remains a quiet night, a slow night. I hear someone having a bad dream. I go to check, and it's the newbie with no family. Very much alone, an old lady they threw away. Mrs. Alberta Bronson, who is depressed, has diabetes, stuck in a wheelchair. I stand near the end of her bed as she moans and farts and shudders.

Miss Maryanne Standage, her roommate, looks at me as I wait to see if Mrs. Bronson is having a stroke or just a bit of a dream. I smile at her. She looks back up at the ceiling. The pictures of her younger self have been turned over tonight on her nightstand. Perhaps she cannot bear to look at herself when she was healthy, young and frisky.

I decide it's not a stroke and leave the two to their own ends. Marsha has been watching, to back me up in case anyone accuses me of anything.

Marsha goes off to tidy the supply cupboard. I go back to continue catching up on paperwork for the state. We have an inspection coming up, so our ducks have to at least look like they're in a row. Ha ha. Ducks. I'm not scared out of my wits by ducks.

I catch a glimpse of something pink from the corner of my eye. I need more coffee and wonder if there was any in the staff room. The kitchen staff would be here around five or so. There'd be real coffee then, despite hulking, whisper-voiced Marsha squeaking about obesity and cancer.

I look up from filling in reports.

There, against the wall, a flamingo, with a single metal spike, and a crack along the neck seam; the general, the leader, the head flamingo. My mother's favorite. She had put duct tape over that crack many a time and once, a bandage.

How was it here? How had it gotten here?

I rose from the desk, having been entering information into the generic file form on the center's main computer. It saved trees, the director had said, at a meeting. It saves trees to use online forms.

Those sly, painted eyes marked me. Those painted eyes marked me as a dead man.

It had followed me here to show I was not safe anywhere. No lock or door or trip to work would spare me the coming wrath of the lawn flamingos.

No god or devil would intervene to write me a pardon or help me in any way against the coming wrath of the lawn flamingos.

The flamingo fell over. It had been leaned carelessly against the wall. I gasped, my bowels filled with hot rats chewing at my insides, hot biting rodents. I slowly moved toward the bathrooms, quite sure an accident would happen before I got to a toilet. That fallen bird watched me, already triumphant. Already confident that it had won, and I had lost.

I slide toward the bathroom, so careful not to turn my back on that plastic commander of a small, powerful, invincible army. It observes me from its place on the shining white floor. Marsha makes sure that the floor is cleaner than the plates in the dining room. My tennis shoes make complaining sighs. Marsha comes from Mr. Appleby's room, checking a worrisome cut on his foot that won't heal up. I've checked it, too. He'll soon be off to the hospital and the morgue, frankly. We just don't say it aloud. He doesn't either.

She asks me what I'm doing as I play some sort of sliding game, apparently, and then notices the flamingo.

Where did that come from? I just love them. They're so weird and cute.

Damn it.

I don't know, I say as I try to escape to the bathroom to empty my rather full bowels.

I thought it was yours, Marsha. Oh, the lie comes easy.

That's the head flamingo general. I know this; the flamingo knows this. This is all for Marsha, who will tell everyone she can that I'm a fruitcake, a cracked fruitcake and crazy as a loon. Marsha has her pet words and phrases for the staff here. She suffers no fools gladly.

No, where would I keep lawn ornaments at my apartment? In the bathtub?

She laughs, goes off to straighten the magazines in the rec room. Perhaps she inventories the adult diapers. She might sort through the donated paperbacks for 'dirty books' she finds inappropriate and not necessary. She's set aside that one about the guy who likes to whip his girlfriend that got so popular and anything by Mickey Spillane, Rosemary Rodgers or Jean M. Auel.

The residents complain. They are adults, they claim, and can decide for themselves what to read or not. But Marsha squashes those rebellions, and continues to do as she wishes, content to be a benevolent dictator and protect her charges, even when they don't wish such protection. She has the skin of a rhino and the eye of a zealot. The world cannot prevail against such a person. Her three children and husband cannot win against her. We are all at the mercy of Marsha. Bucking her has become too tiresome and too against adopted habits of letting her do as she pleases so peace prevails.

I make it to the bathroom. My bowels explode, the sound like a gunshot in the enclosed metal box, booming off the enclosing metal womb. I shiver, my stomach cramping, my other end as open as a Los Angeles super-freeway. Feces pour from me in liquid awfulness.

Oh, how Marsha would have talked about me.

Terry shit his pants last night. I think that guy's crazy as a loon. Who shits their pants these days? No one, that's who, said in her whisper-voice.

Something falls over in the next stall over. There are two in the antiseptically white bathroom, which doesn't actually contain a bath or shower, just two toilets, a urinal and a sink. A paper towel roll in a holder stuck to the wall, a mirror, antiseptic soap for hand washing. The odor of industrial-strength cleaners stains the air— pine and lemon. I barely hear that *scutter* of flamingo meeting floor, not over my relief at the emptying of my body into the receiving bowl beneath. My forehead has a sheen of sweat. I look down.

There, by my foot, is a pink plastic flamingo head. The rest of it is outside my stall, but it has managed to fall just so.

Just so.

Just so that it can peek up at me as I endure a bout of fear-diar-rhea.

I scream, a hoarse, honest little scream. The plastic black eyes roll up to peer at me in amused condescension.

We'll get you, that flamingo promises in a growling voice inside my head.

We'll get you.

I kick at the thing and it slides the short distance to the wall. It wedges in the corner, on the far side of the one urinal.

A faint, barely heard squawking laugh. It's amused by me; it knows the taste of dark victory in its long S-curve throat.

A knock on the door catches my attention before I hear Marsha's whispery plague of a voice.

Terry? You okay?

Yes, I answer back, my bowels still leaking brown sludge the consistency of watery gravy. *Why?*

I thought I heard you yell.

No, I screamed when the evil flamingo general showed up.

No. Just a bit of a bellyache, is all. I'm fine.

I heard her shift and creak. Her work clothes rustle. Her jeans, a long tunic, an apron over all that, one of those Betty Crocker-ish ones, protect her clothes from old people's messes.

Okay, sorry about that. I'll leave you alone.

She walked off, and I noticed the flamingo was back, staring up at me as if I hadn't kicked it. Please, please, I prayed to my bowels. Please.

That black eye moved. I saw it—the slow blink of a plastic bird slowly turning into a real bird. Something else occurs to me. It's a real bird with the brain of some cartoon villain. Aware, amused and wanting vengeance for no other reason than vengeance is always needed.

That pupil contracted. The iris changed to a pumpkin sheen.

My foot came down on that head.

It twisted beneath my foot.

That head twisted and turned beneath my foot. I attempt to crush it. It was as if I had stepped on a struggling chicken or duck or a furious flamingo. Not a brittle, weathered plastic decoration without redeeming artistic value, but a living thing.

I bore down with my foot, encased thankfully in a thick-soled, well-made tennis shoe from Nike.

That thing struggled, I felt it struggle.

I could almost hear the caws and calls from the other twenty-two flamingos, somehow witnessing me murdering their head general. An absurd murder! A monster has a bout of diarrhea while killing one of its own. It was unheard of. It was bordering on *genocide will solve that absurdity.* As if destroying all humans would finally save all plastic lawn flamingos from destruction. This notion was essentially true. Genocide is a sort of severing of the Gordian knot. Occam's Razor. All the nice, pretty words involved in reducing your choices to kill or be killed.

That head broke open beneath my foot. No blood or brains, just poisoned air rushing up at me. I choke. I cough and retch, making me bear down even harder, the reek of my intestine's interiors almost sweet by comparison. The metal legs, two long

pieces of wire to stick into the ground to anchor the flamingo and make it look, somehow, alive . . . beat on the stone floor as if in dying throes. As if the thing somehow had organs and nerves and muscles telling it that it would soon be no more.

I sat there, on the toilet, panting and sweaty. It was dead.

Dead.

After finishing, as there could not be anything left in my bowels to pour out, I broke the bird further with my bare hands. I bent the metal legs. I smashed the hollow plastic body, cutting my hands. I stuffed the remains into the wastebasket and covered that, as best I could, with toilet paper and paper towels. I decided to just take the bag out and put it into the garbage bin out back. There were piles of new liners underneath. The plastic sack bulged obscenely with dead flamingo general remains.

I peeked out. No Marsha.

She'd want to know what was in the sack to make it puff out like that. Why was there a metal wire sticking out through the side?

I got it to the bins out back. I tossed it among the remains of last night's fish dinner, soiled sheets no longer able to survive the harsh detergent or harsher old washing machines. I disposed of my vanquished foe among whatever detritus would not be labeled a biological hazard.

I had crossed a line. I knew that. It had been more of a game until now. They had held back from actually killing me outright. I had not yet done anything unforgivable. Other than that vague sin I had committed, unknowingly, in the beginning. We knew our parts; we played along with each other.

Now their hatred would manifest, bubble over, boil through them. They had loved my mother. I had murdered one of their own.

My head fell forward. I shivered in the cold air. Right before dawn, the world is a dead whore in a ditch: a hopeless, filthy obscenity of a time. Night is beautiful, day is a happy child. That hour right before day shows up again is a dead whore. That hour before dawn rots in a roadside ditch full of slimy water and used condoms.

I walked back inside and finished my shift, numb and absent-minded as Marsha clomped about, always busy. She gave me some Imodium pills she had in her big white purse. I washed them down with decaf coffee, gave her a smile at her odd acts of kindness and thoughtfulness.

I waited for that flamingo general to rise from the dead. I waited. Seven came and the shift change. Breakfast smells. Scrambled eggs and toast today. Cheerful careful voices of Maria, Sandy and Maisy as they checked on residents, got them up and going for the day, gossiped and chattered with each other and with Marsha.

I left, and it was raining a bit, a misting of rain. No coat. I got in my Chevy, sat there. In the back seat, nothing awaited me.

I drove home, so very tired. I had the swing shift tonight.

The flamingos were all gone when I got home. I sat in my car before I turned it off, the engine ticking gently as it cooled. Rain splattered on the roof. Rain made little rivers down the glass. Where were they?

Where were they?

I got out, the rain sizzling on my exposed skin. Winter would be here in two shakes of a lamb's tail. Snow, ice, Christmas decorations at work, nothing here at my little house. My mother decided to share Christmas this year with my aunt. I had prepared that excuse but no one had asked about her. Not even Marsha.

My mother had quit at the grocery store, her heart too bad to let her stand for long periods. I told her it was fine, our bills were small. She told me she'd die soon.

And she had.

I saw the curtains twitch on the window of the back door. As if someone stood there, peering out as secretly as possible at me.

For a moment, I thought it was my mother. Was it me or some salesman, or some earnest robot selling Jesus?

I miss her. She survived life. She had not given way to despair, she had not succumbed to any chronic illnesses. Carleen had done nothing wrong. She had worked, saved her money, voted when asked to vote, raised a child on next to nothing, kept the sink cleared of clogs and the toilet working. Her possessions still lived in her small bedroom. I hadn't yet cleaned them out, sorted through them and hauled most of it off to the thrift stores or the nearest garbage can. Mostly in case someone came looking for a missing woman nobody missed or misses now.

It's what happens to all of us. Our treasures turned into trash the moment we shuffle off the mortal coil.

I put my key in the door. I turn it. The tumblers click and chatter. I open the door.

They stand there, balancing on their various spikes and twin metal endings. They seem bigger, the pink darker, more menacing. Their eyes move and swirl as they fix me with hard, pitiless gazes. The closet is now open. How? How did it get out? My little house overrun with plastic malignant flamingos somehow free of the earth that allows them to stand upright and serene.

Please, I ask them softly.

The flamingos saying goodbye to my mother, gathered about her secret grave, pink heads bent to give her respect. Perhaps even to weep, their grief allowed to flow out of them and out and out.

What if I took them, all of them, to my mother? Buried them in the ground with her? Or arranged them about her grave as a sort of honor guard? I had prepared her for burial. I won't say how, it's best left to imagination what is done to the dead to make them ready to be viewed by the living and then placed in coffins for eternal rest. I have some medical training, I know what happens to bodies after death: the gases, the decomposition, the . . . yes.

The thought of just what to do danced through my brain.

I'd have to capture these soldiers, stuff them into my car, touch them again when I buried them. It seemed fitting to bury them. And I'd have to retrieve the head flamingo and take her as well. A female, of course—that flamingo who had invaded the bathroom during my moments of distress caused by fear and constant paranoia had been female.

Would they let me?

Even as I watched, they crept a little closer, like a weird game of Simon Says or Mother, May I. Except I hadn't given any commands or instructions.

Listen, I say. They listen.

Listen. I'll take you to my mother. You can be with her.

It's a two-day drive. It's far. I strained my back getting her in and out of the car. I took a shovel, some rope, a big tarp. Except plastic flamingos did not rot or flop about. They were already in severe rigor mortis.

I'd go today. Today.

They allow me to make plans. They make plans, too. The shift toward each other, the exchange of avian glances, the soft, nearly inaudible rasp of their newborn voices.

I call in sick to work. Marsha can verify, with everyone, that I was indeed, suffering some flu-like symptoms working Jessica's shift. No doubt that bathroom still reeks, frankly. Stephanie, the on-call person in case of staff problems, will work my shift tonight. As I am seldom sick and cover for everyone, even during holidays, no one minds if I call in, on Friday and claim illness. Nobody thinks I'm headed off for the bars or anything else any fun. I'm a little homebody, as someone once remarked in a cutesy voice. Plus, people need the money these days.

I put the shovel in the trunk. I also included a battered flashlight. How to get twenty-two flamingos in my car. Some on the roof? Yes. I put on my winter gloves. I begin carrying them out to my car. The heads turn on the long, long necks to regard me rather thoughtfully, as if actual thoughts live in their hollow heads. They are planning something. I stop, at the sixteenth flamingo, considering this, with real knowledge that something bad is coming. That something bad will happen to me. Which is nonsense, humans can't know such things; the future stretched blank and pale because nothing has marked that canvas yet. That's science.

And yet . . .

They had gone still and patient. The flamingos allowed themselves to be neatly stacked in my car, arranged, tightly packed together. Some were tied to the roof of my car and I flung a tarp over them, fastened that down neatly. I stacked them against the shotgun seat. Those heads were right next to my arm.

I'm taking you to my mother, I told them over and over and over. I spoke as if to calm an enraged tiger, as if I addressed a bear about to charge me. I spoke low, soothing words in a slow, soothing tone, hoping they forgot I was their villain and devil and archfiend.

Burn them, another voice said deep in my head.

Just stack them all in the front yard and burn them.

And then what, I asked back. They'll kill me before I can douse them with gasoline and throw a match.

Kill you? Are you a man or a mouse?

I'm a mouse, I replied.

Off I went. I had my wallet. I had my shovel, my winter coat. My eyes had turned into gritty marbles in my eye sockets. I dry swallowed a Ritalin from my stash. I had ten left. I had not slept since Wednesday night. My reserves of energy had gone alarmingly low, so I stopped, with my carload of lawn ornaments, which made people laugh and smile—and yes, point—and got myself a quick breakfast sandwich of sausage patty, rubbery egg, fake square of cheese on a soggy biscuit. I got a big giant coffee.

I'm taking them to my mother's place, I said very truthfully to the girl at the drive through. She shrugged her skinny shoulders, tossed her tail of solid black hair and took my debit card.

She's moved, I'm just helping her out.

Onward.

I drove and drove. I'm not a lover of the open road. I am rather a homebody. I like to stay home, people depress and annoy me. I find I cannot follow along with their little sorrows and happy bland joys. Kids and trips and pets and family dinners mean nothing to me. I never had such things growing up. I cannot relate, as they say. I can only stand aside and nod whenever someone tries to include me in the discussions of in-laws, diaper

training, dog-chewed chairs and breaking down just outside Twin Falls, Idaho, on the way to the water park in Utah.

I drive and drive and they wait, the flamingos with their plans well hidden yet.

They will try to kill me.

They can't forgive me, not a real forgiveness, which is so rare. Where you honestly move on after someone almost mortally wounds you. That ability to trust that person again, when you know they are capable of ripping your guts out and laughing while they do it. The flamingos work on eye for an eye level. I am a sinner and they are the executioners. That's all they understand yet of the world they are slowly being born into. They don't understand nuances. Once a sinner, always a sinner is not always true.

They are new hatchlings. Everything is black or white for them.

I won't let them kill me. I haven't yet given in to them.

I stop at work, park far down the street, sneak up like something out of a bad shallow screwball comedy. I nick that bulgy bag, full of head general of the flamingos, out of the garbage. No one, that I know of, sees me do so.

I hit the open road, with all twenty-three flamingos now. It feels right. This feels right. They might not think so and will probably try something awful but they were meant to be with my mother, not plotting my death at the little house.

And this way, I can come off as kind, as the one who took the high road. Whatever judgment comes when my race is won, I will have this decision to treat my enemies with mercy in my positive column. And no one, even the Eternal Judge, or Anubis or Hades or Jesus or Allah need know that I was too cowardly to burn them in my front yard.

As such an act would just . . . give my mother's army strength.

Give them enough power to return and settle with me once and for all.

No, this was better. This act of kindness on my part would put coals on their head. Render them into nothing more than silly birds with a grudge. A grudge for no reason now.

I drove and drove, took the little road that went a hundred miles or more. It crossed the ragged strip of blacktop that led me to the dirt path. This wild horse track led upward into the high desert where my mother's grave was.

People laughed as they passed me, I am a cautious driver. I didn't care. I got gas and coffee. I bought candy bars and hot dogs and beef jerky.

Sometimes they moved and shifted. It was not the car or the bumps in the road. It was them, reminding me time was rapidly ending for me.

I got on the ragged pavement, found the dirt path again. I had marked it with three big rocks, in case, for whatever reason, I wished to visit where my mother slept her infinite sleep.

I had driven all day and night invaded the sky. It was far longer than a couple hundred miles.

The flamingos, slowly becoming more and more aware each passing day and hour and minute, seemed to smile.

I found the spot, after parking and getting out, retrieving the shovel and the flashlight. I had a weapon and tool in one hand, and light in the other. There was the disturbed earth yet, the headstone a slab of desert rock where I had placed smaller rocks in a smiley face configuration, with my mother's name written on a rock, in black letters. Anyone coming across this would stop and wonder, of course. But pass on, I hoped. It looked like one of those markers for a car accident where someone had been killed. No cops would be called over this. And it was far enough off the regular roads that no one would notice this for years.

I kept one eye on the car full of savage unnaturally animated flamingos and my other eye on that grave. What to do? Bury them? Or just stick them about and let them arrange themselves as they wished when I had gone?

I would bury the dead one and just stick the others in the hard earth. Wind moaned and skittered through the sagebrush and weeds, a coyote called, several more answered. I sighed, so tired, so very tired. I would have to drive to a motel after this. I'd not eaten a real meal since the morning breakfast sandwich. It seemed more important to get here, to my mother's side, and rid myself of evil flamingos.

First, I buried the dead one. I dug a hole next to my mother's grave, and placed the bag in it, covered it with a covering of clods, rocks and dry desert earth. No one would suspect foul play, ha ha, if they dug up the sack of what looked like garbage. No one would suspect me or come find me and accuse me of murdering an important general. I thought of taking another Ritalin. I thought of the dead general. Had it been preparing to slaughter me with its metal legs? Deciding which tender part of me to stab repeatedly? Until I stopped screaming and it could claim victory over the one and only foe it knew about, dreamed about, perhaps?

It was almost over.

I had put my back on my car.

I turned, and they were there, alive, fluffing their pink and rose feathers in the cone of the flashlight. I grabbed it from the ground, swung it back and forth. Their beaks opened, and hissing came forth. As only savagely angry birds can hiss. Their long thin legs ended in wide webbed pink-skinned feet. I had the shovel. I backed away, away from the car. They followed . . . I tried to count them. Were they behind me, were some of them behind me, closing me in a flamingo circle of imminent death?

Yes.

I stopped, stood there, trying to be calm. I would not die like this.

Listen, I asked them.

They came closer, not listening. I heard them behind me.

She is right here, my mother is right here.

They stopped, their heads cocking as if they wanted to believe that.

She's right here. Right below our feet. I miss her, too. I miss her, too!

Hisses. Honks. Calls so low I almost could not hear them.

Black eyes blinked at me. No, not black, golden to orange to pale brown with giant pupils, real eyes. They sported real eyes to regard me with. The rustling of the many feathers threatened to drive me into fits. The wrong move or wrong word and they'd fall on me.

My voice quavered. I did not become brave or noble. I am not made of sterner stuff.

I miss her. Stay here and guard her, please.

The many heads in the flashlight's beam bobbed and turned as they consulted and schemed and perhaps argued my fate.

I said nothing further. It seemed patience was needed now as they decided what to do, what to do, what to do. Their own plans seemed silly now, perhaps, or they were torturing me further before rendering me into human jelly. I gripped the shovel's handle, readying myself. Nothing would come to my rescue, no cavalry would ride up. No intervention.

The desert night held wind and coyotes and the soft sounds of flamingos, who'd once been lawn ornaments, deciding my fate.

One by one, they arranged themselves into a big circle. I watched this, my heart clenching and pounding. My bladder seemed full of hot acid.

An opening had been left among their ranks . . . as if a door, an exit, right to my car.

They watched me, they watched me.

This is not your place, they seemed to say. This is not your place now. It's *ours.*

My feet caught at every last little tuft of tough grass, every last little pebble, I made my way to that opening in the flamingo circle.

I walked through and out.

When I looked back, after reaching the car, getting in, locking the door . . . the circle had closed. Just plastic flamingos arranged, for whatever reason, in a circle around a rock with a smiley face in smaller rocks on it. Some weird version of a funeral or a practical joke or aliens visiting the earth to do experiments with stones and plastic decorations. Rather like a version of crop circles, except with lawn frippery.

I wept.

I sat there in my car and wept.

And then noticed one flamingo had not joined the rest. One flamingo waited in the back seat, returned to plastic hardness and stiffness again. Oh, it turned its long head to watch me weeping in the front seat, uncomprehending why I should feel such relief. They had not forgiven me at all. They would watch me and come back.

I would never be free.

The army of flamingos turned in one smooth movement to regard me sitting in my car. The one in the back seat waited calmly for me to start the long journey back to my little inherited house. I would never be free of them.

Never.

I drove. I found a motel. I slept. I made it home, that single flamingo guarding me. Reminding me how very damned I was. I went into my house. Sunday I go back to work, and there are few questions I have to answer. No one much cares. I do a shift, nothing happens, it's just a shift. I drive home, it's clear, cold, dry. My little house awaits me, the lawn now empty of those baleful pink birds.

I unlock the back door, go in, tired. I eat my last can of chicken noodle soup, vowing to go the store. I take a shower, go to bed, my door open. What can they do to me? Watch me sleep? My eyes close before I'm near the pillow. Morning, the alarm. I have the early shift. It takes me a while to wake up.

It takes me a while to realize something is wrong.

There, on my bedroom floor, is my mother. The flamingos had thrust their spikes and wire legs through her bloated body . . . there is dirt in her wide-open eyes. Anyone with any sort of forensic training will know the wounds caused by the spikes are postmortem. But everyone will assume my hands desecrated her corpse . . . that I caused her to be a corpse.

I cannot scream or breathe or think.

The flamingos blink at me, over and over.

I can smell her now, that miasma of decay. The flamingos wait for me to bring her back to life. They somehow got her here for me to fix. For me to make this all right and all better.

I drag my mother's corpse to the front lawn, using gloves and an old sheet. Her fingernails and hair seem longer but that is due to her skin shrinking back, not the growing of her tissues after death. Death means life stops. One eye glared at me, clouded over, the other blessedly closed.

The flamingos hopped and swayed around me, following me. Carleen waited on her own front lawn, still bearing the dirt from her desert grave. She had small holes poked here and there where her devout fanatical darlings had pierced her to bring her home. Rather like a dog digging up the dead cat to place it once more upon the carpet that cat had so once loved.

My hands fetched cooking oil and the box of matches. Cooking oil would burn just fine. I had nothing else to douse her corpse with. I covered her with her books, piling them about her. I tore out pages from her romance novels, crumpled them to use as a starter. The matches did their job, my fingers shaking as the flamingoes watched, their heads tilting as the tiny flames bit and spread across her gray smock. I began to layer her clothes atop her body. The few pictures she had saved, one of Aunt Carol from Florida pointing at a dead gator someone had hung outside a shack. The fire curled, leaped, and danced. The twenty-two half-living lawn ornaments drew their heads together. One broke from the rest, orange eyes rolling for a moment as it regarded the lawn it had inhabited for years. It let loose a low hissing cry, sounding almost like a goose. I saw real feathers along the S-curve neck. It leaped into that fire atop my mother's body. The flamingo writhed and melted in such an obscene way that I had to close my eyes—a parody of lust and seduction that pretended to be grief. I heard it shrieking in pain, in ecstasy. One by one the flamingoes repeated this ritual. They leaped to the center of that fire. They melted down. The next one calmly waited to be turned to a puddle of charred pink goo that bubbled and steamed, before blackening.

The lazy swing of police lights because even distant neighbors would notice the little odd man burning something illegally in his front yard.

Someone whispering they had to wait until the last one had gone, could we wait for the last one to go before going anywhere, please? I whispered that. It was me.

Two had been left, just two.

I sit in my cell, with murder charges pending, among other charges. It's night. I hear the calling for mama, the profanities of the caged, the call of guards to knock it off. I count the click of the doors, hear the changing of the shift. I wonder if Marsha gossips about me yet as she picks what books those under her care can read or not.

I turn my head and the two flamingos in the corner patiently wait their turn to be with their maker. But I fear whatever magic or malice formed them had seeped into the earth. The directed spray of the garden hose turned the plastic living birds into charred, cheap plastic. The police doused the fire of my mother's funeral pyre and the destruction of her beloved disciples.

I held out my arms. The two that had been left so far behind their brethren, now in paradise or hell with my mother, huddled against me. Soon their faint heat would turn cold, they would just be lawn ornaments again.

My head ached so.

They rubbed their plastic heads against me, their beaks finding my cheeks, my nose, my ears. I whispered to them all through the night. I whispered and held them until they turned cold and still, just plastic flamingos with cracks and holes in their sides.

And in the morning, I let them go, and they clattered to the cell floor. One shattered, elderly plastic turned to something like glass but the other lay there, staring at nothing with one painted flat black eye.

Something's Wrong with the Greenhouse

by Zero Saucier

Content/Trigger Warnings

- Disturbing imagery and violence

"Professor?" A small knock accompanied the voice, far too close to be at the door.

"Yes? I'm—" Adam stopped himself as he looked up. The woman standing before him was very small. Well, small wasn't the right word. Short is better. Apart from her height, nothing about her was small. Adam couldn't properly make out her frame, as everything else about her was far too large.

Most of this woman was framed in the giant bright fiery halo of her curly hair. Adam was certain she could store things in that mane. Her eyes were probably already big and only magnified by her thick-lensed glasses. Her oversized gardening gloves and far too large dirty lab coat made her appear as a cartoon mad scientist, which worked well with the pure manic energy that seemed to surround her.

"There's something wrong with the greenhouse. The plants tell me they aren't developing well, and it really seems like they haven't been. I think there's a monster. Nothing has been changed, or at least to my knowledge. I need a second opinion."

Adam sat silent for a second, as that's how long it took to fully receive what she had just said. The words came out a mile a second. It seemed to Adam that she was already forming new words before the old could reach his ears.

"I'm sorry . . . the plants?" Adam cleared his throat and composed himself somewhat. "And you are?"

"Margret, but everyone calls me Maggie. Except one professor, down the hall from you, he calls me Meggie. Think he heard me wrong. I've been a student here—" Maggie paused for only a second, quickly counting on her fingers. "I don't know. I'm with botany. Major. You're Worth, right? Professor Worth?"

Maggie's whirlwind of speech finally stopped, and her with it. Mostly. She jerked into stillness, and Adam could swear her gaze was boring into his skull.

"Oh yes, you can call me Mr. Worth." On instinct he stood and extended his hand to shake. Adam started to wonder if she had blinked at all in the entire time she had been in his office.

Maggie broke eye contact for only a second to glance at his hand and shake her head. "You don't want to touch my gloves." It was the only thing she had said slowly up until this point. She turned and started out at what Worth would call a light jog, but what was probably her normal walking pace. "Come on, need a second opinion."

Worth couldn't find either time or a good way to argue out of this. And quite frankly, he didn't want to find either. It might be fun, something he rarely indulged in. So, he followed, having to keep a strong pace to not lose her. Maggie turned corner after corner, just barely in sight. It was only when she was stopped by a door that had to be unlocked that Adam properly caught up with her.

"You said the plants told you?" Worth ducked, almost in time to not hit the top of the door frame above the stairs. The metal against his skull made a loud ringing *thunk*, and a slight headache started to form. He had certainly never been this way to the greenhouse, not that he could remember. But then again, he had only been once to the greenhouse.

The metal spiral creaked and swayed beneath them, though it did nothing to deter Maggie's pace. Maggie jumped the last few steps and fished in her pocket for a key, leaving Worth on something that felt to him more like a tornado than a stable walkway.

"Of course. A few of them are hooked up, they can type." The key was loud in the lock, louder than Adam remembered keys being. "They keep wanting to do more, connect outside of their little bubble, but we don't want them online. Now help me get this door open."

It took both of them pulling on the door for it to fully squeal open. The greenhouse was bigger than Worth had remembered. Even though he was aware of where he was, Adam found it a bit off-putting to see this much plant growth in the dead of winter. It was mostly green—as the name of the building would suggest—with the only contrast a barely visible corner in the back filled with every color imaginable.

Adam took a deep breath, finally slowing down. The plants must have just been watered. The scent of rain, fresh wet dirt, and leaves filled his lungs. Adam felt himself relaxing more and more, drifting into that missed bliss that spending time in nature had always given him.

A sudden yank on his arm pulled Worth out of his trance. The space was far more open, but Maggie's voice seemed almost twice as loud. "Don't stand too close to the door. Not sure what they're doing with those drosera, but they really need to stop. Shouldn't mess with nature too much."

Maggie didn't let go of his arm though, instead pulling him toward what appeared to be a small sectioned-off compartment. She put in some sort of code for it on a keypad that looked so rough it made Worth wonder how it could still be kicking. Apart from that, Maggie's hand flew so fast it was almost a miracle she didn't have to reenter the code.

The room was very small, and covered top to bottom with what appeared to be weeds, wires, and sticky notes. "This is my section. My baby. I've been working on it for a few years now. It gets a different watering routine, so I really don't need to forget." She seemed to be gesturing to everything, but Worth figured she was referring to the abundance of notes, all in bold capital letters. He wondered on what continent you would have to be on to *not* be able to read them.

"You do know people are going to ask about the wires, not the sticky notes, right?" Worth started to question his choice of following this strange woman. Or maybe this doubt came from his growing headache. He was amazed at how Maggie seemed to know her way around the disorganized clutter of a room.

Maggie began typing something on a computer that was allowed barely any room on the already small desk. "Of course." She paused, scanning the sheet hanging from a shelf in front of the monitor. "That's why I explain the notes. Everyone asks about the wires. Now they'll have an explanation for everything."

"And the plants?" Adam asked, feeling a smile creep its way onto his face.

Maggie turned to him, no emotion in those saucers of hers. "We're in a greenhouse."

The way she said it made Worth feel truly stupid. He coughed and composed himself once again. "Well, what *is* with all the wires? You said the plants could type?"

A wave of regret made Worth shiver as Maggie fully turned to him, her features now somehow bigger with excitement. She started, her hands and arms—and really body—now joining the cacophony of words.

"Yes! Understand, plants are smart. They think. In a way. They always know how to move for the sun or weather. They learned the watering routine, the ones out there at least, I try to not follow a pattern for these in here, so they don't complain when I'm late. They like to complain. Did you know plants complain a lot? Or that's what it seems like."

Worth waved to get her attention. "Hey, plants typing?"

Maggie jolted, looking right into him again. "Oh right. Researchers at MIT made spinach send emails. Monica Gagliano—she's really cool you should look into some of her work—found plants can be trained. Like those dogs with the food bell."

"Hold on," Worth interrupted. "First, Pavlov. Second, they made spinach do what?"

"Send emails! An infrared camera picked up nitroaromatics leaving the plants when they were placed in soil with it. The camera sent an email to the researchers about it. So really, it was the cameras that sent the emails, but the spinach did the heavy lifting."

Maggie looked fully at Worth again. Determination made a temporary home on her face. "But I want to take it a step further. I'm using liriopes as they're an evergreen perennial and easy to deal with. I've got them hooked up and have been teaching them the alphabet, basic language, and abstract ideas. They show high intellect but very little drive. They have yet to fully apply themselves."

Adam just stood there for a second. It must be a bad day, as he very rarely couldn't think of anything to say. Maybe not the best decision to come down here. "So, the plants . . . *text* you?"

Maggie let out a short huff and finally turned away from him to the plants, almost giving them a death glare. "In a broad sense. We have them hooked up to a basic text document that sends me updates through email." Her gaze softened a bit, and it looked to Worth as if she reached out to pet one of the leaves. "They can communicate basic things, need for better soil, upcoming growth, need for water. But you very much have to fill in the blanks and piece the puzzle together yourself."

Worth could almost swear he heard her whisper a little, "but I believe in you" to the wall of growth and wires. Were this anyone else, he might have questioned it.

And back again, Maggie was moving in the cramped space, shuffling over to the computer. "But that's not why I brought you in here. I did figure you would want an explanation for everything though."

She waved her hand, gesturing to everything this time. Her hands flew over the keyboard, scanning the sheet in front of the monitor a few more times. Mainly Maggie just hit the computer case, muttering something about a "stupid" or "old" system.

Then finally, a loud slow whirring overpowered every other noise. Worth instinctively sucked a breath in as Maggie let out a sigh of relief. The lights started to power off one by one, as did everything else. It was only in the silence that Adam was able to process just how loud the greenhouse had been.

"What the hell? Did you do that? Scared me half to death!" Worth was about to laugh at the absurd horror of the situation.

Maggie waved her hands, immediately shushing him. "Quiet. Just wait a second. You'll see," she whispered, already crouching behind the plants, out a view of the windows.

So, he waited a second. Then two. Then three. Then four. At around sixty, Worth was ready to give up. He sighed and started for the door. That is, until something moved outside of the compartment, rustling the plants and creaking the wooden flower beds.

For once in his life, Adam felt comfort while trapped in a little room with someone else. He knew now it *was* a bad idea to come indulge in this little fun. They couldn't get out, so it couldn't get in, right? He wanted to ask, *Whatever could be out there? Weren't they the only ones in the greenhouse?* but everything in Worth told him to stay quiet.

Maggie seemed pleased with this development. She quickly snaked her way to the door—still crouched—only slowing when she grabbed the doorknob and started turning it.

"The hell are you doing? I thought we were the only ones here. If so, *something* is out there," Worth hissed out. He could feel the professionalism quickly leaving his body as panic started to settle in. He had to stop himself from going up the Maggie and yanking her away from the door. That might cause too much noise.

Maggie stopped and looked slightly over her shoulder at Worth. "We were the only ones here. That's kinda what I'm hoping for." She peered up through a section of glass on the door not blocked by plant growth. "Fingers crossed it's out there."

Worth wanted to move, really. He wanted to move to the corner, crouch down, and hide. Wait until the lights and sounds came back, and this all blew over. Then it could be a dream. It wouldn't be real. But a sinking weight kept him in place as Maggie slowly pushed open the door.

Maggie started forward, waving at Worth to get down with her. He instinctively followed suit. She seemed like she knew what she was doing, like she had done this before. So, in theory, she would be able to get them out, right? It dawned on Worth that this was the quietest Maggie had been since they met.

The pair slowly wandered through the greenhouse, still crouched, with Maggie leading the way. Out of the little compartment, the sounds of heavy labored breathing and slow footsteps joined the rustling of plants and flower beds. The air felt colder, and not just because the AC was off. There was something awful about whatever creature was now in the greenhouse with them. Worth wasn't particularly a spiritual man, but he found himself almost praying that Maggie would lead them to the door.

She peeked around another flower bed, but this time she didn't immediately turn back. "Oh, man." This was the calmest Worth had heard her speak. "I think it saw us. Wanna leave?" Maggie turned back to Worth, giving off a look that seemed closer to boredom than fear.

Adam felt his face drain of color and the instinct to throw up come over him. The thing, whatever it was, knew he was there. Thankfully, he didn't puke, as he feared whatever was out there would find them just a bit easier. He quickly nodded.

"Reasonable." Maggie peeked back around the bed to look at it again. "Just don't run—it chases. Follow my lead. The door's this way." She started again, picking up the pace a bit. Even crouched, Maggie knew her way around the greenhouse. Adam noticed that she knew it far too well for being this low to the ground. *How many times had she done this before? Been in this situation?*

Everything was going smoothly, until it wasn't. Worth of course didn't know the path as well; he hadn't spent hours here as Maggie had. So, it wasn't a surprise when his foot caught the bottom of a stack of small clay pots. Despite his best efforts, they shattered as loudly as they possibly could. When Adam looked to assess the danger he had put them in, he finally saw the thing wrong with the greenhouse.

Maggie had been right to call this thing a monster. There was really no other word to generally describe it. It was transparent, really more hazy. There was an obvious general form, but only when quickly glanced at. The longer Worth looked at it, the more abstract it seemed.

But the monster was only mostly hazy. Splotched all across its form were patches of what seemed like flesh. Maybe. It was definitely red, but the longer Adam looked at it, the less fleshy it seemed. Worth wondered if this thing was closer to anything growing in the greenhouse than to him.

And there was something mesmerizing about the creature. Worth wanted, *needed*, to study it. And Worth had never been a man inclined to science. This thing *had* to be understood. It just seemed so fascinating, something that looked so unnatural but must have a solid explanation.

Unfortunately, Worth only snapped out of this trance he seemed to be in when he realized something. This was the kind of thing that one could only tell how truly large it was when it got closer. And it was getting closer. Much faster than Worth would have really liked.

"Remember what I said about running before?" Maggie asked this just as though she were asking for Worth's favorite ice cream flavor. "Ignore that."

Adam didn't need to be told twice. Probably trying to vault over and look cool, Worth scrambled over one of the beds, trying his best to get out of the path of this thing. The monster shot past him. Adam couldn't tell if it was making solid contact with the floor or just racing above it. Maybe both? Its movements were far too fluid and unbothered to be running, but far too rough to be floating.

Worth knew it really didn't matter though. However much he wanted to study, figure out, and understand this thing, it wouldn't play along. At least yet. So instead, he ran, ducking and turning far too sharply for his tastes. All the while frantically searching for any sign of Maggie.

"Professor! Professor Worth! Over here!" Her voice came from his left, so his body started that way. Maggie was held against the door pushing. It didn't seem to want to move as much as they needed it to.

Adam had never been good at processing everything in stressful situations. His friends and family teased him about it all the time. They said he would ask why a room was hot if it had caught fire. It wouldn't surprise anyone that he didn't hear the creature coming up to him from his left. On Adam's defense though, he had formerly noticed that the thing wasn't making as much sound as it should with all the steps it was taking.

Worth must have been a very lucky man though. Through all logic, the thing should have landed on him and either crushed him or—most likely—ripped him to shreds. In short, Adam should be dead.

But he was alive! Adam had started to debate on whether it was a good thing. The creature did get him, though only slightly. It was only able to hit him, more batting him forward than anything. That did help though, as he slammed against the door, hard enough to open it just so they could squeeze through. Or well for Maggie to squeeze through, basically dragging Worth out behind her.

"Get up, wordsmith! If you want to keep your job!" Maggie had already braced herself against the door, pushing again.

Worth thought it more suitable to think of his life on the line, rather than his job. He threw his body against the door too, using whatever strength he had left to help seal some sort of barrier between them and the thing. He could see the creature growing in size as it got closer and closer to the door that wasn't closing as easily as he would have liked.

"WHAT *WAS* THAT?!" Adam yelled when they were finally able to fully shut and lock the door.

Maggie looked at him, calm and direct. Or at least as calm as she had been since they met. "That's what's wrong with the greenhouse."

Worth was only able to get out a small "What?" that he wasn't sure Maggie heard.

She continued, her words seeming almost faster than normal now. "They're playing with nature, the newer ones. Keep trying for something. I'm not sure what they won't say. But it can't be good. You saw it in there. There's no way that happened naturally. See, I said there's a monster in the greenhouse, and you didn't believe me. Though few people *do* believe me with that."

"Was that the second opinion you were looking for?" Worth asked, still a bit distant, trying to figure out what all just happened. His former headache was starting to creep its way back into his life.

Maggie squinted at him, letting out a short *hmm*. "In a way. I thought you'd be better at words. You're English, right? An English professor? Thought you'd be able to put into words what you saw. Well, better words. Better than mine. I just say there' a monster in the greenhouse and no one believes me."

Worth immediately went into revision mode, a learned skill he had yet to figure out how to turn off. "Now let's not say monstrous. Yes, we don't know what it is, and it does look and seem monstrous, but there must be some explanation. And people don't readily believe in monsters." He thought for a second, looking down and tapping his chin. "Say something is wrong in the greenhouse. Maybe an animal got in. Not monstrous, how about horrible?"

"Wait! I'll forget! Write this down!" Maggie yelled, more panicked about finding a pen and paper than she had been against that thing in the greenhouse. She began patting down her pockets, soon flinging out all manner of objects stored inside. Worth questioned just how big her pockets were.

Maggie suddenly turned back to the door. "Aw man, forgot to shut off my compartment behind us," she whined. "The monster might get in." Maggie seemed to Worth to be more frustrated at the idea of the thing messing with her work than whatever the thing was existing in the first place.

"Not a monster. Thing, creature. Those are better," Worth instinctively corrected. A worry quickly formed in his mind. "What about the power?" Maggie looked at Worth, confused by his question. "I mean, the lights, air, watering system, whatever else a greenhouse has. Can we leave the plants in *there* in *that* condition with *that* thing?"

Maggie waved off the ideas as if they had been absurd. "Oh, it doesn't mess with the plants, not that I've seen. And the power should be back on in like an hour? Maybe two? We could call maintenance, but I think they'd send someone to check it out this time. Don't think that's a good idea." She kept looking into the windows of the greenhouse, probably trying to justify going back in to close the compartment door.

The full weight of the situation finally hit Worth, much like the creature had, batting him forward into a whole new set of emotions. A part of him wanted to laugh. Another wanted to scream. Another wanted to cry. Yet another had millions of questions. All of which he knew wouldn't be answered. This was too many parts, or at least more than Adam was used to dealing with.

The last part started to win out. "So, there's a monster—sorry, *creature*—in the greenhouse. And you brought me here to show me instead of just telling me? What is it? How did it get there? What am *I* supposed to do about it? What . . . just what the hell?!" Adam's words sped up as he talked, almost flying as fast as Maggie. All the parts combined into what one could call distress.

Maggie huffed and rolled her eyes. If this had been anyone more reasonable than Maggie, Worth wouldn't be able to believe *this* is how they were reacting. "I did tell you. I said there's a monster in the greenhouse. You followed me here. And I'm not sure what it is or how it got there. I would have explained those things had I known." She let out a sigh, trying to calm herself down from what she saw as nothing to get too worked up about.

Again, Worth was too stunned to speak. It was a bad day, and not just for words. He started away, *slowly*, toward the stairs. He still didn't trust them, but it was a much better chance than staying closer to that thing in the greenhouse.

"Oh, about the second opinion. I need help taking care of the . . . problem in the greenhouse," Maggie called out after Worth as he left. "If you could help, that'd be great. Be even better if you had any ideas." She smiled brightly. Even that was big. "Just think on it, would ya?"

Despite staying as far away from the greenhouse as Worth could manage, the being *inside* the greenhouse could not stay out of his mind. He tried explaining the concept to his partner Jon with the excuse of it being a new monster for an upcoming book, but was met with lackluster enthusiasm about it.

"It's just very . . . different." Jon was precariously leaning outside the small apartment, a makeshift safety rope bound him to the building as he washed the windows. "Not saying that's bad, but you always like to have a 'deeper message' to your monster books, don't you? What could that one be about?"

"Well, I . . . " Adam floundered, not thinking this far into the excuse. "It could be about contrast, two halves becoming whole. Something like that."

Jon leaned his head down to the open portion of the window so Adam could hear him better. "And where did you say this would be set? The middle of the woods?" He laughed. "I love you, dearest, but you confused a black-throated blue warbler for a cerulean warbler the other day. I think you need to spend more time in nature if you are to write about it."

Adam knew Jon didn't mean to hurt his feelings; he *did* often joke like that, but it still stung. "Of course I'll do research before writing it. And I don't have to know everything about nature to write about it. I didn't even say I had started on it yet," he muttered out, crossing his arms and leaning on the counter.

Adam heard a sigh coming from outside and turned to see Jon clumsily crawling back in. "I'm sorry. Truly, Adam, I am. I didn't mean to be mean. I was only teasing." He paused, searching for the right words. "I'm just worried about you. You've been more distant, and now with this new book idea I . . . " Jon cleared his throat. "It just doesn't seem your style. You don't really branch off like that. With your books, I mean," Jon quickly added. He gave Adam a soft kiss on the cheek, and his shoulder a reassuring squeeze, walking off to put up his cleaning supplies.

Adam knew Jon was right. He was predictable. His students had always said he was the stereotypical English professor. The kind to wear neat little sweaters and button-ups, to have a dog, and a husband, and a few published works. To not have bright or garish decorations on his walls or colors in his wardrobe. To live simply.

And they were right. Worth had always thought of himself as not needing much. A simple man with simple wants and a simple life. But where had this led him? He was now unassuming, predictable, boring.

Adam wasn't too much of a fan of this way of life. He much preferred his teenage years, wild and free and uncaring. Doing anything and everything that he wanted to do that seemed exciting. Yes, it was far more dangerous. Adam was often rejected and ostracized, to put it lightly. But it had been fun. Thinking back on it, that feeling of excitement and fun had returned to him a bit that day in the greenhouse.

"Adam!" Jon called out from the other room, waking Worth from his thoughts. "The Christmas market closes soon. Do you want to go by? I think they still have that hot chocolate mix you like."

That settled it in Adam's mind. He was going to do it however he could. Get out of this predictable, unassuming, boring lifestyle. On the way, he might be able to help Maggie with the problem in the greenhouse.

It finally dawned on Worth as he and Maggie were making improvised weapons in his office. "*Can* we kill this thing?"

Worth had invited her there, having to talk to multiple different professors and wait outside of multiple different classes just to catch her. And even then, he had only caught her in a small hallway far away from everyone and everything else. It seemed to Worth that she didn't want to be seen with him. They were going to gather supplies and finalize a plan, hopefully heading out soon after.

"Not sure." Maggie didn't look up from what could loosely be called a homemade spear. "And I don't want to kill it, anyway."

Worth sighed, putting down the clumsy armor he had been sewing together with fishing wire. "Well, what *do* you want to do with it then?" In all honesty, he didn't want to kill it either. It was too interesting, too important. Something like that was far more than a common housefly one would swat at without a second thought.

"Not sure. That's kinda why I asked for ideas. Like I don't want to kill it. Not all too sure if we can. It almost doesn't seem real. But then again, most anything can be killed. I think it's kinda close to plants? In a way. Maybe." She paused, wiggling her spear to test its sturdiness. A good breeze would win against it. "I can kill plants." Maggie finally looked up at Worth. He still hadn't gotten used to her stare. It was just so . . . intense.

"You don't seem all too sure about much right now." This wasn't what Worth had been hoping for. Nothing about this was a good idea. Then again, an idea can't be bad if there isn't an idea in the first place.

Currently, Adam's plan was to extend his hand and offer respect. The thing would be much easier to study, to listen to, to understand if it were on his side. If that didn't work, hit the thing hard enough to knock it out, but not hard enough to kill it. If that still didn't work, hit Maggie hard enough to at least knock her out and leave her for the creature. Worth was sure it would appreciate if something was left for it. Then he didn't have to be fast; he just had to get out. Maybe if Worth was lucky, he'd be able to snag her keys to the greenhouse . . .

Adam shook his head, trying to dismantle the thoughts. A part of himself almost feared Maggie could read his mind. It was silly, he knew, but it was just the way she stared at him with those big unblinking eyes.

"So, what—" Worth tried to break the silence but was beaten to it by his ringtone. The caller ID, *Pumpkin <3*, contrasted with the small, annoyed groan Adam let out. He took a deep breath, letting it ring for just a second longer before finally picking it up.

"Honey, Adam, where are you? It's almost nine, and you're still not home. I'm starting to get worried," Jon asked before Adam could even get out a greeting.

"Hey, Jonny-bear," Adam drew out. "I was just held back going over a few papers. This new class they've put me on is more abstract than most—some students are having a hard time understanding it." Not a lie, he had pushed his office hours to six thirty this semester to help with this new class. "I then got distracted with my writing. I meant to leave at seven, but time just completely passed me. It's that new monster one I was telling you about."

Jon sat silent for a second. Adam started to fear the believability of his excuse. "Have you promised it to a publisher yet? Because I *know* you haven't outlined the story, and you *know* you shouldn't jump the gun like that again."

Adam wasn't able to stop himself from giving an annoyed little huff. "I'm just going off the cuff this time, instinct. Trying something new. Is that so bad? Is there really something so wrong with that?" Adam wouldn't say he was mad *at* his husband yet, just frustrated *with* him.

"Yes!" Jon's voice crackled over the phone, loud enough for Maggie to hear. She kept her head down though, smart enough not to get involved, but curious enough to continue listening.

"You've done this before! It didn't work. You didn't have anything on time, and the publisher dropped you. Do you not remember?!"

Adam's confidence quickly vanished. "Yes, dear, I—"

"Two years."

"Honey, I know."

"You were in a rut for two years and couldn't publish anything. I'm not letting it happen again. You can't go through that again. I can't see you go through that again."

Adam leaned back and rested his head against the wall. It felt as if all of reality had been shoved in his face again. This is why he had changed his lifestyle. Yes, his teenage years were fun, but this was safe. And if Adam was being honest, it was a nice kind of comfortable. "You're right, Jon. I'm sorry. I love you. I'm going to stay at the office tonight. Sleep on the couch."

Jon cleared his throat. "That's all right, baby. I love you too. I'll be waiting for you when you get home."

Worth sighed and threw his phone to the side. His brain buzzed with too many thoughts that he couldn't entirely make sense of. They were familiar though; they had been around for years at this point.

"Aw man, does that mean you won't help me with the greenhouse?" Maggie whined.

Worth laughed. He and Jon were probably going to have an argument next time they saw each other. He had been debating his whole life, or at least the past decade. And Maggie was whining.

He shook his head. "No of course not. I promised, I think. And I don't like to leave a project unfinished. Yeah, I'll help capture your monster."

Maggie brightened up at this, now sitting as tall as she could, not that this was a significant change to her height. "Oh good, cause like you're already here and you believe me. And I specifically chose you cause you've written those monster books. I'd thought you'd have some insight. Ya know, to help."

Worth laughed again. Everything felt different now. Before, his confidence came from the fear that he would have to fight. To look bigger to let the other side fear him more than they should. He still had that confidence, but the background had changed. It was far brighter, more hopeful. The confidence one gets from knowing they will get through to the other side.

Worth stood up and walked over to the broken rolling whiteboard he had propped against the wall. "Ok, so, what's the plan?" He wrote *PLAN* in big letters at the top, underlining it. Unsurprisingly, writing things out had always helped him make sense of his mind and what was going on around him.

"Ok so I was thinking we could make weapons," Maggie nodded at everything laid out around them. "But non-lethal ones, like I said I don't want to kill it. Just like knock it out and contain it." She mimicked throwing her spear. It fell apart in front of her.

Worth wrote *KNOCK OUT* and *CONTAIN* on the white board in neat little bullet points. "Where can we, as you put it, contain it?"

Maggie started toying with the dull tip to her spear. "I was thinking in my little compartment. Like if you've got any rope or like zip ties, we can restrain it and then it'll be easier to get in there. And deal with after."

Worth paused before writing anything else on the white board. "Well, I don't want to hurt it."

"Gotta crack a few eggs to make an omelet," Maggie said almost instinctively. She looked up quickly, a flash of panic striking her face. "We're not cracking any eggs though. We're not killing it." She took a quick breath and calmed herself. "Anyway, it'll be ok. As long as we don't kill it, I'm sure it'll heal"

Adam added a dash beside CONTAIN, putting GREENHOUSE COMPARTMENT next to it. He stood looking at the board for a second and added a check mark, completing that part of planning in his mind. "And how do we knock it out?"

"Move it to a corner, trap it, ya know. Like a king in chess. Then hit it really hard? Didn't really think about it but that's what works for most things. You hit them hard enough and they go down."

Worth, yet again, paused before writing anything on the board. "What if that doesn't work? Is there anything else we can use? Maybe a gas or medicine or spray or something?"

Maggie thought for a second, making a long *hmm* noise as she did so. "There're a few bee smokers stored in the back of the greenhouse. Or well they should still be there. Haha, get it, bee? Anyway, that might work."

Adam gave a polite chuckle to the joke and quickly turned back to the board. He put a little dash beside KNOCK OUT adding HIT, GAS, and a little check mark. Worth stared at the crude plan on the board, nodding his head after a minute. He quickly turned to Maggie, extending his hand to shake. "Plan?"

"Plan," she responded with a smile, grabbing his hand and shaking it in what Worth would call the worst handshake he had ever been given.

The door was just as difficult as before, and because it was long after any reasonable hour, the electronic system lock was set. Maggie quickly swiped her falling apart student ID, but hesitated when it came to putting in the code. Worth realized this was the first time he had seen her question her actions.

"Are you sure? Cause we can come back another time with a better plan. We can get other people too. Maybe I can just do it myself," Maggie spoke hurriedly, like normal, but something was off with it this time. For once, she was nervous.

Adam's mind screamed at him to leave, come up with a better plan. If Maggie was questioning this, and Worth was more stable than Maggie, then Worth should be seriously questioning this. He ignored this though. Adam didn't want to, wasn't going to, listen to these fears that pushed him toward mundaneness. Besides, would they even be able to get others on board or come up with a better plan?

"Come on, what's the worst that can happen? I believe in us." The bright confidence felt so much better than the defensive confidence he had before. So this must be better, right?

Once inside Maggie hurried over to the computer, just as quick to shut everything down. They waited outside the little compartment for the creature to show. Soon a silent darkness overtook everything as the power went out.

It took Worth a second for his eyes to adjust, but he could faintly make out Maggie twirling the metal pipe she had eventually chosen after abandoning her spear. Worth himself paced—not too far, only a few paces—back and forth, swinging the bee smokers in time with his walking. He was about to ask if it had taken this long the last time when the distinct snap of a stem sounded from the back corner with all the colorful flowers.

They looked at each other. There was something in Maggie's eyes Worth couldn't quite place. Maybe he just couldn't see properly in the moonlight. She motioned for him to go first. He didn't hesitate. If Worth wanted to study this creature, he had to be comfortable getting close to it.

He started up, silently, trying to put on a brave show for Maggie. Prove to her—and himself—that he was sure in what he was doing. Worth wasn't able to get too far when he heard Maggie clear her throat.

"Sorry in advance. It just needs to eat, ya know. Figured you'd under-stand," Worth heard Maggie quickly say before feeling something hit the base of his skull.

Adam could still somehow hear the loud shallow breathing of the creature getting louder and louder as it approached over the throbbing in his head. He groaned and instinctively started crawling away.

"Hm, you have a ticker skull than most. Usually that hit, *wham!* It knocks them right out. Must be losing a bit of my strength. Or maybe cause you're taller than the others." Maggie squatted down beside him, cocking her head to look him in the eyes properly. Worth wasn't fully able to process what she was saying, but he could make out a bit of red on the metal pipe she was holding from the moonlight.

She stood, grabbing onto his arm and bringing him up with her. "Come on, let's get up now. There we go."

Adam groggily stood and looked up, just in time to see Maggie straighten herself and get a better hold on the metal pipe. "One more ought to do it," she said in a cheery voice. Well, so much for solving the problem with the greenhouse.

Cleithrophobia
by Isabella J.

Content/Trigger Warnings

- Mention of Cleithrophobia

Cleithrophobia

Sealed,
No escape
Too many barricades
Error . . .

Walls absent of openings
Rooms become deficient
Size never mattering

All exists demonstrate non-existence
I inhale; suffocate, explosions
Creep under oxygen,
Lungs burning, cavity corruption,
Cold dermis silently abandoning,

Bones breaking, everything disintegrates
In tandem with physical accomplishments
To egress whenever.

Death carries my skeleton
In circles longingly, eternally
Trapped between forever in
Walls that exits abandoned.

About the Author

Isabella J. is a writer from Southern California who recently graduated with her bachelor's degree in English and Creative Writing. During her college years, she found her love for poetry inside and outside the classroom while contributing to student art journals and other creative projects. She loves to explore deep and sometimes dark emotions through her work, finding the beauty in reflections and vulnerability. When she's not reading or writing, she loves spending time with her friends, family, and especially her dogs. This is her first publication since graduating and first work published outside her university's creative community, marking an exciting new chapter in her writing journey. You can follow her on Instagram @redinkwriting_

The Last Laugh
by Brandee Paschall

Content/Trigger Warnings

- Graphic Violence

- Psychological Trauma

- Suicide (Mentioned)

- Bullying

- Death of Loved Ones

- Abuse (Mentioned)

- Horror Elements

Prologue

[INTRO—"Roxy Rambles" YouTube Channel: News Segment Voiceover]

Cue eerie synth music.

Title Card: "Wraithwood Massacre: Two Years Later–Trick or Terror?"

[ROXY RAMBLES NEWS REPORT SCRIPT]

Camera fades in on Roxy, standing in front of a fog-drenched, pumpkin-lit path leading to Wraithwood Town Square. Locals bustle in the background, prepping for the annual Halloween festival.

ROXY RAMBLES (on camera):

"Good evening, ghouls and gals. Roxy here, bringing you the weird, the wild, and the downright wicked. And tonight, we're digging up something *truly chilling* from the graveyard of recent history."

Cut to black-and-white footage of police tape, flashing sirens, and a dilapidated suburban home.

"Two years ago, the quiet town of Wraithwood, Massachusetts was rocked by a string of brutal killings that locals still whisper about—the Wraithwood Massacres. The killer? A nightmare brought to life: A masked figure known only as *Barney the Rabbit.*"

Insert sketch of the mask described by police—pink hoodie, floppy rabbit ears, a cartoonishly grinning white-and-pink mask with razor-sharp teeth.

"The only known survivor, then-sixteen-year-old Tyler Marcone, described the killer to authorities with haunting detail. What no one expected? The monster behind the mask was his own father—Barnaby Marcone."

Cut to courtroom sketches. Flash of the mugshot. Then a breaking news chyron: "Convicted. Suicide in Custody."

"Barnaby was arrested, convicted, and later found dead in his cell—an apparent suicide. Case closed, or so they thought . . . "

[CUT BACK TO ROXY – WALKING THROUGH FESTIVAL SETUP]

"But now, two years later, the town is trying to reclaim its identity with this year's Halloween festival. Candy, costumes, and—wait for it—*a haunted house named 'The Last Laugh.'* A wink to the killer's iconic grin . . . or a wildly tasteless PR stunt? Depends on who you ask."

Quick clips of townsfolk setting up carnival rides, haunted maze props, and teens in bunny masks posing for TikToks.

"Some call it healing. Others call it horror rebranded. Either way, Wraithwood's leaning *into* the legend."

[INTERVIEW CLIPS – PRE-RECORDED]

Local Resident #1 (older woman, shaking head):

"It's disrespectful. That boy lost everything. Turning it into a funhouse? Shameful."

Teen in Pink Hoodie Costume (laughing):

"Dude, it's iconic now. It's like Wraithwood's own urban legend. We made it *ours*."

[CUT BACK TO ROXY – NEAR HAUNTED HOUSE ENTRANCE]

Camera pans over the haunted house's façade—an exaggerated cartoon rabbit face with teeth forming the entrance.

"So here we are, standing at the gates of 'The Last Laugh.' The town says it's all in good fun, a chance to face fear and come out laughing. But with the memory of Barney the Rabbit still fresh in many minds . . . is Wraithwood playing with fire?"

[OUTRO – ROXY TO CAMERA]

"This Halloween, we'll find out if Wraithwood can laugh off its ghosts—or if some monsters refuse to stay buried."

Roxy smirks, raising an eyebrow.

"This is Roxy Rambles . . . signing off—but not signing out. Stay tuned, stay safe, and remember . . . not every mask comes off."

Cue outro music, creepy giggle layered in the background.

[END OF SEGMENT: LIKE | COMMENT | SUBSCRIBE | #BarneyTheRabbit #WraithwoodMassacre #LastLaugh]

One

Billie

Blood and carnage were no strangers to me. In fact, one might attribute them as siblings. At the mere age of eighteen, I'd already overcome enough pain and grief to sedate a grieving elephant.

Friday, October 31st screamed at me from the calendar as I plaited my raven hair and let it drop to sashay across my lower back. My aunt sneered at me from the doorway as I lined my almond-shaped eyes with charcoal. Another arrow shot into my back as I schooled my features into an uncaring smirk. That was the only winning achievement I'd gotten after years of torment from my belittling classmates and stereotypical Vietnamese family.

My aunt clucked in disapproval as she crossed the hallway toward the banister, likely going to plate my precisely proportionate breakfast. Behind hollow cheeks, the reflection showed me a pair of jaded brown eyes that were scowling. A singular beauty mark below my right eye.

Grabbing my backpack off the floor, I almost went sprawling as it took a few tries to tug it onto my shoulder.

"Billie Nguyen, you're going to make Liem late." My aunt's voice carried up the stairs.

"Ma, we don't have to leave for another half hour, would ya give her some grace." Liem sighed over his book as I trotted into the dining room. He smiled at me from behind the pages, and I sent him a wink as his mother turned with our plates.

She groaned as I dropped my bag to the floor with a thud and took the vacant seat beside my cousin. Fried shallots and herbs infiltrated my senses, and my mouth watered at the xôi before me. A rare moment of warmth shone in my aunt's eyes as I scarfed down her cooking, and she patted my head before dropping a pamphlet beside my plate.

Yale, Harvard, Princeton, Dartmouth. The closer graduation came, the more she pestered me to decide. Medical school or law school; yellow or crimson.

Liem's crimson hoodie glared at me like a traffic light; an unwavering reminder that either way, I would never live up to him. I would always be cast in his shadow, and those of my parents. Twelve years ago, two pressure cooker bombs detonated somewhere on Boylston Street in Boston, leaving me orphaned and forced to live with my mother's sister. Whose only resemblance was her cooking, something they'd both learned from my Bá.

Liem wiped any remnants of breakfast from his face and stood. "Come on, Billie. I'll drop you off at the coffee shop."

My aunt tilted her head. "Why not at the school?"

Liem grabbed my hand to hush me. "Roxanne took the early shift this morning, so she asked Billie to come walk with her."

My aunt raised a brow at my cousin's answer before sighing in resignation. "I suppose that's all right, as long as you're not spending time with *that boy.*"

Biting my tongue, I nodded before following Liem out to his sedan. Tossing my bag to the floor, I plopped down in my seat and waited until Liem pulled off our street to speak.

"Thank you," I whispered.

He nodded, his hands tightening around the leather-bound steering wheel. "Not that I necessarily like Jaime either, but besides Roxy he's the only one that seems to keep you afloat."

Afloat. For lack of a better term, or perhaps to preserve my feelings. It was nothing short of a miracle that I got the grades I did, along with the offers and prospects from various Ivy League universities. My therapist would deserve a huge bonus if I managed to graduate college, let alone high school, without a homicidal breakdown.

"You help in that department too, ya know." I smiled at Liem.

He shook his head as he turned down Jaime's street and parked in front of his house. He turned his head toward me and squeezed my shoulder. "I help with Ma. I'm grateful I can be there for something, after being absent when it mattered."

Sticky rice broiled in my stomach at the grief that overtook Liem's face momentarily. All things considered, Liem and my aunt were holding it together quite well for the second anniversary of my uncle's death.

Soft, warm brown eyes sparkled behind black-framed glasses as my boyfriend opened my door and beamed at me. Dark curls trickled across his forehead in disarray, and my eyes trailed the fresh ink that began at the base of his neck and traveled down his right arm. Only eighteen with a sleeve of tattoos that would thrill even the scariest of his favorite horror icons. I couldn't blame my aunt for her concern, because on the outside Jaime appeared as your typical bad boy with no possible future.

My hand warmed in his hand as he tugged me out of the car, before grabbing my backpack from the floor and tossing it over his own shoulder. Liem grinned before saluting him and taking off down the road, his moment of grief forgotten.

Jaime pulled my hand, forcing me into his arms. Not that I minded, as the pressure of his embrace immediately made oxygen come easier. Jaime had always been the one I'd run to since childhood. The only one who could make me see reason when all I wanted to do was leap off a cliff and drown myself. Roxanne was and would always be my best friend, but Jaime was the reason I got out of bed in the morning. He was the deep breath I took before every fight, before every test, and before every hard thing I ever had to encounter. When my parents had died, and the bullying had started. I had him. When the massacre happened, and we'd lost friends, neighbors, and my uncle, I had him.

Jaime nuzzled my nose, his glasses cool against my warm skin. "How ya doing today, Bills?"

"Same as any other day. It's been rough," I lied. My Aunt had glowered at me, her expression a stormy cloud of disappointment, and as always, shoved the college papers my way. After everything I had gone through, only a person completely unhinged would be thankful to a serial killer for murdering their terrible classmates and abusive uncle.

Jaime raised a brow, ignoring what he knew was a lie. The only one who saw past my facade and recognized the feelings I hid, afraid they'd overwhelm my classmates at Wraithwood High, was him.

"Get a room, you two," a voice as sweet as honey said from behind Jaime, and I smiled as Roxy gracefully walked towards us, folding her apron and putting it into her bag. With her arms raised, displaying fresh henna tattoos against her dark-almond skin, she fluffed and shook out the curls of her afro.

"Roxy." I faux-fanned myself as she came closer. "Cay n[illegible]ng!"

She twirled for me before striking a pose. "You like? Couldn't pass up celebrating our favorite holiday."

Beside me, Jaime snorted, and Roxy's stenciled eyebrow went up. "Jaime Bernard, our town has a unique history, unlike others, and I intend to interview witnesses at the upcoming Wraithwood Halloween Fest." My friends and I began walking toward the school as Roxy continued on, "Did you see the video I uploaded this morning? It's already got 10,000 views!" Roxy squealed, and I tried not to laugh at Jaime, who pretended to fall asleep mid-stride. Roxy glared at him, before a playful grin overtook her features and she threw him a mint she'd snuck out of her tote.

Jaime caught it with ease and tossed it in his mouth before dusting its sugary remnants off on his dark cargo pants. His eyes darkened as the school came into view, and a lanky guy with bleach-blond hair leaned against the brick stairwell. My steps slowed as he caught sight of me and wrinkled his nose, as if I were merely the dog shit he scraped off his shoe that morning.

Roxy and Jaime boxed me between them, and Roxy's voice got louder as if she wanted Tyler to know she couldn't give a rat's ass about his existence. Out of all the bullies Barney the Rabbit had taken from the world two years ago, I'd wished nothing more than for Tyler Marcone to have been one of them.

Tyler smirked as I got closer, and I saw his eyes flash to Jaime as he opened his big ass mouth. "Kill anyone lately, Billie dearest?"

A low blow, but a common insult he chose. So, the damage wasn't worth the roll. Were it not for my consistent therapy, I'd probably be inclined to agree with him. But Tyler was the one in denial, as his own father had been convicted of the Wraithwood murders only days after the death of his friends. My uncle had merely gotten into the crossfire;

wrong place, wrong time. Though the burn marks on my back itched at the thought of where I would be today if not for Tyler's father. Beneath my uncle's boot, a pathetic bug for him to crush.

Yup. I wish I could meet Tyler's father or send him flowers to show my gratitude for the grace he bestowed upon me, which helped me find the strength to stand beside Jaime and Roxy in the sunlight today. But that would never happen, as a year ago today Tyler's father was found hanging in his jail cell.

My shoulders eased as we entered the school and approached our lockers. Blonde-haired Lucy Graves tossed her hair back and leaned against Matthew Reese, the local football star.

Matthew smiled easily at her, his toothy grin reminding me of playground days and nights at the drive-in movies. His letterman jacket was off and cascaded around the blonde's shoulders before I could comment about the freshman gawking across the hallway.

"Luce, is that skirt from junior high? Come on." Matthew chuckled, pulling Lucy's skirt down as much as he could without revealing the opposite end. "They'll get you on dress code for sure."

Roxy laughed. "It's Halloween, Mattie. They don't give a shit today; otherwise they'd have to send the whole school home."

Jaime leaned against the locker beside mine as I put books in and took some out for first period. "They should've just called school off for today. Nobody is going to be able to think straight with the haunted house tonight."

My skin chilled. Wraithwood, Massachusetts. Population 999. Known for two things: The Wraithwood murders featuring local serial killer, Barney the Rabbit (a.k.a. Barnaby Marcone), and The Last Laugh. The most popular haunted house on this side of the continent, featured yearly at the Wraithwood Halloween Festival. Each year they did a new theme, but the one unending character they kept was that fucking clown.

As I looked over at my boyfriend, who was grinning, the locker door rattled. He knew how much I despised that clown, and yet every year he made me look into that madman's empty eyes. To say the least, Jaime was obsessed with horror. He had enough scary movie-themed shirts to wear a different one each day of October. Today was the only exception as he dawned a black shirt with *WHF* on it. The one I'd bought him at the previous year's festivities. The festival and house ran the entire month of October, and were even open for a few weeks in September. But Wraithwood was nothing if not community-oriented. So, on October 31st, they shut down the festival to anyone who wasn't with a local, or a local themselves. Kept the streets safer, they said. Not that it had mattered the night of the murders two years ago.

Lucy's fingers snapped an inch from my face, a sneer and cocked hip greeting me as I plastered a patient smile on my face for the cheer-leader. Matthew chuckled as he sprawled himself over his girlfriend's shoulders and shot me a lopsided grin. The kind of grin that had every teenager within the vicinity drooling over him and daydreaming about the sculpted abs that hid beneath his shirt.

"Earth to Billie." Lucy's high-pitched voice echoed through the halls. She winked at me as I gestured for to continue whatever she was babbling about. "I'm gonna order our tickets online during lunch, so is it a party of five again or—" Her eyes trailed lazily to Roxy with a raised brow.

Roxy rolled her eyes as she continued tapping away on her cell, most likely DMing one of her many followers. "No, I do not have a date, Lucille. And no, I do not want you to set me up with some rando. I don't have time to placate someone who thinks they want my attention."

Lucy sighed, shaking her head and she shot off a text to whoever she was planning to set Roxy up with. Matthew pursed his lips. "We'll nail down numbers at lunch, babes. Let's go before we miss the second bell."

The group dispersed as Jaime grabbed the books from my arms and laid them atop his own. "Time for class, Bills."

I reached up on tip-toes, placing a kiss on his cheek. "I love you."

"I know." He winked, guiding me through the crowd of students toward our first class.

Two

Billie

As Roxy and I went through the Wraithwood Halloween Festival gates, the air was thick with the smell of hay and cheap makeup, while The Last Laugh watched me menacingly from the distant trees. Hay bales and Jack-o'-lanterns lined the walkways between vendors and food booths that were selling anything from candy corn necklaces to candy apples and face painting services. Innocent and festive compared to the cartoonishly large bunny head that formed the entrance to Massachusetts' most renowned haunted attraction.

Roxy made a tsking sound as we approached the line of locals already forming in its queue line. "I know all the victims were assholes, but isn't it poor taste to make Barney into such a celebrated town figure?" Her eyes widened as she turned toward me, forgetting whose company she was in. "Sorry, Billie. Not that your uncle was an ass!"

I smiled reassuringly, holding within the bitter taste of the public's feelings toward my uncle. It was always a wonder to me that someone so rotten inside could hide it beneath a sugar-coated smile and a respectable business card.

Our friends waved us over, already halfway up the line, holding our spots. Jaime's eyes softened as I came to his side instantly, their soft warm depths an anchor to my jaded heart. As he wrapped his arm around me, Matthew and Lucy argued about something incoherently. A muscular guy, about the same size as Matt, emerged beside them with a sigh and an apologetic smile. His tanned skin glowed, and something about the way he carried himself was familiar.

"Hey, sorry to insert myself into your group for the night. I'm Jacob Doe." He scratched the back of his cropped hair. "Matt's cousin."

Jaime held a hand out to him. "Good to have ya, man. Puts another body between us and the creeps inside."

Jacob shook his hand with an expression of apprehension. "Not sure if that makes me feel better or worse about going into this house."

"First time?" Jaime asked, and the two were off on a conversation about the different horror attractions they'd been to.

Roxy crossed her arms and glared as Lucy came to stand beside us. "Did you do this? Bring this guy to set him up with me, Luce?"

Lucy gawked. "Of course not. I didn't even want him here, but Matthew insisted."

Roxy pursed her lips at the blonde, not believing her. The ground shifted beneath me as I went flying into Jaime's shoulder, and Roxy fell and was shoved the other way into Lucy. Blond locks flashed across my vision as Tyler Marcone shoved his way between us toward his friends. He smirked at me over his shoulder, a wicked gleam in his blue eyes. Roxy began cursing up a storm under her breath, collecting purse and the things that had spilled from it during the collision.

"Well, that guy is a prick," Jacob assessed. "Friend of yours?"

Matthew scoffed, "That's local legend Tyler Marcone. Don't mind him—he's just living up to the reputation of his father."

Jacob's eyes widened as he continued to watch Tyler mess around with his friends, his eyes flickering to me occasionally. The line shifted closer as Jacob asked, "Rabbit Jr., huh?"

"Not likely." Jaime snorted beside me.

The front hostess for the house came into view, scanning and punching tickets in a black-and-white clown costume—complete with black pom-poms and face paint. Another drop of innocence to a place dripping with ill intent. And another reminder that I was about to come face-to-face with none other than Ludwig the Clown again. Though they hired new actors yearly, something about Ludwig was different. His eyes never changed, always that eerie and soulless black.

Jaime rubbed a hand up and down my arm as the hostess took our tickets and ushered us through the rabbit-shaped doorway. Music crept in from overhead, a mix of ominous dripping water sounds and circus music. Lucy tucked herself into Matthew's side, almost shoving her entire face into his armpit. I wasn't sure how she'd be able to see anything. Roxy and Jacob brought up the rear, murmuring about the house's intricate design, with Roxy also remarking on the town's investment in such an unappealing project.

The dark hallway began to shift as the lights flashed in a strobe-fashion above our heads. The walls flashed to black-and-white stripes. I screamed when something crashed, and a masked person appeared from the shadows; they were wearing torn clothing and holding a wound on their chest, which had fake blood flowing down it. They screamed again before retreating back into their hiding place for the next group.

On and on we continued into the house, jumping every time some ghoul, zombie, or clown popped out from the shadows. Mist began to spray down on us as we changed hallways and passed through a doorway, the red light casting the illusion of blood raining down.

The room transformed into a dilapidated circus tent, and my skin tingled. It featured a stage and bleachers stained with fake blood and corpses that looked as if they were twitching unnaturally. A singular spotlight spun around the zoom until it landed on a shimmering red curtain. My breath hitched, waiting.

A deep chuckle bounced around us, coming from different speakers hidden within the gore of his circus tent. The curtain moved, and before anyone could react, a metallic scraping and the sound of electricity filled the air, as six figures appeared wielding chainsaws that shattered my eardrums. I covered my ears quickly, cringing away from the scare actors and into Jaime's chest. I cursed under my breath, kicking myself for not taking the earplugs that lay on my dresser at home.

The group scrambled around the room as we attempted to outrun our faux attackers, hands grappling the walls for the hidden exit that shifted each year. A chill from my damp clothes ran down my spine as Jaime tapped against the curtain and a door opened beyond it.

Prepared to leave the chaotic scene, I turned to address the others, and found myself staring at the one person I hoped to avoid. The only horror figure that made me never want to run into an actual psychotic killer clown.

I looked up to see a grin of yellow teeth, which were wet with saliva that dripped to the ground. Red stitching, pom-poms, and a suspiciously dirty neck collar sent me spiraling as his exhales heated my face. A quick flash of my parents' funeral crept across my vision as the scent of embalming fluid and dead roses burned my nostrils.

His sharpened grin widened as my breathing became erratic, and his hand slowly raised to my ear before he squeezed the balloon on his metal horn.

Snap.

I questioned whether I would feel less fear towards the minimum-wage scare actor and more fear towards the sadistic serial killer in a silly pink hoodie with rabbit ears if my brain functioned like a typical person's. Or was I doomed to be seven shades of fucked up in a straitjacket somewhere?

Ludwig towered over me, appearing to grow taller by the second. Perhaps it was because my knees struck the ground, or the concussion I was bound to get after my head hit the hard floor and I saw stars while he laughed like a madman.

Billie

Soft music danced across my skin as I shifted to my other side and smacked my aching head against a car window. Cursing, I rubbed at the lump I couldn't find and stopped at the water bottle being handed to me from across Jaime's truck.

Streetlights illuminated the packed cul-de-sac in front of the Reese residence, teenagers covering Matthew's lawn and the lawns of his neighbors. My head objected as I grabbed the bottle from Jaime's hand, and I met his cautious gaze. I smiled as he worried his bottom lip between his teeth.

"I'm okay," I croaked. "How bad was it?"

Jaime's eyes darkened. "Tyler Marcone showed up as you passed out, got the whole thing on tape."

I groaned, leaning my head back against the headrest. "Sometimes I wish that guy would just move away."

"Or jump off a cliff." Jaime nodded, gazing out at the teenagers who were either high, drunk, or pondering their life choices. "I'll take care of him, Bills. Don't worry."

I reached a hand out to ruffle his dark curls. "No, it's fine. I don't want you to get hurt, or in trouble. We'll be out of this wasteland of a town soon enough."

Jaime grinned, turning toward me with a raised brow. "Make a decision yet?"

I swallowed, my throat coarse as sandpaper though I'd just chugged a bottle of water.

Harvard or Yale. Crimson or yellow. Doctor or lawyer.

"Cornell University," I whispered, something in my chest easing at telling someone my choice. *My* choice.

Jaime's head snapped to mine, his eyes lighting up as he grabbed both my cheeks and pressed his lips to mine fervently. Pulling back, he laughed; the sound full of pride and relief.

Cornell University was the farthest Ivy League school on the map from Wraithwood, Massachusetts. But that wasn't the main reason I chose them, oddly enough.

"That's only a two-hour drive from UR!" Jaime beamed, and everything within me solidified that I'd made the right call. His lips smashed into mine again, the air in the truck turning to steam around us as I crawled over the center console and straddled him. His hands were cool as they whispered beneath the seam of my shirt, and my breath quickened as he—

"Bills," he hissed, his voice wanton and full of lust .

Bang. Bang. Bang.

"Hey, lovebirds," Roxy yelled through the glass. "Hasn't Tyler gotten enough footage tonight? I don't think we need to add porno to his ammunition."

Jaime groaned, whispering, "Fuck me, Roxanne."

Roxy's grin turned feral. "You wish, Bernard. You wish."

Jaime sighed as I giggled and pressed the button to push down the truck's window.

"What is it, Rox?" I asked, raising a brow.

Roxy smiled sweetly. "So . . . we need to go back to The Last Laugh." Matthew, Lucy, and Jacob snuck up behind her with suspicious grins and dark clothing. "I think I dropped my phone when Tyler bumped into us."

I glanced at the clock on Jaime's radio. "You're telling me you made it until after two in the morning without your phone, and you just noticed?"

Roxy bit her lip and shrugged. "Girl, I was distracted." She winked at a tall ginger girl that passed and waggled her fingers at her.

"Cay n▯ng, Roxy!" I giggled.

Pushing myself off Jaime's lap, he groaned again as I took the passenger seat beside him. He gritted his teeth as blond hair flashed across the front of his truck.

"Yo, Barney Jr.!" Jaime yelled from the window, which made Tyler Marcone halt and scowl at my boyfriend. "Since you're at fault for her losing the phone, you should help us look for it."

Tyler snorted, turning to leave us but running into Jacob and Matthew with crossed arms. He grimaced, his small, lanky form humorous next to the two fit athletes that towered over him. He cursed, searching for sight of his friends but finding none.

"Let's go, Marcone." Matthew's usually boyish grin was gone, and replaced by something older and stoic.

"Jaime, you don't have to do this. Just leave him," I whispered.

Roxy frowned. "No, he's right. We can't let him keep walking all over us."

Us. Not just me. *Us.*

I breathed out through my nose, relaxing into the seat and making myself smaller as Tyler, Roxy, Matt, Lucy, and Jacob crammed themselves into either the cab's back seat or the truck bed. After all, on Halloween nobody really cared in a town this small if we were wearing our seat belts. Just like nobody seemed to care about the teenagers shotgunning beer in Matthew Reese's backyard . . . two years after a mass murder of teenagers. I hated this town.

Three

I began to question my friends' true nature and their criminal expertise after I hopped some fences, evaded a cop, and broke a lock.

I also wondered if my friends were really my friends as I found myself back inside a pitch-black hallway somewhere in The Last Laugh.

Tyler groaned as he shone a flashlight on one of the fake corpses. "I didn't even hit you guys in here. We were in line. Why are we looking in here?"

"Because"—Lucy clung to Matt's side—"it wasn't out there, asshat. Maybe she dropped it when we carried Billie out."

Heat rose up my neck and face as Tyler began laughing obnoxiously. "You fell out like a limp noodle!"

Jaime's teeth clicked beside me, his eyes darkening into slits. "Keep laughing, Marcone. I fucking dare you."

Tyler's lips thinned as he held in the laughter that made nails on the chalkboard board sound soothing.

Jacob shone a flashlight at us from up ahead. "Here's the tent where she fell. Come on."

The group scurried into the tent, shining their lights on the abandoned circus from hell. Jaime kissed my forehead tenderly as he passed by, hopping onto the empty stage and peeking behind the curtain, as if Roxy had somehow launched her phone back there.

"Not back here!" he hollered, stepping fully behind the curtains and out of sight. My nerves lit aflame at his absence.

"Not over here either," Matthew called from the bleachers.

Roxy began pacing in front of me. "Shit. Where could it be?"

"Maybe lost and found picked it up." Tyler shrugged, "nothing we can do now but go home." He started toward the entrance where I stood, not wanting to enter Ludwig's domain again.

Suddenly appearing on the stage, Jaime whistled. "Don't even think about it, Tyler, we—"

The lights began to flicker above us, and the speakers blared to life with a screeching version of the earlier circus music. My heart began to slam against my chest as we all ran for the middle of the room and clung to each other.

"Jaime!" I yelled, sweat breaking across my back.

A cool hand touched my back and guided me out of the arms of Tyler Marcone, who wiped his hands on his shirt after realizing who I was. Jaime squeezed my hand. "I've got you. The security guy probably turned the power on. We need to get out of here."

"You don't have to tell me twice. Let's go!" Lucy whisper-shouted, running for the doorway.

Matt grabbed her arm as soon as she reached the doorway and blocked it with his body. "We should go the other way—the guard probably came through the main entrance."

Jacob nodded, shining his flashlight toward the secret doorway from earlier. "You're right. Come on, guys."

A scream pierced the air as we all started to move toward the hidden door. Jaime cursed under his breath, his hand tightening around my arm as everyone began screaming.

As his eyes rolled back, Matthew's knees gave way, and in a drawn-out motion, he hit the ground on his side, an axe decorated with patriotic colors embedded in his forehead. Blood splattered across Lucy's gaping face, coating her pale pink dress as her knees wobbled.

Jacob cursed, pulling her back and away from the leering clown. Ludwig stepped into the tent, placing a blood-coated clown boot over Matthew's head to yank out the axe. Lucy screamed again as Jacob lifted her into his arms, and we all went running for the hidden doorway.

No thoughts formed in my head, no emotion toward my fallen friend. The only thing I could do was run; my head began to swim from forgetting to breathe. Up ahead, the hallway split like a fork in the road, and Jacob hauled Lucy to the right with Roxy close behind. The music got louder, almost making it unbearable to hear anything but it.

Jaime tried to yell something, but it blended with the music. Tyler paused beside us, looking over his shoulder to see if Ludwig had followed us. Jaime yanked my hand and tugged me toward the left hallway, away from Roxy and the others. Tyler tried to say something, but shook his head at the volume and followed us.

The darkened hallway and striped walls shifted into a room of glass and mirrors. My eyes began to blur as I clung to Jaime's back, and somewhere in the house a scream pounded across the maze. Tyler raised a shaking hand, pointing toward something in the distance. Jaime and I held our breaths as we leaned over and looked through the glass in front of him. At the far end of the maze, Jacob held Roxy behind him as they slowly backed away from another window coated in blood. Tears slipped down Roxy's face, stuck in a silent scream before Jacob grabbed her hand and they disappeared out of the maze and into the next darkened hallway.

From the blood-coated window, a gloved finger began to smear letters in the sticky red liquid.

COME OUT AND PLAY, BARNEY!

Ludwig wiggled his fingers above the blood before smearing a gaping hole in the fluid and sauntering off in the same direction Jacob and Roxy had gone. Beyond the gaping hole he had left was a blonde girl twitching on the wall. The same axe that had killed Matthew was lodged in her cheek, pinning her to the wall.

"Lucy." I choked on a sob.

Jaime's hand squeezed mine, and resolution turned his brown eyes to steel.

"Let's go back the other way," Tyler said, grabbing my other hand and pulling me from Jaime's grasp.

"Take your filthy hand off her, you prick." Jaime's voice was different, dark and full of rage. Tyler dropped my hand with a rolled eye.

"Whatever, man. Let's just go." He turned back the way we had come.

"We can't leave Roxy and Jacob," I whispered.

Tyler slammed a fist against one of the mirrors. "I don't give a fuck about them, and neither should you. We go after them, and we're all dead."

Jaime's voice was ice cold. "Leave us, and you're dead, Marcone."

Did Jaime suspect Tyler of something? Did he really think he could be behind Ludwig when he was standing right here? Was Tyler really going to be the next Barney Jr. after all?

Thought after thought flung through my mind, distracting me as Jaime stormed past me, squeezing my shoulder as he went.

"What did you say, Jaime?" I blinked, suddenly standing alone as I watched Jaime disappear back into the forked hallway . . . to follow Tyler.

Shit.

I glanced either way. Did I follow Jaime to keep him from fighting Tyler, or did I go after Jacob and Roxy? My gut told me I shouldn't go the same direction that Ludwig had gone, at least not alone. I whipped my head back toward the way Jaime had gone and started back through that side of the maze.

A blood-curdling scream pierced the air behind me, and I cursed. Changing direction, I hauled ass through the maze and toward the feminine voice. Roxy needed me.

The maze shifted into another dark hallway, and whimpering sounded from my right. The room opened into what appeared to be a jail cell, complete with a silver sink, dirty metal toilet, and bunk beds attached to the wall.

Roxy sat on the floor, guarding an arm to her chest. She looked up quickly as I entered, eyes wide and ready to scream again. Her shoulders eased when she recognized me, and I dropped to my knees before her to examine the wound. It wasn't bad, just a couple of cuts and some bruising.

"I ran into a wall." Roxy laughed over a hiccup. I nodded, ripping off the bottom of my shirt to wrap around her arm. "I wish I had my phone."

"Why?" I asked.

"This would so go viral on my channel." She laughed, grimacing as I tightened the fabric around her arm.

I giggled, shaking my head. "Roxy Rambles with an eyewitness account."

She winked. "You know it."

My numb smile turned into a frown. "Where's Jacob?" Something in my stomach chilled at the look she gave me.

"Billie, ru—" She was cut off as something flew through the air past my ear. Three colorful balls the size of grapefruits smashed into Roxy's chest, cheek, and forehead. Blood flew from Roxy's mouth as her head lulled, and her eyes closed.

"No, no, no!" I cried. "Roxy, please, no! Wake up!"

Crunching sounded behind me as something stepped into the room, and anger boiled within me as I turned and stood in front of Ludwig. He towered over me with a leering smile, his teeth sharp and coated in blood. His hand rose slowly, and I closed my eyes to prepare for the inevitable hit.

Honk.

I blinked open my eyes and saw that fucking balloon horn by my ear. I ground my teeth, grabbing the horn from him and launching it at his stupid makeup-covered face. Ludwig's smile fell. The lights flickered. And I ran through the darkness, leaving Roxy in the jail cell with him. All I had left was Jaime. I needed to get to Jaime.

"JAIME!" I yelled through the dark hall, "JAIME!" His name ended in a sob.

The hallway opened into another room, one with pews lining either side of the aisle. White linen brushed over each pew and waved ominously in the breeze. A door opened on either side of the front of the room, and footsteps fell before two forms barreled in.

Tyler and Jacob, both coated in blood and looking worse for wear, launched themselves at me. Both talking a mile a minute, with no room for comprehension. Jacob yelled, shoving Tyler so that he'd stop talking for a moment.

"He killed him!" Jacob shrieked, "He killed Jaime! I saw him!"

My heart stopped, time slowed as I turned my chin toward Tyler, who was arguing something with Jacob. The music played, but I couldn't hear it. Couldn't comprehend a world without Jaime in it.

Tyler's fearful eyes met mine, a moment of apprehension making him back away from me. A smile tugged at my cheeks. "You're dead."

Tyler's eyes widened. "I didn't do it, Jaime! It was Jacob, not me! Jacob did it!"

I moved closer to Tyler, ready to punch him repeatedly in the chest, but I wasn't tall enough to hit his face with as much power as I intended.

Jacob coughed, and I spun around to witness blood spilling from his mouth while he clutched at the axe embedded in his abdomen.

Ludwig stomped into the room, and something within me burned to kill this stupid clown. I didn't know who had taken Jaime from me, but it was this stupid motherfucker in a red wig's fault.

"Are you nuts?" Tyler yelled, grabbing my arm and dragging me away from the looming clown and down one of the side halls. A door was ajar halfway down the hall, and he dragged me through it and into the backstage area where cleaning supplies and scare actor costumes hung on hangers.

The door exploded open behind us, Ludwig closing in on us with his axe back in hand and his grin twitching with anger. Tyler and I both began to back away from him, wondering which target the clown would choose this time. My foot caught on something with wheels, and I went sprawling, my head smacking against the wall and sending stars in front of my vision for the second time tonight. I cursed the skateboard beneath my foot. What did they need that for in a haunted house?

Ludwig charged toward me, axe raised and ready to chop me into pieces. Ludwig's arms froze midair as something bounced off the back of his head. He blinked, turning slowly toward his assailant, and my breath hitched.

Leaning against the doorway with a foot propped against the frame was a man I'd only seen in pictures. Black cargo pants, a pink hoodie with rabbit ears, and a white-and-pink mask with razor-sharp teeth. Lazily he stepped into the room, bouncing one of Ludwig's juggling balls in his hand. Ludwig charged him, axe in the air as Barney popped his neck and launched the ball at Ludwig's head.

The clown froze, staring down at the ball and began to laugh. The sound echoed off the walls as Tyler dropped to my side and began digging through my pockets.

"What the hell are you doing?" I asked.

"I need your phone, so I can prove it wasn't my dad." He pulled my phone from my pocket and shoved me back to the floor as he stood to record to oncoming fight. Gun shots burned my ear, and smoke glistened the air as Tyler dropped to his knees with two bullet holes in his forehead.

My head swam and Barney turned his gun back toward the clown and emptied the barrel. The clown's legs wobbled, and he fell to one knee. Changing course, Ludwig reinforced his grip on the axe and launched it toward me. Yelping I went prone on the floor, the axe flying precariously close over me before sticking itself into the wall behind me.

Stars danced as I sat up quickly, and Barney the Rabbit kneeled before me with an outstretched hand. I blinked, scanning the empty space behind him. Ludwig was gone, slipped out of the room or vanished into thin air.

The exit sign above a nearby door suddenly eased on with a low hum. I turned my attention back toward the serial killer and my vision blurred, and only got my hand partly to him as my body went limp.

Barney caught me in his arms and gazed down at me and I laughed, the sound sounding further away.

"I got ya, Bills," the rabbit spoke, his voice soothing and familiar as he removed his mask. Soft, brown eyes met mine behind black-rimmed glasses.

My heart skipped before darkness called.

Epilogue

"We Were Wrong About Barney the Rabbit – The Last Laugh Wasn't a Joke"

Follow-up to: "Wraithwood Massacre: Two Years Later–Trick or Terror?"

[INTRO—"Roxy Rambles" YouTube Channel: News Segment Voiceover]

Cue ominous synth music.

Title Card: "The Last Laugh: What Really Happened Inside Wraithwood's Haunted House?"

[FADE IN – NIGHT. ROXY is standing in front of the charred ruins of what was once the haunted house. Her tone is grave. Smoke still rises faintly in the background. Police tape flutters in the wind.]

ROXY (on camera):

"Hey, everyone. Roxy here. If you've been following my channel, you already know what I reported yesterday—Wraithwood's bold attempt to reclaim its haunted history with a Halloween festival and a so-called 'funhouse' called The Last Laugh."

[FLASHBACK CLIPS – B-roll from previous video: locals setting up decorations, laughing teens in bunny ears, the creepy cartoon rabbit facade.]

ROXY (V.O.):

"We thought it was tasteless. We thought it was in poor taste. But what we didn't think—what none of us wanted to believe—was that history would repeat itself. Only this time . . . worse."

[HARD CUT – Black screen with glitch effect. Then: cell phone footage of sirens, screaming, the haunted house *engulfed in flames*. Police shouting. Chaos.]

[CUT TO: ROXY BACK ON CAMERA – visibly shaken, now seated indoors, wrapped in a blanket, face lit only by a flickering screen.]

ROXY:

"I was inside. Along with Jaime Bernard, Billie Nguyen . . . and four others who didn't make it out. The haunted house was supposed to be fake. Animatronics. Actors. Mirrors."

"But the screams? Those were real."

[INSERT – Security footage still: grainy silhouette of a tall, lanky clown with blood dripping down his white gloves. Then: a figure in the background wearing a pink hoodie with rabbit ears, barely visible in the shadows.]

ROXY (V.O.):

"Two figures. One we recognized from urban legend: Ludwig the Clown. A forgotten nightmare from the 1989 Carnival Slaughter. Presumed dead. The other? A name Wraithwood *knows all too well*—Barney the Rabbit."

[CUT TO: FILE FOOTAGE – Barney's mugshot. Then a still of his corpse in a body bag, zipped shut. Then: a clip of Roxy holding the rabbit-ear jacket.]

ROXY:

"I reported his death one year ago. I stood by the tape, said the words: *'Suicide in custody. Case closed.'* But now? I'm not so sure he ever left."

[FLASH FRAME – Hazy, slo-mo phone footage of someone screaming "RUN!" and a giant cartoonish rabbit mask crashing through plywood walls.]

[ROXY BACK ON CAMERA – Her voice lowers.]

ROXY:

"We don't know what brought them back. We don't know if they *are* back. Maybe it's a copycat. Maybe it's possession. Maybe it's something else entirely."

"A cult. A curse. Or the town itself, hungry for tragedy."

[INSERT – MAP OF WRAITHWOOD with glowing red markers: 1989 Carnival, 2023 Marcone Residence, 2025 Last Laugh grounds.]

ROXY (V.O.):

"These events aren't random. They're ritualistic. Three locations. Three bloodbaths. All connected by one recurring image: the pink-eared jacket, left behind like a calling card. Clean. Untouched. And now . . . missing."

[CUT TO: BILLIE (recorded video message, tear-streaked, looking over her shoulder)]

BILLIE (panicked):

"Roxy, the jacket—it was gone this morning. I swear I zipped it in a bag. It's not—wait, someone's at my door—"

[CLIP ABRUPTLY CUTS OFF.]

[ROXY – now lit by a single candle, her expression cold.]

ROXY:

"We tried to tell the story before it wrote itself again in blood. But now, we're part of it."

"This is no longer just a town legend. This is a living nightmare. And it's *not over.*"

[DRAMATIC PAUSE – then: Roxy leans in toward the camera.]

ROXY:

"I survived. Jaime survived. Billie . . . maybe."

"But if you're watching this—if you see anyone wearing the ears, or hear that awful laugh in the dark—run. Don't look back."

"Because in Wraithwood, the joke's not on the victims."

"It's on the survivors."

[OUTRO – Static buzz. Then the familiar creepy giggle from earlier videos, now warped and slowed. Text fades in:]

THE LAST LAUGH WAS JUST THE BEGINNING.

[END OF SEGMENT: LIKE | COMMENT | SUBSCRIBE | #BarneyIsBack #LudwigLives #WraithwoodWhispers #RoxyRambles]

About the Author

Brandee Paschall is a paranormal and fantasy romance author based in West Tennessee. With a passion for the mystical and the magical, she brings to life captivating tales that blend heart-pounding romance with supernatural intrigue. Brandee is the author of *The Keepers of the Sacred* series, a gripping paranormal romance saga that invites readers into a world of ancient secrets, powerful beings, and unforgettable love stories. When she's not writing, Brandee enjoys exploring folklore, connecting with fellow book lovers, and finding inspiration in the enchanting beauty of the South.

Follow Brandee to learn more: linktr.ee/brandee_paschall_books

The Forgotten Doll

by E.R. Sano

Content/Trigger Warnings

- Implied abuse

- Childhood bullying/violence

One

Sunrays sliced through the windowpane and landed on the short coffee table, illuminating the room and chasing away most of the shadows. The heat, caused by the magnification of the glass, intensified on the grain, warming the table and the room above that of the temperature outside. Yet the glass itself somehow felt cool, as though the light never touched it. Under the bare table, just out of the reach of the sun's eager fingers, lay a doll. Its lifelike eyes watched the crows glide through the air and land on the treetops, their black silken bodies disappearing beneath the green leaves. The doll remained motionless, neither wondering nor caring where the squawking birds had gone. Though once capable, it didn't notice the difference the sun's influence made on the temperature of the room. It simply remained, hoping it would not be alone for long; that *she* would come back for it.

The rest of the house lay empty; bare as the day its construction had been completed. Not long after the furniture had been removed, painters transformed the canary and violet walls into blinding white. Men in overalls replaced the brown kitchen and bathroom cabinets with new white ones, and even a plain white banister replaced the black, ornate one which originally accompanied the stairs. Where once the house showed signs of life, it now felt dead and forgotten. The wooden floors had been ripped out and replaced by a pale, scratchy carpet, which no longer allowed the footsteps of inhabitants to echo along the hallways. No creaks or moans from aging wood gave away the presence of movement, somehow making the lack thereof even more deafening. The house remained still. Every trace of its previous tenants erased, except for the wooden table and the forgotten doll. Still, the house waited in eager anticipation for life to return to it, for people to fill its rooms with furniture and sound. At least, that is what the doll assumed. In the few moments it spared to think about the shelter, the doll imagined that the house felt quite lonely, which made the structure relatable in some small way. They both watched. They both waited.

The sun slid across the floor, coming ever closer to the doll but never touching its delicate white porcelain skin. Outside, life continued. Squirrels scurried up and down the brown trunks of the trees, only to be chased away by fierce crows. The bickering between the two species could be heard in a series of shrill chirps and clicks. The noise only ceased when the squirrels found refuge in holes and bushes; the crows returning to their nests in a victory they neither celebrated nor understood. Waiting in the tall grass, neighborhood tabby cats with fur the color of orange sherbet, flicked their tails in anticipation as the birds neared the ground. All the while, the sun continued its slow route across the sky, unaware of the activity below. The doll watched in silent agony.

Behind the glass and wood, the air inside the house remained still, the sounds that reached the doll's ears all coming from the outside. No buzz of tiny insect wings, no faint tap of spider legs. In the darkest corners of the house, no webs could be found. As though the house and its precious few occupants had been cut off from life itself. Seasons changed; time passed.

As another sunrise began to peak over the horizon, the click of a key within a lock accompanied by the deadbolt sliding away from the doorframe filled the stale air. Metal scraped against the remaining entryway wood, and all at once the house filled with life. For a moment, the doll allowed itself to hope, to believe an end had come to its waiting. Its optimism shattered when the thud of work boots dulled on the thick carpet. *She* would never walk in such a heavy-handed manner.

Unable to turn its head, it relied on the reflection of the glass to see and felt disappointed to find the surface only projected back an empty hallway. Movement flickered between rooms, but the people did not stay long enough for the doll to discern their features. A deep, throaty sound resonated in the empty space, and the footsteps retreated out the door onto the concrete walkway. The deadbolt slid back into place, leaving the house still once again.

By the time the sun moved into its afternoon position, and its light spread as deeply into the living room as it would ever dare tread, the door opened again. Many more soft padding footsteps entered the house. A woman immediately set about opening the windows to chase out the stuffy air. In the reflection, the doll could see men carrying large wooden objects to different rooms and up the stairs. They brought in pine furniture only. No one entered the living room, but the woman looked down on the spacious area from the loft, scrutinizing the coffee table. Her sharply sweet voice penetrated the silence as she pointed and motioned for the table to be removed. Watching the reflection, the doll feared it would share the same fate, but instead the woman slithered away from the railing and continued to explore the higher level.

Men entered the living room, lifting the dark-brown table and removing it from the house. No one seemed to notice the doll lying there, though their feet navigated around it with little hesitation. Night began to fall once again, and the people left. Outside, the dark creatures hunted, unaware of the change which had taken place during the day. For the first time in many moonrises, the doll could hear the tiny taps of insect feet on the walls and glass. The noise began slowly at first, timid and uncertain. The shrinking sliver of moon gave less light to see by than on previous nights, but it did not affect what the doll could see. It wished to blink, to block out the sights, but could only stare at its own dead, life-mimicking gaze.

The dark sky slowly morphed into a variety of red, orange, and blue colors as the sun rose once again over a horizon the doll could not see. This time the people entered quickly, prepared with boxes already in their hands, each one the same two-by-two cube of brown cardboard. They began to fill the living room and other areas of the house. Covered feet continued to pass by the doll, but their owners appeared to be oblivious to its presence. It longed for someone to pick it up, to hold it, but it remained unfulfilled.

Anger and confusion rose up from the depths of the doll's awareness. How could they pass over it like that? Could they not see it lying there so peacefully on the white carpet? Could they not understand its need to be touched, to be moved from the awful position it had been stuck in for so long? It thought that the blue dress and long, neatly styled black hair should have been more than enough to catch their attention. Yet still they passed over the doll as though it didn't exist, their feet skirting it as though hitting an invisible barrier.

Vibrations in the floor drew the doll out of its thoughts as a darker shadow covered it. In the reflection, it could see a pine-wood couch with white cushions being placed over the spot where it lay, effectively erasing the doll from sight. The crisp, tangy scent of a pine tree, as though the couch itself had just recently come from the forest, filled the doll's nose. The sun reached the side of the couch and warmed the wood, leaving the doll in shadow. Its glistening eyes viewed the outside through the gaps between the side legs.

Movement around the house blended into a single sound of life. No longer did the people leave when the sun set to the rising moon, though the doll now only heard two sets of footsteps rather than dozens. Instead, the new occupants retreated upstairs until the bright day broke through the eerie night. The house seemed to sigh in satisfaction, its purpose once again fulfilled. The doll continued to watch the vibrancy of the outside; the changes between night and day until they, too, blended together and became as indiscernible as the sounds. From the blur of color, visions from its past emerged.

Two

Like so many of its kind, the doll had been assembled by dirty, long-faced people who grumbled under their breath about low wages and long hours. None of them spoke to each other, each one focused intently on their work. At any given time, fifteen craftsmen worked on the dolls. Piece by piece, they molded eerily human body parts and placed them carefully together, taking their time to ensure each detail met facility standards. Despite holding no enthusiasm for their jobs, the dollmakers handled the delicate material as they would a precious keepsake. They shaped, painted, and fired each doll with care, as though their lives depended on the outcome of each creation.

It did.

The doll felt nothing, saw nothing, heard nothing, until its maker secured its eyes into the sockets of its head. Awareness suddenly bloomed as it gazed out into the world, meeting the stare of a disgruntled man who visibly shivered. Involuntarily, he pulled away from the doll, nearly knocking it from the table. With a shaky breath, he looked around nervously before pulling his seat toward his work once again. The doll watched him with curiosity. It wished to speak but somehow knew it couldn't. In this den of silence, a voice would never be allowed. Yet the doll could hear the occasional low murmurs; could understand their words. It could smell the sweat, the decay, and the burning materials.

In fourteen identical stations around them, other men worked on various stages of dolls, creating creatures of unique and beautiful human replication. Skilled hands molded arms, legs, torsos, and heads of varying shapes and sizes. Behind each station, through a window in the wall, women worked at desks designing and creating outfits for each of the dolls, tailoring them to the wishes of their dollmakers. The space between each station discouraged any interaction—there would be no whispering among staff here—but also enabled them to keep an eye on each other. Occasionally, one of the men would walk to their seamstress' station, hand her a sheet of paper, and point at various items within her cubical. As far as the doll could tell, no verbal exchange occurred. The dollmaker would nod his satisfaction at the end of it and return to his work.

The doll looked at the woman sitting behind its maker and wondered what kind of outfit would be chosen to cover its forming body. The maker's eyebrows drew together in concern, and he glanced at his seamstress, as though following the doll's gaze even though its physical eyes could not move. His mouth drew into a further frown, but a moment later he shook his head and returned his attention to shaping an arm.

Movement drew the doll's attention to a dollmaker making his way across the vast room to a man sitting behind a large desk. The worker carefully handed over a doll, using both hands to hold the delicate creature. A strange mixture of longing, sadness, and fear displayed on his face. The other man inspected his creation while the dollmaker stood watching, hands wringing nervously in front of him. As the inspector turned the object in his hands, one of the shoes fell off its little foot. Everyone in the factory froze, all attention pulled to the inspector's table.

"Please, I can fix it."

As the dollmaker reached out his hand to retrieve his creation, the inspector discarded the doll carelessly into the bin next to his desk. His eyes never left the man in front of him. The sound of shattering clay broke the silence. Still, no one moved. The doll watched in fascination while the offending dollmaker collapsed to his knees, tears streaming down his face as he visibly shook. From somewhere deep inside the building, a door slammed. Footsteps echoed down the hallway behind the inspector's desk, growing steadily closer until a short, beefy man with a red face appeared.

"What's going on here?" the new arrival demanded, pointing to the shattered doll in the bin. Collectively, the dollmakers and seamstresses held their breath.

"This oaf failed inspection, sir."

"Please . . . He didn't give me a chance—"

"Did you approach this table with a faulty product?"

"It . . . it was just the shoe," the dollmaker stammered.

"You know the rules, do you not?"

The dollmaker nodded feebly, his eyes downcast. Without another word, the stout man signaled to one of the armed men patrolling the factory. Together, the three of them disappeared back down the hallway. The doll gazed at the bin that contained its fallen comrade and briefly wondered if it also held sentience and felt pain as its newly crafted body broke apart. It looked to its own maker, who, like the others, had begun his work once again.

Please get me right.

Its maker eyed it wearily but didn't stop his work. Three sharp, loud bursts disrupted the air, the sound reverberating down the hallway. The others barely flinched, eyes drawing tight but otherwise not reacting. One or two moved their lips—a silent prayer?—but uttered no sound. A few moments later, the man with the gun reappeared and resumed his patrol.

Three

Behind the doll's maker and to the left of his seamstress, stood a large door with the words *Keep Out* printed in bloodred lettering. The men patrolling the factory took several steps toward the center of the room while passing this door, giving it as much berth as they could without being too obvious. Occasionally, a dollmaker would glance up and eye the door nervously for a moment before resuming the task at hand. Those working on the heads of their dolls glanced up more frequently than the others, though the doll's maker did not glance up at all.

What is in there? the doll wondered, appraising the side of the door it could see. *What makes these men so afraid?*

To the right, a dollmaker removed a piece of porcelain from the kiln next to his desk. Inspecting it carefully, he turned the unpainted and eyeless head over in his hands, checking every square inch. Once satisfied, he fitted it to the body, pausing only once to glance at the forbidding door, sitting up straight and admiring his work. The moment his hands fell from the half-created doll, the shriek of unoiled hinges cut through the room.

Beyond the open door stood only darkness. From the shadows, a cloaked figure emerged, wheeling a single-tray cart with a set of brown eyes, and the doll felt a shudder go through the room. The figure had no discernible features, the hood of the cloak covering the face underneath in shadows as deep and dark as what it had stepped from. Bone-white hands grasped the handle of the cart.

"No one knows where they come from," the maker muttered under his breath, barely audible enough for the doll to hear him. It didn't know if he spoke to it or himself. "But each time we're ready for them, the eyes just appear. Most fill us with sadness, but sometimes they fill us with dread or fear. We have many theories, but all we really know is, there's something not right about the eyes."

The figure pushed the cart to the dollmaker with the freshly completed head and lifted the cushion holding the eyes. The dollmaker hesitated for a moment, seeming to want neither to touch the skeletal hands nor the eyes, before grasping each eye gently between a finger and thumb. His face filled with sadness, and he carefully turned away from the cart bearer and back to his desk. The other returned from whence it came, and the door swung quietly shut, concealing the darkness beyond once more. The soft whoosh of air leaving lungs floated gently through the factory as the collective breath released.

The maker returned to his work, now shaping a second leg. The other limbs lay on the table, waiting to be fired. The doll wanted to ask questions, to learn more about the place, but its uncolored lips couldn't move. Besides, its maker already seemed wary of it; it feared how he would react if it began speaking. So instead, it resumed observing all that it could, frustrated by the limits of its vision.

At the end of the workday, marked by the dimming of the already low light filtering in through cracks in the wooded walls, the dollmakers simultaneously placed their work down on the tables and began tidying up their spaces. The seamstresses disappeared from their windows, to where, it did not know. On this side, it could see no doors within the small rooms in which they worked. In single file, the men passed by the guards, who inspected them before letting them out of the doors located on the opposite side of the factory. The doll had seen the exit only once when its maker had turned it around in its stand to work on something on its backside.

It watched its maker leave each day until he disappeared from its field of vision. The inspector and stout man, who only seemed to show himself if a problem occurred, followed. Once all the men had left, the doll looked at the other dolls around the room. It called to them with its mind, hoping for some response or indication that they could also see, hear, and feel. No response ever came; however, it still felt a presence somewhere in the room despite all the humans leaving—at least as far as it could tell. Not even the guards who patrolled during the day seemed to remain at night.

This night, after the lights died and exit doors locked, the doll watched in surprise as one of the dollmakers emerged from the hallway behind the inspector's desk. The men would occasionally walk down this hall during the day for brief periods of time, though never going as far as the stout man. Instead, they ducked into another offshoot, their footsteps never going far, and would return moments later. Earlier in the day, the doll had seen this dollmaker slip into the hallway but hadn't been interested enough to realize he had not reappeared before quitting time. Now it focused intently on him.

The dollmaker glanced around the factory nervously, sticking close to the shadows. When he emerged into the low light, the doll knew it had been right; not even the guards remained in the building at night. The fear he evoked seemed to give the stout man confidence that none of his employees would be foolish enough to remain after hours and eliminated the need for checks in the evening. The doll appreciated the dollmaker's gall. For several long moments, he remained at the mouth of the hallway, silver-blue eyes glancing between the forbidden door and the exit the doll could not see. He took a step into the factory, shook his head and stepped back.

"I want to know. I want to know," he muttered to himself, trying to build his resolve. He took a step toward the forbidden door and abruptly stopped. "If they catch me, I'm dead. Is the knowing worth it?"

He glanced at the exit once again, taking a deep breath. The doll watched the man's indecision with fascination, also desiring to know what lay beyond the door.

Go on, you've come this far. Don't back down now, it silently willed the dollmaker to take the chance. Sandal-covered feet slapped against the concrete floor as he made his way quickly to the forbidden door. He barely touched it, presumably looking for a handle, when the door swung silently open, revealing the same darkness beyond.

A shiver of dread tickled the doll's back. The silence of the rusted hinges seemed somehow more ominous than the shriek they'd omitted earlier, as though the door itself did not want to attract attention. It watched in delighted fascination as the dollmaker jumped a step backward, body visibly quaking in the low light.

From somewhere beyond the darkness, the doll felt a beckoning pull.

Without a second glance, the dollmaker staggered into the black. A few steps in, the doll heard a frightened gasp and could barely make out the man as he fell to his knees, hands on either side of his head.

Of its own accord, the door swung shut.

Four

The dollmaker never reappeared from behind the door. The doll felt disappointment, watching day and night for some sign or indication, hoping that if he came back, he would have news about what lay beyond. It tried to focus on the dress its maker ordered—a blue Victorian-style outfit trimmed in white—or on communicating with those like it. Yet its attention continued to slide back to the door. Occasionally, it would notice its maker's eyes glance uneasily backward, as if somehow aware of his doll's focus.

"It does no good to dwell," he muttered one day while carefully spreading glue across the doll's bare scalp. His face hovered mere inches away from his creation, the nearest he would ever get to it. The doll couldn't help but notice he remained further away than any of the other dollmakers to their art. Again, it wondered whether he spoke to it or himself. "Around here, to know is death, so it's better to remain ignorant."

Once finished with the glue, the maker lifted a mass of wavy black off a pedestal and began to carefully affix it to the adhesive, starting with the crown and working outward. The doll felt the gentle pressure of his fingers, and the pleasurable tingling slowly drove its thoughts away until nothing engulfed its consciousness.

It didn't know how long it floated in the black. The gentle tugging of its new hair brought its awareness back. Its maker strategically tested sections of the wig to make sure every millimeter had stuck. His brown eyes focused on his work, never meeting the doll's, even when he nodded—a minuscule curt movement—his satisfaction with the wig, and began applying its makeup. Within itself, the doll felt a hole; a darkness, like that beyond the door, that grew with its sadness and bitterness.

When its maker completed the painted face, he stood and walked to his seamstress. She lifted the tiny dress out to him along with some other materials, and he thoroughly inspected each one before bringing the lot back to his worktable. Somehow the doll knew that any imperfection would be his responsibility, and it felt privileged to be in the hands of the best dollmaker in the place. At least, so it assumed. Why else would he be tasked with its creation?

The maker slid the doll into its dress, conscious of its small fingers that could inadvertently pull on the material to disastrous results. Underneath the dress, he added white, fluffy pantalets, giving the skirt a fuller appearance. Light blue socks with a tiny blue bow slid onto its feet followed by white, strapped shoes. White gloves covered its hands, leaving only the porcelain of its arms and neck showing.

He picked the doll up and turned it on its stand so that it faced the other side of the room and covered its body with a cloth. Sweeping half of its hair up into a ponytail, leaving a few strands in the front to frame the face, he began to curl its masses into ringlets. The doll heard a strange hiss behind it as a chemical scent filled the air. Droplets of some kind of liquid splattered across the table around it. It stood this way for several long minutes before the maker turned it back around, placing a cloth over the doll's face, and the hiss briefly returned.

The cloth slid silently to the table as the maker placed it back on its stand. With a grim look of disgust mixed with pride, he pulled out a mirror so the doll could look at its own reflection. It gasped inwardly, staring transfixed at what it had become. Though its pouty lips wore a small smile, it did not reflect the joy the doll itself felt.

It's perfect, the doll thought. The maker shuddered and placed the mirror face down in the drawer from which it had come. Inwardly, the doll frowned, disappointment replacing its happiness in an instant. Why couldn't he take pride in the wonderful piece of art he created?

Performing one last thorough inspection, the maker lifted the doll by its stand from the table. For a moment, he paused as the doll swayed precariously from the momentum, and it wondered if he would let it fall. Then his other hand wrapped around its middle, steadying it, and he carried it over to the inspector's table.

A gruff, frowning man with thick-lensed glasses and calloused hands took the doll with almost as much care as its creator had used and began looking it over . The doll held its nonexistent breath, uncertainty squirming unbidden within. What if this man rejected it like he had the other doll?

No, it thought, scoffing at the very idea. *I am flawless. You're wasting time with this charade, but do as you must.*

For a moment, the inspector paused, a brief look of confusion passing over his face. With a subtle shake of his head, he continued his work. Occasionally, he would produce a flashlight or a magnifying glass. He lifted the clothing to inspect the joints underneath. He pulled carefully but firmly on the seams of the dress, around the hairline, and the limbs. The doll's impatience grew, and it seemed to it that the inspector made a more thorough job of his task with it than it had seen previously. Deep down, it felt its fear start to surface once again and glanced briefly at the discard box, the corner of it barely visible in the doll's periphery. Finally, when everything remained in place, he nodded a single time, emitting a low grunting noise, and handed the doll gingerly back to the maker. Without a second glance, the inspector returned his attention to other projects on the table before him.

The doll and its maker released a simultaneous sigh of relief, and he glanced down at it cautiously. In that moment, the doll thought it felt a desire from its maker to rid himself of his creation as quickly as possible. He carried the doll to a table near a set of double doors; the ones it assumed everyone used to enter and exit the building. He placed it gently in the center of the table, next to a pretty, brown-haired doll. As he stabilized it in its stand, the doll took one last look around the factory and felt a pang of jealousy. The other dollmakers did not regard their creations with the same disgust its maker had shown. Sadness, but also care and pride, filled their faces as they created—to its mind—inferior products. They touched their dolls freely and did not seem to have the same hesitation, the same fear. He had created perfection and could barely even look at it. For a brief moment, as its maker pulled away from his work for the last time, their eyes met.

With me, your work is complete.

The maker flinched; eyes rounded in fear. He quickly held a hand up to one of the nearby foremen before turning and striding away, his feet gliding swiftly over the concrete floor. Adjacent to the corner of the inspector's desk, his feet hesitated slightly, almost imperceptibly. Instead of returning to his worktable, he walked down the hallway, disappearing down the offshoot. One of the guards followed behind, stride set with purpose. Minutes later, wiping his hands clean with a towel, the guard re-emerged. The maker never did.

A man came in from behind the doll, setting boxes next to it and its companion on the table. He placed the other doll gently in the first box, wrapping it carefully in material that would protect its delicate body. For a moment, the doll thought it felt a tremor of excitement coming from its companion, but then the lid covered it and the feeling dissipated. As the man began to lift the doll, the shriek of hinges announced the presence of a new set of eyes. Before it disappeared into the box, the doll caught a glimpse of silver-blue.

Five

The awareness of others, human and otherwise, so clearly felt while the maker did his work, could not penetrate the walls of its container. It left the doll in complete isolation for the first time since it became conscious. With the world cut off by the plain, brown cardboard, except for the sensation of movement, the doll eventually fell into a sort of stasis; aware of nothing but a sense of longing. It did not know how long it remained this way or anything about its journey from the factory to its eventual home.

An unfamiliar sound pulled the doll from its dreamless state, bringing its consciousness back into sharp and abrupt focus. It remained surrounded by cardboard and soft packaging that kept it safely in place. Something thin and papery tore outside its cocoon, causing excitement and trepidation to flutter through the doll. The longing intensified like a fire reaching eagerly in anticipation of its next meal. Somehow it knew that everything it had waited for lay just on the other side of its tiny prison.

Bright, blinding light broke through the cracks of the cardboard as the lid lifted away in agonizingly slow motion. As its sight adjusted, the doll's gaze focused on the face of a small human child no more than seven years of age. Curiosity gave way to excitement as the child's mouth turned upward, parting the lips with joy. Without hesitation, the girl reached into the box and pulled the doll tightly to her chest, and all at once the doll felt complete. The warmth of the child filled it, banishing the dark hole it carried for so long and, in an instant, it understood love and belonging. This girl would never allow harm to come to it; would never leave it.

"Careful now, Alice, sweetheart," the girl's mother chided softly, her silky voice full of warmth. "That's porcelain and very fragile."

"Fragile?" the girl inquired, loosening her grip the smallest of fractions.

"It means it could break easily if you're not careful," a small boy near her replied matter-of-factly, not looking up from his own treasures.

Strewn around the small room, the shredded remains of green and red paper and discarded colorful bows decorated the carpeted floor. Alice leaped to her feet, the doll held tightly in the crook of one arm as she rushed to her parents, small feet kicking the debris carelessly away.

"Thank you," she exclaimed, hugging each one with her free arm in turn. Her parents simply offered indulging smiles full of love. Happiness filled every corner of the room as the family celebrated together. The doll felt the warmth of love continue to seep into its very being, and it knew it had found companionship. It watched as the family continued opening their gifts, sitting comfortably in its girl's lap. Once all the presents had been unwrapped and the toys given an obligatory amount of attention, Alice's brother looked up and noticed the doll for the first time. The smile fell from his face, eyebrows knitting close together, reminding the doll briefly of its maker.

"Its eyes are creepy," the boy commented in disgust, the tip of his tongue sticking out of his closed lips.

"Samuel," the father admonished gently, his smile never faltering.

"They are," the boy argued, his gaze flickering between his father and the doll. "They look real."

"That's a porcelain doll, sweetie. They're supposed to look like that."

The doll gazed at the boy, the joyous feeling beginning to fade, a speck of dark returning.

"Well, I love it!"

At this proclamation, the doll's irritation instantly melted away. Nothing mattered but its girl's opinion. Alice lifted the doll and turned it to face her, their eyes meeting. "You're the most beautiful, wonderful thing I ever saw."

"I've ever seen," her mother corrected gently. Alice glanced up and echoed the older woman with a nod of her head before returning her attention to the doll. She hugged it close to her once again, its feet dangling just below her hips. The immediate bond the doll had felt strengthened between them. In that moment, the doll knew without a doubt: they belonged to each other, and nothing would ever come between them.

Six

From that first morning on, despite its fragile nature, the girl carried the doll everywhere she went. It sat in her lap during meals, rested on a small chair nearby while she took a bath, and slept next to her at night. From its perch, it watched as the family engaged in meals, games, and arguments. Before the end of the day, these tiffs ended in apologies and hugs, no matter how many tears had been shed over the cruel words that slipped through quivering lips. Sometimes the little girl and her brother engaged in physical altercations—he pulled her hair, or she hit him—but they never remained angry at each other for long. Through it all, their parents continued to be attentive and involved in the activities of their children. They encouraged homework in the afternoons, healthy meals in the evenings, and read comforting tales of far-off places as they wished their children goodnight. The doll watched it all with fascination, its arm clutched tightly in the little girl's fist, or its body nestled softly in the crook of her arm. She kept the doll constantly within her reach, and it reveled in the love and attention it received.

One evening toward the end of the school year, the family went out to a restaurant to celebrate the coming summer break. Everyone dressed in their best clothing, and the family sat in a booth around a large table. The doll sat in a booster seat on the bench next to the girl, its own little plate next to the girl's. The waitstaff kindly adhered to her insistence that the doll be treated as real. Only Samuel seemed uncomfortable with this behavior, casting furtive glances at the doll, but kept any commentary to himself.

Throughout dinner, the family told stories and laughed, the doll silently joining in, soaking up the warmth and love. Where it had felt jealousy and bitterness at its inability to communicate in the factory, it felt connection with this family; the girl gave it a voice, its laughter expressed within her own. Toward the end of the dinner, the little girl said she needed to go to the restroom.

"Wait for me," she said to the doll. For a moment, it felt confused. The girl had never left it behind before. It reasoned that unlike the bathroom at home, there might not be a clean surface on which to set it at the restaurant. Reluctantly, it accepted that the girl would be back as she disappeared hand-in-hand with her mother into the ladies' room. Time passed slowly as the doll waited anxiously for the girl to return, its gaze fixed on the door. Hours seemed to pass, the server coming and going a couple of times. Then the boys stood up, and the doll expected one of them, likely the father, to pick it up. Instead, they moved to the front of the restaurant, leaving the doll alone in the booth.

Please, don't leave me, the doll reached out with its mind. Samuel glanced back briefly, a small smile tugging at his lips, but he turned back to his father without a word. Shortly after, the girl and her mother exited the restroom, and upon seeing their party, moved to the doors. Samuel locked arms with his sister and pulled her from the restaurant, a flurry of excited chatter and laughter.

It watched helplessly as Alice left it behind. Inconceivably, she had forgotten it; had not even spared it a glance or realized no one else had it with them. Minutes passed before the waitstaff came to clean the table and realized the doll remained. The woman looked around in astonishment, and the doll wished it could tell her that they had already left. Instead, it could only watch as she checked the restroom and out the front door before returning to gather the doll.

"Sorry, little one," she muttered, though her tone seemed to contain a small amount of distaste. She wouldn't look at it directly. "I'm sure they'll be back for you soon."

She placed the doll in a small cupboard in the podium near the front door. It listened to the people coming and going until the traffic began to slow. Then came the sounds of cleaning and the restaurant staff goofing around, their laughter lancing its insides. Eventually, the light between the cracks disappeared, leaving the doll in darkness. While it waited, the doll felt the cold sting of loneliness tear into its heart; abandoned and unloved. Thoughts began to creep into its consciousness.

It's their fault, they made her forget you, a voice from the darkness within it whispered coldly, mockingly. *Even if she does come back for you this time, someday she'll leave you behind forever.*

That's not true, the doll thought angrily. *She loves me.*

The way your maker loved you?

Before the doll could respond, it heard the swoosh of the door opening and the light returned. A face it didn't recognize peered into the cabinet.

"Ah, here it is," the man said, pulling the doll out and handing it to the father.

"Thank you so much," he said, taking the doll's arm in his hand and holding it carefully by his side. "My daughter wouldn't go to sleep without it. You've saved our night."

Warmth chased the cold feeling away, amplified once it returned to the girl's arms. After a squeezing but gentle hug, the girl held the doll out at arm's length, gazing into its eyes. In that moment, more than anything, it felt its desire to be by her side always.

"I'll never leave you behind again," the girl promised as she pulled it close to her.

Seven

During the hot summer months, time passed blissfully for the doll. Together, it and its girl spent their days with little to no interruption, watching television, playing games, and exploring the neighborhood on daring, make-believe adventures. One midsummer day, they sat outside at a small table, having a tea party.

Alice lifted the small teapot from the center of the table. Carefully holding it by the handle and using a towel to support it under the nose, she slowly tilted the small opening over the empty teacup in front of the doll. From between her lips, a small *pshhh* sound, like liquid falling into an empty container. She repeated the steps for her own cup.

"Careful, it's hot," she warned, picking up her own teacup and lifting it carefully to her lips, blowing on the invisible contents.

Thank you, Alice, the doll thought, imagining itself lifting its own cup.

"You're most welcome—" a rush of gray and black fur surrounding narrowed green eyes sailed over the table. Padded feet landed squarely on the doll's chest and knocked it to the ground. Despite the soft grass landing, a small crack slid up its white leg, from knee to hip, concealed by layers of fabric. To the doll, it felt like nothing more than a strange, burning itch.

Alice screamed, jumping to her feet and immediately chasing the feline away. Anger and hate filled the doll as it watched the cat slink over the fence. The girl returned, hugging it tightly before she brought it up to face her.

"I'm so sorry," she began, stopping shortly when their eyes met. The concern drained from the girl's face, leaving an expressionless mask. For a moment, the doll thought it could see its own hazel eyes through its girl's ice-blue ones. It allowed all the bitterness and fear it felt to flow into the girl, images of revenge flashing within both of their minds. Somewhere within the girl, the doll felt a sense of disgust and horror.

It must be done.

At dinner, Alice didn't speak and barely touched her meal. Her parents exchanged worried glances, but when her mother touched her head, she found it to be warm and helped Alice climb into an early bed-time. Later that same night, when the snoring of her father reverberated throughout the house, the girl slipped out of her room, doll in hand, down the stairs and into the backyard.

The next day, the neighbor came to their door, asking if they'd seen his cat, which hadn't shown up for her morning meal.

"She goes hunting at night, but she's always at the back door first thing." The parents exchanged helpless, sorrowful looks and simply shook their heads. The girl held the doll tight to her chest, her eyes shimmering with unwept tears over the thought of the lost animal. Samuel stayed in the shadows and looked fearfully at the doll but said nothing until the front door closed on the distraught man.

"It was the doll," he whispered to his parents anxiously, thinking he had them to himself in the kitchen. On the other side of the door, the girl and doll listened. "The cat attacked it yesterday, and it became angry."

"The cat became angry?"

"No, the *doll*," the boy insisted, his voice pleading, too young to understand his parents' skepticism, but old enough to know they didn't believe him. Silence followed this claim, as though neither adult had the words to explain that the doll simply couldn't feel without potentially causing their son to lose his childlike wonder and imagination. The doll felt its own resentment and gratitude build. Before it could hear the rest of the conversation, an upset Alice whisked it away to her room.

From that moment on, Samuel became serious whenever he found the doll in his vicinity. One moment he could be seen laughing and having a good time, and then the doll came into view, and his good cheer would suddenly disappear. The doll felt him watching it, silent and waiting. It wondered at times if the boy could hear its thoughts or sense its intentions. At times, it would think about hurting something, just to see how he would react. Samuel might have been keeping tabs on the doll, but it watched him as well.

Eight

Time continued forward, days passing into months, which slipped into years. The bright yellow paint of the hallways began to chip and fade; Christmas trees no longer appeared bright and cheery, despite their multicolored lights and sparkling ornaments. Laughter no longer filled the house, dishes went unwashed for days, and dust gathered on the furniture. The doll didn't care about these things, perfectly content in its bubble with its girl.

Alice's parents' concern about the deteriorating quality of their daughter's schoolwork and social life began to grow. It started as nothing more than small comments asking her how she enjoyed school and if she liked her classmates, and grew to whispered conversations behind closed doors.

The doll went to school with Alice, and for a while, no issues arose. Alice and her friends played with their dolls in the classroom while the other children played outside. Yet the doll couldn't stand the lifeless toys the others brought. It sensed no consciousness from them and didn't understand why any of the children would want to play with them instead of it. Slowly, one by one, the girls abandoned their toys. On a rainy day in the third grade, one of the girls had brought a multicolored spring. Everyone gathered around to see how the colors changed as the flexible metal moved. The doll sat alone, observing the show with growing scorn. Off to the side, one of the boys watched, a sneer plastered across his face. Looking at the boy, the doll thought about how much it would love to see the slinky destroyed. Suddenly, the boy crossed the room, ripped the toy from its owner's hand and began twisting it out of shape until the thin metal snapped. Astonished, the little girl cried, and the little boy shook his head, as though coming out of a dream. Alice and the others returned to the doll, playing as though nothing had happened.

Her fifth-grade teacher called early in the year to express her concern about the doll to Alice's parents. They did not permit toys in the classroom, and yet Alice insisted on the doll sitting in a chair next to her. It had caused issues with attention and focus, not just for Alice, but for the other students as well.

Her parents tried to talk to Alice about their concerns, but she refused to leave the doll behind. She told them that she had made that mistake once and would never do so again.

"Leaving your doll at home isn't the same as leaving it behind in a restaurant," her father said, a note of exasperation in his voice. "She'll be here for you when you return."

Alice conceded and stomped off to her room, doll in tow. Its panic rose, thoughts of spending the days alone in isolation flooding its mind. Again, the voice within the inner darkness whispered that one day she would leave it for good.

"What can I do? They might take you away if I don't do what they say," Alice whispered in the softly lit confines of her room.

You can't leave me.

The next day, to the doll's delight, Alice slipped it into her backpack. As soon as she cleared the schoolyard gates and the prying eyes of others at the end of the day, she removed the doll from her pack, and it became her sole focus. She confided in it, telling it about her day and the secrets of those she called friends.

They're not your friends. They're just stupid people who want to get in the way of our friendship, the doll would remind her during these occasions. Jealousy stirred each time she talked about other people. She had it—why would she need anyone else? *I'm your only true friend. I'll always be here for you, Alice.*

"Sometimes," she admitted one day as they sat in the park near their home, "I wish they would all die so I don't have to impress them. Then it truly would just be you and me."

A sense of unease grew within the house. The more her parents tried to separate Alice from her doll, the more time she spent alone with it. In trying to break the bond, her parents encouraged her to write in a diary, but she continued to use the doll as a confidant. Troubled by her fixation and concerned that she would be held back a year in school, her parents threatened to take the doll away until she finished her homework.

"I'll do my homework," Alice cried, clutching the doll to her chest. "Please don't take her away from me."

She sat with the doll, asking it to help her, and completed her assignments. Behind their bedroom door, her parents expressed that they felt at a loss, recognizing the unhealthy attachment but not knowing how to help their daughter. In the dead of night, through the adjoining wall, the doll focused feelings of ease and complacency. It recognized that Alice could not live without her parents, but it tired of their interference. In the morning, when they discussed the situation again, they agreed to leave her alone, each expressing hope that she would grow out of the phase.

Meanwhile, Samuel's dislike of the doll grew, and he frequently remarked that he could feel the eyes watching him, plotting to hurt them all. Several times he threatened to throw the doll away if she did not remove it from the table, stating that he hated the way it stared at him. She twisted his arm behind his back and demanded he retract the statement, but he only called the doll creepy and evil in response. He claimed the doll placed malevolent thoughts in her head and that without it, the family would return to normal.

Even as their fights grew more severe, their parents did nothing to intervene.

During Alice's eighth year at school, an unfamiliar face of a boy peering into the backpack surprised the doll. He pulled it from the bag roughly by its arm, the porcelain scraping against itself, and held it high for all to see.

"Alice still plays with dolls," he mocked, and those around him took up the chant. Fear flooded the doll, and it searched frantically for its girl, calling out to her with its mind. It watched Alice break through the laughing crowd, slamming her fist in the boy's stomach and catching the doll as he released his grip. She snatched the strap of her pack and scurried down the hallway, fleeing the school. The doll never knew if they chased after them; it only heard their laughing, mocking voices echoing in their wake.

Once back at home, Alice encountered her father, confusion and anger plain on his face. She grasped the doll tightly in her arms as wet streams ran from her eyes, dripping onto the doll's silky hair. At the sight of his daughter's tears, the father's face softened, and he kneeled beside her. The doll felt a sudden jerk, its legs rattling together, as Alice turned to the side. Her father only placed his hand gently on her shoulder and asked what had happened. The words fell from her lips as they did when she confided in the doll. She finished relaying the incident, and he told her to go to her room, his voice flat and devoid of emotion.

When her mother arrived home from work, the adults had a long conversation concerning the situation. The doll watched from the bed as its girl tried to listen through the wall. In an exasperated voice, she expressed her fear that they would take the doll away; a fear it shared with her.

An eternity seemed to pass before the adults entered the room. Alice grabbed the doll from the bed, clutching it tightly to her chest as though holding a shield.

"Alice," her mother began tentatively, "after many difficult discussions, we've decided it would be best to make a new start in a different town. This doesn't feel like home anymore, not for any of us, and we're hopeful that if we start over, we can find our joy again."

"We've been thinking about this for a while now," her father broke in. The doll didn't care about the details; it just felt thrilled about the possibility of a new location. As its excitement grew, so did Alice's. "Another company has offered me a better job, and I think I'm going to take it. I think it will be better for all of us. What do you think?"

Alice cried out with glee and ran to tell her brother; the doll still clutched in her arms.

"Sammy!" She skidded to a stop just inside his room. He turned, a tentative but warm smile on his face; it had been ages since he'd heard his sister call him in such a manner. "We're going to move!"

Immediately, his smiling face melted into confusion and disdain. As his eyes fell on the doll, his lip curled up toward his nose in a sneer. Alice seemed oblivious as she stood in his doorway, humming with anticipation.

"I don't want to move!" he screamed, face contorting into a mask of rage. "I have friends here. This isn't fair. Why should I have to move because of you and that stupid doll?"

Before Alice could react, Samuel pushed her from his room and slammed the door in her face. The doll glared at the wooden surface, feeling its hate toward the boy grow. How dare he ruin their happiness! Alice stood for several minutes, staring blankly in confusion and hurt. By the time she returned to her room, her parents had gone, leaving her alone with the doll. For a brief moment, the first in their time together, the doll felt almost disconnected, as though Alice felt lonely, and the doll did not fully fill up the space inside her.

The doll shook itself, dismissing the idea; it and its girl could never be separated and would always have each other. As the doll cast the dark aside, Alice also seemed to come back to life, rolling out her shoulders and smiling. She held the doll in front of her.

"Sammy is stupid," she confided with a single nod of her head. "He doesn't know what he's talking about. This move is going to be great."

Nine

Samuel continued to fight with his parents and his sister throughout the following weeks. He locked himself in his room and only came out for school, where he seemed to linger longer and longer. Boxes began to appear all over the house, filling with their belongings. Their parents took advantage of Samuel's absence by packing up his room, donating items he'd outgrown but wouldn't let go of himself.

One afternoon, when nearly everything had been boxed, donated, or trashed, Samuel came home unexpectedly early from a friend's house. Upstairs, the doll could hear the parents packing up the kitchen, soft clangs of metal cooking tools interrupting the beat of their music. It heard the front door open, its fear and anger growing. Alice sat in her room, humming contentedly as she brushed the doll's hair.

Alice, something's wrong, it hissed, trying to get her attention, to warn her, but Alice remained focused on her work.

The doll heard the soft whisper of socked feet on carpet just moments before Samuel snatched it out of her lap. Swinging helplessly from his hand, it watched as Alice jumped immediately to her feet, turning on her toes and giving chase down the hallway toward the stairs.

"Sammy," she screamed, feet pounding after him, tears filling her eyes. The doll could feel her fear as it amplified its own. The noises from the kitchen paused. "Give her back!"

As he approached the banister overlooking the living room, the boy dared a glance back at his sister. His foot caught the corner of a box, sending him sprawling forward on his belly, his momentum sliding him to the railing. The doll flew from his grasp, sailing over the banister and to the living room below. Falling in slow motion, it searched frantically for some sign of rescue—maybe one of the parents would emerge from the kitchen and catch it just in time—but found none. Its damaged leg collided with the hardwood floor first, the existing crack spreading and splintering up across the rest of its delicate frame. Time suddenly sped up as the rest of its body landed and shattered across the floor. Its girl hung over the railing above, her arms outstretched but too late to help.

The image would be the last memory the doll retained before finding itself alone in the house.

"Noooooo," Alice wailed and raced down the stairs. Behind her, Samuel climbed clumsily to his feet and stared down at the scene below, relief and shame warring for control of his features. From the kitchen, the parents emerged, their footsteps hurried. For the first time in years, they appeared fully engaged and alert. The mother scooped Alice up before she could reach the doll, doing her best to comfort her inconsolable daughter. The father wrapped his arms around his wife and child, beckoning with one hand for his son to join them. Together, they sat on the floor, feeling and sharing the words they could not speak. The doll could sense the emotions of the family yet felt somehow disconnected.

Once the tears had been shed and the children returned upstairs, the experienced hands of the adults set to work. They picked up the sharp pieces and disposed of them unceremoniously into a garbage bag. Despite the care they used, the porcelain managed to slice through exposed areas of thin skin. Once all the larger pieces had been removed, the vacuum sucked up the smaller slivers, making the carpet safe for bare feet once more. At dinnertime, the siblings emerged for their favorite meal of takeout chicken nuggets and fries. Crossing the living room, a stray shard found its way into the soft skin of the girl who held the doll so dear. As her mother carefully administered first aid, doing her best to remove what she could of the thin sliver, Alice cried. The doll cried with her, unable to understand why she hadn't picked it up.

While carefully searching for any other missing pieces, Samuel found the doll's eyes underneath the coffee table, where they had rolled once free of their porcelain prison. They remained completely intact, and for a moment, the boy stared into disembodied eyes. With a shudder, he stood and retrieved a small wooden box from the donation pile, and, careful not to touch the shining orbs, placed the eyes within.

The next day, as the movers loaded their belongings into a truck, Samuel smiled as he buried the doll's eyes in the backyard. Alice stood beside him, offering her goodbyes to her fallen friend. Hand-in-hand, they turned to the house and walked to join their parents in the front, their heavy footfalls becoming lighter as they left the shadow of the doll behind.

Still, the spirit of the doll remained in the place where its body had shattered, no longer connected to the eyes which had originally given it meaning. Long forgotten, it would continue to wait for its friend, unable to understand the reason she left it behind. It watched as the sun continued to make its trek across the floor, followed hours later by the moonlight. Yet the couch that stood over it blocked any hope of being found, filling the doll with irritation and sadness. It imagined the large piece of furniture sliding back.

In the stillness of the night, the couch moved.

Slowly it slid across the floor until the doll no longer felt its shadow. Surprise warred with relief, and for the first time since it gained consciousness, the doll felt a smile tug at the corner of its lips. Looking around the room, it wondered what else it could do while it waited for someone to notice it; to bring back the girl who had loved it so much.

About the Author

E.R. Sano grew up in the mountains and valleys of California where a love of books and adventure developed into a passion for storytelling. Currently residing in the Pacific Northwest—at least for now—she spends her days studying human behavior, exploring nature, playing video games, and finding new ways to creep out others. An avid world traveler, E.R. rarely stays in one place for long. Terrified of dolls since her older sister regaled her with a tale of an evil doll during their childhood, *The Forgotten Doll* seeks to share her caution of these life imitators with others.

Playing with Chemicals
by Chloe D.

Content/Trigger Warnings

- Guns

- Death

- Blood

- Some Elements of Gore

- Mentions of Human Trafficking

- Sexual Assault

Claire could not get enough of the plain white ceiling, the open window and the soft breeze, and the dark covers of her bed. She wanted to stay there forever.

"You have to get up."

Someone was talking to her. She didn't care. She couldn't see them; they did not matter.

"You're safe now."

The voice felt thick, enveloping her. It was rich and soft. She remembered loving it, but she was too stripped of emotion to feel that now.

The breath of the voice grew closer and quieter. The words hot against her cheek.

"I still need you."

"Don't kill him! Don't you dare!" Claire cried, sprinting out of the break room, half-eaten sandwich in hand. "Don't—"

"Claire." Kris raised his hand in front of her, blond hair falling into his eyes. "That's not what I'm doing."

Kris held a purple needle—indicating the liquid contents were lethal—over the poor dog's leg. This was a place of experiments, and far more often than Claire liked, the dog had to die. But today, she didn't understand why the dog had to die, which made it different.

"Then what are you doing?"

"Injecting an illness into him. Our department has been assigned to the illness going around the power plant."

Claire nodded and looked at the dog. "So we're getting him sick to test the vaccine on the dog?"

"Precisely." Kris stuck the needle into the dog.

The dog didn't bark or flinch. It occurred to Claire just then that the dog had been drugged with a small enough dosage that he faded in and out of awareness.

"Finish your break, Claire," Kris muttered and carried the dog back into his cage.

Claire turned back, wishing she had her white lab coat on so she could hold herself together better. She had not meant to react like that. In fact, Claire had gotten used to it since starting as an intern at the lab years ago before becoming a lab assistant. But it seemed that she had not gotten used to it enough.

There was only one window in the break room, one table, and a shelf of assorted books. It had always reminded her of a prison. The gray walls, the dim fluorescent lights. She felt secluded as she ate her floppy, damp ham and cheese, staring out the small window on the scratched-up wooden door.

Wind tugged at the trees outside the lab, threatening to break them down and wreak havoc on the electricity. This lab was the only one on the island. A land that had only just won its independence fifty years ago. Claire was lucky to be living in a new nation that had stabilized itself and was prospering.

The timer on Claire's phone went off. Break was over. When she re-entered the lab, she was greeted by Brax. He grinned as she entered, rubbing the stubble on his chin.

"Heard about our latest project yet?"

"Sort of." Claire shrugged. "We're testing that illness at the power plant."

Brax's voice dropped to a whisper, something she could never imagine coming from him, as his voice always carried too loudly. "Did you hear what it does to people?"

At that, Claire shook her head. She had learned of the illness only last week. The government wanted to keep it under wraps until it was better understood. This was the nation's first-ever disaster, and no one craved the negative publicity that it could cause.

"Their skin turns purple and peels off." Brax's face never showed much emotion, but his eyes held a sort of fear Claire had never seen before.

"Skin peeling? Like leprosy?"

Brax shook his head. "Don't know, but I've heard it's much worse. So far, everyone who has contracted the illness has died. And there are also tremors, sickness, and severe migraines. And so many other things. Anyone who contracts the disease is put away because it's contagious for the first three weeks."

"Put away? Where?"

Brax shrugged. "Don't know. Good thing we don't work in the plant, right?"

Only Brax could find some excuse to smile at the current moment. Claire just wanted to puke.

Kris poked his head into the lab room and pointed at Brax. "You. We need your help with another testing phase."

"Sounds good." Brax jogged to the next room over, his broad and tall figure having to hunch together just to get through the door.

High heels clicked through the various laboratories until they reached the office Claire was in. "Mrs. Mardock?"

"Claire," Mrs. Mardock greeted her and set a folder on the table. "I want you to analyze these files today after work. Also, I want you to go home early. We had an accident on the third floor and have to send everyone who isn't cleaning it up home early, for safety measures."

"Okay, thank you." Claire took the folder, flipped through a few pages, and set it down. "I'll pack up really quickly and be out of your hair."

"Oh! And Claire?" Mrs. Mardock arched a sharply sculpted brow. "Don't discuss with anyone outside of the office—that means those two and me—about this project. Understood."

"Sounds good." Claire nodded absentmindedly as she cleared her workspace.

And with that, Mrs. Mardock vanished.

When Claire stepped out of the lab, the cool air hit her in the face first thing. The October air was nice to feel as the final leaves fell out of the trees and swirled to the ground. What was not nice were the clouds hovering over the island in dark bundles. They made everything feel suffocating and gloomy.

"Claire." The call behind her made her look over her shoulder as two lab assistants came from behind. Mary and Colin. Sporting a fresh new buzz cut and sunglasses, Colin, the one who had called her name, was waving in a crazed sort of manner. He was the type of person who loved himself in a way that told you he had never suffered from low self-esteem in his life.

Claire turned around and raised her arm to greet them. "You guys still working on the old project?"

"Yeah." Mary sighed and rubbed her forehead while scrolling on her phone. "We've gotten nowhere with the bacteria in the plumbing, and I don't think we'll be done for another month."

"Ugh, that's obnoxious." Claire walked with them through the maze of the parking lot that zig-zagged around the whole building.

"We were just testing bacteria, again," Claire shared, heeding Mrs. Mardock's warning.

Colin changed the subject right before they lapsed into silence. "So, you guys got any hopes for the weekend?"

"My hope is to finish enduring Friday." Mary unlocked her car and walked away. "See you tomorrow."

Colin and Claire waved goodbye and walked to their cars at the end of the parking lot.

Colin, always grinning, muttered, "Huh, looks like we parked together."

"Guess so." Claire nodded along. "I wish I had taken tomorrow off instead of yesterday. I am so tired and behind on all my paperwork."

Colin chuckled. "Jokes on you."

Claire squinted her eyes, "Why are you laughing like that?"

He shrugged and grinned like a fool. "Guess what?"

"What?"

"Your husband and I are going to the arcade on Monday. We're both off that day."

"When'd those plans come about?"

"Oh, this morning during break."

"Goodness. You guys know how to keep yourselves busy."

"And you can, too, with all your leftover paperwork."

Claire glared at him and unlocked her car. "See you tomorrow."

"Yep, see ya." Colin smiled at the sky, the way he always did, and marched to his car, the very last one in the parking lot, right by the entrance.

With a sigh, Claire pressed her head against the steering wheel and stared at the little horn symbol on the top of the horn pad. When she was at work, she never really had much time to think. Between paperwork and experiments and research and analysis and meetings, everything was too hectic to think about anything more than the next thing on the schedule. She had to have at least five minutes of thought just to herself before she started driving.

Claire flipped the phone over in her hand and looked at the time. Three-oh-one. She had three texts from Sammy, probably entailing all his weekend plans with Colin. They had been friends, those two, for a long time. At some non-work sanctioned staff get-together, Colin had introduced her to Sammy back when she had first started her internship at twenty-three. Four years later, here they were, living in the same house and married for almost two years. Claire fiddled with the gold band on her left hand. She loved it. If she had to save something in a fire or bring one possession to a deserted island, it'd be that ring.

Leaning back in the driver's seat, Claire looked out the window at the city landscape in front of her. The island country had a basic structure; it was a large city in the center and suburbs all the way out until the surrounding sea. Rising in technological development, it was the first place to develop a power plant using the new element they had discovered, which was cleaner and more efficient than nuclear. Marabidium, named after their island, Marandia. If the element did not exist, their nation would not have run, and they would not have been able to claim their independence all those decades ago.

What everyone prided themselves in when it came to marabidium, was that extracting the chemical from the stones through a phosphorylation process to create the energy needed produced more energy than nuclear power. The waste from the phosphorylation process was good enough to be turned into more energy after. Though it took more time and effort, it was worth the powerful results.

It was hard to admit the island was perfect. No, the sky was a little foggy around the factory, but it was still clean. Though they had a national curfew, there was no light pollution after eleven at night until five in the morning. Still, Marandia was an ideal place to live. And with its short history, Claire could not be disappointed by it.

And yes, imperfections came, like the new factory disease. This imperfection worried Claire in particular.

The pictures she spun in her mind, imagining the peeling skin and the welts she had heard about, caused her stomach to churn. But what worried Claire about the most was that the flaw they identified in the marabidium could harm the workers. And among those workers was Sammy, her husband. If something were to happen to him, she wouldn't know what to do. She'd be alone on this island since her parents had retired in a richer nation far away. All she had were her friends here. But without someone at home on this island, she would be entirely lost.

As long as they contained the disease, everyone should be fine. Claire convinced herself of that much. They were enforcing isolation, health procedures, and more. She'd read the papers while leaving the office. Claire knew she shouldn't worry too much, but she couldn't help it. Sammy's health was important to her.

But this was a scientific procedure they were following, and she trusted science. Claire exhaled, smiled, and reversed her car out of the parking lot. She was glad it didn't take long to ease her mind.

She had to remain quiet. That was the most important thing at the moment. Quiet and hidden.

Claire peeked past the oak wood that separated them, crouched on her knees, tiptoed over just slightly, and then lunged. Throwing her arms around his shoulders, she yelled, "Surprise!"

He flinched, stifled a scream, and leaned over the sink, eyes widened. Then, Sammy looked over his shoulder, smiled, and laughed. He leaned his head back so it was touching hers.

"How was work today, love?" When he smiled with all his teeth, his face always had a different glow.

Claire pressed her head to his shoulder; it helped her recharge. "Tiring as always. What about you?"

"Easy. I got out of work early. No heavy-lifting or anything, just operated machinery."

"That's good." Claire yawned. "Is there anything good to eat here?"

"Dinner's in the fridge. Salad and the frozen pizza we bought yesterday."

"Ooh, pizza." Claire let go of Sammy and opened the freezer.

"Wow, I'm hurt." Sammy turned away from the sink, crossing his arms. "You left me for pizza real quick. Imagine what you'd do if—"

"Imagine nothing." Claire hurried over to him and planted a kiss on his cheek. He wrapped his tanned arms around her, and they stood there for a while. "What were you doing standing by the sink?"

"There's a cute little hummingbird that's always fluttering by the roses outside. It's such a free little thing. I want to keep it."

"That's so funny," Claire chuckled.

Claire looked up at Sammy and smiled. He wasn't as tall as most guys and she was on the shorter side, so she easily fit into his hugs. His soft brown eyes and small dimples; he was the sweetest person she had ever met. She closed her eyes briefly and brought her lips to his. That was her favorite part of their evening routine.

When their lips parted, something flickered in Sammy's eyes that Claire wanted to ask about, but his next sentence came too soon for her to say anything. "Want to finish the pizza together?"

"You'll eat the majority of it, I know it," Claire teased, grinning up at him.

Claire stared at Sammy's back in the dark of the room. She could easily make out his shoulder blades and back muscles. With the tip of her finger, she liked to trace over them slowly, mesmerized by all the bumps and dips and his soft skin.

Sammy was still tense; she wondered why. What had been floating around in his head? What if it was the power plant illness?

"Sammy," she whispered. "Are you asleep yet?"

"No, what do you need?" he whispered back.

"Can I tell you something important?"

"Yes."

Claire waited for Sammy to turn over and face her, but he didn't.

"It's really important."

"What is it?"

"You can't tell anybody about it."

"I won't."

"You promise?"

"Promise."

Claire took in a breath. "Did you hear about the disease at the factory?"

This time, he turned around, sitting upright in an instant, spinning the covers around his legs with him. Shocked, Claire stared at his sudden movement; she could just barely see his face in the moonlight that slipped through the curtain.

"How do you know about that?" Sammy's voice was glazed in panic.

"I'm looking into it at work."

"Oh, I see." He fell back in bed and looked up at the ceiling. "How long have you known?"

"Since today."

"Don't talk to anyone else about it, okay? The government does not want that type of attention, and we don't want to get in trouble. I'm sure it will all be resolved soon."

"I know. It's just, I'm worried how the marabidium affects you at work."

Sammy flinched slightly and then grabbed her hand, squeezing it. "Don't worry—my department is unaffected."

"That's good." Claire inched closer and wrapped her arms around him, dropping a kiss on his shoulder.

"Not right now." His eyes trained on the ceiling as he whispered.

"Why not?"

"I just—not right now, okay, Claire? I just want to sleep."

"Fine," she huffed and turned her back to him.

He was still holding on to her hand, though. She hadn't noticed that.

Sometimes Sammy could be confusing. They could be perfectly fine together, and then he'd start pushing her away. Claire didn't want to think it was the topic's fault. They had discussed worse things, but it felt like in the past few months, he had been slowly pushing her away. She didn't understand why they were not as intimate as before.

"I'm not mad," Sammy whispered into her ear. He had turned in her direction and had wrapped an arm around her waist. His arm was cold to the touch. Sammy's words fell flat and were void of the emotional rise and falls she was used to.

"It's all right," Claire said, but she still felt disappointed from before. Even though he was right next to her, skin touching skin, she still felt as though they were not close enough and he was still trying to hold his distance.

"Claire," the call came from the walkie-talkie. "You're needed in the lab."

She was not sure how she would be able to get through the rest of the day at this point. Three pointless meetings and too much paperwork, and now the lab needed her.

The door to the lab was locked. How odd. Usually, for safety purposes, it was wide open. There must have been something extremely important for the researchers to have locked the door. Pulling out her keys, Claire opened the lab and stepped inside.

"Lock it," Kris called out, his back still turned to her. Claire did and noted that Brax and Mrs. Mardock were also there.

"What is it?" Claire asked, but no one was facing her direction. They were all blocking a small island counter in the middle of the lab. On the ground, an open cage door swung between open and closed on weak hinges.

The dog.

"Want to see the marabidium disease with your own two eyes?"

Claire couldn't say a word; she couldn't think. It was a miracle that she could even shuffle her feet all the way over to the counter where the dog sat. The second she saw the poor thing, she wanted to turn around and barf.

"Fascinating, isn't it?" Kris asked, slight amusement sneaking into his words.

"That's one way to put it." Brax's uneasy smile did not suit him, nor did his green face. At least she wasn't the only one who was uncomfortable about all of this.

Claire forced herself to look at the dog again as Kris took a small sample of the dog's illness. Mrs. Mardock viewed the whole process from the top of her five-inch heels. It was the first time she found herself hating a colleague or her boss. Sure, at times she was bothered by some of them, but at this moment, she felt such a burning form of hatred.

Finally, Claire took note of the dog's features and mentally recorded them. Purple welts peeling all over the skin, shedding fur, bleeding from the nail beds, and whimpers of pain.

"Joint pain is quite common." Kris nodded at the dog as though reading her mind. It made Claire feel sicker. He carefully set up a sample under the microscope. "One of the symptoms we can't see is the pain in his joints, which is caused by the tearing of ligaments."

"The marabidium does all that?"

Kris nodded and pushed the microscope toward her. "Want to look?"

Against her better judgment, Claire took a peek under the microscope. The purple-hued bacteria squirmed around. She zoomed in and focused the image and saw that all the little slug-like bacteria were covered with spike proteins.

"I can't wait to break open and look at the inner structure of these things. Hey, Brax, come take a look."

"Sure." Brax nodded, his stoic expression back in place. He walked over to the bacteria, looked through the microscope, nodded, stood back up, and stared into the space before him. "Cool."

"It truly is," Mrs. Mardock commented from the back corner. Her lips pulled back into a tight smile. "Remember to put him out when you guys are done."

She whipped out of the room, her long coat trailing behind her like a cape. Claire did not know how to describe the thick feeling that traveled opposite her digestive system, climbing up her esophagus, and through her throat, tickling the back of her tongue.

When they finally left that forsaken laboratory, Claire felt she could finally breathe. She preferred paperwork over this, she now realized.

"Hey, I know that was rough to see." Kris looked back at them as he walked to his desk. "Since we're all set here, you guys can just go back home early. And take an energy drink with you."

"Do you have grape?" Brax asked, walking to the vending machine. "Oh, sweet! One more left. Want me to get you one, Claire?"

"No thanks."

"All right." Brax snagged the drink after it tumbled out of the vending machine. He opened it in a second, tilted his head back, and jugged.

Claire and Kris laughed, and Brax cracked a smile. She could really feel herself start to relax in the office, finally. The dog issue was behind them, and they were a step closer to solving the illness of the factory. Maybe this week would shape out to be better.

As Claire went through the office, she smiled. When she saw Mary's blonde hair, she caught up to her.

"Mary, we made such good progress with our project today."

But Mary didn't seem to care enough. Instead, worry lined her eyes. "Have you heard from Colin today?"

"No, why?"

"I texted him, but it looks like the messages can't be sent because he's not 'connected to Wi-Fi,' and I called him four times. It's like he's gone MIA."

"He told me he was going to the arcade today."

"But there is nowhere in this country that doesn't have a Wi-Fi connection." Mary's face was grim as she stared at her phone.

"Maybe his phone died."

"I don't think that's it. I'm really worried about him. Was he with any friends?"

"Yeah, Sammy. I'll ask him when I get home and update you as soon as possible."

"Thank you, Claire." Mary held a hand to her chest. I've never had this happen before. "I'm sure it's nothing."

"Probably, but it's always fine to check."

"Yeah, see you tomorrow," Mary called out as she walked to her car, unlocking it.

Claire walked in silence to her vehicle, thinking about the things Mary had said, but her mind wandered to the dog over and over again. No matter how hard she tried, she couldn't forget it. And soon, she had sculpted a mental image of Sammy, covered in those welts and skin peeling. His dark hair is shedding, and he is lying in bed, unable to move from the pain.

At her car, Claire held the door handle tight. She closed her eyes and tried to banish those thoughts, but failed over and over again. Why could she not ignore those images in her head? Half of them were not even true.

"Claire."

In an instant, her eyes were open, and she saw Sammy standing on the opposite side of her car, doubled over, panting, sweat running down his forehead.

"Claire."

"What is it, Sammy?" Claire raced over to the other side and held his shoulder.

"Claire, is that—" Mary stood not too far behind them, her car left running right next to them with the driver's door open and music still blasting. The upbeat tune did not match the moment.

Claire turned her attention back to Sammy. He leaned against the car, still working on catching his breath.

"Sammy, where'd you come from?"

"The arcade."

"You ran all the way here from there? That's like ten miles."

"I-i-it's because, because—"

"Samuel, please, spit it out!"

"Colin. He's—"

"Dead."

Mrs. Mardock's voice pierced the air. Claire turned around and saw Kris standing not too far behind.

"You three should come inside with us."

The three of them sat in a small office space with blinds covering all the windows, and the room was dimly lit. They all sat on short stools, which made them feel at a disadvantage compared to Kris, who stood towering as he watched over them.

It felt like hours before the door to the office space finally opened, and Mrs. Mardock, carrying some sort of bundle to her chest, and Brax entered. There was something wrong with the latter, however. Brax was pale all over, and his skin was visibly dry and crackling between the folds of his hands and elbows. He had not looked like that just an hour earlier. But looking at him closer, she could see the purple welt that slowly formed on the back of his neck.

"Observant, aren't you, Claire?" Kris asked. "Don't worry. If you didn't grab anything from the vending machine all week, you're all set."

"W-what?" Brax's eyes widened, and he leaned against a window and grabbed his temples.

"Dizzy? Fascinating. See? This is the importance of a human subject." Kris's pupils constricted, and a grin covered his face. Claire felt hot and dizzy in her seat. "The progression of the illness is speedy for humans, isn't it?"

"I'd like to inform you of the disease that has been going around the factory. I'm sure, Samuel, you are quite aware of it." Mrs. Mardock smiled at the edge of the room.

Claire turned to her, eyes wide.

"Sammy," she whispered cautiously, tugging on her husband's sleeve.

"What's going on?!" Mary cried, standing up.

Kris grabbed her arm and yanked Mary back to the seat. "Just listen, will you?"

Mrs. Mardock quickly summarized what had occurred in the past few days to Mary. "But that was all a hoax. This island is a hoax. If you weren't paid or brought here by an agency, you're here because you're clueless. Everything we do is to test how to spread this new illness across the globe. We still haven't created a cure, but when we do, we'll have the ability to take over nations. We'd be powerful."

"Do you really believe that?" Mary interjected. "Viruses have crippled nations, but no organization has ever managed to overpower them."

"They did not want to. They did not try to. But this is different; this could ruin them enough for anyone to take over. No one is powerful against it. The best thing is that one cannot catch it; it must be injected."

"That's terrible, that's—" Mary doubled over and groaned.

"This was bound to happen." Mrs. Mardock clicked her tongue. "You should not have used the vending machine."

Kris pulled the weak Mary out of the room. Slowly, Claire began to comprehend the situation. They would not make it out of here alive.

The room darkened, and Claire noticed the weather outside. Suddenly, a rumble came from the dark clouds. Right, it was supposed to rain today, thunder and lightning.

Kris came back. Mary did not. They all knew too much; Colin must've known something too, and that's why he wasn't here. They all knew too much. They were doomed as long as they stayed stuck in this room.

Claire tugged Sammy's sleeve. He was still sitting upright, frozen. She whispered his name under her breath over and over. Thunder crackled again, and a tree branch brushed against the window. Claire just wanted to curl up and cry.

A baby started crying. The one sitting right on Mrs. Mardock's chest.

"What?" Claire muttered.

"It's my heir." Mrs. Mardock smiled. There was a glint in her eye as she looked at them, as though she meant something more than what she said. "When all is destroyed, she will be the next queen of the globe."

No doubt Mrs. Mardock was dangerous and delusional. She believed she could take over the world. And that type of psychotic behavior would kill them in seconds.

"When that happens"—Brax's words came out slowly—"can I be first?"

"First?" Kris echoed.

"To die. It hurts a lot."

Mrs. Mardock shook her head firmly. "Kris, you know what to do."

In two steps, Kris moved to Claire's side and grabbed her arm. Thunder clapped and a gun clicked behind them. Sammy held out the handgun, pointing it at Kris.

"Like you could shoot me." Kris scoffed and yanked Claire's arm while she tried to push away so she couldn't follow him.

Lightning flashed and Sammy struck. Brax jumped in front of Kris. With a grumble, he fell to the ground.

"Finally." He sighed, blood seeping to the floor from the left of his chest. In only a few more breaths, his eyes rolled back, and his shallow breaths began to stop. The room was quiet, and even the baby had stopped sobbing at that moment.

Without hesitation, before anyone could twitch a muscle, Sammy shot again, and Kris went down this time. A bullet through his head, he smashed against the white wall, staining it red as he slid to the ground. His body stopped working faster than Brax's had.

"Goodness." Mrs. Mardock smirked. "I did not know you were one for violence, Samuel."

Sammy moved toward the door. Mrs. Mardock backed away, cowering. This time, Sammy smirked.

"Are you not going to shoot?" Mrs. Mardock asked as her child started sobbing again.

"You're nothing without followers. After today, this island will be nothing."

"Impossible. In seconds, this place can start swarming with our highest-equipped military."

"You wouldn't want them to know. Now would you?"

Sammy was right. As long as Mrs. Mardock didn't act, they were safe. She couldn't get to them through anyone else but herself. Slowly, stepping over the bodies on the ground, her shoes and pants now stained with blood. She felt like a ghost of herself, and walking through the small office space took too long. She felt dizzy enough, though she knew she wasn't sick. Claire reached for Sammy's outstretched hand, but she still couldn't get the image out of her head of him shooting at Kris. Killing Kris and Brax. He was threatening, and she had never seen that side of him; it was too foreign. What was worse was that her naivety had blinded her from what other odd things she must've done in the lab to help Mrs. Mardock. She couldn't come up with anything now, but no doubt she had helped with the disease in the past few years she had been here.

But only Sammy could be trusted right now. Right? He did have to know marabidium was fake, didn't he? He had been working there for a while; what if he was just as complacent in all of this as she was? But he knew about it. Still, Sammy had defended her, and there was no one else she could turn to.

She clutched Sammy's hand as he opened the office door. They walked through the labs, Claire leading them out of the building. They passed Mary's body, slouched along the wall somewhere, and Claire tried her best to ignore her body. The whole place was quiet after hours, which made them quite lucky.

As they reached the exit, Mrs. Mardock's heels clicked as she followed them through the dark hallway. This time, the child was in a stroller, and she carried a handgun pointed at them. "Now we're even."

Sammy whipped out his gun and pointed it at Mrs. Mardock. Claire was finding it harder to breathe. She thought they would be out of here soon. Sammy stepped away, letting go of Claire's hand as he held the gun with two hands.

"Would you really hesitate, you—"

Lightning flashed, and the gun went off. The crack left an echoing sound through the empty, dark halls. The baby started crying again. Sammy dropped the gun to the floor and ran to the baby, pulling her out of the stroller and carrying her out to the parking lot.

"Come on, we need to unlock your car."

Claire, too shocked for words, followed Sammy outside. Obediently, she listened and followed his orders to drive to the ports.

And the whole time, her mind couldn't stop going as she drove through the evening traffic.

This whole thing was a hoax. I was a part of it. Sammy knew that. He killed three people, not hesitating. We're in big trouble. But this is all a hoax, so we're not. No one really knew what happened. And if Mrs. Mardock didn't want trouble, then could the cameras be fakes to make people like me believe this reality? So, everyone on here, except us, is on her side? Was Sammy on her side before?

"Stop here." Sammy got out of the car the second Claire parked it. She hurried to catch up to him as he chose a boat, boarded it, and got it running, the baby hanging on to his neck. It had stopped crying. Lightning and thunder were gone. The city seemed distant and terrifying. How had she gotten here in just a few days?

Claire got on the boat and stared at the shrinking island as they left. She fell to the ground. She wanted to cry, but couldn't. Why would the tears not come?

"Claire." Sammy sat beside her once the island was too small a dot and they were stopped in the middle of the gentle seas. The baby slept in his lap. "I need to tell you something."

"You knew about this all along."

"I did."

"Why would you?"

"I grew up in a third-world country. Impoverished and easy to manipulate without parents around. No family at all. And when I got a job, when I came here, I loved it. So I followed the leadership blindly. Only when I turned sixteen did I start getting involved in...stuff here."

"What sort of 'stuff?'"

"I-it's hard to talk about."

"Can you try? Sammy. For me?"

Sammy looked away, sighed, and looked to the sky. "Don't hate me, please."

"What is it?" Claire pleaded. "I'm your wife, shouldn't I know these things about you. I don't. I can't believe I'm such a fool."

"You're not a fool." Sammy folded her in her arms. "You did what you could with what you knew, and at the end, you knew who you couldn't trust."

"Can I trust you?"

"I want you to. I need you to." It seemed more like a plea, a cry for help, than a command.

They stayed like that in silence, Claire's eyes starting to get wet, but they did not stay wet for long. Something had broken in her today, and she didn't know where.

"She started selling me to others at sixteen. Sometimes labor. Sometimes something else. She took advantage of it, too. It's how I met Colin." Sammy paused, his words heavy in the air. "The kid's mine too."

Claire understood; she didn't need him to elaborate. He'd been doomed when he had thought he was saved. He'd been hurt and destroyed. And now, he was sitting next to her, vulnerable. She was too conflicted. She wanted to trust him after knowing him for four years of her life, but now, after learning all this, the distance between them was gaping. It was hard to ignore. She could feel herself moving closer and closer to one side of the scale. Further and further away from Sammy.

"It's okay," Claire whispered, but she didn't really know if it was the right thing to say or if she meant it. She still struggled to comprehend what was going on and here she was in the middle of the sea. Holding onto Sammy didn't make it better. Claire was still lost at what to do next and how to feel. The realization that Mrs. Mardock had destroyed both of them, had such villainous plans, and until tonight, Claire was absolutely blind to it, she felt like a fool.

"There's a cot if you want to go to sleep inside. I can drive us to the mainland by morning."

"How do you know all this? Sailing and the mainland?"

"I forced myself to learn, I wanted to get away."

Claire nodded, and a thought occurred to her as she twisted her band on her left ring finger. "If you were under their control, how, why'd you marry me?"

"I wanted to try to live a normal life here since she had dropped me and moved me to handing out injections. Well, as normal as possible. I made it my goal to marry the first person I met."

"Oh." Claire pushed him away and stared.

"But I don't not love you. I fell for you at some point, but I just didn't want them to see it. I wanted them to—it all sounds so stupid now. Claire, I mean it. I do love you. You're the only one who ever cared for me. Ever. And, you were the thing that made my heart hurt in a good way for once. Like a little hummingbird, I just felt drawn to you, your sweetness. And you loved me, and I just wanted to be able to return that feeling truthfully for once in my life."

"Sammy," Claire stood up and shook her head, "save it for another day. I'm tired. Just get us to safety."

"I can do that."

Claire headed to the cot inside the cabin. She lay down, running the whole day through her head. The only person she could trust was Sammy, and he had been hiding so many things from her. She really could never trust him. And he was hurt, and she wasn't sure if the love he felt for her was genuine or desperate. And she had been lied to, and she was foolish, and she was so, so lost. Her eyes became wet.

Slowly, tears slipped out of her eyes. She could not breathe. Everything hurt. The ship lurched and carried them through the waters. She cried, her breath coming out in short bursts as she curled into a tight ball under the scratchy covers on the dirty mattress.

The ceiling was white. The walls were white. The bed sheets were a deep black. Why, she didn't know. She looked at the face before her. No longer blindsided, he stood, trying to make eye contact with her.

It was hard not to see anything when truth had removed the blind over her eyes.

"I need you."

And she started to cry.

The Eyes Behind Our Own

by Eric Still

I saw them whenever I closed my eyes. As if peering from within the darkness, they glowered with unknown intent. Eyes not my own, alien and unreadable.

They say there is the devil you know and the devil you don't, but what if it isn't a devil at all? Could be something worse. Evil I can understand—however cynical. Kindness, too. But there is a layer between—the *gray area,* many call it—that can pave the way for dastardly enigmas I'd rather not entertain. I'd rather the eyes staring from within be easily distinguished as one or the other, but that would be too easy.

Eyes reveal many things—like the anxiety I ignored. They reveal lies and things unsaid, obscured behind insincerity and words revealing only partial truths. What of the things yet voiced? Perhaps that is what I perceive the most when I stare into their depths. But the greatest lie of all is the one I can't see.

I can see the truth peeking from behind all eyes—all except my own. They are the greatest of impostors, whose impervious cloak I can never remove. I suppose that means I lie to myself more than anything, in spite of my best efforts at introspection. I tire of looking inward and strive to understand others better instead.

Glittering jewels or lusterless obsidian, I found them all interesting enough to unearth. Behind those eyes, I saw who people truly were. I preferred knowing my devils like that. Maybe to have met an angel too, but I hadn't succeeded at the latter.

It's suffocating peering into your eyes in the mirror and not knowing which of the two you are.

That morning, I was strangely numb to the question rousing in their depths. Hazel, like always. Our gazes exchanged curiously, but I learned nothing—such was the plight of Omari Wilson. When I blinked, the game was over.

Ignorant yet again.

I left the bathroom, shutting the light off behind me. The cramped halls always reminded me of how old the home was. Chipping beige latex paint formed patterns reminiscent of the brocade curtains around the home. However, unlike the chic curtains, the emulation was stark against the matte white beneath. My siblings and cousins had been haphazard with everything in Mom's house in our childhood, and much like other transitions into adulthood, the damage was crudely covered up. The parallel was even scarier, considering we couldn't paint over the cracks in our mental health, but Mom tried at least.

She was there in the living room with a steaming mug—Folger's instant coffee with some cheap off-brand creamer and an abundance of sugar, no doubt. The smell alone reminded me where my caffeine addiction began. Much like the truth behind eyes, sugar, too, is a gateway drug many ignore. When I caught Mom's attention, I could at least see she was sincere in her love for me.

"Son," she began.

"Mother," I returned with a smirk. We liked to joust with such references.

"My baby ready for his first day of college?" she asked, tone saccharin as she sipped her coffee.

"Probably more so if you could drive me instead of making me take a bus at the butt-crack of dawn." I had a car already, funnily enough. A graduation gift of a piss-yellow station wagon. It was a year younger than me, but still old by car standards. I had put half the money down with my grant, but she pretended she'd paid for all of it. Mom hid the key somewhere. Otherwise, I would have driven it. As if reading my mind, she gave me a shit-eating grin.

"It's nearly nine a.m., boy. Quit being dramatic," she sneered. "Besides, you'll have your license next week, then you'll be complaining about gas prices instead."

"I hear you complain enough already," I muttered, shaking my head as I crossed the living room and grabbed my softshell jacket from the basket of unfolded laundry next to her.

"Maybe I should complain more about teaching me to use the washer and dryer, if complaining works."

"It doesn't," she said, setting her mug down beside the folded laundry on the coffee table. She dug into the pile of clothes on the couch and resumed folding them. "I need to teach you and make things easier for me. You're not a baby anymore, just *my* baby."

"Yeah, yeah," I dismissed, and she stared hard at me for a few moments. Sun rays shimmered across my face, peering through the crudely tied drapes.

"Always reminding me how pretty your eyes are. So colorful today," she said, and I dug my fingers into my palms.

Mom always reminded me how pretty my eyes were. With my chubby form and learned insecurity, it was the only compliment I'd ever earned from others. She always told me how handsome I was, but I thought her insincere, or more so just never had others affirm such a claim. Still, seeing the genuine praise through her matching hazel set Grandma had gifted me through her, a smile tugged at my lips as I shrugged my jacket on and tightened the wrists' Velcro straps.

I had fifteen minutes until my bus arrived, but procrastinating was all too common for me, and I was actively working to improve my punctuality. Five minutes was better than a scrambled sprint to the bus while it was boarding passengers.

"Well, off I go for my edumucation," I said, earning a chuckle from Mom as I raced toward the foyer

"All right, big man. Go get me a Nobel Prize to brag about."

The neighborhood was always so tranquil on Monday mornings. The mid-August heat simmered on the freshly cut grass, and with its scent came nostalgia. The tingling of allergens on my skin after an afternoon of playing in the grass, usually football. If not for dislocating my knee in middle school, I'd have tried sticking with it, but my high school hadn't even had a football team.

For the final two years, Mom forced me to start taking the bus to school, and I resented everything about taking the bus. They were never clean, for one. Two, there were a lot of *interesting* scents aboard, and I preferred boring in that department. Then there was the regiment you'd build around the schedules. Despite my lack of punctuality, I somehow managed my own more effectively—more of an indictment than a boast.

Upon reaching the bus, I boarded and crammed myself into one of the seats. An odd assembly built throughout the ride, and I felt nauseous thinking about the bombardment to my senses as I shrunk into myself. That was hard to do with how big I was.

One more week, I kept repeating. I receded into daydreams about my college journey ahead. Engineering paid well in my city, or so I had been bashed over the head with from the job sector being endlessly hyped up. In truth, I only cared about working with interesting machinery. The pay was only a pleasant aside. Coming from a frugal middle-class upbringing, I valued money and wished I had disposable income, but I planned to focus on getting a job after my first semester.

The campus was large compared to my meager high school, featuring several sections for the different departments. A large strip bisected the center. On one side, it branched into the classrooms and educational facilities, and the other was the epitome of capitalistic dis-integrity in the education system: overpriced administration centers, a campus store, and a cafeteria at the end.

The fact that it looked nice was quickly negated the moment I was reminded of my insubstantial allowance. Somehow, the nagging of having *food at home* suddenly seemed the most sensical thing Mom had taught me.

I awkwardly fumbled with the paper map given to me the week prior at the orientation. Tension crept up my throat as I struggled to navigate with it to my first class, and I was woefully reminded of my inability to navigate. Even if it wasn't relevant to my curriculum, the inadequacy of being unable to understand maps jumbled with my uncertain expectations to disorient me.

I was a sweating mess by the time I pushed through the classroom door of my intro to engineering class. I shuffled to an empty seat on the side of the class and kept my head down as if that would erase my hurried intrusion.

An awkward greeting and an examination of the syllabus later, and my nerves settled enough for me to realize just how mismatched the inside of the room was from the exterior of the campus. If looks could kill, I'd live forever with how tacky the too-small all-in-one desks were atop the weathered vinyl flooring. They probably once reflected the fluorescent lighting above, but their original color was hardly present. Unsurprisingly, it wasn't redeemed by the *smart* whiteboard that would only ever know a marker, seeing as the geriatric professor would struggle to operate a decade-old projector, let alone that confusing mess of unnecessary tech.

As much as I'd prefer to continue scrutinizing the college, my class was soon compelled by our professor to speak with each other in preparation for future projects. Nobody caught my interest in the class. Glittering, cocky gazes devoid of introspection surrounded me. Comments of their summer projects reeked of both entitlement and a lack of empathy the more they downplayed the things I deemed difficult. It was apparent I had graduated from high school and had been sent back to freshman year with how pretentious they all were.

At least the humanities class I enrolled in proved far more friendly. Sure, nobody really stuck out, but they weren't irksome like the engineering students. That was until I was greeted by Ahreum Baang from Philosophy 101, who insisted on being called Ahri.

She was a cute Korean girl with a bubbly personality, but more than that, her eyes captivated me. Through the thick rims of her glasses, dark moons stared back, and suddenly, I felt as if I was gazing into the night itself. Elusive, but beckoning my understanding more than usual. Maybe it was just how cute she was, but I was immediately interested in what she had to say.

Her insights themselves weren't incredibly interesting, per se, but the passion behind her tone invoked an energy I was drawn to. I watched those eyes shift the more she spoke about her desire to bring cultural liberation and awareness into her writing, however vague she was when I dared to probe deeper.

"I think . . . that science is awesome and needs to be appreciated outside of cultural prestige," I remarked in an attempt to complete her meandering thought. Her eyes lit up, and she nodded eagerly.

"Yeah! Like, appreciate their discoveries rather than the fact that they have a degree or prestigious title or something," she affirmed, folding her arms over her chest with a smirk. She caught my gaze, head tilting for a moment as her lips pursed, and I suddenly tugged at my jacket sleeves to brace myself.

"You okay?" I shyly asked, and she gave a small nod.

"Your eyes are scary," she bluntly said, and my heart shrieked in my chest. I nearly had to wrestle for breath, but an insincere laugh forced its way out.

"What?" I remarked with a wry smile. As her gaze burned into mine, I couldn't help but feel foolish for entertaining any deeper connection.

"Yeah. Like . . . I just feel like you're tearing me apart with them, but not in a creepy way or anything," she said, and my smile melted.

Again, I thought. My eyes were one of the things I'd ever felt secure in, but now, ironically, she sundered them in her scrutiny. Their alleged beauty mattered not in that moment, but I feared what she saw was something else.

Self-determination was all I could ever rely on—affect. What she saw? I was powerless to change. Eyes so elusive, yet begging to be known. Eyes, like my own, that didn't wish to invoke fear. Eyes that yearned for safety.

Suddenly, I was staring at myself in the mirror. My own eyes were where hers once were, and as I held her gaze, I was on trial again. They bored through me, driving anxiety into my veins like a needle. The failure to wrench myself open, just as I had failed to understand her, strangled me, and phantom guilt crept in as I suffocated.

What I could have said to assure her of my intentions? Nobody ever understood, no matter how much I explained. I definitely had a habit of overexplaining, and something simple was usually what was required, but many failed to understand then, either.

My silence would have become an admission of guilt. I had to say something—anything.

"Oh . . . I've been told I have an intense stare, is all," I lied, shaking my head. It was all I could come up with.

"If you wanna know more about me, just ask," she said, smirking knowingly. "Omari need not be afraid." She shifted her pen as she dragged its cap along the horizontal lines of her notebook page.

Ironically, now it was my turn to be torn apart by those dark moons. I might as well have been sundered by the night and evanesced into its alluring darkness. Thinking in the poetic way I did, I suddenly thought of the band I used to brood around the house listening to, but the immediacy of Ahri's scrutiny called me back.

"What if I am?" I sheepishly retorted, my gaze drifting away.

"Don't be," she answered immediately, chuckling. "I'm not scary."

My former anxiety was sentenced by her—condemned to daftness along with my self-effacement, but that, too, could have been foolish of me. Habits died hard, my mom always said.

"It's funny. You said my eyes are scary, yet, I'm the one who's afraid," I said sardonically.

"Well, you're nice and interesting," she declared, and for a moment, she scrunched her face as she leaned into her seat. "I'll let you prove you're not scary, is all I'm saying." Having spoken her piece, she snapped her notebook shut before shoveling it into her shoulder bag.

As class ended, the professor informed us of our first assignment to read the first assigned book about logic and rhetoric in preparation for our next meeting. The book had sounded interesting enough to me, but I was a self-proclaimed *try-hard* when it came to matters of philosophy. I wondered if Ahri would agree with enough time.

I shuffled out of the class with her. She was heading off to her English class next, whereas I had calculus waiting for me. Math was the bane of my existence. It was the biggest hurdle for me to overcome in my program, and based on her snide remarks, English was the same for her. However crude a thought, a part of me cynically considered us tutoring each other in the respective subjects. She was already two leaps of math ahead of me, and I was a leap ahead of her in English. With my meekness, I suppressed suggesting such a thing for at least another two meetings with her, but I didn't get the chance.

"You help me, and I help you?" she suggested, as if tearing the initial thought from my head. Doubling back, I composed myself and nodded eagerly.

"Yeah, sure. I was thinking the same thing," I admitted in my scrambled thoughts.

"Deal," she said, but when I held my hand out to her, she gestured with her finger and poked my palm. Upon further inspection, she had formed a finger gun, and before I could process it, she snapped her thumb down.

"Bang!" she said before lowering her hand.

"Huh?"

"Bang! Like my last name. A lot of people made puns with it, so I held on to the best one. Ahri . . . *bang*," she said and shot me again for emphasis as she retreated. Instead of a bullet, I was hit by her smile, and I shot her with a smile in return.

"That bangs."

I could easily say I was beyond giddy as I curled up in bed, perhaps a bit more effeminate than I'd ever be around others, but then again, I cared little for arbitrary gender expectations. I was comfortable.

That bangs? I repeated in my head, wincing at myself with irony etching my thoughts. I always tried to be superfluous with my words and presentation, but the vernacular of my upbringing creeped out in my excitement. I'd have been harsh on myself about it, but the fact that she had giggled only encouraged me. I thought of a running joke I could make with my last name. I had once been bullied for it, along with other characteristics kids had singled out about me.

Limerence was a dangerous thing. It wrapped around the mind and enshrouded the heart in a tangle of temporary irrationality. I gravitated to her again and again, no matter how I tried to conjure a healthier mindset. When I liked a woman, I felt vulnerable, but perhaps I was just a masochist like that. I yearned for such a feeling while my rational mind admonished me for it. I couldn't deny that it cut the cynic in me just a bit.

Thinking of those dark eyes, I was soon asleep with the ambiance of melodies on a YouTube playlist lulling me under. It was dark. *Too dark.* I was afraid of the dark, despite my efforts to overcome the fear. The TV cast its glow over the room long enough to bring me under, but that same light didn't fill my slumber. Bit by bit, I was suffocated in it until . . . I wasn't.

It stared at me.

A singular eye emerged, juxtaposing the depthless abyss I drowned in. It only stared, unblinking, all-knowing, and all-consuming. I had nothing to give it, I thought, but it yearned more than any other. It tore me apart. It shredded me in a way that only the dark could. And just as my heart drummed and my formless being panicked, I was perceived by it.

The darkness was usurped by flashing colors, all too unnatural. I'd have preferred the dark, but I was tossed into a rumbling of these colors as I convulsed. Even as an atheist, I prayed and pleaded for some measure of divine intervention, but I was constrained to the colors brought forth by the eyes until I wasn't.

I awoke. Mute and resigned to remembering. I didn't want to, but I didn't consider not. I thought continuously about it until I was a zombie dragging myself from bed to get ready for my driver's test.

I drowned out Mom's unsolicited yammering about how to do the test. I was just numb. Not nervous—numb. Like many times of strife, I drowned my expectations and accepted the present for what it would bring.

Upon staging my car in line for inspection, Mom handed me the key and wished me luck. The large man—larger than me, even—checked off boxes on his paper to ensure my car was road-ready, and I watched blankly as he instructed me to get behind the wheel. Check signals, brake, seatbelt, start the car.

We were on the road before I knew it, and my muscle memory kicked in, allowing me to glide through the test perfectly. In my periphery, I saw his eyes boring into me as we approached an intersection. His voice, muddied by his insistence on repeating things quickly, confused me.

"Left lane at this light," he said. I flicked my blinker on and veered left. "Left lane, not this light." I faltered, face scrunching. "Left lane at this light." I hesitated.

As my wagon slowed, half straddling the left turning lane, the car barreling up from behind me honked loudly, and the instructor yanked my steering wheel left, pushing us out of the way in time as he fumed at me from the passenger seat.

I failed then and there, but as my heart shrunk in my chest, I could only see that chastising, all-too-familiar leer casting all blame on me. The cynicism was reborn again.

Mom was oddly quiet driving me home, but her gaze suggested she was disappointed or maybe worried. I didn't care which.

"Gotta pay more attention," she said in at least five ways over the course of the ride, but I gave basic regard to what she said as I sighed heavily.

"I'm done with the bus," I concluded, eyes narrowing as she pulled us into the driveway. I had class later that day, but taking the bus again was not an option. "I can drive well—that stupid instructor fucked me up with his lack of enunciation," I spat, and Mom shot me a concerned look.

"Omari," she began, but I cut her off when I marched inside and tucked myself into my room to prepare for class later. I yearned for that additional hour of sleep the bus schedule took from me, and it was only three weeks until I would take the test again, anyway. I doubted I'd get pulled over when in bumper-to-bumper traffic to and from the campus.

Mom didn't push the matter as far as I could tell she wanted to. It was my mistake to make, I imagined she thought. She didn't argue it, and much to my vindication, it went exactly as I said it would. In just a few weeks, I had my license with a more competent instructor, and I was self-reliant again.

The end of the semester approached, and I was out studying with Ahri over sushi. It wasn't a date. I had to keep reminding myself. I only considered one-on-one outings to be a date if I explicitly expressed that during the invitation. We were just studying, but I'd be lying if I said there weren't precursors of interest. Probing questions and the like.

I was far from altruistic, in my mind, but I thought to use my talents to give a voice and reason to the madness. Be it articulating the plight of my community or taking incoherent babbling and deciphering it, I was there for it.

Ahri was more refined than when I'd first met her. She wasn't so vague now that she could express her thoughts with the rhetorical tools I introduced her to. I can't say I was much better in the math department, however. The more I listened and witnessed her mind and philosophies she bared before me, the more I gravitated to her. I convinced myself that I cared about her passion and ideals more than her looks. Still, I admired everything about her.

"Are you going to Kawaii Expo next month?" she suddenly asked me while holding nigiri to her lips. I gripped the California roll with my chopsticks, hands trembling from my efforts not to demolish the fragile piece. I was clumsy with chopsticks.

"Yeah, actually. I got a two-day pass with my friends—what about you?" I asked, aware she was into shoujo more than any other genre.

"Just one day. My job doesn't pay well," she sighed, but I smiled as I consumed the roll in my grip.

"I'll be cosplaying a nameless ninja from *Shiitake.*"

"Hell yeah! I'll be cosplaying Evelia from *Sinisisters!*" she proclaimed excitedly. I vaguely knew of the anime, namely because of how men fawned over Evelia. A risqué nun outfit would do that to a guy, and I was hardly better. I would be lying if I said the thought of her in that outfit wasn't enticing. "I'm not driving there, though," she continued. "I'm still too new to driving on the freeways here." She scowled.

Ahri had gotten her license just a month ago, but didn't have her own car. Her mom was agreeable, but she was well aware of Ahri's limitations. Driving in the city was one thing—the coastal freeways were a different beast to kill. I learned that the hard way.

Admittedly, it was difficult to meet with Ahri very often off campus. For all of her strengths, she was a bad planner and often ended up flaking more than I cared for. I didn't judge her too harshly over it, but the yearning it left did irk me just a bit.

"I can be your Uber," I offered with a smile, half convinced she'd decline. She mulled over the thought, chewing on another piece of sushi as she nodded triumphantly.

"If you're sure!"

"I'll pick you up and take you home. Actual Ubers are a million dollars on con days," I informed, and she snickered.

"Settle for me buying you boba after this as payment?" she offered.

"You drive a hard bargain, Miss Baang." She pressed a finger gun to my chest and pulled the trigger, and I played dead in my seat as she blew on her finger with a smug look.

"Still gotta get you to pass the final, though. We've got a week left to study up," I reminded her, and she pouted as she picked at a piece of salmon.

"Yeah, but I'm not sure how to feel about my chances. But being with you is reassuring," she said, meeting my gaze.

"That so? Guess my eyes are not so scary now, huh?" I challenged. She smirked and looked down at her plate, spinning her chopsticks.

"Nope. Definitely still are," she said before devouring the rest of her sushi.

Though I was cosplaying as a shinobi, I felt more like a canned sardine in the packed halls of the convention center. It allegedly was built to host up to 100,000 attendees, but it wouldn't have surprised me if they had oversold the tickets. *Something, something profits.* The only boon would have been getting to hold hands with Ahri as we weaved through the packed crowds to reach the center we were interested in browsing. It was more than nerve-racking; I could have easily crushed her delicate hand if I wasn't careful.

Ahri hardly seemed concerned. The occasional glance with her dark eyes suggested as much to me, but I could tell she was eager to break into the open area of the exhibition hall. Reminiscent of a layered carousel in its layout, the sprawling circles might as well have been a maze to us. It was my third time coming to the expo, but I was a notoriously bad navigator. This had been Ahri's first time, as she'd volunteered the more we bantered on our journey through the crowd of cosplayers.

To no surprise, Ahri was stopped pretty regularly for photos. Some were with random attendees, and the others with characters from the series. I found it amusing, but I was honestly a bit jealous. I hadn't cosplayed a specific character, and posing with a big guy in a cheap, generic ninja cosplay and shades wasn't the first thought most had when they saw me. I didn't think I could pull off an official character.

Ahri and I found ourselves in line as she chatted with the friends she'd mentioned. They were nice enough, fairly unassuming, even. If not for my shades, I'd have felt naked with how my eyes drifted off in dissociation. I tended to do that when excluded from conversation. I overheard glimpses still; the new shoujo being announced, some generic romance manga I had negative interest in, and some dreaded words that woefully snatched my attention.

"He doesn't like me being into K-pop; says it's shallow and stupid," Ahri complained to her friend, fingers curling tighter around the rolled-up poster in her hands.

"Who?" I asked, abrupt in my return to reality. Her friend gave me a look, nervously glancing at Ahri as she enthusiastically smiled at me.

"Oh, my boyfriend. He's not into anime or anything like that. He doesn't even know I'm here."

Or here with me, my mind finished, but my shrouded eyes were impervious to the damning information given. I could only consider her a liar. It had been just a few weeks, and she already had a boyfriend? It always seemed so simple for women, but I was just being cynical.

"Ah, gotcha," I replied simply. Though my venomous thoughts swarmed, I quelled them quickly and forced a smile, and that seemed to ease Ahri's friend.

"You'll have to meet him. I haven't told him about you."

No thanks, I thought and spaced back out. Neither Ahri nor her friend seemed to want to push the subject or probe into my distance. Could have been that I was her ride home, or maybe it was something else I couldn't possibly understand. I wouldn't have deigned to either. I hated trying to understand all the things that made my blood boil.

She owed me nothing, not her friendship or something more. My expectations were my own, I kept repeating, but I couldn't make those words ring true no matter how sensical it all was. Each glance she gave from then on was not with her own eyes, but with *those* eyes.

Maybe it was a panic attack, but the air in my lungs tickled a bit, settling into dancing spines and a queasy tightness. I was ignored, so they didn't even notice as I silently hid the unsettling feeling.

Before me, eyes drifted, staring from within the clamorous crowd drifting by. The world became mute, and I was on trial at the most inauspicious of times. They couldn't speak, but I could hear that voice so clearly. *What did you expect?* I heard as a whisper in my ear. The voice wasn't clear, but it was familiar. Regardless, I had no answer.

She owes you nothing, the voice continued, and I bit my lip hard—almost enough to draw blood. Those eyes grew larger and more prominent. With it, light fled, and I was submerged in that nightmare once again. Eyes everywhere. Around, above, below—*within*. When I shut my eyes, they were waiting for me behind my lids.

"Ninja, ninja," Ahri's voice blared through the muteness, and I looked into her dark, insidious eyes. "You okay? Need an exorcism?" she playfully quipped, holding up the glimmering rosary on her neck with an amused smile, as if she could never take anything seriously.

"Nah, just . . . thinking is all," I told her truthfully in spite of my vagueness. Her friend pursed her lips, glancing away.

"You sure?" Ahri persisted, but her friend grabbed her shoulder and gave a wry smile.

"He seems chill. Don't worry," her friend said, and they exchanged glances before continuing their conversation.

I was always a terrible liar. And before those damned eyes I hated so much, no such lie was possible. No shades could disguise my festering disdain. I was always okay with just being friends, but the reveal felt insidious. Insincere and oblivious to the obvious harm waiting ahead.

My estranged dad had been a player, and I didn't have enough fingers to count his affairs. Anything even broaching infidelity was reprehensible to me, and Mom never would allow me to forget how much she'd hate me if I cheated on a woman. This was more complicated, but it settled all the same.

Between abstaining from the overpriced food truck and the summer heat, my expression had become visibly disturbed. The day's end was approaching as we bounced from event to event, and Ahri had more than taken notice of my resigned silence.

"I should get going. I'll just take an Uber home," she murmured, but I perked my head up and shook my head. "I said I'd get you home. Ubers are gonna be at least ninety dollars at this time," I informed her, well aware of what surge pricing could do to a wallet.

"You sure?" she asked, and I nodded.

No matter how spoiled my mood was, I could never shake the altruistic bones from my skin. Maybe I really was just gullible like that, but meeting her eyes, I was reminded that it was more of a divorced obligation in my head as opposed to some deeper emotion like I had entertained prior to learning of what this all had been.

Those eyes that usurped her sockets were not fooled, I could tell. Cynical and damning all the same, colors awash and scorning my mind, I relived that nightmare over and over again until I broke eye contact and guided her through the crowd. Snaking around several blocks, we walked as I texted my friends to meet once I'd drop her off. Ahri offered tepid thanks for the accommodations, and I gave an equally disinterested response to downplay the inconvenience.

In truth, it would be more convenient the sooner I dropped her off. The car ride was hardly different, and she hummed themes and melodies to fill the silence. My heart almost wanted to soften, but each time it thought to calm, those eyes resurfaced again and again to scorn any *mercy* mustered. I hated thinking this way.

I came to a stop before her home, and she clenched the rosary close to her chest as she glanced at me.

"Thank you so much for a journey well enjoyed," she spoke in character with a bemusing smile.

I doctored a yawn and smiled at her, but our eyes betrayed us.

"Of course. Glad to have gotten you home safe with your wallet intact," I joked, perhaps the sincerest thing I could have offered. *She knows*, I convinced myself. But that smile was impervious to the alleged lies of the accompanying gaze.

"I'll have to treat you to sushi next time, 'kay?" We exchanged nods, and she reached over to hug me, but I couldn't fake it enough to return it and awkwardly played it off with me being tired.

I watched her skip inside before I drove off, and the drive to my friend's house was an unnerving, bitter end to it all. Of course I had checked out, giving a spliced recap to my friends. Mostly guys, they offered the typical generalizations, corroborating my cynical subconscious, but I didn't need that. I was their ride to the convention the next morning, and I opted to sleep over to save on time, lest I be robbed by the surge in parking fees if we ran late.

The others slept adjacent to me on their air mattresses, the emptied-out living room looming with its dark ceiling and only the light of my phone as I looked over Ahri's and my text messages. Lamenting was unhealthy, I knew that, but the call to the void was too strong to resist as the others slept. Soon, my vision obscured as I drifted off with my cellphone clenched in my hand.

My own eyes had always eluded me in ways that made no sense. They were my eyes. *My eyes.* I should know myself best, if anybody could truly know someone. I knew others well, better than they knew themselves sometimes. Obliviousness and empty minds alike were married and refused to divorce.

Such ignorance compelled disgust within me. Knowing less was being lesser, and lesser was weakness. I would never allow myself to be buried under such considerations again and again. That's what those eyes conveyed to me.

They bloomed in the dark, bright and indicting in their fathomless judgment. Irises illuminated the damnation that gripped my limbs and froze me before them. Such a magistrate wouldn't be forgiving; I could tell. No words were spoken, like always, but I knew what they conveyed as their leer atomized me.

All too knowing, all too discerning, all too yearning, all too burning.

Again and again, I was diminished until I was left curled up in fear before them. My brain rumbled, and my eyes retreated into my skull. Shadows wrapped around my vision again and again, and soon, I stared at him. The scared, shriveled person cowering before my gaze.

He had always stared at me. I knew it. Always trying to unearth me in ways that challenged all I knew, all I was. I had always been scared when he did that, but he seemed oblivious to how he scorned me. But here . . . he cowered before me? My eyes aren't scary, I promised, but he couldn't hear me.

But neither could I.

When I awoke, I stared blankly at the ceiling again. Not quite the abyss it was at night as the light of dawn offered a semblance of a glow to keep me from losing myself in it. Maybe it was just my vampiric tendencies, but the light kept me from ruminating so much. It was a weird parallel that my aversion to superstition didn't allow me to explore.

I was a man of commitment, even when my mind was in a drought. I drove my friends to the convention and pledged to pick them up later. Sometimes, twenty dollars extra in gas was worth having a little quiet to think. Mom thought so too the moment I entered the house.

There she was, watching her daytime television programs on the big screen while doing her lotto scratchers at the coffee table. I gave her a wry smile as she greeted me, but she saw through me quickly.

"Omari," she began and set an old penny down. "You ain't going to the expo today? You got a two-day pass, didn't you?" she asked, raising a brow.

"Yeah . . ." I sheepishly said and shoved my hands into my coat pockets. "Head ain't right for it today. I dropped the gang off, and I'll pick them up later."

"Boy, wasting that money. Could have got three pastramis with a single day there!" she quipped playfully, flashing a smirk. I couldn't help but chuckle, shrugging.

"If you want a pastrami from Keeps, I can go—"

"Boy, shut up. You know that ain't why I'm saying that," she said and patted the seat next to her.

I approached slowly, pursing my lips as I dropped the tough-guy act she hated.

"What about that girl you kept talking about?" she asked. She knew me too well for my ego to prosper.

"My fault for getting my hopes up. Has a boyfriend now. Said she didn't tell him about me," I sighed out, burying my face as I released the breath I'd held in since yesterday.

"Omari . . ." Mom began, shaking her head.

"I can't do what you tell me to do. Forget her and just move on or whatever. I don't want to think it was malicious or on purpose, but goddamn, why does this kind of thing always seem to happen? How else am I supposed to see it?"

"I don't know. I don't have your eyes to tell you," she said.

"I try to find out how I should see it—how I should react. I stare into my eyes to find out why I can't stop seeing it all as this . . . fucked-up thing, but I can't."

Mom grabbed my hand, lifting it to her lips as she tucked my head into her chest. She was terrible at consoling me usually, but she tried as any mother should.

"I come from a different time, you know. That kind of thing . . . wouldn't be received well by anybody, but you ain't like my daddy. You ain't like *your* daddy. You're softer than I even meant to raise you, but that just means you gotta find your own way of looking at it," she said, stifling a chuckle as if she felt embarrassed to say any of that.

I raised my head, sighing heavily to release the tension I held. I didn't have to pretend to be unbothered or stoic like I had with Ahri. Maybe I shouldn't have then, either. I didn't have the answers or knowledge to be greater in that instance. I could only pray that it was all right—that I wouldn't be diminished in suggesting I didn't know how to feel about her still.

I shifted to sit up, and Mom grabbed her lotto scratcher, pensively eyeing the numbers she revealed with careful scribbles. She lost, and cursing under her breath, she tossed the penny in the coin jar next to the flower vase.

"Could have been rich if my eyes weren't so scary," I joked, and Mom gave me a look, scrunching her face.

"Boy, yo' eyes ain't scary. Intense, but not scary."

"Well, they scare me whenever I look into them," I admitted, pursing my lips. "Gotta be honest with myself if I hope to win at this whole life thing," I facetiously countered. Her gaze bore through me, and after a moment, she scoffed and hit my arm before standing.

"Not when you're looking at yo'self. That's a staring contest you'll always lose."

Darling, Don't Play in the Woods at Night

Carter Elise Key

Content/Trigger Warnings

- Death

- Hunting

- Mild blood imagery

- Knife mention/use

Heat lightning flashes across the cloud-covered sky, illuminating the tops of the trees and odd angles of the telephone poles. It hasn't started raining yet, so I have to act fast if I want this done.

Flashlights speckle the forest ahead, an indicator that they are looking for me.

Someone is always looking for me.

The knife in my hand is frigid. With no body heat to warm myself, I twirl the weapon between my fingers. I'm careful, though—I won't cut myself.

I won't give them a trail right to me.

A branch snaps. It's maybe twenty feet north of me, and I'm only partially sure that it's another one of my kind. I bob and weave to try to see them through the shadows. They stand there, in a pocket of darkness of their own making, statuesque. Glossy hair reflects the moonlight, and their pale skin is mostly covered in leather. They have a mask on to cover the lower half of their face, but I can still see their eyes. They're red. Hungry.

Our gazes meet as they feel me watching them. She goes through the same assessment I did, and I flash her a smile, the points of my fangs obvious against my cherry-red lips. She returns the smile, and we refocus on the humans in front of us.

"I know I heard one of 'em comin' this way. There's even practically a trail to follow—and my wife said they don't make it easy."

"Paul, maybe if you shut your trap, we'll be able to actually get 'em out of their hiding."

Paul, I assume, snorts. "They're already dead; not like they can do much more harm."

His companion takes a second before he responds. "I dunno. People have been disappearing in these woods for a few months now. Best not to take our chances."

I twirl the blade again behind me, so that none of the limited light can glint off the shining metal. Just because I've returned here doesn't mean I'm going to have sloppy or lazy habits. I keep my stash clean as a whistle—there's no use in having anything of value if it's just going to rust or stick to itself after a few uses.

Paul and his friend get very close to where I'm standing. Maybe even on the other side of the same tree. I inhale, savoring the scent of their fear and the sound of their hearts, and then exhale as quietly as I can.

Lightning strikes. Nowhere nearby, but the thunder that follows is loud enough to make the two grown men jump. The sound of the leaves crunching under their boots as they land is like music to my ears.

Now I just need to get them separate.

I know that my own eyes are a deep shade of maroon. It's been nearly a decade since I've feasted so much; it's been difficult to stop myself. With the presence of the other, I'm glad to know that I'm not the only one. These woods are full of stupid people with stupid goals. There's no shame in showing them what happens when they mess with our territory.

The other woman, confident in her ability to wield shadows, sends a wave of them in my direction. I nod, flashing another smile in her direction. She dips her head in acknowledgment, still refusing to remove her mask. Smart.

"Paul? Where'd you go?!"

"I'm right here, Rudy, chill out."

"You disappeared!"

"I did not—just look to your right."

I move, slowly at first. I don't want to interrupt their calls for distress; that would cause more suspicion than necessary.

"I'm looking to my right and you're not there," Rudy yells, his voice echoing off the trees.

Paul stumbles backward, in line with where I am. He takes a moment to swing his head back and forth, surveying the new-to-him area. Once his eyes land on me, they widen. His jaw goes slack, and the unlit cigarette between his lips falls to the forest floor.

Now, my smile turns wicked.

He tries to turn and run away, but he can't take his eyes off me. I can't blame him; I am a sight to behold.

I advance. One step. Two.

He falls on his ass, tripping over one of the tree roots that's made its way to the surface in search of a more reliable water source. I huff out a laugh at the irony. I love being one with nature.

I stand above him, my feet on either side of his knees. He whimpers, and I kneel, my knees caging in his hips. My hands slide up his torso to his neck, the blade of the knife raking his clothes open in its path.

I can smell his fear.

It's exhilarating.

I move my hands to rest on the ground by his face, truly caging him in now. He tries to cry out, but it's pathetic, and I slap one of my hands over his mouth to keep him from doing it again. Unfortunately, Paul starts to squirm, still trying to release himself from me. Silly Paul—nobody likes to play with their food.

I sit back, my groin pressed into his. Lightning strikes again, and it lights up my face. Now, he can clearly see the hunger in my eyes. My nostrils flare, and my septum jewelry flashes. My cherry-red lips are painted into a smile. And as soon as he sees me, he's plunged into darkness again as the light disappears.

Paul shrieks, but it's too late. I drag my tongue up his chest and to his neck, pressing the blade of my knife against the other side. It's right at the sensitive bit of skin where your jaw connects to your neck, and he shivers. He wants to tell himself that it's from fear, but I can tell that there's some excitement there.

Once my lips trace up his jawline, he whimpers again, and this time it's from a lack of contact. I give him one open-mouth smile, and my fangs elongate. The hungrier I am, the longer they get—and they're hovering above my bottom lip with my jaw hanging open. The moonlight flashes in his eyes, and if I had a heart that still beat, I'd probably feel pity for him.

A twig snaps, and I whirl around to see where it came from. Rudy, Paul's friend, stands behind me, shaking. He's got his gun raised and ready to shoot.

The other is nowhere to be found.

"Y-you got my uncle there!" he shouts.

"Rudy, git!"

"N-no, I . . . I won't let you! I won't let you have 'im!"

I give him a moment to realize how ridiculous that statement is. He can't do anything to hurt me; I'm immortal. Never ending. You can't kill something twice.

Unluckily for him, the other appears from his shadow. They take a moment to wrap their hands around his short neck, and the boy's eyes nearly bulge out of his head. Sure, her skin must be cold, but it can't be that bad.

Swiftly, she snaps his neck.

Paul screams, and I plunge the blade into his artery. The noise doesn't last very long.

I sigh. "It's less fun if they're already dead when we eat them," I mutter.

The other laughs. "Much easier though, if they aren't trying to run away."

We share a grin, and she sits next to me. They lift the body with their shadows, turning them solid enough to move matter, and bring it closer. It's impressive, but I don't waste time telling her that. We're both hungry and must be satiated before holding a pleasant conversation.

Now, we may feast together.

About the Author

Carter Elise Key, otherwise known to their students as Noble Tutor Carter, is currently working toward their MA in Creative Writing from Seton Hall University. When they're not penning flash fiction or poetry, they're likely researching small ways to better the community around them and sending photos of their ESA to burnt-out peers and students. They hope to pursue a PhD in Creative Writing and continue nurturing the spark of creativity in others, just as their teachers and professors have done for them.

My Beatrice

Jay L. Scaffa

Content/Trigger Warnings

- Implied Sexual Assault

- Assisted Suicide

- Murder

- Suicidal Ideations

Bea was twenty-three the first time she saw it: gaunt and ghostly, faint enough for her to try to pretend it wasn't there—to pretend it was a trick of the light, a manifestation of her guilt. She averted her gaze, just for a moment, and wiped at the tears staining her cheeks, smearing blood across her freckled skin. Her eyes blinked rapidly as they followed the shadow's movements, watching closely as it knelt across from her.

She tried to speak, to plead her innocence to this creature, but nothing came out—her words stuck like tar in the folds of her throat. Her chin quivered. Hands shook as she pressed them into her bare knees, turning the skin beneath them white. Surely this was her punishment; this creature was here to take her life in return for what she had done.

Black hair pooled into the hollow of the spirit's clavicle, a dense fog over still water. It tilted its head slowly, as if it were possibly taking a moment to assess the situation in front of it. A broken lamp. A man with thick blood oozing from his skull. A woman with glass stuck in her palm, kneeling beside him, crying, crying, crying. It was obvious, wasn't it?

She had only wanted him to listen.

She had only wanted him to *stop*.

Eyes, black and empty, turned up to meet her. A chill struck her spine like lightning, pinning her in place. Its eyelids fluttered, narrowed, and its gaze locked onto Bea as its head rocked slowly from side to side, the motion eerie and unnatural. Bea couldn't stop staring back—a thin outline of a pupil was barely apparent in the abyss as the spirit sat close and leered at her, never looking away from her eyes.

It appeared to be emaciated, the lines of its face and chest and shoulders narrow and sharp. It disappeared into too-big, ripped robes, only its bony fingers poking out from the wide sleeves. Its skin was roughly textured and ashen, almost transparent, and the shift of its joints were practically visible through the flesh.

"What—" Bea's voice broke as it leaned in closer. "What are you?"

Its chapped, thin lips parted, but no words came out. It simply opened and closed its jaw—loose on its hinges, blackened teeth clicking together uselessly. It sat back farther from Bea as it leaned down to press its gnarled mouth against the skin of the man lying dead between them.

"I . . . didn't mean to . . . " she whispered, scooting herself farther away from the body. "I didn't . . . I didn't . . . "

It only deigned to look up at her when her back slammed into the nightstand and something heavy fell to the ground next to her. Being farther away from it somehow felt worse, like its eyes were leaving gashes just under her skin to bleed her dry—like the only way to stop the pain would be to disappear inside its shadow and agree to let it consume her. She thought maybe she should let it. What life would there be after this, anyway?

Instead, it stood and lifted one arm, pointing to the doorway. It seemed to be telling her to leave, showing her mercy, and Bea wasn't sure she deserved it. Then something unfamiliar washed over her. A cold chill, a lightening of the air around her, an itching feeling deep in her chest that told her it would all be okay. She didn't know what it had done, but she suddenly felt safe; protected. She knew she couldn't stay here much longer.

It gestured again, she left without another word, and her life carried on as if nothing had ever happened.

As if she hadn't just been changed from the inside out.

"Hello," Bea says, forcing a smile as the door opens. "How are you today, Mrs. Calder?" A weight, unfamiliar and aching, bears down on her chest as she steps through the threshold. She scratches an itch tickling the back of her neck.

The door latches behind her, and the exhausted woman rubs at the bridge of her nose.

"He's been unresponsive all night." There is the barest hint of relief tinging the despair coming from her words, a combination that has become more and more familiar during her experiences with home care families. "I think it's time." She wipes under her eyes in a futile attempt to hide the emotions written all over her face. "His breathing has been kind of ragged. Should we stop the oxygen?"

Bea shrugs off her jacket and hums, pressing a reassuring hand onto the woman's shoulder.

"I'll go check his vitals and see where we're at. We can decide from there." She straightens the front of her scrubs and heads toward the bedroom. "Do you want to come with me?" Mrs. Calder shakes her head and points to the kitchen, saying something about lunch. Bea nods and waits for her footsteps to disappear before she opens the door slowly. "Hey, Frank," she hums. Her words are artificially airy. "Heard you're not feeling so well today."

There's a flicker in the corner of her eye; a shadow that seems only slightly out of place as she sets her bag down on the stool beside the bed. A shiver prickles at her spine when she turns to try to catch it. Nothing. Her imagination.

"Let's get you checked out." The slight sheen of sweat across his forehead parts as she swipes the thermometer across his skin. He has a fever, and Bea frowns at the number blinking up at her. She goes through the rest, checks his pulse, his oxygen levels, his blood pressure; weak, shallow, and far too low. "It is time, isn't it, Frank?"

A sigh escapes her as she slips the oxygen mask from his face. His lips and nose are chapped, and a dull red line presses into his cheeks. A wet breath reverberates from the back of his throat, and Bea swallows against the knot forming in her own. She hasn't been present for a patient passing yet, and she wasn't sure she was ready for it. Wasn't sure she'd ever be ready for it, actually. Was anyone?

Sucking in a gulp of air, Bea reaches to adjust the bed and move Frank into a more upright position, hoping that will help with the rattle knocking around his ribcage.

"Want me to get your family in here?" she asks, knowing there won't be a response. "You're looking a little dry," she continues, pulling the family's chosen assortment of balms from a basket on his nightstand. Comfort is always at the top of her mind, even at the point when her patients probably can't tell the difference. "There." Her fingers swipe softly over his skin, with the moisture soaking in almost immediately. "That'll feel better."

The door creaks open just slightly, and Bea turns to see who has decided to join her.

"Hey," she starts, pausing as she notices that no one is in the doorway. "Hello?" Bea recaps the balm then heads for the door and breathes out a soft laugh. "Must be your grandkids, huh, Frank? Little rascals." As she swings the door fully open, Bea half expects to see the smiling face of the youngest looking back up at her, but frowns when no one is there.

"Mrs. Calder?" she calls as she checks the handle to make sure it will latch next time.

"In the kitchen."

Something feels wrong, but she can't explain it. It's almost as if there is a dark shadow looming over the family, over Frank; like a dark, heavy blanket of something unpleasant has trapped them within the house. Is this what being so close to death feels like? Could it really be this palpable? This thick? She shrugs it off and steps through the foyer, poking her head around the corner into the kitchen.

"Did you call your husband? And the kids?"

Mrs. Calder freezes, her shoulders tensing as she stops what she is doing and turns to face Bea. "Yeah, they're on their way back from school now." A sad smile pulls at her lips. "So, it's definitely time?"

"I think so, yeah." Bea nods. "But I'll be here with you, and will do whatever I can to make this transition easier for you and your family."

The bedroom door swings shut with a startling thud and the women both turn toward the sound. Bea can feel confusion painting her features as she tries to brush off the discomfort making her hair stand on end. She takes in a breath and wipes her expression to be as neutral as possible before turning back to Mrs. Calder.

"You may want to get that door checked," Bea laughs, trying to calm the obvious unease that is growing in the room. She presses a palm against the chill on her skin as Mrs. Calder shakes her head.

"It swung open on me earlier, too," she sighs, crossing her arms over her chest.

"Maybe it's a ghost." The look on the woman's face sternly implies that she does not find this possibility funny. "Or . . . not, sorry. I don't know why I said that."

Mrs. Calder turns to switch the burner off. "It's fine," she says. "I . . . like to believe that our loved ones stick around. It's"—She pauses to wipe her hands on a towel hanging from the stove—"comforting."

"I agree," Bea says when a car pulls into the driveway and immediately shuts off the engine. Only a minute passes before the door slams open and a young boy throws himself into his mother's welcoming embrace. Bea's heart cracks a little more.

"Well, your dad is ready when you are, if you want to say goodbye." The tension hovering around them is thick as Mr. Calder shuts the front door, his oldest daughter's hand clasped in his own. Bea recognizes the fear painted on her round face; of the unknown, of death, of seeing it. "He's just sleeping right now," she says warmly, attempting to help ease the scrunch of her face without addressing her directly. "He's very comfortable, I promise."

The children are instructed to leave their school bags, jackets, and shoes by the door before the family files into their grandfather's bedroom. The kids are brave and do not hesitate to stand right by his bedside. The moment is private and grievous, so Bea turns to busy herself with something else. A few sniffles and whispered words escape through the door, still slightly ajar, and Bea wipes her fist under her nose.

A breeze tickles the back of her neck like a featherlight kiss brushed across her skin. A whisper, almost a hello. Bea whips her head around to once again find an empty room. There is only a shadow she cannot seem to catch lingering at the edge of her vision. The bedroom door opens wide, and something moves within it, something just outside of her perception; alluring, tempting, pulling her closer. She steps through carefully, and then—

Long black hair pours over the spirit's shoulder, delicate as a waterfall, when it leans over Frank's body. A gentle hand runs softly across the crown of his head as his breathing turns into gasps. Then, with just a soft press of its plush lips to his cheek, right at the corner of his nose, he lets out his final breath—visible, as if it were freezing—and the family begins to weep. Bea knows she needs to pronounce him, knows she needs to help make necessary calls, but she cannot drag her wide eyes away from the thing standing beside the family. The thing that presses a hand to the shoulder of the child that is staring up at it. Suddenly he looks around confused, as if it were no longer there, and then buries his face in his mother's shoulder with a soft whimper.

But it is; it is there, standing right beside Mrs. Calder, and its gaze is boring into Bea's soul.

It looks vaguely recognizable as the thing she had seen ten years ago, but it is softer, more ethereal, more . . . peaceful. There is a new roundness to its face, to its body. Its robes drape over it as if they were made specifically to fit the spirit's perceivable form. It parts its lips as if it wants to say something, but they snap shut and it begins walking toward her. Bea backs up, pressing her spine into the door as it steps closer, but there is no fear; a thrill is rising within her, a memory she had buried, a safety in its energy, a desire she could never explain. Closer, closer still, until she could touch it, if only she would dare to reach out her hand.

And then it is gone.

"Beatrice!" Mrs. Calder snaps, frustration evident in her tone. When Bea's eyes meet hers, she gestures toward her now deceased father. "Can you please . . . ?"

"I"—Bea's eyes dance around the room, seeing four sets of tear-filled eyes all staring at her—"I'm sorry, yes," she blurts out as she moves quickly back toward the bed. "Time of death . . . "

She swears can see it all the time now. It lurks in the shadows near the most terminal patients; it glides down the corridors, but only in her periphery. Bea cannot catch it long enough to be sure, but she feels it in every room where someone is close to the end.

Bea knocks swiftly on the door before cracking it open to take a look at the new patient in her rotation. An elderly woman is sitting by the window with a well-loved book in her hand, but there is something about her that feels youthful and serene.

"Hi there," Bea says, smiling. Her eyes glide from corner to corner of the room, seeking out a familiar shadow. "I'm Bea. I'll be helping out today." This woman doesn't outwardly look like she belongs in the Palliative Care Unit, but Bea has seen stranger things. The woman turns to face her as she steps through the door. "Mrs. Teague, correct?" They lock eyes, and the woman gives her the warmest smile Bea thinks she has ever seen.

"Oh, honey," she says, a deep rasp in her voice, "Elaine is fine." She sits up further in her chair, closes the book in her lap, and gestures for Bea to come closer. "And honestly, my husband was a bastard who doesn't deserve for me to continue to use his name."

Bea can't help but laugh.

They get to know one another as Elaine takes her medications, they share a lovely moment over one of Elaine's anecdotes as Bea remakes her bed in fresh linens, and Elaine pats the back of Bea's hand very tenderly before she moves to gather what she needs to take from the room. There is an almost-instant connection to Elaine that Bea can't quite explain—like Elaine was the mother she had needed so long ago, who wouldn't have abandoned her in her weakest moment—and happily requests to be her caretaker as often as possible.

"Do you have a boyfriend?" Elaine asks her one day as Bea is taking her vitals. She simply lets out a breath of air from her nose, almost a snort about how ridiculous an idea that could be. "Or . . . a girlfriend?" Elaine's words are smug. A smirk pulls at the edge of her lips while Bea's cheeks flush bright red and she stammers over her words.

"You know, my Matty is gay. His husband is a darling. The only men in the world I still care about."

Bea simply clamps her mouth shut and proceeds to collect the data she needs to record. "Mhmm," she hums, nodding as she connects a Vacutainer to the end of a tube to start a blood draw.

"I think they're soulmates," Elaine continues as she sways back and forth in a slightly dreamy fashion. "There were so many times they just missed one another before they finally came together. Like, they were even in the same high school! They just never quite met. Maybe it just hadn't been the right time before. I really do think we meet the right person at exactly the right time, you know what I mean?"

The rubber tourniquet around Elaine's arm snaps back to slap Bea's knuckle when she pulls it from Elaine's arm too quickly. "Sorry," Bea mumbles, squeezing her fingers.

"Do you believe in that, dear?" Elaine is completely unfazed.

"Believe in what, Elaine?"

"Soulmates."

Bea's words catch in her throat before she manages to stammer out, "No, I don't think so"—at least not in the traditional sense—"I mean, it'd be nice though, right?" She fidgets in place, trying not to let her mind wander too far to the shadow lurking around the corners of her imagination. "It would be nice. Someone almost guaranteed to be yours; someone, or something, that the universe was always pushing you toward . . . Or pushing toward you."

A chill runs down her spine.

"But I don't think so."

"Ah, I'll just have to believe enough for the both of us, then."

A few weeks pass like this before Bea finally runs into Elaine's son and his husband as they are heading out to speak to a doctor. The air around them is stale, as if they are already in mourning. Bea opens the door with a heavy breath and prepares for the worst. She feels the hair on the back of her neck stand up as the cold air from the room rushes out to kiss her nose.

"Elaine?"

A black corner greets her, weighted in its emptiness, before she snaps her head around to look at the bed.

"Don't let them keep me alive, okay?" Elaine looks so small, so weak and fragile as she lies there, and there is a darkness that seems to hover over her head. "If all I am is a body on a tube, don't let them keep me alive."

The rapid pounding of her heart beneath her ribs has Bea close to a panic. "Elaine, I'm sure your son will do what's best—"

"He won't."

Bea snaps her mouth shut.

"He's too attached to me, my baby. All we had for so long was each other. He won't let me go. But you have to make him let me go." Tears are flowing down the corners of Elaine's eyes as she fiddles with her IV and the electrodes attached to her chest, as if she is already planning her escape. "Promise me."

"How am I—"

"Promise me."

A heavy weight is pressing into Bea's chest, but a hazy fog of need is pulsing at the back of her mind. What if . . . If it's Elaine's wish to die . . . to not be kept on life support . . . wouldn't she be doing what's right to help her? Isn't it her job to make sure that her patients are as comfortable as possible? It would only be a bonus that she might see—

"Please."

She could . . .

"Okay," Bea nods. A familiar fixation floods her every thought. "I'll do what I can."

It is only a week longer before Elaine is intubated. Every time her sedation begins to wear off, Bea can see her fighting; she gurgles around the tube shoved down her throat, her discomfort evident. A subtle pain is always etched into her features.

Her son barely leaves her side.

The shadows grow heavier in the room; watching, waiting.

Three days in, the doctor suggests he go home and rest.

Three nights in, Bea sees the only chance she will have to help.

"Elaine," she whispers as she sneaks into the room, ensuring that no one sees her. "It's me, Elaine. I'm going to take care of you." Bea's words are wet with hurt, but she is ready to do this; ready to see if she has been right. "Thank you for your love and kindness these last couple of months." She feels it again, the familiar kiss at the base of her skull, but as always there is nothing there when she whips her head around.

She turns everything off with haste, aiming to prevent alarms from blaring out to alert the on-staff nurses and doctors that anything is wrong.

And then she does it.

Elaine's breathing slows until it stops.

Bea's breathing quickens as her eyes dart around the room. Please. Please. She needs to see it. Losing Elaine can't be for nothing—she can't lose the only friend she has made in years for *nothing*.

A minute passes. Another. Another, and tears well up in her eyes. She can't be wrong. She knows she has felt it just over her shoulder; she *knows* she has. Maybe Elaine hasn't passed yet. That must be it. Bea presses her ear into the woman's chest and begs to hear a heartbeat.

Nothing echoes within Elaine's ribs, at least nothing that Bea can decipher, and a sob breaks from her throat.

She had been so, *so* sure.

But she waits, continues to wait, forces herself to embrace the silence of the room for as long as she can bear it because she needs to know without a shadow of a doubt.

Then the lamp on the bedside table flickers until it turns off with a sharp snap, startling Bea up from her grief. A chill tickles her spine as a calm washes over her, and then it appears; standing across the room and angelic in the moonlight, the creature is here, tall and beautiful and everything Bea had remembered it to be. It looks almost human in this sterile environment, silver light bouncing off every ridge and valley of its body.

It tilts its head to take Bea in and satisfaction blooms through her chest. It steps closer, and the sweet taste of vindication washes over her tongue.

She knew she was right. She had been so *sure*.

Bea sees it more frequently after that day; in the dark corners of her patients' homes, reflecting in glass around the hospital, just out of reach and taunting her. It is always lurking, always nearby, as if it were desperately waiting for a reason to be near her again. It comes to her when a patient passes, each time taking in more of her, lingering around longer, getting closer, barely resisting touching her. Bea keeps her composure when others are around—simply basks in the feeling of refuge that comes with its presence—and lets its breath and aura prick at her skin until it takes the deceased and disappears once again.

But she can always feel it; can always see a piece of it. It follows behind her and shows itself in mirrors and glass. It waits outside of rooms for her, softly caressing her skin as they cross paths. It watches her closely, always near, always humming just behind her.

There is safety in its shadow, comfort in the way it appears every time another life burns out in her care, and it is only when she is finally able to see it clearly, able to see it every single day, that they take it from her.

It has been three years.

Thrumming music and strobing lights sharpen Bea's senses as her eyes dance around the room.

It has been three years since she last saw it.

Three years since the people around her had begun to suspect that something was not quite right. Three years since she had chosen to leave before they could rip the fragile lives of the already dying from her fingers; since she had the opportunity to call it whenever she wanted to without guilt. Three years of trying to come by it somewhat naturally once again.

Three years of watching her back, of trying to stay afloat.

Her gaze locks onto a man who has clearly had too much to drink and does not seem to care that he is making the young women around him uncomfortable. His so-called dancing consists only of gyrating hips and putting his hands all over their bodies, trapping them in place. He's disgusting. He's abhorrent. He's perfect. So, Bea approaches.

Three years of waiting. She is so, *so* tired of waiting.

A tremble of anxiety tickles the space between her shoulder blades. Bea flutters her lashes as she takes the man's hand and guides him away from the girls. Gratitude washes over their faces and they move quickly to the other side of the club.

She offers him a sly smile as she places his calloused, sweaty, horrible hands onto her hips. "Hi there," she says, pulling him closer. He reeks of cheap liquor and stale cigar smoke. Bea fights the disgust that is crinkling her nose. "What's your name?"

He mumbles something generic like Jack or Jake or Josh—something she can't be bothered to hear or remember—then squeezes her ass, and he laughs.

It is easier than it should be; it is easy to convince him to leave with her, it is easy to get him angry, it is easy to shove the knife into his stomach, and it is easy to sit beside him as she waits. Adrenaline pumps through her veins as his life weeps out of the jagged wound, and she waits for the heavy weight of Death's presence to wash over her. It won't be long.

It has a routine that Bea can't help but recognize: a flicker in the corner of her eye, the dense feeling of fog thickening around her, a whisper of a kiss across the back of her neck, and then it steps out of the shadows.

She scrambles to her feet.

"You're back," Bea sighs, wiping her bloody hand against her cheek. The sharp metallic scent of blood floods her nostrils. "I'm so glad you're back." It doesn't respond to her—it never has—but its eyes linger on her, longer this time than ever before, until it looks down at the body between them. "He"—Bea swallows—"he was going to hurt me, didn't you see? Weren't you watching?"

Its hair has grown more ragged over the years, ends broken and brittle, and its eyes are set further into its face. Robes hang softer over its thinning body. Feminine curves disappear into bone. It is no longer as youthful and ethereal as it once had been, but Bea can see the real beauty in its new form; the vulnerability of it showing her who it really is. Who it was the night they first met.

It bends down on one knee and takes the man more swiftly than Bea has ever seen it take someone. No kiss, no guidance, simply a wave of its hand across the man's chest. Quick, boring, dutiful.

"Where have you been?" Bea asks, dropping to her knees to meet its eye level. It looks at her, the soft glow of a fresh soul settling behind its pupils. This close, she can see everything new: wrinkles, rot, decay. It fuels her. "I've . . . I've been waiting for you." There is a waver of a plea on the edges of her words. "It's been so long . . ." It stands, and she stands. "I—I didn't want to do this, but you—you weren't coming! You weren't—" It stares, and Bea feels small. "Why did you go away for so long?"

There is a hesitation; she can almost see a debate flickering through its stoic eyes. Then it reaches forward, and it touches her.

It touches her for the first time, so gently, so softly. Its hand cradles her cheek. It is cold, but it is burning her. The knife falls from her fingers and she reaches up, desperate to hold it there. As her hand rests over Death's, it begins to move slowly. The drag of its fingers leaves stinging lines across her skin as it traces down her face, her neck, to rest solidly on her sternum. The crook of its thumb cups her throat. Bea steps closer, begging it to stay, stay; maybe if she holds onto it hard enough, it would this time.

But it doesn't. She thinks it never will.

A heavy breath forces its way into Bea's lungs as soon as the hand is gone from her chest, like it had been leeching the air out of her without her even noticing. She gasps, presses her own hand to the skin that is still stinging, and feels unfamiliar ridges and valleys under her palm. Shuddering as it vanishes completely, Bea drags her phone from her pocket and turns the front camera toward herself.

There is a painting left across her skin; fingerprints and scratches like bold brush strokes. A marking that makes her Death's.

It has claimed her, and she belongs to it. That is enough.

It comes to her more often again, always clearly, but never close. Just enough to appease her insatiable desire. It lingers outside her windows and walks in step with her across the street. It lurks nearby when tires screech into almost accidents, or when pedestrians do not pay enough attention.

For years, it is there, just out of reach. She knows it could be closer, but the sacrifices she would have to make feel too big—too permanent—now that she is settling into a new life. For years, she is satisfied, knowing it will always be right there, knowing that she will always belong to it.

For years, Bea sees it at least once a week, until she doesn't.

Beatrice is thirty-seven the last time I come to her.

Her razor-shorn hair is matted and wild around her red-smattered face as she breathes heavily. Soaked strands stick to her lips as she stares up at me. *What have you done, you stupid girl?* I want to yell at her. *What have you done?*

"Just take me!" she screams, standing up and ignoring the squelch of her sneakers in the blood pooled beneath her feet. "I know you want to!" She steps over the bodies and throws her knife to the ground. "You keep coming back to me and showing me the real you—I know you feel this too, so just take me!"

The rot of my touch is still puckered across her skin. She has never tried to hide it, and every glimpse I have gotten of it since that dreadful day has wound something within me even tighter. I cannot be with her. I cannot give her what she desires; I cannot even bear for her to be near me. That is why I left.

And yet . . .

A violent mixture of anger and desperation and obsession is woven through her features as she comes closer and closer still. "Touch me and take me," she begs, stopping only an inch short of me. "I want you to. I don't want to live without you anymore."

I do not live, I want to tell her. I am no longer flesh, and I am not capable of reciprocity.

"Please," she almost cries as her knuckles whiten under the pressure of her fisted grip. "Please!"

I look behind her at the shattered faces of people who should have loved her. I feel the pain radiating from my beautiful Beatrice, and I crumble. I am weak. I had been whisked away the first time I saw her;

small, soft, and suffering. So human, so unlike any I had known before. I am desperate to console her. I wish to speak, but I cannot while her soul is not yet mine. I drag these bony, useless fingers up to her face, past her ear, to push locks of her loose hair back out of her eyes. These lines left upon her skin are worse, more rotten than the last time, but she does not seem to mind as she leans into my touch.

After all, there is no return for her now. No chance of a peaceful life nor a restful death. Would it not simply be a mercy to take her with me—to keep her under my watch, under my guidance? My Beatrice, who has not been handed kindness. My Beatrice, who simply ached for someone to love her as she is. My Beatrice, who sacrificed the only person she had managed to trust just to see me again.

My Beatrice, who has been mine as long as I have been hers.

My eyes wander past her, and I step away. I must take care of them first. These people are innocent in the eyes of the universe, and they should be innocent in my judgment; but I cannot be impartial, not to those who did not care for my Beatrice the way she had deserved. So, I will send them someplace where I will not be the judge or the jury. I try to take care with each one, providing a gentle transfer to a different plane, and I hear movement behind me as their souls dissipate from the earth.

"Please," she whispers, so soft and weak and innocent. My Beatrice, standing before me, begging me to love her. "Please. I want to go with you. I can't do this anymore." Her hands wrap around mine, and I wonder how long I have been able to feel empathy; how long I have been able to feel anything.

Not once since I became this; until I met her.

I lay my fingers against the rot that already scars the edges of her face, unwilling to mar her further, and I nod. Once, just once, and she knows she is safe. The relief that washes over her is so strong, so potent, I can almost picture how it would feel vibrating through my own bones.

My thumb drags over her throat, and tears well up in her eyes.

I still remember how I was taken all those centuries ago—how my beloved Reaper had taken me as a protégé in lieu of passing me on to the ether. Under its tutelage, I learned the dangers of attachment. It warned me that every soul must be fleeting; that impermanence was what made it possible to help them pass on.

I do not think it ever felt affection for me—that is not why it kept me—and I do not believe it was right. There is beauty in attachment, in wholly loving something precious. Beatrice is meant to be with me, she is why I was placed here. I am certain of this.

She is mine for eternity. She is mine, and I am hers.

I tuck my fingers into the hair behind her ear, ignore the singe burning into my palm, and lean in closer.

Closer, still. Closer, until my lips meet hers.

This is the first time I have taken the soul of someone still living. The first time I have taken something I have wanted. She is pliant and giving and warm as I try to imagine what she might taste like, if I could still taste anything. The faintest memory of the sugary sweetness of candy rolls across my tongue, and I am sure that would be it.

A whimper escapes her. The last dregs of her life weep out from her throat as she clings to me. Her body goes limp in my arms, and I hold her tighter.

I have never before felt a soul so devoted. I have never had a soul warm my own from the inside out. I have never held onto one before.

Never, until her.

About the Author

Jay L. Scaffa, a non-binary writer originally from Long Island, New York, has spent many years seeking out queer joy, horror, and everything in between. It doesn't take much to garner their interest—if there are lesbians, then Jay is in. While they normally focus on writing more wholesome sapphic romance, "My Beatrice" is their first foray into exploring tragedy and obsession.

When they're not creating their own stories, Jay spends most of their time either consuming others' stories through books, video games, television, and film, or getting lost in various new artistic endeavors. Whatever they are doing is usually accompanied by cuddles from their two cats, or a fight over whether or not the Lego pieces on the table are actually new cat toys.

You can keep up with their work on Instagram: @jay.l.scaffa.

My Dearly Beloved
by Heena

Content/Trigger Warnings

This novella contains **dark and gothic themes** that may be triggering for some readers. Please proceed with caution if sensitive to the following:

- **Death & Ghosts** – depictions of hauntings, graves, and supernatural encounters.

- **Violence & Gore** – references to severed body parts, strangulation, hanging, and other forms of death.

- **Suicide & Self-Harm** – characters struggle with depression, suicidal ideation, and overdose.

- **Abuse & Exploitation** – emotional manipulation, family neglect, and sexual assault.

- **Substance Use** – alcohol abuse, drug use, and sleeping pill overdose.

- **Psychological Trauma** – gaslighting, grief, obsession, and mental instability.

This work explores the shadows of family, memory, and vengeance. Reader discretion is strongly advised.

Author's Note

My Dearly Beloved is a work of gothic fiction. While it draws on familiar tropes of haunted mansions, cursed families, and lingering spirits, it is ultimately a story of loss, betrayal, and the dangerous ways love can twist into something darker.

Though the events and characters are entirely fictional, they explore very real themes of trauma, guilt, and survival. None of these depictions are intended to sensationalize or glorify harm — rather, they reflect the brutal emotional landscapes of the characters themselves.

Readers are encouraged to step carefully into the world of the Ashfords. The story is one of shadows — but in those shadows, the truth of human desire and despair often lingers most.

One

Inside the sugared roses and layers of sponge of the birthday cake -two of her fingers were found. She had anticipated this, but it took ten winters for the haunting to start. Waiting and watching how the colors changed on each of their faces when they discovered the fingers inside the velvet-red offering. Blood almost matching the filling.

Ashford Mansion, where it would all begin, loomed in silence atop the hill, smothered by a mournful mist that clung to the earth like a grieving child to its dead mother. The storm rolled in without mercy, a grim omen crawling across the sky. The mansion was always like this during the celebration of Bianca's birthday family dinner, this year being no less.

The cake, amid it all, stood like a silent, doomed dancer waiting for the curtain to rise. Something about her stillness promised a spectacle not meant for the living.

Maria hummed a silent melody, peering over her grandpapa's shoulder and sensing the hike in his blood pressure. Too much strain for bones that old. Her grandmama had paused mid shriek unable to look away from the cake. While her three step-siblings lingered in the corner, whispering like cowards and wearing the masks of adulthood, her beloved stepmother crept toward the cake with leaden steps. Bile clawed its way up her throat, the cloying sweetness in the air rotting into something foul.

The only person not shaken up by the ordeal was her dear father but in all the years she had known him, nothing ever had. He quickly pulled out his phone and dialed his lawyer. Of course, the hauntingly beautiful Corbin Graves. Ah, the gray, soulless eyes that man had. Maria had coveted the same eyes from the minute she laid her abyss-like black eyes upon him.

Martin Ashford had a powerful legal team, but cleaning up his dirty work was always Corbin's duty. Her elder brother Raphael, who must have been lingering somewhere in the room's dimly lit, inky darkness, also depended on Corbin whenever his psychosis flared up.

"Corbin, my child, come up to the family dining room. Looks like someone's been pranking again," he said, looking at Derek, the notorious one of all the children raised under Father's scrutinizing gaze.

He sighed and hung up the phone. Looking at each and every one, especially a stern glance at Derek, he spoke again, *"This year didn't we decide to behave like proper Ashfords before Bianca joined the company? Then why is this atrocious thing happening before my eyes?"*

No one dared to break the silence, and the air thickened with tense, almost desperate anticipation for the only person who could quell the fury that was Martin Ashford.

Maria twirled around in her laced blue dress that had seen better days, dancing on her tiptoes and singing the lullaby Mother once sang to her even on her last breath. Her black, lifeless hair—an eerie legacy from her departed mother—trailed like a shadow in her wake.

**"Hush thee now, the moon glows red,
The wind has found a sorrow dread.
Hearts do ache 'neath mourning's veil,
For softest breath, a soul so frail."**

No one paid attention to her, no one except Raphael, but that could be because they shared a soul connection. He held a tiny smile, hidden from the lot and watched her enjoy the scare each passing minute gave to the other people in the room. Even though Raph, her soft-hearted brother with his forest green eyes and head full of dark hair, resembled their father, his tanned skin reminded her of their mother.

Raphael hated birthday parties since their mother, Camila Duarte, died and Father decided to get married to the beautiful Miss Stella Richardson, the florist from the next town over. He said the flowers she grew forged a fragile connection between them. But even Maria, only thirteen, quietly understood the harsh truth—he was seeing her while Mother lay coughing blood, trapped by a family curse no one spoke of.

Beautiful, wasn't it? Father had defied Grandpapa's rigid demands in his youth by marrying a woman of color he loved. When Mother quietly slipped away, he gladly embraced the presence of Miss Stella Richardson and her three children from a previous marriage—Simon, Derek, and Bianca. He offered them a love that sometimes felt deeper than what he showed his own blood grandchildren. There was something in their features, a quiet echo of Grandpapa's own—a resemblance that stirred in him a sense of belonging and legacy, unlike the distant faces of the grandchildren he had grown up around.

As she neared the corner Raph sat around, he whispered, *"Careful, or you might cause Grandpapa another heart attack with all that humming."*

Maria chuckled softly but lowered her voice, for Raphael was the only one who spoke to her, and she couldn't bear to dishearten him.

Before she could take another traced another silent arc across the room, the Ashford Butler James announced the last guest for the night, her sweet, sinisterly handsome man, Corbin.

He glided toward the gathering with the cold assurance of a lord returned from the grave to reclaim what was once his. The rest—silent, small—might as well have been his obedient shadows. His icy blond hair was sculpted to cruel perfection, and his gray eyes swept the room like a winter storm, lingering briefly where Maria stood . . . before locking, unblinking, onto Father.

He . . . he can see me? thought Maria. It must have been a fluke. All these years, she had drifted between the light and shadow of the old mansion, watching him grow into a man of imposing stature—yet never once had his gaze touched her. How could he see her now? Perhaps it was only the lightning outside, casting cruel illusions and playing tricks with her tired mind.

Maria dragged herself to the tall French windows that overlooked the dark forest—where her mother's grave lay among others, half-swallowed by the earth. Outside, the mist had given way to a heavy downpour, and lightning slashed across the sky like the muse of a heartbroken painter. The dense foliage devoured the landscape, all but one strange exception: a lonely gremlin statue, placed long ago by some eccentric great-great-great-great grandpapa to display both his wealth and his madness.

She remembered when the gardens were once lovingly tended under her mother's eye. But after her death—and Father's newfound devotion to his second family—the children had been sent to the next town for their education. Grandpapa and Grandmama became little more than monthly visitors, though Maria never missed them much. They'd never been particularly loving to Raph or her.

"Do you think it belongs to someone?" Sweet Bianca's voice floated up behind her, making Maria turn her head. Bianca clung to Corbin's arm as if he were hers alone—her knight in shining armor, summoned just for her. A sharp pain bloomed in Maria's chest, followed by a flush of heat that surged through her heart and head alike, leaving her shaken and afraid of what it meant.

She had known of Bianca's growing affection for Corbin ever since that summer—twenty years ago—when Bianca first laid eyes on him through Father's study window. Maria had been beside her that day, watching the same boy who had played with her since they could both toddle.

Corbin was the son of their former butler, sweet Uncle Carson Graves—the man who used to slip her cherry-flavored candies that turned her tongue red.

Corbin and Maria, childhood sweethearts, or so she liked to believe. She remembered the fragile flower crown she had carefully woven herself—the one she wore as a child when she made him promise a life full of love. It was a moment from when she was only six, during a pretend wedding long forgotten by everyone else but forever alive in her heart. That memory lingered softly, like a whispered secret from a time when hope felt endless and the future still unwritten.

"No, it might be one of those Halloween decorations left over that might have somehow gotten into the cake batter. You know how irresponsible the cooks are," Derek spoke up for the first time since he was accused of such malicious intent.

How dare he . . .

Maria seethed in silence, but there was nothing she could do. After all, she was merely a soul, lingering within these walls, clinging to whatever strength remained. Darla and Raymond—fantastic cooks—were the only ones Grandpapa allowed Mother to keep, even after her death, as if they were heirlooms rather than people.

And Derek? Just a spoiled child, convinced his slice of the inheritance made him some vital limb of the family tree.

"Don't be absurd. Darla could never make such a blunder," Simon said, stepping in as the ever-dutiful mediator—the responsible sibling always eager to overshadow Raph and play the golden boy.

But only Maria knew the monsters he kept buried, the ones that stirred when no one was looking. *"Besides,"* he added with a smile, *"it's just a cake. Let's not ruin a lovely dinner—and celebrate my dear sister's thirtieth."*

"Simon is right. Let's not ruin the evening—dinner should continue," Corbin said, his voice calm, composed. *"I'll have the cake removed and a new one prepared before dessert."*

It was the first time in years Maria felt that his voice carried something more—a hidden truth nestled behind those lips, a secret she would never be allowed to know.

At his signal, James quietly removed the cake—the object of everyone's quiet dread—and Corbin gently guided Bianca toward the dining table. She followed like a lost pup, and the rest fell in behind her. Miss Stella, pale and silent as a graveyard dove, dragged out a chair and sat before anyone else could. She looked by far the most shaken.

"I've lost my appetite for the night," Grandmama murmured. *"You lot continue. I'll have James bring me some soup in my room."* With that, she exited, her faint, mothy scent trailing behind her until it faded completely.

For the first time in years, Grandpapa followed her—perhaps to prevent another "attack," the last one having been blamed on Derek. Though only Raph knew the truth: **it had been Maria who orchestrated that little shenanigan.**

"I'll take my leave as well. I've had too much to drink, and my stomach's feeling a bit off. Happy birthday, Bianca. May all your wishes come true," Raph said, rising to his feet.

He took a slow, deliberate look at each person around the room—one by one—until his eyes landed on darling Bianca last of all. She received the dirty little sneer he'd always reserved just for her—the same venomous look he'd worn since the day she arrived at ten years old. At fifteen, he already knew with cold certainty exactly what she was meant to replace.

Maria contemplated following Raph back to his room but knew he'd be a bore at this late hour—while her own desire to dally was just beginning to spark. The remaining company was far duller—well, except for Corbin—but she had no patience to endure Father's drone about market trends and sinking investments. Simon tried to join the conversation too, but unlike Raph, he lacked the sharpness in finance that made Father respect him—the only one Father truly feared in business matters.

Miss Stella and Derek barely grazed their food, lost in their own thoughts, while Bianca's gaze lingered on Corbin's side, as desperate and longing as a deer finding the last drop of water in a scorched forest.

Maria knew about the contract signed last Tuesday, the one that made Corbin officially part of the family—but not in the way she had hoped. Bianca and Corbin were to be wed next spring with great pomp and ceremony, a plan hatched entirely by Corbin and Father. The knowledge only deepened Maria's bitterness toward Bianca.

She was no mature adult—just a child watching the person she loved most in the world slip away to become the least favored. And she was powerless to stop it.

Maria had sat, staring at their heads for hours as they discussed the contract. And with every passing second, Bianca's joy grew, Maria vowed vengeance.

"You know, I noticed something," Derek murmured, lifting his gaze from the plate with a glint of curiosity. *"One of the fingers wore that old emerald ring . . . the same gaudy thing Maria used to parade around—the one her dancer mother left behind, wasn't it?"*

Everyone froze, forks and spoons suspended midair, staring at Derek as if horns had suddenly jutted from his skull.

"Don't spew nonsense just because your mouth is free," Father's voice boomed, a command wrapped in thunder. Another bolt of lightning cracked across the sky, its glow casting eerie shadows along the walls—shadows Maria was certain Derek felt in his bones.

Stupid boy. Or rather, stupid man—he was thirty-three now, the same age she would have been . . . had she lived. Of course, it was her ring. Of course those were her fingers, that were once adorned with blood-red polish every day of the week. Everyone had seen it, but no one dared speak. Derek spoke up only because his courage had a habit of arriving at precisely the wrong moment.

Still, Maria was thankful. His foolishness had unlocked the first door, whether he realized it or not. Now, at last, she could begin Part Two of her plan—and there would be no turning back.

This moment proved too much for Miss Stella, and she placed her soup spoon back onto the plate with trembling hands. She looked at Bianca and said, *"Help me back to my room. I think I'm full."*

Though reluctant, Bianca nodded—unwilling to drop her sweet facade in front of Corbin—and moved to her mother's side. With a quiet *good night*, the mother-daughter duo exited the room.

Watching them together reminded Maria of the days when her own mother would sprain her ankle practicing new dance steps, and Maria would help her to bed, gently applying ointment. *What good old days they were.*

Derek, sensing the rising tension, also chose to retreat—before Father could dig up his latest folly and reprimand him in front of the guest.

Yes, it was true. Deep in their hearts, both Simon and Derek detested Corbin—perhaps even more than Raph on certain days. The simple reason was this: he had lived longer in Father's good graces than either of them ever had.

What burned more was what they refused to admit: Corbin had the mind to outthink them, the charm to disarm, and the patience to make it all look effortless. Even Grandpapa—cold, unswayed, a man who measured worth in silence—had grudgingly tipped his head in approval.

Corbin rarely smiled. He didn't need to. The room leaned toward him anyway, as if pulled by something they couldn't name but couldn't resist.

Perhaps it was what he learned at Eton, where Father had sent him at the age of ten—alongside Raph, as they were in the same class. Maria always believed it had been a calculated move—one designed to sever the quiet bond forming between her and Corbin. A bond that may have become love. A love that frightened Father's principles, even though he himself had once crossed such lines.

He had no qualms about binding Bianca to Corbin—after all, she wasn't his blood. But the rules for Maria had always been different. Father once looked at Maria with tenderness—at least until Bianca appeared. Now, she was just a memory, a shadow. And Bianca had become his new pawn for social acclaim.

Maria understood the thoughts behind every face at the table—well, perhaps all except Raph and Corbin. So little surprised her these days. But the marriage proposal? That had struck like an arrow to the heart.

And when Corbin kissed Bianca beneath the stairs two nights ago, smiling as though Maria had never existed—it ignited the frozen pit of her heart. And those flames, once lit, would burn through everything in their path.

Two

Raphael knew what he had to do next. He had skimped on his duties since Maria left, letting them pile up like dead leaves in an autumn gutter—forgotten, soggy, and rotting. But now, with the weight of guilt clawing at his insides and the silence echoing too loud in her absence, he had planned to fulfill it all in one go.

Helping Maria get her revenge was the one thing he could do without hating himself for his existence.

It wasn't about redemption anymore. That door had closed long ago—maybe even before he found her lifeless body hanging beneath the beautiful blue-sky-painted ceiling of her room. No—this was about loyalty. About debt. About finally answering the question that had haunted his sleep every night since she'd gone: *What would it take to make it right?*

He knew the names. He knew the faces. Every last one of them who had played a part in breaking her spirit, in tearing down the fire she used to carry in her eyes. Raphael had watched that fire go out. And now, he would light another—a different kind. One that burned everything left behind.

This wasn't just about vengeance. It was about finishing something *for* her, because he never had the courage to do it *with* her. And if he had to become something monstrous in the process, so be it.

She had given everything. Now it was his turn.

Tampering with the cake was merely the first whisper of vengeance.

He wanted them all—every last conspirator—to drown in the same cold, suffocating fear that had once wrapped its fingers around Maria's heart and squeezed until it barely beat. To feel the slow, elegant unraveling of their own minds—the quiet horror of watching sanity slip away, thread by thread—as cruelty smiled at them, wearing the tender, lying mask of friendship.

Hundreds of forgotten graves lay scattered around Ashford Manor, like broken memories buried in the dirt. Digging up a few fingers—and adding that ring—was the cherry on the cake. Literally.

Raphael let out a cold, hollow laugh at the thought as he swirled the brandy in his glass, its amber hue catching what little light dared to enter the room.

His chamber remained cloaked in shadow; not even the flicker of a single candlestick could pierce the oppressive darkness.

He knew Maria wouldn't disturb him this late—she was too busy fawning over and hating that scum of the earth, Corbin.

In the beginning, Raphael had felt only a distant sympathy—perhaps even a flicker of pity—for Corbin. He, too, had seemed like nothing more than a pawn, moved across the board by the withered hand of Martin Ashford, the rotting patriarch who fancied himself a king.

But that illusion shattered the moment Corbin began his slow, serpentine ascent—climbing the blood-slick rungs of ambition. He whispered alliances with players far darker and more powerful than Ashford had ever dared to summon.

Poor Maria had adored them both—blind, sweet Maria—never seeing how quickly they carved up her inheritance like carrion, sealing contracts over the smoldering ruins of her heart.

He was certain Maria would stay downstairs tonight—maybe even linger in the guest room where Corbin slept. That is, if Corbin hadn't already surrendered to Bianca's sweet, poisonous charm.

Oh, how he had detested the way they shook hands and smiled so gracefully at each other that evening. He loathed that all he could do was stand there and offer his congratulations to Corbin—knowing full well the pain behind Maria's transparent tears.

One night, Maria woke him in tears, her voice cracked as she spoke of Corbin and Bianca's reckless display of love that tore at her heart. In that moment, he vowed silently—no matter the cost, he would do everything to see her smile again.

Now, for the final act of the night, he rose slowly from the futon, each movement deliberate, as though the air itself had thickened with expectation. His bare feet made no sound against the cold wooden floor as he moved toward the antique drawer—so very different from the rest of the furniture in the room. It stood out like a relic, misplaced and unwanted, its dark wood carved with fading roses and faint scorch marks at the corners.

That drawer was the only thing he had left of his mother. The only thing Miss Stella had allowed him to keep after the fire—after the great purge she justified with her quiet superstitions and tightly pursed lips. Maria had gotten the family ring, of course. A cruel token perhaps, but one she wore with reverence.

The rest of their mother's things—photographs, letters, even the silver-backed hairbrush she used to carry—had all gone up in flames, consumed not by accident, but by design. Miss Stella had insisted it was for the best. She never said the woman's name, only referred to her as that dead woman, as if even the memory of her bore some unspeakable stain. A stigma too heavy to live alongside.

But the drawer remained.

And tonight, it contained the one thing that could put the final nail in the Ashfords' coffin.

For years now, since graduating summa cum laude with a mind as sharp as a dagger's edge, Raphael had mastered the art of deception. He had carefully woven a tangled web of lies and cunning deception, manipulating both his grandfather and father with calculated precision. Through his schemes, he drained their fortunes dry—convincing them it was all for the grand purpose of expanding the family empire. Like ravenous gremlins possessed by greed, they had blindly followed his lead, unaware that with every coin they relinquished, the noose around their necks tightened

Behind veils of secrecy, through shadowed intermediaries and silent transactions, Raphael siphoned their wealth into hidden coffers. The Ashford estate itself—once a proud monument to lineage and legacy—now teetered on the brink of ruin, its fate sealed by the cold, relentless hands of the impending auction.

He had already donated most of the funds to various charities, big and small, ones his mother and Maria had loved and cared for. Especially to the Little Butterfly Sanctuary, where Maria had volunteered for one too many summers—something to preserve her legacy, a fragile light in the darkness.

The remainder he kept, tucked away and guarded, reserved to complete his plan with one of his most trusted men, who awaited his command to carry it out.

Yet, a single thread still held the house from falling into strangers' hands: the binding contract of a marriage—bitter, strategic, and suffocating—woven tightly around their fortunes. It was a cage, yes, but for now, it kept the darkness at bay.

Corbin was no fool. He sensed the decay gnawing at Martin Ashford's empire, the slow erosion of power and coin. But the true riches—the old patriarch's secret vaults, the money carefully parceled out to each child—remained firmly clutched in Martin's iron grip. Corbin knew that to secure his place in this collapsing dynasty, he had to worm his way deeper into its rotten core.

For him, gaining favor was not just about wealth—it was about influence, about carving out a throne amid the ashes. The whispers of old money, of inherited power, promised clients and connections that would secure his future, no matter how tainted.

Raphael watched all this unfold with cold amusement, his plans set in motion like a slow-burning curse, ready to consume them all.

He took out the bottle of sleeping pills—filled to the brim—and stared at it in silence. He knew what he had to do. His forthcoming death needed to look suspicious enough to shake the foundation stones of the old house . . . and the monsters who walked its halls.

Maria had been his only tether to the world, the only light in its choking fog. And after her death, he had long since given up hope of ever truly living.

But then—*he saw her.*

A hysterical vision, drifting like a sorrowful ghoul through the beautifully blue-painted room she had so painstakingly repainted every few years. That room had always caught the light in strange, celestial ways, thanks to their mother's careful hand with paint and glass. At first, Raphael had thought he was finally going mad.

But the vision never left.

Every time he stepped into that room, chasing the ghost of a girl he couldn't forget, Maria would be there—waiting. As real as memory, and yet as untouchable as mist.

At first, neither of them understood what had happened. Maria had always believed in the unseen, in the soft whispers of magic that laced the world. And they were both reminded of one of their mother's favorite sayings:

"Magic is never lost—it is merely hidden. And when the time comes to find it, it will appear and hold your hand."

Perhaps it was their mother's love that bound the siblings together—even from the gates of heaven and hell. Something ancient and aching had tethered Maria to the world of the living, and in that fragile thread of magic, Raphael had found a reason to breathe again.

Ten years ago, the rage in him had burned bright enough to light the manor in flames. He had planned to kill every last one of them—the ones who had broken Maria. He had dug the graves in his mind, chosen the weapons in his dreams. But Maria had stopped him.

"Don't destroy your life for something already lost," she had whispered. *"This . . . this strange gift of being able to see each other—this is enough for me. I'm not ready to let go yet."*

And so, he waited. And watched. And lived half a life in the shadows of the dead.

But now—*now*—she had asked him. She had looked at him with those tearful, radiant eyes and begged him to help her find peace.

How could he ever say no?

After creating the perfect scene, Raphael laid back on the futon, with the bottle of pills waiting beside him. He closed his eyes, not in despair, but with quiet resolve—drifting back into memories of laughter, sunlight, and the days when his heart had known warmth.

Tomorrow, the reckoning would begin.

Three

Blinking red and blue lights sprawled across the driveway, still cloaked in a thin blanket of mist. Some of the officers clutched their amulets, muttering prayers to whatever gods they believed in—hoping to make it out safe and sound, without any lingering apparition clinging to their backs.

A hollow laugh escaped Stella as she watched the scene unfold. How ridiculous they looked—grown men and women who had likely seen countless mangled bodies in the wreckage of their careers. Now, they were reduced to frightened children by the sight of a crumbling mansion wrapped in fog and shadow.

How had she lived in this place all these years?

Even she wasn't quite sure anymore.

This was supposed to be her ticket out of hell. Her lifeline out of the gutter her parents had raised her in.

God, how *satisfied* they'd been with their small, shabby lives—how it drove her nearly mad. At first, she told herself she'd take the noble route: study hard, get a job, and slowly climb her way toward the life she dreamed of.

But each paycheck was swallowed by debts—crumbling and bottomless. Her desperate overindulgence in clothes, perfumes, and dinners she couldn't afford was a pathetic attempt to claw her way onto society's golden ladder. The ladder, as it turned out, had greased rungs.

And soon enough, there were three useless children. Screaming, needy, clinging. Little weights she'd never planned for, dragging her deeper into the pit.

So, she took a detour.

A very dark, very bloody detour.

She had long since realized that no amount of honest labor would deliver her into a life of luxury. The world wasn't built that way. If she wanted silk sheets and a house with chandeliers, she'd need to play the game differently.

She gathered everything life had taught her—bitterness, desperation, charm—and crafted a strategy both dangerous and, in its own way, deeply fulfilling.

She had learned the art of seduction early. The power of a glance, a touch, the tilt of her voice. She used it when she needed to—but not too much. After all, she had *morals*.

Or so she thought.

But when those morals stopped paying the bills, she killed them.

Killed them right along with her sweet, smiling parents.

It was actually . . . quite easy.

She tinkered with the brakes on their car—just enough to avoid suspicion. Gave them their favorite wine that evening, smiled sweetly as they drank, and watched them leave, half-drunk and full of love.

Not before taking out multiple insurance policies in their names, of course. It was easy to convince them. They adored their grandkids, after all—those loud, sticky-fingered burdens.

She played the grieving daughter well. Black dress, trembling lips, a tasteful sob or two at the funeral. People called her brave.

She called it *winning*.

Then the money came—and this time, she played it strategically.

She moved a few cities over. Somewhere a little more expensive, a little more polished, but full of opportunity. She opened a florist shop—small, elegant, perfumed with lilies and roses. Her green fingers, inherited from the father who always smelled of warm pies and baked for others with love, found purpose in soil and petals.

The shop attracted the *right* kind of men. Some came in with the dazed expression of the newly in love. Others with guilt on their lips and bouquets meant for wives, girlfriends . . . or mistresses. A few didn't need a reason at all. They came simply to see her—that curvy figure bending gracefully over the counter. Sunlight caught the golden strands of her hair, making them glow like spun honey. And those icy blue eyes of hers seemed to pierce through silk and bone alike, holding a gaze that both mesmerized and unsettled.

But what she *wanted*—or more precisely, *who*—had yet to appear.

Until she saw him.

He stepped out of the hospital across the street—tall, dark-haired, and impeccably dressed, with hints of silver threading his temples like war medals earned in silence. His suit whispered of wealth—tailored, expensive, cut from fabric she'd only seen in the pages of high-end magazines. And on his wrist, a Patek Philippe—the kind of watch that didn't just tell time, but told the world who you were.

She didn't need much more.

Her assistant made the introductions—innocent, effortless. When she overheard mention of his wife's diagnosis and her slow, impending death, something cold and calculating settled behind her eyes.

A perfect catch, she thought.

She knew he wouldn't be easy. Men like him rarely were. Grief and pride made them guarded. But that only sharpened her resolve. This would be her greatest performance yet.

A challenge, yes—but one she was more than willing to accept.

To tell the truth, Stella had seen the wife once, when she went to run a flower delivery errand to one of the hospital wards. The woman must have been gorgeous enough to tempt Zeus—if the cancer hadn't taken away each breath like a thief in the night. She'd also spotted two children loitering nearby, but that wasn't any of her concern. Getting rid of the kids would be the easiest part.

What actually sealed the deal with Martin was when she introduced him to the finance megamind Mr. Crawford, one of her regulars, who took a certain fancy to Martin's fool-like behavior and decided he'd make the perfect new pet.

Martin's desire to reach new heights and prove his father wrong at every step added fuel to the fire. Soon, they were spending their evenings in each other's arms, in an apartment overlooking the city's beautiful lights.

He used to say she was his anchor in the dark, his only benefactor in a cruel world that always seemed to take from him.

Stella knew better than to take those words to heart. That could come later—*after* she had earned the title of Mrs. Martin Ashford.

She held her breath, slow and heavy, waiting for the day Camilla Duarte took her last. And finally, it came.

The rest passed in a blur: the funeral, a short and solemn mourning period, and then a grand wedding held in the mansion. Fortunately, the elder Mr. Ashford had taken a surprising liking to her children and was like putty in her hands.

Her only real resistance came from Martin's mother—but she was a subdued little mouse, far too quiet to cause any real damage.

Years passed by in a blur. There were constant rifts between both sets of children, but Stella never had to pick a side—other elders in the house did that for her. Camilla's children were always left in the lurch.

She had tried to charm them, of course, as she did with everyone—but something in them had caught on to the darkness coiled inside her. Perhaps because it looked too much like their own.

For the first time in her carefully constructed life, Stella was truly terrified.

Then came the day that changed everything—the day that shattered the pillars of her well-sought fairytale.

Maria had just turned twenty-three. Ethereal, like a nymph out of a forgotten myth, she turned heads at every gala the family attended. Raphael had the same magnetism, but something about Maria always *pinched* Stella in a place she couldn't name.

And because of Maria, her daughter Bianca was so often pushed aside. She had no real talents, was passably pretty, but never enough to hold anyone's attention for long. Not in a house where Maria moved like moonlight and spoke like music.

Stella couldn't stand it.

She had worked too hard to be overshadowed by the child of a woman she'd killed.

Bianca was her soft spot. Of all three of her children, Bianca was the one she would gladly take dangerous steps for—again.

The party was in full swing that night—laughter like clinking glass, the air heavy with wine and perfume. Most guests were drunk to their very souls. But Stella's heart had carried a sinking feeling since the night before.

She knew, somehow, that her world could come crashing down at any moment. And yet, a few fragile threads of hope still held her upright.

A few nights ago, she had drunk herself into oblivion after discovering Martin's latest affair—this time, with his boss's wife.

She had let her guard down. After all these years, she had fallen in love with him. *Stupid, reckless love.*

And it was in that drunken stupor that Stella had begun to ramble. Unfiltered, unhinged confessions spilled from her lips—and they were overheard by none other than sweet, unsuspecting Maria.

Ramblings where she confessed to the murder of her own parents. And, unsurprisingly, to Camilla's as well.

She had snuck into the hospital on a thunderous night when the city was plunged into darkness by a freak power outage. Her plan had been simple: convince Camilla to divorce Martin, leave quietly, and make space for her new life.

But Camilla hadn't begged or wept. Instead, she wasted her final breath calling out Stella's mistakes—speaking with the calm judgment of a woman who had nothing left to lose.

It drove Stella mad.

In a flash of fury, she smothered her. With her own hands.

When it was done, she slipped out of the ward, her hoodie drawn tight over her head, just in case someone caught a glimpse of her face. But the corridor was mercifully empty, and the gods—cruel as they were—had been on her side.

There were no cameras then. No eyes in the dark.

And no one had ever suspected.

Until now.

Now, with the camcorder gently resting in her hands—an intimate gift from a friend who truly understood her dreams to dance, travel and photograph the world—Maria captured the very moment.

Though no threats were made outright, there was something in Maria's voice that made Stella feel unhinged—like a mind slowly fraying at the edges.

"Father wouldn't mind knowing about you, Miss Stella," she said with a dark smile. *"After all, he's been looking for younger women to stroke his fragile ego—and something else—for a while now."*

Stella knew she needed that camcorder. And that party night, she got it—along with a final silence from Maria.

She had taken Simon with her instead of Derek. Derek couldn't keep a secret to save his life. Simon, on the other hand, was both useful and easily manipulated, especially when drunk—and Stella knew well about his barely concealed lust for Maria.

They found Maria in her walk-in closet, changing. Without hesitation, Stella signaled Simon to keep her quiet while she searched the room. She could almost feel Simon's hungry eyes as he approached Maria, but time was short, and Stella had no room for morality.

She found the camcorder, and just before leaving, she shut the doors behind her—muffling Maria's screams. The loud music from the gala swallowed every shriek, every sob, especially when Simon was done with her.

Simon believed something had begun between them that night. But Stella knew the danger he posed. That same evening, after assuring the guests that Maria had simply retired early, she dismissed the servants and carefully crafted a noose from silk.

Maria never saw the dawn.

As for Martin—Stella knew exactly how to handle him. She dangled the affair like a poisoned gift, using it as leverage to pin the entire crime on Simon. It wasn't difficult; Martin had always cared more for his reputation than for the truth. And perhaps somewhere deep down, he had already begun to resent Simon.

After that night, Martin never looked at Simon the same way. The easy camaraderie between them vanished, replaced by a quiet, lingering distrust. Stella saw it all happen—calculated it, even. She knew the bitterness would fester in Simon, but that suited her perfectly.

To the outside world, she played the role of the helpless mother—burdened by a wayward son and betrayed by a cheating husband. It was a story people were quick to believe. After all, grief and innocence wore the same face when tailored correctly.

Fate added a final touch when Martin was diagnosed with erectile dysfunction. From that point on, Stella slowly began to take over—not just his feelings, but his life.

A small triumph, perhaps.
But hers nonetheless.

And now, it was all crumbling down again. Her dreams—once vivid and bright—had mostly curdled into nightmares since that night ten years ago.

The police had been called before anyone in the house could even make sense of what had happened. Butler James had found Raphael's body early that morning, just as he was bringing in the usual cup of coffee.

Martin and Corbin were desperately trying to keep the police from entering the estate, but it was no use. Raphael, it seemed, had made arrangements in advance—ones that would require more than slick words and old money to undo.

The scene inside looked like something out of a crime thriller. The air had turned unnaturally cold, sharper than January wind. Stella sat frozen, feeling as though someone—or something—was leaning on her shoulders. Not quite comforting. More like . . . draining. Cold, invisible hands tugged at each breath she took.

She gasped loudly, breaking the silence—and startled the older Ashfords seated just a few feet away.

"Could you please calm down?" Martin's father snapped. *"We're already knee-deep in disaster—we don't need another corpse on our hands."*

He rubbed his temples and muttered bitterly, *"What have we come to? No money, no connections . . . And overnight, everyone's cut ties with us. There'll be nothing left soon. Nothing for any of us."*

Derek sat at the far end of the living room, smoking a joint and staring blankly at the wall, as if trying to bore a hole through it with sheer will.

"We're cursed," muttered the older Mrs. Ashford, her voice laced with bitterness. *"We've been cursed since the day that woman—that*

dancing hippie—stepped foot into this house. Had she not charmed my son, he would've married one of my friends' daughters. We wouldn't be tangled in these endless shenanigans."

She scoffed, shaking her head. *"Then he marries her—a woman who's been calculating since the moment she laid eyes on my poor boy."*

Derek chuckled at the comment but didn't bother to look up, much less engage.

Outside, Bianca hesitantly stepped toward the garden, hoping Corbin might offer some comfort. But one sharp glare from him sent her right back inside. Stella watched the exchange and shook her head. Her daughter had no control over that shrewd, self-serving boy—whose only goal in life seemed to be a warm, accommodating lap.

Stella had seen it before—with Maria. The way that girl had devoted herself entirely to Corbin, and how he, in turn, kept her close just enough to benefit. Maybe, Stella thought grimly, she had more in common with Corbin than with any of her own children. None of them had turned out like her.

Now, all she could do was wait for the inevitable.

And the inevitable was near—lurking just around the corner, watching, waiting . . . ready to open its dark jaws and swallow them whole.

Finale

Four

Maria watched as Derek and Simon were loaded into one of those shabby police cars. They had always detested unclean environments—ever since they'd gotten used to the luxury of the Ashford estate. And now, watching them return to the kind of place they truly belonged gave her a flicker of satisfaction.

Not much, though. The rage still burned hot inside her. If it were up to her, she'd have set every last one of them ablaze.

Martin and Corbin were pacing, shouting into their phones—desperate to reach someone, anyone who could help. But deep down, they knew the truth. The damage was done. Somehow, Simon's long history of assault and abuse had surfaced—reaching the media, the courts, and every household in the country . . . maybe even beyond. His name was being cursed in every language. The company he'd built with such vanity collapsed overnight.

There would be no coming back from this. Not without irreversible ruin.

Derek was another story. Special in his own way. His name had been in the police database longer than anyone had suspected, but Corbin had always been there to clean up after him. Not well enough, it turned out. The same pattern of cover-ups had finally come back to destroy them all.

Maria stared at the car until it rolled past the gates and disappeared from view.

She turned around.

The Ashford monarchy—already cracking—was collapsing faster than she'd imagined.

Grandpapa and Grandmama sat slumped in the drawing room, looking like they were teetering on the edge of madness. With no money left, and the mansion sold off to cover legal fees and fines from Father's dirty dealings, a nursing home was next. And knowing Miss Stella, Maria was certain she'd make that decision with a smile.

Father, meanwhile, was flailing. Trying to liquidate his investments, drain stocks, anything—but nothing bore fruit. The empire was dust in his hands.

"That's it! We're penniless! Destroyed! Gone—all the Ashford pride, gone!" he screamed, his hair wild, face red with fury. *"For once, be of some use, you low-level bastard!"*

Corbin scoffed and pointed at him. *"Me? Who was the one throwing money into every goddamn pipe dream? I told you—not before consulting me. I've cleaned up after your messes for years. This one's on you."*

Neither of them looked stable anymore. And watching that—watching their anger and helplessness swirl like poison in the air—made Maria love Raphael even more. It was as if, even in death, he'd finally taken the revenge she never could.

Miss Stella and Bianca were another story.

They sat together on the velvety sofa. *That* sofa Bianca had specially commissioned during her interior designer phase. It was hideous. Gaudy. But somehow still prettier than the two women perched on it.

Maria remembered everything. Every look. Every lie. Every betrayal. Raph might have handled the men, but the women? They were her territory.

Especially Miss Stella.

Oh, how unbearably sweet it would be to watch her squirm—to drag her through endless torment, so slow, so deliberate, that every gasp for even a fleeting second of peace would be cruelly snatched away. She would writhe, desperate and broken, drowning in suffering without relief.

As for Bianca, Maria pictured tearing her wardrobe apart, piece by merciless piece. Then she would haunt her relentlessly—stalking her every waking moment, driving her to madness with fear so sharp, so constant, that her downfall would be as ignoble as it was inevitable: a heart attack, drowning in her own blood and filth.

Ironic, really. The woman who tried so hard to be proper, undone in the most improper state imaginable.

And Miss Stella deserved something . . . *special.*

Maria pictured her mind unraveling, slipping in front of everyone, her public composure cracking like glass. Her next stop? The asylum. Alive, but unwell. Kept right on the edge of madness—courtesy of Raphael.

Father had already lost the things he clung to. But pushing him off that final edge? That would be a gift.

For years after her death, Maria had held back. She hadn't troubled any of them. She'd simply helped Raph collect evidence, piece by piece, believing—hoping—that maybe, somewhere deep inside, they had loved her. That maybe, in some buried corner of his heart, Father still missed Mother.

But dreams crumble when you leave everything to fate.

And when they do, you're left on a path so lonely, so desolate, that returning seems more daunting than walking it forever.

A noise coming down the stairs pulled Maria from her thoughts.

Four police officers were carrying Raph . . . or rather, his body.

Somewhere deep in her heart, Maria had already sensed the night's grim turn. She had found a letter addressed to her, carefully placed on her bed just as she was settling down, humming Mother's lullaby in search of peace.

She knew who had left it. And the reason behind it felt like a heavy burden.

Dear Maria,

My sweet sister—one named after the mother of the Lord.
Mother chose your name so carefully, just as you yawned

with such grace at two days old. She knew of your soft heart but also feared the darkness it might carry if left unchecked, if not carefully channeled. She loved us both deeply enough to calm our storms. But her passing took away that safe cocoon—the place where we could heal.

After she was gone, I couldn't protect you as I wished. For that, I will always blame myself. When they wheeled your lifeless body past my eyes, I swore to destroy everything that hurt you. I had already planned it all, but then you came back to me, reached out and held my hand, and I found myself in the same space of solace again.

For years, I depended on you to save me from the horrors inside my mind. But when you came crying silently, it unleashed the darkness once more.

Don't worry about the people in that house—I have arranged everything for them. If you wish to toy with them, do so without remorse.

I'm sorry, my little dove. I tried to stay by your side forever, but I found more peace without breath in my body. I hope you can forgive me for leaving you. And if given the chance, I'd love to come back—to run around the pond and climb the trees with you once more.

Your loving, yet selfish brother,
Raph

Maria couldn't blame him. He had stayed by her side for so long, never once complaining. And now . . . it was her turn to do something for him.

All she wished for was one last goodbye. But she knew—if she saw him again, really saw him—her resolve would shatter. She would try to pull him back. Keep him here. And she wasn't that selfish.

Not with Raph.

His body was already stiff as it passed by her, covered in white cloth. She reached out, just wanting to pull back the sheet and glimpse his face one last time.

Her hand passed through.

Broke her heart into a million pieces.

All she could do was stare at their backs with misty eyes, whispering to no one: *"Why the hell is a ghost so emotional?"*

Raph—the one who shielded her from Miss Stella's wrath behind Father's back.

Raph—who would step between her and Simon, or Derek, whenever they tried to toy with her.

Raph—who quietly cleaned her wounds when her fights with Bianca left her hopeless.

Raph—who stood by her when the world forgot she ever existed. When even her name faded from memory . . . only he remembered.

She watched the squad leave, their footsteps echoing through the hollow halls. Only a few officers remained behind, sifting through drawers, bookshelves, and corners—searching for anything that could bury the Ashfords further. The family stood there, hopeless, watching their empire crack and crumble in real time.

Once they loaded Raph into the van, Maria wiped her tears and turned back toward the house, already planning how to end this circus of lies once and for all.

This time, her eyes finally landed on the *chess piece* that had fueled the fire—a fire that had left them all teetering at the edge of ruin.

Corbin.

He sat hunched, running his fingers through his hair, lost in thought. His posture screamed denial—he wasn't ready to accept defeat. Not yet. Not even close.

Maria studied him. The contortion of his face, the ugly grimace, twisted something that once looked so polished—so beautiful. She wondered how she had never seen it before.

Then again, Corbin had always been the first to master the art of polished treachery.

How did he end up like this?
Had he always been this two-faced devil, hiding behind charm and designer smiles?

He stood and walked toward the window, trying to calm his mind—maybe even trying to think of a way out.

Maria drifted toward him. Slow. Silent. Purposeful. She was ready now. He would be her last, and maybe her most deserving, purpose for vengeance.

He stared out the window, breathing heavily.

Just as she reached him—ready to freeze him with her ghostly touch—his eyes lifted.

And *met hers.*

Not directly. Through the reflection in the window pane.

His eyes widened in disbelief. Then he squeezed them shut, shaking his head violently—as if trying to shake off a hallucination.

Maria froze.

How?
How is this possible?
He wasn't supposed to see her.
But neither was Raph.
Have the fates turned on me again?

Though long dead, Maria felt a sudden, jarring pulse in the hollow place where her heart used to be.

Taking another step forward, she reached out, hoping it was all just a dream—that her plan would continue as usual. But before she could touch him, Corbin turned on his heel and left the room through the far end of the hall, maybe heading toward the back gardens.

Maria hesitated. There was nothing left in this room that required her attention. The people inside were already broken—perhaps they deserved a moment to catch their breath before she dragged them deeper into the hell they'd earned.

She followed Corbin silently, watching as he walked through the overgrown garden, his expensive leather shoes now stained with dirt. Then he turned toward the family graveyard.

Why the sudden interest in the graves?
He hadn't even visited mine after the funeral.

Slowly, cautiously, Maria followed. But when she saw him stop—at her grave—her breath caught again in her throat, even in death.

He visited her? Was he here for something? Maybe forgiveness?

No, it's all in her head. He must be here to taunt her or to curse her like she did to them.

Corbin sat down in the grass without a care, releasing a long, exhausted sigh.

Only her grave and Mother's had a bit of clearing around them—Raph had always taken care of that, no matter the weather. Now, Maria wondered who would do it next. Raph would soon be buried beside them.

"You know I never meant all this to happen," Corbin said softly. *"When we were young, I had plans to marry you. That way, I could have had my future . . . and you with it. But you left me in this world to fend for myself. I had no choice but to marry Bianca—just to stay close to this place. You understand the sacrifices I've made for you, don't you? You were the only one who truly understood me . . . my darling."*

He spoke with such tenderness that any stranger would've thought he was heartbroken—still in love. And maybe she would've believed him too, if she hadn't already seen his truth.

"I thought I'd find peace by living here again," he continued, staring into the distance. *"But lately… I've seen you. Twice. Am I finally going mad? Have I loved you so madly, my dearest?"*

And with that, Maria knew: *he could see her now.*

Just like Raph had.

But she wouldn't fall into his trap—not now.

Instead, *she would make him fall into hers.*

Slowly. Carefully. And then all at once—with no way out.

She sat beside him and gently rested her dainty head on his broad shoulder.

Let the world think he was alone. Maria would know better.

From now on, she would be with him in every breath.

In every dream that twisted into nightmare.

In every sigh he made when pretending to care.

She would be there when he played the charming man, luring new prey.

She would lay her ghostly hands over his as he sat through operas he loathed but watched for show.

She would be there when he made love to another blonde, or brunette, or maybe a redhead this time—close enough to breathe down his neck.

And just as madness began to crack through the surface, she would embrace him.

And make him feel the cold she had felt all these years.

With those thoughts lingering in her hollow chest, Maria began to hum again—*her mother's lullaby,* this time with even more sadness than before.

"Hush thee now, the moon glows red,
The wind has found a sorrow dread.
Hearts do ache 'neath mourning's veil,
For softest breath, a soul so frail.

The roses bloom with darkened hue,
Where once they flushed in morns dew.
Now petals weep in heavy dread,
For love long lost and words unsaid.

No candle burns upon her graves,
Just ivy curled where her dream caves.
And in the hush, the shadows start—
Still lingering in her broken heart."

THE END

The Dark Secrets of Family Business

by Jimmy Daleson

One

"MOM! MOM!" I bellowed, trying not to drop the wet child or slip in the shower.

Mom cracked open the bathroom door, poking her head in. "Is Small Child ready?"

"She is. Take her."

Mom stepped into the bathroom, snatching a half-dry towel from the floor. But Small Child protested unexpectedly as Mom reached to pluck her from the shower.

"Mom! I'm not done yet! Dad didn't wash my butt!"

Mom and I both chuckled at that. "Trust me, Darcy, your father is a professional butt-washer." That did make me laugh, which drew the attention of Big Child, the 12-year-old Barkley. She came marching into the bathroom, sleuthing what all the shenanigans were about.

"Hey, B! I've told you—now that you're a twelve-year-old sixth grader, you've been trained up in sex ed and can't see your dad in the shower anymore!" I turned quickly so she couldn't see me hiding my grin.

"Daaaaaaad!" Whiny baby voice. Blech. She knows I can't stand that voice, but I had earned it by teasing her on a sensitive subject. Her adolescence required her to be shy about sex ed class, but also thoroughly embarrassed by anything and everything her father did. Trouble compounded in that I teach middle school—at her school! So she's just embarrassed by me all the time. And I love it.

"Darcy, what's wrong with your leg?" It's shocking how fast my wife transitions into a medical professional at the slightest injury to one of her children. Me though? Forget it. She'll hang me out to dry to solve my ailments all alone.

"Looks like heat rash from her socks," I piped up, toweling myself off.

"You think that's all it is?" Mom leaned in to scrutinize the red skin and tiny welts dotting Darcy's leg. "You don't think it's a reaction to something?"

"She's been in ski boots for the last four days, and she's never done this before. So, yeah, it's those thick socks and too much sweat."

I'm not sure what transpired next, but Darcy was suddenly hyperventilating and screaming, and it wasn't about her legs. Apparently, it was her stomach. But Doctor Mom's first thought: UTI. Mom was trying to soothe the child, but this was obnoxious. The four of us were crammed into a Club Med hotel room, so the pealing squeals of a seven-year-old were unacceptable.

"Hey, cut that out!" I barked, not giving the child an inch. My ADHD's adverse reaction to loud noises kept my tolerance for such drama very thin.

"Dad, cut her some slack. She's not feeling well," Barkley chimed in.

"Good grief, don't play into it—either of you!" I eyeballed Mom and Barkley both, then dramatically grabbed my sweatshirt, book and phone. "I'm leaving. I'm not sticking around to hear this nonsense."

"Dad, don't leave me to deal with this," Mom implored, but I was having none of it. "We have laser tag in twenty minutes."

"Laser tag? With that noise? Forget it. Brush Darcy's teeth and send her to bed." More squeals and crying, but I anticipated that. I tossed open the hotel door and stepped into the hallway. It was eerily quiet out here—the sound of solitude. I loved it. Dad had successfully escaped.

I hadn't been in the lobby for five minutes when Mom sent me a text. "Dad, Darcy and I are headed down there for laser tag. What should Barkley do?"

"She's twelve. Let her hang out on her own."

"I dunno. There's so many people here. Do you think that's safe?" *Mom, cut it out. Stop being such a ninny.* But I couldn't translate my thoughts into a text without sparking a war, so reluctantly I caved.

"Send her down with her iPad. She can hang out with me. I'm in the lobby near the DJ booth."

"Ok. I'll do that."

A number of texts quickly followed about an impending government shutdown. Mom wasn't mad at me anymore. The temper she lashed me with was deserved, but I knew it wouldn't last. That was just one of the married couple snipes thrown at each other when one is frustrated by

. . . just life. Parenting is chaos, yes, but the absurdity of it can get the better of you. That's when tempers flare, things get said, whatever.

We were too good of a team to let petty things like tonight burst our bubble. Just yesterday we spent the morning lost in search of green runs Mom could handle at one of the largest ski resorts on planet earth. And since it was Christmas break, the early season snow in Tignes, France was thin enough that only select runs were open. Unfortunately, the run we needed to get back to Club Med wasn't one of those open runs. That meant we had to figure out how to cross miles of French Alps without killing Mom. It was tense, but we landed back at the hotel with just enough time to pick up the kids from ski school for a family lunch date.

We sent the kids back for afternoon ski school and gave each other a shared look of understanding that we had had enough skiing for the day. Afternoon sex and a dip in the outdoor hot tub was more like what we needed.

"You know," Mom said amid the frothing bubbles, "this is the first vacation we've had that feels like an actual vacation. The kids are engaged, you don't have to cook, and the two of us have had two afternoons of adult time. Have we really taken thirteen years to figure this out?"

"Better late than never," I casually responded, distracted by her large breasts floating just at the top of the water.

"I knew you'd say that." Mom smirked, happy and content with our Christmas vacation.

"That's what I always say," I snarkily replied. "Did you schedule me that massage?"

"Of course I did. I always have to do it for you."

"That's the way I like it. You're awfully good at being Mom, you know that?"

"I know." Her big, happy smile was the best Christmas present I could ask for. That, and a massage.

Two

Who knew laser tag could be so . . . dramatic? Mom had taken Darcy back to the room while I sat in Club Med's lobby. It's not really a lobby, but more like a great room for families to congregate on comfy, convertible furniture. It also doubles as a children's theater, something Mom is wildly enthusiastic about. This Club Med is her dream come true, with one child activity after another. What Mom cares about most in the world is that her family's needs are met, and Mom and Dad's needs can't be met if the kids aren't taken care of first.

I had been reading S. E. Hinton's *The Outsiders*, prepping to teach it in January with my eighth grade, when Barkley rolled up. Fresh from laser tag, face flushed, looking surly. Something didn't feel right.

"Dad, we need to leave . . . now!"

"Uh oh. Laser tag sucked or something?"

"No. I just want to use profanities, and there are too many adults around. I don't want them to hear me." I could see from the look on her face that she needed to vent.

"Let's head back to the room and you can tell me all about it."

As we walked, she spun a yarn about a couple of younger girls, probably nine and ten, and a group of aggressive teenage boys. She directed her tirade at the boys, claiming they were cheating in laser tag. Plus, some of the boys were a bit too touchy-feely for her tastes.

"Lame. I was hoping you'd have fun," I said sympathetically.

"It *was* fun. There were just a couple of shitty boys I had to deal with." I asked also about how long the laser tag lasted, as she'd been down there almost two hours. Apparently, the kids had gone back to a teen room with pool and foosball tables and sat around talking.

"What did y'all talk about? You were down there for a long time."

"We just talked about whatever. Like, we talked about what we were all doing at Club Med, where we are from, how long we'd been skiing, that kind of thing. One of the boys was bragging that his dad is in the Mafia."

"Really? Do you know what the Mafia is?"

"I've heard about it in books and movies. It's like a gang or some-thing." Nonchalant, she didn't really care about this tidbit of information.

"Where did this kid say he was from? Was he just bragging about Mafia connections? That's serious stuff."

"I don't remember where he said he was from. I think he was just trying to look cool."

"Maybe. Point him out to me. Anything else happen down there? Are you planning to go back tomorrow?"

"I dunno. We weren't friends or anything. And the two girls are younger than me."

"You know what, Bark? I admire you. I would never have been able to go down and sit with a random group of kids when I was twelve. I was too shy. You have amazing courage and confidence in yourself." I tossed an arm around her shoulders as we walked, feeling proud to be Dad to an amazing teenager. "You're growing up, kid. I'm trying to give you space this week so you can do that."

"I know. I appreciate it too, Dad."

"I have some parameters for you to work within, but they're pretty loose. What are Dad's two rules?"

"Be kind to others, and under no circumstances am I to go to any-one's room."

"Cool. I'm proud of you!" Berkeley had a good head on her shoulders. I admired this young person whom I knew would responsibly explore the person she's becoming. "Just remember that your little sister is sleeping, so let's not be too loud when we get back. I know you'll want to tell Mom all about the evening, but keep the volume down, ok?"

"Gotcha. I'll try at least." Barkley is like me—louder than normal people. She's also a theater kid, so when she gets animated, it's like watching a play performance. She's serious about her stories too, but it's funny to watch, and she gets mad when we giggle at her antics.

Three

It was snowing hard the next morning, almost white-out conditions. Mom and I decided to let the kids sleep a bit longer and check in with ski school later in the morning. That meant we'd have to be sneaky about our intimate adult time, getting the job done before the kids woke up. What a nice way to start a day.

Breakfast was slow this morning. Apparently, we weren't the only ones having a slow morning, balancing needs for snow and ski time with vacation laziness. But I could see that Barkley was apprehensive about something.

"What's on your mind, kid?"

"Dad, that's the punk who was talking about the Mafia last night!" She whispered fiercely, flipping her head in the direction of a well-dressed family at one of the big tables. This was classic money-family on a ski trip. The father was dressed in expensive ski gear, never taking off the enormous gold watch on his left wrist. His outfit suggested he was skiing with the kids and knew what he was doing on the slopes.

The mom, on the other hand, was there as part of the unspoken ski vacation fashion show. These pageants of opulence pit wealthy women clad in designer snow outfits against each other to see who has the best drip. The only thing they have in common is zero intention of actually stepping outside. These peacocks prance around, showing off their fancy clothing, immaculate hair, and expensive makeup. Growing up in Colorado, I had seen these runway models too many times, and never once did I find them impressive. In fact, the whole getup spoke volumes about this family.

Taking seats at our little four-top, I leaned over to suggest a clandestine conversation. "B, they do look like the Mafia. Better be careful with them. Maybe they have some dark secret you'll stumble upon..."

"What do you think they're up to?" Barkley couldn't help herself and kept glancing over at them.

"Hey, stop looking over there. They'll know we're talking about them."

"What do you think they're doing? Something bad?" Bark really was concerned. This wasn't part of her dramatic theater persona. Another quick glance . . .

I looked up at that point too, and noticed the teenage boy she had originally pointed out staring straight at me. He leaned over and whispered something to his father. "Uh oh, Bark. We'd better be careful. They know we're talking about them." I watched the dad acknowledge his son with a nod of his head, then his eyes lifted and spotted me as well. We made eye contact for a brief moment before he casually looked away. He didn't look friendly, and he didn't look happy that we were spying on them.

"All right, family, finish up. Let's get out of here." We had worn out our welcome. The only thing that was guaranteed is that we'd spend the rest of breakfast stealing nervous glances at the Mafia table, and no good would come from that.

"Why? We aren't done yet," Mom inquired, sensing that something was going on she didn't know about. Nothing bothered Mom more than when she felt like we were keeping secrets from her. We were, under no circumstances, allowed to plan anything without her approval.

"Barkley had a run-in with that kid over there, so we're going to take off," I said, trying to sound casual. "I'm gonna get her out of here. We'll head back to the room to finish getting suited up for ski school." Mom glanced over at the Mafia table, but shrugged without concern.

"Ok. Darcy and I will finish up and then meet up with you downstairs at Club Mini Med. Darcy is ready, but make sure Big Child puts on deodorant." Mom gave a sagely look, then rolled her eyes with a smile as Barkley stormed off in a huff.

Four

"You know, the strangest thing happened," Mom said as we re-grouped in front of the ski school. "The lady at that table you pointed out came over after you left and said she was looking for a yoga partner at today's 9 a.m. stretch class. She wondered whether I'd like to join her. She said her son spoke highly of Bark, and she was just extending a friendly invite from one mom to another."

Barkley's eyes popped open at this. "Mom, you are NOT going. You can't."

"Why not? I said I would."

"Uh oh, B. Looks like Mom just made friends with the Mafia," I chuckled, trying to sound dramatic and ominous.

"No, seriously, Mom. You can't go. That boy is the ringleader of the *Assholes*!" Bark was getting fired up. She was turning on some serious theater, ratcheting up her volume.

"I'll be fine, Barkley. We're just going to yoga. Besides, I'm trying to do anything other than actually ski." Mom jabbed me in the ribs when she said that.

I took a deep sigh, realizing this was another day I'd be skiing by myself. Resigned frustration was about to take over when I noticed the Mafia family walk into the bay of ski lockers with their youngest daughter. The younger kid at breakfast with them, a girl probably ten years old, was registered for Club Mini Med as well. She wasn't in Darcy's class though, as some previous ski experience had her placed with advanced students.

Mafia Dad wasn't alone, though. A younger guy, late twenties maybe and pocked with the residue of teen acne scars, stood just behind him. This guy was wearing a black leather jacket and looked like a bodyguard. He was skinny but tall and had a look about him that screamed he'd grown up behind bars. The nasty scowl snarling across his face was directed at me.

We got the kids checked in to ski school, then headed to the Club Med ski lockers. "Mom, I don't like the look of those Mafia guys. They're shady."

"You've caused quite a bit of trouble yourself, so don't get too worried about it. We're not joining the Mob." Mom rolled her eyes.

"Just be careful today. Don't say anything to Mafia Mom that will let them know who we really are. Think about your diplomat training and how to keep your identity secret."

"Whatever, Dad. You just watch yourself out there and try not to crash." With that, she turned and strode off for a day of yoga and low-budget Hallmark Christmas movies.

Five

Suited up, I marched with skis in hand out into the morning sun. I loved those days just after a nasty snowstorm, where the sun shined brightly and the world was covered in powdery fluff. Today was going to be a great day.

WHAM! I was almost knocked off my feet by someone walking past, up from behind me. It was the young Mafia bodyguard kid. He never even looked back, just kept on clomping in his ski boots, poles in one hand and skis in the other.

"Geez, man, that was a slam, huh?"

I looked over and saw my early morning coffee buddy, Luca. We met on the first day in the lobby, where the complimentary coffee machines were. Early birds tend to flock together, and the two of us had enjoyed quiet mornings every day we'd been here. He was tall and skinny, and I had accused him of being American because of his accent—it had zero percent European tilt to it. Turns out, he was an Italian who had grown up as the child of UN staffers. So he traveled all over the world at a young age. I understood that predicament immediately, as Mom and I are doing the same thing with our kids. But Mom is an American diplomat, not a UN worker. Luca had grown up at American international schools, which explained his accent. He had also spent significant time at Club Meds, and this one in particular.

"Yeah, it was," I said, rubbing my shoulder and stretching my neck.

"Be careful with that one, Jimmy. That guy is connected. You know what I mean?"

"Connected, as in *Mafia* connected?"

"Yeah. I'd stay away from him if I were you." Luca glanced up at the bodyguard walking away. "He was here last year as well, probably protecting Gavrilo Abate, a high-ranking Italian Mafia don. Abate's wife and kids are here this week as well."

"You know about these guys?"

"I do. I might not have grown up in Italy, but I'd always go back for school holidays. The Italian Mafia has a long history, and they're all over the place in my hometown, Venice. Abate hails from Rome, but it's all part of the same extended family."

"What is he doing here? Just on a ski vacation?"

"I know that his oldest daughter is handicapped, and Club Med Tignes hosts an international Special Olympics every year around Christmas time. They've been setting up the slalom course for the event just over there, beyond the ski school."

"That's what the gates are for?" I had seen plenty of race courses, having grown up on ski mountains in Colorado. I even participated in weekly amateur races in North Conway, New Hampshire, when I lived in Maine. I spent a season working at a ski resort that hosted community events, where every Wednesday you had to show up and do your run. Your time would be posted in the paper the next day, and teams would compete casually for bragging rights. It was fun, and most of the local participants showed up shit-faced to race and then stayed to get even drunker in the mountain's ski pub. That's about as close to competitive skiing as I ever got, but some people take this sport very seriously.

"Why would a Mafia don be concerned about me? I'm just a middle school teacher."

"Dunno, but it looks like you've been sent a message. We don't want Jimmy Daleson in tomorrow's paper, suffering a tragic 'accident.'"

"Well, I think I'll put some distance between the two of us by hitting the rental shop. I've got a solo day on the mountain, and I'm going to rent a snowboard. I'll catch you later, Luca. Probably for coffee tomorrow morning."

Six

We both chuckled and issued goodbyes before I turned and headed back inside. Stopping briefly by the locker bay to change out of my ski boots, I excitedly strolled into the rental shop as I hadn't been on a snowboard in several years. Sleeping in today was a good idea, as most of the morning crowd of eager skiers had already left.

"Puis-je vous aider?" a round-faced ski tech asked, looking up at me from tweaking a ski binding.

"Um . . . yes?" I responded. Even though we spent four years living in Senegal, my French sucked. I blamed COVID for my lack of French language skills, even though I taught at the French school in Dakar. In all honesty, I struggled with all the silent pronunciations of French words. If you're going to speak, then actually say the word—don't whisper it.

"Ok," the ski tech said, with a heavy French accent. "How can I help?"

"I'd like to rent a snowboard and boots, please. S'il vous plaît." I may not know much French, but I can say please and thank you. And ask where the bathroom is—all the important stuff.

"Sure thing. What's your level on a snowboard? Your *experience*?" He struggled with the word experience, with his French accent getting in the way of his tongue.

"I've been snowboarding for thirty-seven years."

"Ooh! Ok! So you know what you're doing. Where have you done all that snowboarding?"

He was clearly impressed with my snowboarding history. "I grew up in Colorado, in the US. I started skiing when I was three, and started snowboarding when it came out in the late-80's. Most Colorado resorts didn't even allow snowboarding at the time, thinking snowboarders were punk knuckle-draggers."

He laughed at the snowboarding insult. "I've heard about Colorado. Big mountains out there!"

"Yup. Very big. Great place to grow up for a kid that loves snow sports."

"Uh oh. It looks like someone is watching you . . . " Ski Tech nodded his head toward the door, and I stole a quick glance in that direction. It was Pocks! He was lurking by the door, clearly spying on me.

"Hmmm," I muttered. "I'm not sure why that kid is following me."

"You better be careful. The family he travels with caused trouble here last year."

"Oh yeah? What kind of trouble?" I asked as I pulled on a snowboard boot for fitting.

The tech whispered like he was sharing dangerous secrets. "Someone died here last year . . . mysteriously. One of the ski racers who participates in the Special Olympics we host every Christmas. She was set to win the gold medal, but she had . . . an 'accident.'"

Uh oh. That's what Luca had warned me about too. I wonder why he didn't mention this little tidbit of information if he was here last year as well? "Do you know who that kid is?" I asked without looking up.

"I think his name is . . . " Tech gulped and stopped speaking. I looked up from my boot and noticed the color had drained out of his chubby face. He was staring at the rental shop entrance where I noticed Pocks clandestinely shaking his head. *No* was what he was indicating.

"Hey, kid, no more info. Let's keep some distance from that guy. He's clearly trouble."

"Ok," tech said, clearly relieved. "Thank you. How do the boots fit?"

"They'll work. Let's ring this up so I can hit the slopes."

"Okey dokey," the tech said, smiling. "Isn't that what you say in America?"

"Something like that," I said, chuckling. As I headed toward the register to pay, I saw that Pocks was gone. What a creepy dude—definitely not someone I wanted on my tail. With snowboard in hand, I marched back out into the sun for a second attempt at hitting the slopes. I'd been looking forward to this for eight years, and nervous about my back holding up. I laughed at my struggle just trying to strap in. I was heavier than I used to be, and bending over to buckle snowboard straps was tougher than I remembered. But getting onto the lift, I felt like I was being watched. Not just by Pocks, but by everyone here. It was disconcerting, and I couldn't shake the feeling.

Seven

Ski school ended at 4 p.m., and we'd spent these first two days meeting as a family to tackle the afternoon. Club Med did a pretty good job of bringing out snacks and cocoa around 4:30, knowing that families were regrouping and needed a pick-me-up. Actually, this place was totally family-oriented, and there weren't many people here *without* kids. The atmosphere was lively, with pop music booming through the lounge and all the families re-organizing the modular furniture to suit their needs. Mom was enthralled, and her needs were being met 100 percent.

"I love this place, Jimmy," she said, eyes glittering as she looked around. "I've never been to a place that is so family-friendly. Look at how everyone has re-organized the furniture."

"Too bad you're lactose intolerant because these little cakes on the snack bar are the bomb," I said, stuffing another huge bite into my hungry maw. I'm actually worried about how much I've eaten in the last couple of days.

"So, Mom," I casually asked, knowing I was poking the bear. "How was yoga with your new friend? Is she really a Mafia moll?"

"A what?" Barkley piped up, curious about anything Mafia-related. "Dad, keep your voice down!"

"Yes, you should watch your volume, Dad," Mom replied, clearly not impressed with my attempt at digging on her. "Allegra is quite pleasant. She told me all about her family and kids. Her eldest daughter is competing in the Special Olympics tomorrow!"

"So I've heard. I bumped into Luca downstairs while I was heading out. He told me about it. Actually, I didn't bump into him, but rather the thug trailing along with the Family."

"Who bumped you?" Mom asked, looking concerned as only a mom can.

"The younger guy that's tagging along with the Family. Luca thinks he's a bodyguard."

"A bodyguard? What in the world do you think is happening here? We're at a family resort, not some Atlantic City casino. It's not a movie," Mom said, incredulous.

"Hey look, the kid slammed me from behind and almost knocked me down. Luca told me to be careful with him." Mom and Bark both rolled their eyes. Why did no one take Dad seriously?

The music suddenly cut, blanketing the lounge in unexpected quiet. Every family must have had the same awkward reaction we did because a hush fell over the room. The head of the ski school program and seemingly social coordinator for the Club Med family events climbed onto the theater stage, mic in hand.

"Friends, I have some unfortunate news," he said first in English, then quickly in French. This was a common way to address the crowd, bouncing back and forth between languages so everyone could understand. "Marco, one of our rental shop technicians, was severely injured in an accident today. Please keep him in your thoughts tonight and let's hope he's able to pull through. He's in surgery right now."

"Oh, that's awful . . . " Mom said, clutching her hands together.

I wasn't paying much attention to her, as the projector flashed a smiling picture of Marco on the movie screen. It was the same kid who helped me rent a snowboard. I glanced around the room and saw pretty much everyone else looking flabbergasted as well, with one exception. Luca, wine in hand, was happily talking to Gavrilo Abate. It seemed like the two were old acquaintances from their revelry. Then I noticed Pocks, sitting in a lounge chair next to Barkley's laser tag boy. He had one leg casually propped over the other, and was rubbing one fist into his other hand. He was staring straight at me. I won't forget his smirk for a long time.

Eight

Nervous. Shaking. Trying to hide it. I spent the rest of the evening anxious about what was going on at this Club Med. For some reason, our family had run afoul of the Italian Mafia—not like a Hollywood version either. This isn't *The Sopranos*—this is the real-deal, old-school *Family*. I needed to understand how we got in their way, and now I was worried about asking Luca. How close was he? Luca and Gavrilo sure seemed like old friends. Who was I supposed to trust?

The dinner hall was packed as usual, and we'd decided Table 22 was our camp. Darcy ran over and claimed it, and that's when I noticed that we were just a few tables away from the Abates. Allegra and her younger daughter were sitting, and everyone else must have been up hitting the buffet. The two moms saw each other, beamed brightly, and Mom went walking over. Allegra seemed tickled to see her, and I tried not to stare as the two women talked, laughing about something. The daughter was giggling as well, and I saw my wife turn and address her as well.

I hurried to claim our table with Barkley's sweatshirt, then scooted the kids toward the food. I knew Darcy wanted pizza and noodles—that was all she ever wanted—and I herded her toward the Italian section of the Club Med grand dinner buffet. There were a ton of different options, and I should have realized that the Italian Mafia would probably be in . . . the Italian section, where else? *Great.* Walking up, I noticed Barkley's teenage companion from laser tag, the kid that she had been so upset about. He just didn't look friendly—at all. Dark, dour expression, scowling eyes—this kid was the quintessential surly teenager. Probably spoiled rotten too, filled with the knowledge that his Family has power. Real power. He glanced up and saw Darcy and me, and his eyes squinted with hatred. *What the hell did we do to this kid?* Bark wasn't telling us the whole story.

I helped Darcy get a couple slices and some cheesy pasta, then sent her back to our table. I meandered around distracted, too many thoughts in mind to properly build a plate. I ended up back in my seat alongside the kids with an eclectic mix of sliced sausages, cheese cubes, and crudités. *Whatever.*

"Dad, is that really all you're eating?" Barkley asked, sounding concerned.

"I dunno, Bark. I've got a lot on my mind tonight. Tell me what happened at laser tag—the whole story too. That boy you mentioned *hates us,* and I want to know why."

She hesitated, then timidly said, "He tried to kiss me, Dad."

"Yeah? What was your response?"

"I was scared."

"Uh huh, and then what?"

"I might have . . . you know . . . slapped him."

"You slapped him?" I could feel the color draining out of my face.

"Yeah. But not very hard or anything. I was just trying to get him away from me. I don't know him, Dad. Don't tell Mom, ok? Please?"

"I won't tell Mom," I said, trying to give Bark some honesty and support. "But we're now on the shit list for that Family. The boy—what's his name? He's really mad, and his thug bodyguard has been following me around. I think he did something to the rental shop guy who was injured today."

Barkley got wide-eyed when I mentioned the ski tech. "Dad, do you think he did something? Why would he do that?"

"Well, I went down to rent a snowboard today. I was trying on boots when the ski tech kid saw the bodyguard lurking by the door, and he told me the guy is bad news. Like, he may have killed someone here last year."

"What?" Bark was getting her dramatics going, as only a twelve-year-old theater kid can. "Dad, that's crazy!" She was excited and scared at the same time and spoke a bit too loud.

"Shhhh! Keep your voice down, kid!" I stole a glance over at the Abate table, which had become mostly populated with the Family. The only one missing was Pocks.

Then Mom showed back up. She was furious and had food spilled all over her shirt and pants. "You won't believe what just happened!" she loudly declared. "Some guy just elbowed my plate all over my shirt!"

Allegra hopped out of her table and hurried over to help clean Mom up. "Oh my, Katie, what happened?" she said as she tried to wipe my wife's shirt off with a napkin. The rest of the Family was looking on, the son seemingly amused at the misfortune.

"Someone just bumped me and I spilled my plate."

"I'm so sorry. It's such a lovely shirt as well." Allegra sounded genuinely sympathetic. She was either not a thug like the rest of her Family, or just really good at hiding it.

"Thank you—oh. That's him. The guy who just sat at your table is the one who bumped into me."

"Oh no! You mean Ludovico? I'm so sorry. I'll replace your shirt."

"That's ok, Allegra. Thank you." The two women issued niceties, then Allegra went back to her table and Katie sat down.

"That guy they're with is an asshole. He bumped me on purpose." Mom was trying to keep her cool, but she was clearly rattled.

"Mom, that's the bodyguard. The one that's been following me," I said in a hushed voice. "I think he bumped you to send me another message."

Barkley's eyes were wide with fear. "What do you mean, *another* message? What else happened?" Mom asked, deeply concerned now.

"You know that rental shop technician that got hurt today?"

"Yes? What about him?" Mom replied.

"I think *Ludovico* happened."

Nine

I bolted upright, suddenly awake. Cold sweat. Heart racing. Nerves tingling. The only sound in the hotel room, aside from my gently snoring wife, was the blustery wind outside whipping clouds of freshly fallen snow across the seventh floor balcony.I had a nagging feeling that I woke up for a reason. I laid back down in bed quietly listening for anything unusual—aside from the fact that the world was dark and immersed in holiday slumber. Too much exercise learning to ski, too much heavy French cuisine on the all-you-can-eat buffet, too much . . . Club Med. Too much anxiety. Thoughts just churned through my head. *What time is it?*

I climbed out of bed to hit the john, checking my phone for the time as I walked past. 4:48 a.m. Being a middle school teacher, this was my normal time to wake up so I was ready to go. The main lobby's coffee bar was proving to be a great place to plan my classes for after the holiday break. Classes start up in early January, which means I always spend holidays working to make sure I'm prepared. Teaching is lame like that, it just sucks away your family time. Luca was the only other person awake at this hour and we'd had some nice conversations over the last few days. It was actually quite a nice way to start the day—meeting a friendly stranger enjoying their holiday.

But why was Luca chatting with the Mafia boss yesterday like they were old acquaintances? Luca had told me to be careful with the Family's bodyguard, Ludovico, or Pocks as I call him. What did Luca *really* know? Was he hiding something? *Maybe I could find out*, I thought. The idea of investigating what this Mafia family is up to terrifies me—I'm no detective or private eye—I teach middle school!

I pulled on some sweats, grabbed my computer and phone, and headed for the door, trying to be as quiet as possible. Even the slightest interruption to my wife's sleep turns her into an angry momma bear and I didn't want to start the day with an animal attack. Opening the door let in just enough light from the hallway to display an unexpected surprise.

There was an envelope on the carpet, just inside our hotel room.

Seriously? Like a Hollywood thriller, I'd been slipped a note. Bending down to snatch it made my heart race. What in the hell was going on? My skin crawled reading the contents:

Be careful with your coffee

I stood rooted to the spot—skin crawling, clutching the letter, reading it over and over. Was something going to happen to me if I went to get coffee this morning? For a moment, I thought about not going down. But I wanted coffee, and I wanted to slyly investigate Luca and see if I could get some additional details on the shenanigans going on.

Steeling my nerves, I stuffed the letter into my pocket and headed for the elevator. The early morning's serenity had been shattered by the revelation that I may be walking into a calamity. But I needed to face it. I had to. In some awkward way, I felt a burning desire to prove that I could not be broken. I figured that being ubiquitous would show that I'm determined to figure out what's going on. Come hell or high water, I was in for the long haul.

The elevator dinged its arrival, and I stepped into the first floor's dark hallway. Few hotel patrons were awake at this hour so I could talk to Luca without being fearful of eavesdroppers. The male housekeeper's buzzing vacuuming filled the living room area though, almost making me break concentration. But I saw Luca's tall, skinny frame near the breakfast bar and strode pointedly up to the self-serve coffee machine.

"Whoa, buddy! You look intent on getting some Joe this morning!" Luca exclaimed brightly, ribbing me for the way I marched up and grabbed a mug.

"Good morning, sir!" I responded, trying hard to keep my smile natural. "How are you doing, Luca?"

"I'm pretty good. Got a big day ahead of me."

"Oh yeah?" Maybe this was going to be easier than I thought, especially if I could keep him talking. "What's on your agenda today?"

"You've seen all the Special Olympics racers on the mountain? I'm headed out with a couple of them for some slalom practice today. I've got a couple friends in those sit-ski's and I can't even keep up with them."

"I've seen those guys!" I said enthusiastically. "There's a couple of them here this week that are crazy good—really carving up the mountain."

"Exactly! I'm headed out for some runs this morning, and then spending the rest of the day watching qualifiers for tomorrow's races."

"Cool, man. Sounds like a great time. Are the Special Olympics formally starting tomorrow then?" I was almost as excited as he was. I love winter sports and find the Special Olympics enthralling. What courage those racers have. Tenacity. They make me feel small and unaccomplished.

Luca and I exchanged a few more pleasantries, then I took a table nearby and worked on my sixth grade class planning. "Work" isn't the right word—I was too distracted by all that was going on to stay focused on work. I'd never been stalked by the Mob before and it had gotten the ski shop kid hurt. Was I just in over my head? I didn't honestly think I could tell anyone what was going on. What would happen if I made a claim about a Mafia boss without any specific proof? I feel like I'd spend the rest of my life looking over my shoulder or wondering if there was poison in my food. But at least I knew what Luca would be up to for the next couple of days. I decided to follow and keep an eye on him. *Jimmy Daleson, Private Eye.* Kick ass!

I was equally relieved as I was excited. Whatever had been warned about in that letter hadn't come to fruition.

Ten

"Why do you seem distracted?" Geez man, I cannot be sneaky around my wife at all. It's like she knows I'm up to something if I'm even just thinking about it. I'd only been back long enough to take a morning shower before getting the kids dressed for breakfast and skiing and she'd already busted me for thinking I'm a spy.

"I'm not . . . distracted." Shit. She knew somehow. "Are you doing yoga this morning with Allegra?"

I withered under her scrutinizing look. Several seconds went by before she responded. "I was planning on the 9 a.m. Yoga Stretch class. I need it if we're skiing again today."

"Ok. I think I'll go out this morning and ride some of the harder stuff. Then I can go out with you after lunch?" *Perfect.* I had a chance to actually follow Luca around unencumbered.

"Sounds like a plan . . . but what are you up to?"

I shrugged dismissively, channeling Barkley's theater expertise. "Just skiing." Again, that hard stare made me turn around so I didn't have to acknowledge it. I pretended to fiddle with my snow boots instead.

"All right, who's ready for breakfast?" Both kids shot up their hands. "Let's roll then, people. Mom, I'll take the kids if you want to meet up with us."

"Table 22?" Mom said merrily.

"Somewhere around there," I said, shooing the kids out the door. Immediately they started bickering with each other about who got to tell me about their ski school plans for the day. "Cool it," I said. "That's enough. Dad doesn't want to hear you two fighting about who gets to talk. Darcy's the youngest so she goes first. Darce, start talking."

The girls bounced back and forth on the way down to the dining hall, but I didn't hear much of what they said. I was looking for Luca, and sure enough, I spotted him almost as soon as we walked in. He was conveniently over by Table 22 as well. Close enough to keep an eye on. Perfect.

Katie showed up about half an hour after we did, so the kids and I were mostly done. I noticed Luca was about done as well and started getting nervous that he'd leave and I'd lose him.

"Mom, I'm about done. I think I'll head out and get an early start today. Can you get the kids to ski school by yourself?"

"Sure. What time should we meet back up? Lunchtime? How about you get the kids and I'll meet you back here?"

"Ok, that works. Let's plan on meeting here right at noon when the lunchroom opens." I was elated that this sleuthing plan was actually working out. Not even working out—more like falling into place. I better not get cocky though.

Eleven

It wasn't hard to follow Luca. I didn't know his room number, but everyone at Club Med Tignes has to pass through the locker room where all the skis are kept. Everyone has a wooden locker to hold skis, boards and boots. The place bustles like a Grand Central Station, everyone eager and anxious just before the lifts open. I ran down and grabbed my skis, then stepped outside to wait casually. The ski school area was right by the door so I casually walked over and pretended like I was waiting for the kids to show up.

There was a sizable crowd milling about but Luca was easy to spot. The guy was 6'6" and weighed about 125 pounds, so he stuck out. I saw his bright red jacket yesterday too, so it wasn't hard to find him. And sure enough, he was with a handful of people organizing sit-skis. Maybe Luca was honest after all? Maybe I was chasing ghosts, and I was making up a fictional crime drama. But then Pocks walked up and joined the group. What the hell was he doing with them? I turned slightly so it wouldn't look like I was just watching them and pulled my goggles down over my eyes. I better hide my identity or the gig is up. And then, like a little flock of angels coming to my rescue, ski school poured out of the building. Forty or fifty kids, ages six through twelve, was a small army. Rowdy and boisterous, they provided a perfect distraction so no one would focus attention on me. Bark noticed me standing by the ski school fence and ambled over, walking like a robot in her ski boots.

"Hey, Dad. Whatcha doing? I thought you left already."

"I suited up early so I can make the first chair on the lift. We got fresh snow last night so I want to hit the powder before it gets skied off."

"I have no idea what you just said." She was the perfect illustration of an emo teen.

"That's because you don't know how to ski yet. Fresh snow is amazing."

She shrugged, clearly not understanding what "powder day" meant. I glanced up and to my horror, Luca's group was gone! I frantically searched the crowd, looking for the beanpole in the red jacket. Luckily I found him, but he was just about to get on the lift!

"Bark, I gotta go. I'll see you later—lunchtime!"

She yelled something, but I was too focused and determined not to lose Luca. I saw his group sit down on a chair and off they went, zooming up the mountain. *Shit! Hurry, Jimmy. What kind of private eye are you?*

Team Luca had a sizable head start, about a dozen chairs ahead of me. But then again, I didn't want anyone to think I was following. I scanned the area as my chair approached the top and Luca's group was pretty easy to spot. They were just starting their run and moving fast. Duh! These are Special Olympics racers, and they're quick! I struggled to catch them and was worried about keeping up from a meaningful distance. What fun though! These guys are a blast to ski with and the skills required for sit-ski are truly amazing. Resilience and stamina to the extreme.

We skied all morning—them about one hundred yards ahead of me. I stayed about a dozen chairs behind on each lift and we went all over the mountain. Luca had said they wanted to slalom, so I figured that they'd want to be on the race course that runs just under the lift. But the group only did that once and spent the rest of the time just carving up regular runs. Good times. It's too bad I was playing spy because I would have liked to have joined Luca for the day. He had Pocks with him though . . . *why did he have Pocks?*

I peeled off from the group just before noon so I could pick up the kids and meet Mom for lunch. I passed the mark group as I was heading toward the lodge and noticed something odd. I saw Pocks hand Luca a thick yellow envelope. Cash? Did I just see a payment? I was too focused on the scene and didn't realize that Pocks had spotted me. I glanced up as I skied past him. Even from a distance, I couldn't help but notice his hand gesture. He was making the unmistakable sign of a gun: thumb up, index finger out. Firing, right at me.

Twelve

"Hey Dad, isn't Mom supposed to meet us?" Darcy may be young, but she's observant.

"She is supposed to meet us. Maybe she's taking a nap?" My concern grew as lunch passed by. We finished eating, and I took the kids back to Club Mini Med. I was trying to keep cool, but the only thought on my mind was: "Where is Mom?" She skipped lunch.

I dropped the kids and headed back to our room. "Hello?" I called out, stepping cautiously into the suite. I could see her feet hanging off the bed and one of them still had its snow boot on. I rushed in and found Katie sprawled across our bed—unconscious. "Katie? KATIE!" I yelled, slapping her face rapidly. She groaned, which let me know she wasn't dead. She was also more than just asleep.

Another message. I was with Pocks all day, so he didn't send it. Was it . . . Allegra? Is Mafia Mom capable of this kind of shit? This is serious—drugging another mom and for what? Is this really because her spoiled brat of a teenage son didn't get to molest my daughter? My anger was tempered somewhat by Barkley's slap of the kid's face. That'll teach you a lesson, you little fucker.

Mom stirred and sort of rolled over. Her eyes groggily fluttered open, and she drunkenly asked if it's time for lunch. I gingerly sat on the bed and stroked her hair. She smiled and started going back to sleep. She'll be all right, but I'm gonna get the bastards that did this.

I gathered myself for the battle ahead, and marched out the door, intent on finding out what was really going on. The afternoon Special Olympics races should be starting up soon, and the older Abate girl was supposed to be racing. I intended on being there to watch.

I was met by the morning vacuum guy as soon as the elevator opened on the first floor. We made eye contact, and as I shuffled past him, I heard him whisper, "Did you get my note?" I spun around and he desperately tried to shake his head. He had a push cart of housekeeping supplies and motioned that I should walk with him. "What did you mean that I should 'be careful with my coffee?'" I asked, keeping my voice hushed.

"The man you've been meeting for morning coffee isn't who you think he is. He's part of the Mafia family—an uncle. He's Mr. Abate's brother," Vacuum said quietly.

I was floored. That is absolutely not what Luca had told me. That meant Luca was in on whatever crime was transpiring here. "Is the Family here just for the Special Olympics?"

"They come every year, and have since she was a teenager," Vacuum responded. "And she's won every race she's ever been in. *Every single one*. And every single one had the leading competitor . . . *drop out*." He raised his eyebrows when he said that last part.

"Drop out, or got taken out?" I asked, boggled at what I was suddenly involved with. Pocks had handed Luca an envelope. What was in it? "Do you know what room my coffee friend is staying in?"

"He's in room 315. Do you need to get in there?"

I chuckled at the room number. "Room 315. Third month, fifteenth day." I taught history classes before I taught language arts and my passion was Roman history. "The room number is the Ides of March."

"Let's get you in there. I just saw him leave his room. I'll take the stairs and meet you in the hallway."

I nodded and headed back toward the elevator. Rattled nerves had me shaking and I could barely push the 3 for the third floor. *Deep breaths. Let's settle down.* A moment later the doors chimed and slid open but it wasn't Vacuum standing there to greet me—it was Pocks! He grabbed my stunned body and slammed me against the elevator's back wall. Oof! Instinctively I brought a knee up and rammed it into his balls. He scooched his hips back, which I anticipated. What he didn't expect was the left uppercut that I smashed into his chin, rattling his teeth and spilling blood from his mouth. He must have bit his tongue because blood poured out all over the elevator's gaily carpeted floor. I must have rang his bell too, because he dropped like a sack of potatoes. He fell backward, just as the doors shut on his head. I stomped on his chest, and he doubled over gasping for air. Another hard kick—right in his ass—released his bowels all over in a stinking mess.

I thought the fight was over, but Vacuum was suddenly there with a towel rolled up. He wrapped it around Pocks' throat and twisted. Pocks kicked his feet and scratched at the towel, but it was over in a minute. His eyes glazed over, his muscles relaxed. He was dead.

Jesus Christ! Did I just kill a man? *Holy Shit!* Vacuum looked up at me and I could see that he was more than just a housekeeper. He was a plant, but I wasn't sure what kind. "Let's get you into that room—I'll take care of this," he said, motioning to the dead bodyguard.

I nodded in agreement. "Thanks . . . for everything." What are you supposed to say to a hotel housekeeper who's just killed the Mafia hitman tailing you? Fuck if I know!

Vacuum handed me a swipe card, and I hurried toward 315. I opened it slowly, not sure what I'd find on the other side of the door. The room was clean—like there was never anyone here. It wasn't just that housekeeping had made the beds and changed the towels. There was oddly no luggage either, except for a briefcase and laptop on the desk in the main room. I opened the briefcase and there was the envelope. It was filled with Euros.

"What are you up to, Luca?" I said aloud, trying to talk myself through my bewilderment.

"I thought you had figured it out by now," a voice responded.

I spun around, and there was Luca, flanked by Barkley's teenage stalker. "No. I actually haven't figured it out. Why don't you enlighten me."

"I'm afraid I haven't been entirely honest with you, Jimmy," Luca started, choosing each word carefully. "We have been coming here every year for a generation, ever since my father made Don. That brings certain . . . perks. We've always loved Tignes and when my brother Gavrilo's handicapped daughter fell in love with skiing, we decided to fund and host Special Olympics for her."

"So you're the one that sets all this up?"

"We do, as a *Family*." He made sure to emphasize family.

"Why all the sneakiness then? Why not just declare that you're responsible for hosting the games? That's a great way to support athletes who need recognition."

"See," Luca beamed, "I knew you were different. You see the value in what we're doing. But the Abate name is . . . tarnished. We don't have the best reputation. So we can't really go flouting the games the way we'd like to."

"So you fix them so Gavrilo's daughter can win." I shook my head in disgust. "What should be beautiful games is nothing but a crime scene."

The teenage boy spoke up then, muttering something in Italian.

"Don't be so glum about it, Matteo," Luca said to him.

"And what does Matteo have to say about it, Luca?" I asked, curious to know what this kid's beef is.

"Matteo is frustrated that his sister always gets her way, and he seems consistently forgotten about."

"Is that why he's so mad at my daughter? He's a bit too aggressive, from what I hear."

"Your daughter made a grave mistake in striking an Abate. No one does that . . . without consequences." Luca turned and said something to Matteo, who eyeballed me hard.

"He's got a lot to learn about girls. Or maybe you think that since you're an Abate you get whatever you want."

"Ah, there it is, see? I knew you'd figure it out. We Abates always get what we want. *Always*."

"What's the cash for, Luca?"

"That's for our . . . *helpers* out on the race course," Luca said, chuckling. "We've got a couple of friends that tune skis. It's not pretty when a ski racer's ski comes off—especially when they only have one leg." He chuckled darkly.

"And what happens if they don't get their payment," I asked, shaking the envelope at him.

"Oh, they'll get their money. Of that, I'm sure."

A whistled tune in the hallway made all of us look up. Vacuum was out there, casually organizing his cleaning cart. How long had he been standing there?

"Housekeeping. Need any fresh towels?" Vacuum asked, looking Luca square in the eye. I had a distinct impression that Vacuum's identity was about to be revealed.

"No. I don't need any fresh towels, thank you," Luca said gruffly, clearly annoyed that the housekeeper had shown up. Then he squinted hard at Vacuum's housekeeping cart. There was a Converse sneaker sitting on it. There's only one place—or person, rather, that the shoe could have come from. And Luca recognized it.

Luca was about to say something when Vacuum took a few steps into the room. He was squared off as if ready to brawl. Then another man appeared in the doorway—the emcee for Club Mini Med. This was also Marco, the ski tech's friend.

"Sir, I'm calling the authorities. My friend here, Alain, and I have been on your trail for two years, and now we've got the proof of your crooked deeds." MC held up his phone, wiggling it like a threat. "I've been recording your conversation with Mr. Daleson. I have your whole scheme to rig the Olympic races recorded—in your own words."

Silence. Then Luca turned and looked at me, head hanging down. "I admire you, Jimmy," he said, lifting his eyes just enough to meet mine. "You're just a middle school teacher caught up in Family business. But you've got the balls to actually do something about it. I admire that courage."

"Am I supposed to say 'thanks?'" I asked, incredulous at the scene unfolding. Luca was right—I was just a middle school teacher that got sucked into Mafia business during my Christmas break. *I didn't ask for this!* Had it really started because Barkley slapped some random kid? No matter . . . now we could spend our last two days at Club Med Tignes not worrying about being followed. Or killed.

Thirteen

Club Med swarmed with police activity that day, but the MC for Club Mini Med made sure it took place just after lunch and during ski school hours. That meant hardly anyone was around to see it. None of these families wanted a crime drama unfolding. They wanted to blissfully enjoy their Christmas ski vacation. Their kids were in ski school, the parents were in the hot tub and little French pastries were on the snack table. Families were there to escape and that meant willful ignorance of trouble. And the MC knew it. Apparently, so did the housekeeper, Alain.

The Special Olympics continued and young Lady Abate took fourth place in the downhill. Fourth place is just a step off the podium. It was the worst possible outcome that a competitor could get. Served her right. She might not have been the one pulling the strings, but she was the recipient of foul play. A fourth place finish showed everyone that she was just not good enough for a medal.

I never did find out what happened to Luca. Honestly, I didn't really care. With deep Family connections to the legal system though, I imagined that he didn't get much of a punishment. Sometimes I wondered if he was upset with me so I'd been keeping an eye out for new variations of Ludovico. One thing is certain though: we won't be going back to Club Med Tignes ever again.

About the Author

Jimmy Daleson teaches middle school language arts. He's always been a storyteller, but only recently began to write them down. A group of 6th graders inspired him to follow a "passion project," and he wanted to figure out how to become a published author. So he started sending stories to different competitions. A couple wins later and he can't stop! Writing is how he processes his life's journey and many of his stories are memoirs of his crazy childhood. There's a bit of real life experience in each of his stories, and it's up to his readers to decide which is truth and which is...well, not true.

Acknowledgments

It takes a village to write an anthology. That's how the saying goes, right?

What Hides in the Dark is EJL Editing's second anthology and has been a joy to edit and publish. I am in awe of the diligence, compassion, and creativity of all the authors involved and I urge readers to go follow their favorites. They might just have a backlist waiting for you!

Thank you to Maddi for your unwavering friendship, patience, and stellar edits. There's no one else I'd rather share a brain cell with!

Thank you to our phenomenal anthology interns: Ollie and Shruti. I am in awe of your dedication, empathy, and precision. It's been so much fun working with you on this project and I know you'll both be amazing editors!

Thank you to Vic for keeping business moving even when I couldn't.

Thank you to Val (Aethrastic Designs) for donating our stunning covers!

Thank you to my family, friends, and everyone else I bully into buying and reading *What Hides in the Dark.*

Finally, one more time, thank you to every author of *WHitD!* We wouldn't have an anthology without you.

Looking for your Favorite Author?

Volume I

- Camilla Zahn

- Jane Humen

- Bryanna Bernice

- Christopher J. Brice

- Eleanor Hall

- Noah Johnson

- Vera M. Sidney

- Cisco Bautista

- Luke Van Amburg

- Ann Wuehler

- Zero Saucier

- Isabella J.

- Brandee Paschall

- E.R. Sano

- Chloe D.

- Eric Still

- Carter Elise Key

- Jay L. Scaffa

- Heena

- Jimmy Daleson

Volume II

- Hannah Phillips

- K. Beyer

- Brianna Dingeldein

- Jessica Daniliuk

- Eden Fanning

- Kit Oregon

- L.E. Guerrero

- Rhianne Rivers

- Nesi L Stone

- Micaiah Blakemore

- Amaru Starling

- Anna Cunningham

- Marwa Hussain

- Jess Lynnae

- Jalen Tellis

- Brian Wayne Bingham

- M.S. Ray

- Melissa Rivera-Jovel

- Morgan Bridges
- Onika Howdyn
- Pandora Cress
- Alyx Barter
- Amie Glazier
- Sapphire Lynn Johnson

Volume III

- Madame Envy
- Laramie Cummings
- Carliann Jean
- Kathleen Boston
- A. P. Cooper
- E. L. Canney
- B. Childs
- Olivia J. Bennett
- Breanna Sumiko Teramoto
- A. Marie Cantrelle
- Tyler Whetstone
- A.C. King
- Cassandra Aston
- John North

- Mason Monteith

- Shin Sano